John Harvard Biles

The Design and Construction of Ships

John Harvard Biles

The Design and Construction of Ships

Reprint of the original, first published in 1908.

1st Edition 2023 | ISBN: 978-3-36849-857-3

Verlag (Publisher): Outlook Verlag GmbH, Zeilweg 44, 60439 Frankfurt, Deutschland
Vertretungsberechtigt (Authorized to represent): E. Roepke, Zeilweg 44, 60439 Frankfurt, Deutschland
Druck (Print): Books on Demand GmbH, In de Tarpen 42, 22848 Norderstedt, Deutschland

THE DESIGN

AND

CONSTRUCTION OF SHIPS.

BY

JOHN HARVARD BILES, LL.D., D.Sc.,

PROFESSOR OF NAVAL ARCHITECTURE IN THE UNIVERSITY OF GLASGOW.

VOL. II.—STABILITY, RESISTANCE, PROPULSION, AND
OSCILLATIONS OF SHIPS.

With 316 Illustrations, including 4 Folding Plates.

LONDON:

CHARLES GRIFFIN AND COMPANY, LIMITED.

EXETER STREET, STRAND.

1911.

PREFACE.

This volume, like the previous one, embodies the Lectures on the subjects dealt with as given at the University of Glasgow. It was intended to have completed the subject of the title of the book, Design and Construction of Ships, in two volumes, but the rapid growth of material which should be included in the subject and the decline of available time to devote to such work have together delayed the completion of it, and have made it desirable at this stage to publish a second volume. The parts of the subject included in this volume are Stability, Resistance, Propulsion, and Oscillations of Ships.

In ship forms the determination of Stability is usually made by methods of calculations similar to those explained fully in Volume I. To these methods many persons have contributed, but probably few will be disposed to grudge to the late Mr F. K. Barnes the honour of having laid securely the foundations upon which Sir William White, Sir Philip Watts, and others have built up our very complete mastery of this subject. The methods at present used are very different to those used by Mr Barnes and his coadjutors. The introduction of the planimeter, the integrator, and the integraph, calculating instruments invented by Amsler and Coradi, has broadened our grasp of this subject by making easy the calculations upon which Sir William White and Sir Philip Watts and others in their early days spent many weary hours. These instruments have made it possible to have stability calculations made by a much less highly skilled class of calculators. The author remembers with much pleasure the ease with which, at Clydebank, Mr Archibald Campbell, now at Ferrol, Mr John Paterson, Naval Architect to Messrs John Brown & Co., and Mr A. W. Stewart, Electrical Engineer, and others, then lads fresh from school, used Amsler's integrator when it was first applied to stability calculations.

The purely geometrical side of the study of stability, *i.e.* that side which is connected with *theorems*, and not with *actual values*, owes its existence almost completely to the French writer Dupin. Extensions of the geometry of stability have been made from time to time by other writers. Methods of proof of Dupin's propositions and the later extensions are here given, differing in many cases from the original proofs, because the methods seemed to the author better suited to the purpose of the student. To the methods of obtaining *actual values* the author has devoted considerable attention, with a view to producing simple processes which can be used by operators of small experience, and with much less labour than the older processes.

The work on Resistance and Propulsion cannot fail to be largely an adaptation of the published work of those who have been fortunate enough to have the use of experimental tanks, from which alone such results can be obtained. The work of the late Mr Wm. Froude and his son Dr R. E. Froude has been largely laid under contribution. Some of the adaptations have been made by following the original closely, rather than by making changes of doubtful advantage to the student. This has the advantage of occasioning less frequent references to the original text of these writers, an advantage which it is hoped will be of value to students, as the size, cost, and inaccessibility of the volumes of the Transactions in which the work originally appeared are considerable. The work of Mr D. W. Taylor of the American Navy, read before the American Society of Naval Architects, has largely been used in a similar way, but since this volume has been in type a valuable collection of his work has been published. Professor Sadler's work in the University of Michigan on Resistance of full forms (read also before the American Society of Naval Architects), and that of others, has been also given. Messrs Denny of Dumbarton have from time to time given the author information as to the Resistance of specific forms, and in some cases the information is embodied in Chapter XIV. in diagrams, giving for each of a series of speeds the H.P. required to drive any required displacement.

Propulsion has, by the gradual increase of revolutions of engines, become one of the most important subjects in Ship Construction. The experimental work in connection with the determination of Resistance has been in advance of that of Propulsion for the last forty years, but now they are nearer than ever to being abreast of each other. This is due to the work of Dr R. E. Froude and Mr D. W. Taylor, and to Messrs Denny, whose work is none the less real and valuable though it cannot be exactly appraised, as much of it has not been published.

The work on Oscillations of Ships is in the least fully developed state of the four divisions of this volume. The work of the elder Froude has had little of value added to it since his time. The epoch-making discovery that small stability and great steadiness were correlated has been acted on in all navies. The extreme cases with which he dealt are all that have been fully investigated. They are, first, where the periods of the wave and the ship are equal, in which case excessive rolling takes place. Second, where the ship's period is indefinitely great compared with that of the wave, in which case the ship remains practically upright. Third, where the ship's period is indefinitely small compared with that of the wave, in which case the ship's mast follows the wave normal. The second and third are unreal cases, and the first is very unusual. The intermediate conditions have not been investigated theoretically, though at sea many of them have been practically experienced in all kinds of ships.

To Mr A. Cannon, Assistant in the Naval Architecture Department of this University, the author is indebted for assistance in the collection and correction of the Lectures on which a considerable part of this volume is based, and for the correction of the proofs, and for some valuable suggestions.

Regrets are offered to those who may have been good enough to have expected that this volume would have been issued sooner, and that it would have completed the work on this subject.

The work on Design has proved to be much more voluminous than was expected. It is an elusive subject. Types of ships vary from year to year. The kind of knowledge accumulated and stored in the first two of these volumes is increasing rapidly, but its application to Design not only causes additions to our knowledge, but produces changes of type of ships and improvements in results which make the wisdom of a few years ago the folly of to-day. Much less help can be given by others to the student in matters of Design than in other parts of the subject. He can only become a competent designer by making designs ; and while theories and data can be given to him, their application can only be his own work. An attempt, however, will be made in the next volume to put some information and examples before the student to which he may refer for assistance at present, but to which in the future he will probably look back with the same reverent or irreverent feelings as we look back upon the work of our predecessors.

To those Reviewers who noticed the first volume the Author is grateful for the uniformly kind way in which it was received.

JOHN HARVARD BILES.

March 1911.

CONTENTS.

PART IV. STABILITY.

PART V. RESISTANCE.

PART VI. PROPULSION.

PART VII. OSCILLATIONS OF SHIPS.

THE
DESIGN AND CONSTRUCTION
OF SHIPS.

PART IV.

STABILITY.

CHAPTER I.

RIGHTING ARMS AND MOMENTS.

In Part II. Vol. I. the methods of finding volumes and centres of gravity of solids have been discussed. In this chapter it is proposed to consider fully the action of the forces upon a ship when at rest in still water, and when slightly disturbed from this position of rest to another position.

In fig. 1, suppose B to be the centre of gravity of the volume of water V displaced by the ship S S S (called the centre of buoyancy, or C.B.), and suppose G to be the centre of gravity of the whole of the material in the ship (called the C.G.). At rest, the weight may be considered as concentrated at G, and the buoyancy or supporting force at B. The weight and buoyancy forces are equal and opposite, and act vertically in the same line.

Suppose that some force F, whose point of application is b, inclines the vessel until she is again at rest in the position shown by the dotted section S¹ S¹ S¹.

The point G will move to G¹, the same position relatively to the structure as before, and the volume displaced will probably be of a different form to that in the upright position.

If the force F displacing the ship from its upright position of rest be acting in some direction, say A b, other than horizontal or vertical, we may resolve it by the parallelogram of forces into horizontal and vertical components F$_H$ and F$_V$ respectively, acting in D b and C b. The vertical component will cause an increase of volume of water displaced equal in weight to this vertical component. The centre of gravity of this increase of volume may not act in the same vertical line as the vertical component of the applied force.

If W L be the position of the waterline in the vessel when she is upright, and $W^1 L^1$ be the position of this same line when the vessel is inclined, and $W_1 L_1$ be the water surface in both conditions, we may cut off from the ship $S^1 S^1 S^1$ a volume below $W_1 L_1$ equal to the increase of volume which the vertical component F_V causes to be displaced. The horizontal component F_H will tend to move the vessel bodily to the right, and must be resisted by some force R in order that there shall be equilibrium. If this force R be resolvable into vertical and horizontal components R_V and R_H respectively, the former

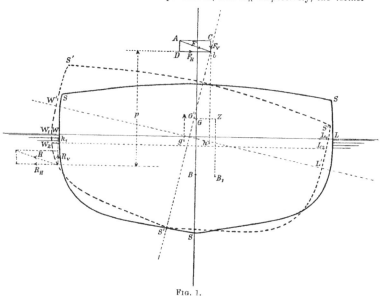

Fig. 1.

must be treated in the same way as the vertical component of the applied force. Let $W_2 L_2$ be the waterline parallel to $W_1 L_1$ which the resultant of F_V and R_V cuts off in volume. If its centre of gravity is at g we shall have a couple formed by the force F_V and the leverage $g h$ and R_V with leverage $g h_1$ tending to overset the vessel.

The force R_H must be equal to F_H or the vessel will move bodily. This force R_H will form a couple with F_H. Its moment will be $F_H p$. The weight of the ship will act downward through G^1, and the buoyancy, equal in amount to the original buoyancy in the upright condition, will act upwards through B_1, the centre of gravity of the volume below the line $W_2 L_2$, which volume is the same as that in the upright condition. These two forces, the weight and buoyancy, form a couple $W . G^1 Z$; W being the weight of the ship.

If the point B_1 is to the right of G_1 the couple tends to bring the ship back to the upright, and *vice versâ*. We have thus the following couples in the figure as drawn.

1. An upsetting couple due to F_V and R_V and the buoyancy of the layer.
2. „   „ F_H and $R_H = F_H \cdot p$.
3. A righting couple „ $W = W \times G^1 Z$.

If there is equilibrium, the algebraic sum of these must be = zero.

The case may be simplified by assuming that both the applied force F and the resisting force R act horizontally and are equal, and, in consequence, the volume of displacement remains unchanged. For equilibrium, the value $W . G Z$ must equal the moment $R . p$ of the inclining force. This value varies

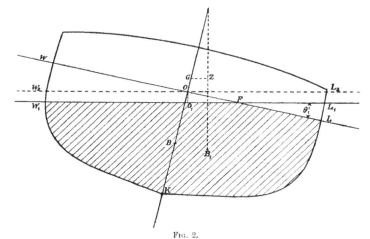

Fig. 2.

with the angle of inclination, and when known for all angles it is possible to determine the angle at which equilibrium will exist for a known inclining moment. With a fixed position of G the problem becomes one of finding the position of B_1 for a given inclination. This would be easily done were the volume of displacement at a given angle determined. We know what it ought to be, viz. the same as in the upright position, but to know exactly where the waterline is that will cut off, at a given inclination, a given displacement, is not so easy. Turning to fig. 2, suppose W L and $W_1 L_1$ to be the positions in the body of such a waterline in the upright and inclined positions, the angle of inclination being θ. The volume $W K L = W_1 K L_1 = V$ the volume of displacement. $W_1 K L$ is common to W K L and $W_1 K L_1$, so that

$$W F W_1 = V - W_1 K L$$
$$= L_1 F L$$
$$= v, \text{ say.}$$

v is the volume of the wedge of emersion or submersion, and therefore the wedge of emersion $W F W_1$ is equal to the wedge of submersion $L F L_1$. If B_1 is the centre of buoyancy of the volume $W_1 K L_1$, then V. G Z will be the moment of the buoyancy causing the vessel to return to the upright. This quantity V. G Z is expressed in units of weight, each equal to the weight of a unit of volume. This moment is called the righting moment, and is the measure of what is known as the stability of the vessel at the particular angle of inclination θ.

If the vessel be of such a form that all waterlines cutting off equal volumes pass through the point O, it will be easy to find the exact form and position of the centre of gravity of a volume of the solid which has constant displacement V. But generally this is not so. The waterline $W_2 L_2$ cuts off from the upright solid a wedge $W O W_2 =$ say v_1, and adds a wedge $L O L_2 =$ say v_2. The volume $W_2 K L_2$ then equals $V - v_1 + v_2$, and this is (as drawn) in excess of V by the layer $W_2 W_1 L_1 L_2 =$ say A.K (where A is the area of the waterline $W_2 L_2$ and $K = O O_1$).

Hence $V - v_1 + v_2 = V + A.K$

∴ $v_2 - v_1 = A.K.$

Hence the volume of the layer $W_2 W_1 L_1 L_2$ (known as the correcting layer) is equal to the difference of the wedges v_2 and v_1. If we know this volume A. K and find A, we can find K, which will enable us to determine the true position of $W_1 L_1$. It is evident that we may find the volumes v_1 and v_2 and the value A by the methods of previous chapters.

Had v_1 been greater than v_2, $W_1 L_1$ would have been above $W_2 L_2$ instead of below it.

We can also find the position of B_1. Suppose, in fig. 3, g_1 and g_2 to be the centres of gravity of the wedges v_1 and v_2 respectively. Join $g_1 g_2$ and drop perpendiculars $g_1 h_1$ and $g_2 h_2$ upon $W_2 L_2$. Take moments of volume about the line O H drawn perpendicularly to $W_2 L_2$. B P is horizontal and perpendicular to O H.

Starting with the volume V and moment V. B P we first take off v_1 with the moment $v_1 O h_1$, then add v_2 with moment $v_2. O h_2$, and finally take off $W_2 W_1 L_1 L_2$ with moment $(v_2 - v_1) O c$, c being the foot of perpendicular let fall from C the centre of gravity of the correcting layer upon $W_2 L_2$. The result of these changes is to leave us with the volume V ($= W_1 K L_1$) and its moment about O H, viz. V. P R. Expressed as an equation, treating moments which turn as the hands of a watch as positive, and reductions of volumes as negative, we have,

$V B P - v_1 o h_1 - v_2 o h_2 - (v_2 - v_1) O C = - V P R$

∴ $V(B P + P R) = V B R = v_1 o h_1 + v_2 o h_2 + {}^{*}(v_2 - v_1) O C$.   .   . (1)

Taking moments about B R,

$V(B_1 R) = v_1(g_1 h_1 + O P) - v_2(O P - g_2 h_2) + (v_2 - v_1)(O P - C c_1)$

$= v_1.g_1 h_1 + v_2.g_2 h_2 - {}^{\dagger} C c (v_2 - v_1)$ (2)

---

* This sign will be + if the excess of volume of one wedge over the other belongs to the opposite side to which the C.G. of correcting layer is in relation to O P. It is generally remembered by the expression "like sides give negative." This means that if the volume is a submerged excess with the C.G. of the connecting layer on the submerged side of the O P the sign will be negative. Similarly, an emerged excess on the emerged side will be negative. The other two combinations will give a positive sign.
† This sign is always negative.

Hence we may at once find the position of B laterally and vertically if we know the positions of g_1 and g_2 and the volumes v_1 and v_2.

$$\text{BR} = \text{BN} + \text{NR} = \text{BG sin } \theta + \text{GZ}$$
$$\therefore \quad \text{BR} - \text{BG sin } \theta = \text{GZ}$$
$$\text{V.BR} - \text{V.BG sin } \theta = \text{V.GZ}$$
$$\therefore \quad v_1 oh_1 + v_2 oh_2 + (v_2 - v_1)OC - \text{V.BG sin } O = \text{V.GZ}.$$

To find the position of B_1 vertically we have similarly

$$v_1.g_1h_1 + v_2.g_2h_2 - (v_2 - v_1)Cc = \text{V}B_1\text{R}.$$

A particular case of this equation for V. G Z is known as Atwood's formula.

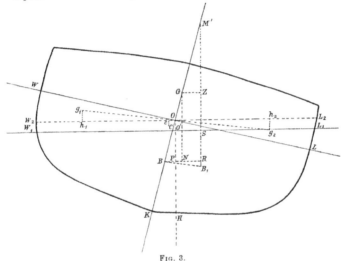

Fig. 3.

It is obtained by direct investigation, as Atwood obtained it, or by substitution in the equations (1) and (2) of $v = v_1 = v_2$, when we obtain

$$\text{V.BR} = v(oh_1 + oh_2) = v.h_1h_2$$

then
$$\text{V.GZ} = v.h_1h_2 - \text{V.BG sin } \theta \qquad \qquad (3)$$

or
$$\text{GZ} = \frac{v}{V}.h_1h_2 - \text{BG sin } \theta \qquad \qquad (4)$$

and
$$B_1\text{R} = \frac{v}{V}(g_1h_1 + g_2h_2). \qquad \qquad (5)$$

B M from Atwood's Formula. — Suppose θ to be small, and the vertical through B to intersect the vertical through B_1 in the point M (fig. 4).

$$\text{GZ} = \text{GM sin } \theta = \frac{v}{V}h_1h_2 - \text{BG sin } \theta \text{ from (4).}$$

Suppose O W or O L represents y, the half ordinate of the load waterline. For a small angle, the area of the small triangle $L O L_1$ is represented by $\frac{1}{2} y^2 \theta$. If we suppose this triangle to have a small thickness dx in a direction perpendicular to the paper, we may express the volume of the wedge by

$$v = \int_0^L \tfrac{1}{2} y^2 \theta . dx,$$

the limits for x being from zero, up to L, the length of the waterplane.

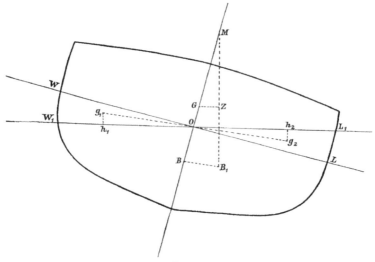

Fig. 4.

The moment of this element of volume about O is $\frac{1}{2} y^2 . \theta \times \frac{2}{3} y = \frac{1}{3} y^3 \theta$, and the moment of the transference of the wedge v is $v . h_1 h_2 = 2 \int_0^L \tfrac{1}{3} y^3 . \theta . dx.$

Hence we may write $GM \sin \theta = \dfrac{2}{3} \dfrac{\theta}{V} \int_0^L y^3 . dx - BG . \sin \theta.$

If θ is small, $\sin \theta = \theta$

and $GM = \dfrac{2}{3V} \int_0^L y^3 . dx - BG$

$$BG + GM = BM = \dfrac{2}{3V} \int_0^L y^3 . dx.$$

The point M is known in shipshape forms as the metacentre. It has been fully defined in Chapter IX, Part II.

This expression is
$$BM = \frac{\frac{2}{3}\int_0^L y^3.dx}{V}.$$

We have seen that this expression $\frac{2}{3}\int_0^L y^3.dx$ is the form of expression for the moment of inertia about O X of an area in the plane X Y and symmetrical about the O X axis.

Now the axis of O X is in the direction of the length of the form, that is, it is perpendicular to the plane of the paper, and the y ordinates are the ordinates like O L. Therefore $\frac{2}{3}\int_0^L y^3.dx$ is the moment of inertia of the whole waterplane W O L about an axis through O in the direction of the length.

Calling
$$\frac{2}{3}\int_0^L y^3.dx = I,$$

we have
$$BM = \frac{I}{V}.$$

If we obtain a series of values of G Z for a series of angles of inclination and a given displacement, we may set off the results in a graphic form thus :—

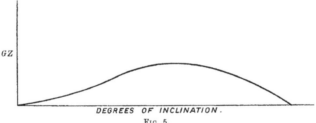

Fig. 5.

This curve is known as a Curve of Righting Arms, or more commonly a Curve of Statical Stability. We may call it a curve of G Z's for constant displacement and constant position of G, and for varying angle of heel.

Suppose we have three axes at right angles to each other, as represented in fig. 6. Suppose at each value of V for which we have a curve of stability (with a constant position of G) we set up the curve of statical stability. It is evident that it is only necessary to have a series of curves for a sufficiently large number of values of V to make a surface of statical stability. If we cut this surface by a plane parallel to the plane through Z O Y such as in $P_1 P_2 P_3$, the curve $P_1 P_2 P_3$ will be one of G Z's for varying displacements and constant angle of heel (measured by O h). If by an independent process of calculation we could obtain a series of curves such as $P_1 P_2 P_3$ we could obtain the same surface of statical stability as that obtained by the series of curves of statical stability (or curves of G Z for constant displacement and varying angle of heel). Such curves as $P_1 P_2 P_3$ are called Cross Curves of Stability.

The difference between a curve of stability and a cross curve of stability is that the former is a curve of G Z's for constant displacement and varying inclination, while the latter is for varying displacement and constant inclination. In the surface above dealt with it is assumed that G is unchanged in position.

For each position of G there will be a separate surface of statical stability.

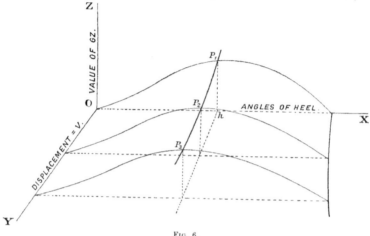

FIG. 6.

Suppose we have a known form of ship at a given inclination, and find for a waterline $W_1 L_1$ (fig. 7) the volume of displacement V and the position

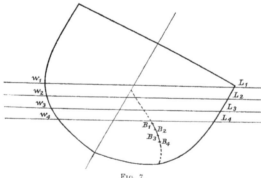

FIG. 7.

of C.B., say B_1, by any of the methods described in an earlier chapter. It is evident that we have only to find V_2 and B_2, V_3 and B_3, etc. for other water-lines $W_2 L_2$, $W_3 L_3$, etc. in order to be able to obtain a curve $B_1 B_2 B_3$ from which we can determine such a curve as $P_1 P_2 P_3$ (fig. 6). If we find a series of such curves for a series of angles of inclination, we can completely determine the surface of statical stability for a known position of the C.G. of the ship. For every position of the C.G. there will be a separate surface of stability, but they will all be founded on the positions of the C.B.'s for the different volumes and angles of inclination. Hence it is desirable to find the C.B.'s for all volumes and all angles of inclination, and then surfaces of statical stability can be found for determined positions of G.

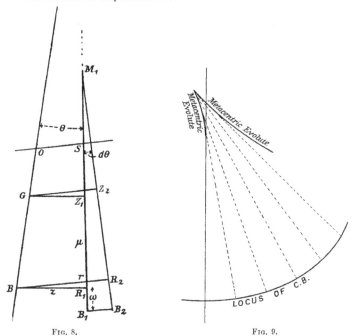

FIG. 8.   FIG. 9.

Hence we see that the determination of the stability resolves itself into finding volumes and C.G.'s of volumes, and may in all cases be dealt with by the methods described in Part II., or some modifications of them.

Metacentric Evolute.—In fig. 8 let B be the position of the centre of buoyancy in the upright. Let B_1 be the position of the centre of buoyancy after the vessel has been inclined through an angle θ.

Let B_2 be the position of B after the vessel has received a further inclination through an angle $d\theta$.

Draw the verticals B G, $B_1 M_1$, and $B_2 M_1$ through the points B, B_1, and B_2 respectively.

If the vessel is symmetrical about the midship section, i.e. if it is double-ended and the vessel be inclined about a fore and aft axis, fixed only in direction, the centre of buoyancy for all transverse inclinations will lie in the midship section, but if the ends are not symmetrical, there may be a tendency to change trim when the vessel is inclined. The verticals through the centres of buoyancy corresponding to two consecutive positions may not intersect, but they will be in vertical planes perpendicular to the axis of inclination, i.e. parallel to the plane of inclination. The intersection of the projection of these two lines in a transverse vertical plane may be called the metacentre, and the locus of this point is called the Metacentric Evolute (fig. 9). M_1, the intersection on the plane of the paper (parallel to the plane of inclination) of the projection of the verticals through B_1 and B_2 (fig. 8), is a point on the metacentric evolute.

For transverse inclinations it involves generally only an inappreciable quantity if we consider these verticals to lie in the midship section and to intersect at a point M. Its amount is small, because in most forms the departure from symmetry about the mid section is small.

Later we shall see that the term metavol is suggested for the locus of the intersection of verticals (or their projections) through the centres of buoyancy.

In fig. 8 draw perpendiculars from the points B and G on the verticals through B_1 and B_2.

$$\text{Let} \qquad R_1 M_1 = \mu$$
$$R_1 B = z$$
$$R_1 B_1 = w$$
$$\text{The angle} \qquad R_1 B R_2 = d\theta.$$
$$\text{Now} \qquad r R_2 = dz$$
$$\therefore \qquad \mu.d\theta = dz$$
$$\therefore \qquad z = \int \mu.d\theta.$$
$$\text{Again,} \qquad r R_1 = dw$$
$$\therefore \qquad z.d\theta = dw$$
$$\therefore \qquad w = \int z.d\theta.$$
$$\text{Hence} \qquad w = \int z d\theta = \int\int \mu.d\theta.d\theta.$$

If we have a curve of $R_1 M_1$'s or values of μ in terms of θ we can get the curves of $B R_1$ and $B_1 R_1$ by integration. Integrating once we get the curve of values of z or values of $B R_1$. Integrating this curve we get the curve of values of w or values of $B_1 R_1$. These three curves are shown in fig. 10.

We have seen that

$$B_1 R_1 = w = \frac{v}{V}(h_1 g_1 + h_2 g_2), \text{ equation (5), p. 5.}$$
$$\therefore \qquad \int z d\theta = \frac{v}{V}(h_1 g_1 + h_2 g_2).$$
$$\text{But} \qquad z = B R_1 = \frac{v}{V} h_1 h_2, \text{ p. 5.}$$
$$\therefore \qquad \int h_1 h_2.d\theta = h_1 g_1 + h_2 g_2.$$

Dynamical Stability.—The work done in inclining a vessel through an angle $d\theta$ is $W.GZ.d\theta$, and therefore the total work done in inclining a vessel from θ_1 to θ_2 is $W \int_{\theta_1}^{\theta_2} GZ\, d\theta$.

The dynamical stability of a vessel at any angle is defined to be the work done in inclining the vessel from the upright position (in which she is assumed to be in statical equilibrium) through that angle. The expression for the dynamical stability is therefore $W \int_0^\theta GZ\, d\theta$, where θ is the angle through which the vessel has been inclined.

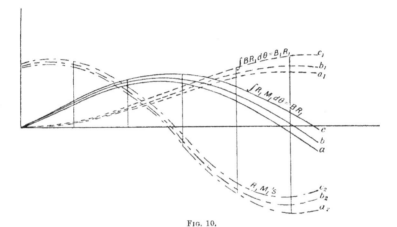

FIG. 10.

The dynamical stability $= W \int_0^\theta GZ.d\theta$

$$= W \int_0^\theta (BR_1 - BG \sin \theta)\, d\theta \text{ (see fig. 8)}$$

$$= W \int_0^\theta BR_1\, d\theta - W \int_0^\theta BG.\sin \theta.d\theta$$

$$= W.B_1R_1 - W.BG(-\cos \theta + 1)$$

$$= W(B_1R_1 + BG. \cos \theta - BG)$$

$$= W(B_1Z_1 - BG).$$

Hence the dynamical stability is $= W(B_1Z_1 - BG)$.

The expression $(B_1Z_1 - BG)$ is called the Dynamical Arm, and is generally written h, so that the dynamical stability is represented by $W h$.

A method of showing directly that this is the work done in inclining the vessel is as follows (see fig. 3, p. 5) :—

O G is distance of C.G. above or below the waterplane W L in the upright condition.

O B   ,,   C.B. below the waterplane W L in the upright condition.

S Z   ,,   C.G. above or below the waterplane $W_1 L_1$ in the inclined condition.

S B_1 ,,   C.B. below the waterplane $W_1 L_1$ in the inclined condition.

Original distance between G and $B = BO + OG = BG$.

Final distance   ,,   G ,, $B = B_1 S + SZ = B_1 Z$.

∴ Distance by which these two centres of force have been separated during the inclination of the vessel $= (B_1 Z \sim BG)$.

Here, since $B_1 Z$ is $> BG$, the distance $= (B_1 Z - BG)$.

∴ Work done in inclining $= W(B_1 Z - BG)$.   (Fig. 3.)

And $(B_1 Z - BG)$ is the quantity previously denoted by h.

I.e. work done during inclination $= Wh$.

Relation between the Statical Curve of Stability and the Dynamical Curve.—The statical curve is a curve of values of G Z, and the dynamical curve is a curve of values of h.

We have seen that $W \int GZ.d\theta = Wh$.

$$\therefore \quad \int GZ.d\theta = h.$$

∴ The dynamical curve is the integral of the statical curve, and it can be obtained directly from the G Z by ordinary integration.

CHAPTER II.

STABILITY OF FLOATING BODIES GENERALLY.

In this chapter will be investigated the stabilities of bodies in general, that is, of any form.

It has been seen that the displacement of a body is equal to its weight, and on the assumption that the weight is constant and that the C. G. can be suitably shifted, the body will float in equilibrium in many positions. In other words, for every plane cutting off from the body a volume of the liquid displaced whose weight is equal to the weight of the body, we have a possible plane of flotation. For each volume so cut off there will be a centre of buoyancy.

If we imagine a body to be slowly rotated about an axis through its C.G. and fixed in direction, but free to move vertically, the body will adjust itself vertically so that the weight of the displaced fluid will be equal to the weight of the body at every point of the revolution. Hence we shall have an indefinite number of planes in the body which can be planes of flotation cutting off constant volume. Each volume corresponding to a plane of flotation will have a centre of buoyancy.

When the revolution is completed, the centre of buoyancy will coincide with that at the beginning of the revolution.

The whole series of centres of buoyancy which have corresponded to the series of constant volumes submerged during the complete revolution will form a curve beginning and ending at the centre of buoyancy in the first position. In other words, it will be a closed curve.

If we now rotate the body about another axis fixed in direction, but otherwise free, as in the former case, we shall obtain another closed curve of centres of buoyancy which will be different to the former one if the direction of the axis of rotation be different. We may take an indefinite number of axes, all having different directions ; in fact we may start with an axis pointing to the north, and take every point of the compass between north and south for the direction of the axis, and to every direction of axis there will correspond a closed curve of centres of buoyancy. These obviously will, if taken closely enough, form a closed surface, which may be called a surface of buoyancy. Hence a surface of buoyancy of a body may be defined as the loci of centres of gravity of constant volume cut off from the form. We may, for convenience, call this surface of centres of buoyancy the *isovol* surface, that is, the surface for constant volume and varying inclination.

Suppose the chosen axis through the centre of gravity to remain fixed in direction only, as before. Also suppose the whole volume of the body to be

13

unchanged, but its weight to be changed gradually from nothing to the weight of its whole volume of the liquid in which it is immersed. In other words, let the body be at first without weight, just touching the water surface, and be gradually increased in weight until it is just completely submerged, change of position taking place only in a vertical direction. To each volume submerged there will correspond a centre of buoyancy ; and if the volumes cut off be taken closely enough together, these centres of buoyancy will form a curve, beginning at the point of no immersion and ending at the centre of buoyancy of the whole solid. This curve may be called an *isocline*, and may be defined as the locus of centres of buoyancy corresponding to volumes cut off at planes perpendicular to a fixed line in the body.

Suppose there is a datum line in the body passing through the centre of gravity of the whole volume, and making a known angle with the assumed vertical already referred to. We may have an indefinite number of lines, each of which may be a vertical making the same known angle with the datum line, and for each of these verticals we may have an isocline. These isocline curves will form a surface which may be called an Isocline Surface of Buoyancy for the known angle. There may be an indefinite number of angles, to each of which would correspond an isocline surface, and these surfaces in all would make an isocline solid which will correspond to the solid formed by the enveloping surface of the body.

Similarly, for each volume cut off—from that of no displacement to the whole displacement of the body—there will correspond an isovol surface. These will form a solid, which could be called an isovol solid, but that it is the same as the isocline solid and the enveloping surface of the body. The isovol surface corresponding to no displacement will be the enveloping surface of the body, or the surface which all the tangent planes to the body which do not cut it would form.

Let us first consider some of the properties of the isovol suface of buoyancy, the isoclines and other curves.

1st. It has been seen that *the isovol is a closed surface*, and must lie within the limits of the enveloping surface of the body.

2nd. *The tangent plane at any point of the isovol is parallel to the waterplane corresponding to that point.* For, the direction in which, for a small inclination, the centre of buoyancy changes, has been shown to be parallel to the straight line joining the centres of gravity of the wedges of emergence and submersion. When the angle is indefinitely small, this latter line coincides with the waterplane, and the former line with the direction of the tangent. As this is true of all directions of inclination, a change of direction of the centre of buoyancy takes place along the tangent line parallel to the waterplane, and therefore in a tangent plane parallel to the waterplane. Hence all points indefinitely close to the original centre of buoyancy are in the same plane with it, and that plane which is a tangent plane is parallel to the waterplane.

3rd. *It has no re-entering parts.* If any part of the surface had re-entering parts, a tangent plane in some point of the part would cut the surface, but it can be shown that a tangent to an isovol surface can never cut the surface.

We have already seen that a change of waterplane caused by inclining the body through a small angle (displacement remaining constant) is equivalent to taking a wedge of volume from the emerged side *below* the waterline, and placing a wedge of the same volume on the submerged side *above* the waterline. This necessarily causes a rise in the centre of buoyancy relatively to the waterplane.

As the waterplane is parallel to the tangent plane the centre of buoyancy will always move relatively to it in the direction of the waterplane, and, therefore, its curvature will always be towards the waterplane, and away from the tangent plane. Hence the surface can never have a re-entering part, and a tangent plane cannot cut it.

This can also be seen as follows :—

If the isovol surface has a re-entrant part, then some tangent plane at B_1 parallel to a plane of flotation must cut it, and, in the vicinity of the tangent plane B_1, the adjacent centres of buoyancy would move away from the plane parallel to the waterplane, which is impossible. Further, there would be

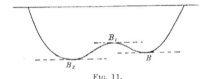

Fig. 11.

another tangent plane at B_2 parallel to the same waterplane as that corresponding to B_1, and we should have a solid with three positions of centres of buoyancy, which is impossible.

4th. *For every isovol there is a complementary isovol similar in form, but with corresponding radii at* 180° *from each other.* The pole of similarity is the centre of volume of the whole solid.

If V be the volume of displacement and B its centre of buoyancy, the volume v of the remainder of the solid and the position of b will be related to each other by

$$v . bH = V . BH,$$

where H is the centre of volume of the whole solid. Since B and b are points on the isovols of V and v volume their loci will be similar, since $bH = \dfrac{V}{v} BH$ and $\dfrac{V}{v}$ is constant. The radius bH is at 180° to BH.

The limiting isovols are (1) the enveloping surface of the body, (2) the point H ; so that the complementary isovols which approach very near to the total volume of the body and to no volume, approach very near to the point H and to the enveloping surface of the body respectively. The point H in the limit has the same shape as the enveloping surface, but with all its corresponding radii at 180°.

5th. For the same angle of inclination, the tangents to the isovols at the centre of buoyancy for the same solid and angle of inclination will all have the same inclination, as they are parallel to the waterlines of the same inclination. Hence all tangents to isovols along an isocline are parallel to each other. Fig. 12 shows a set of isovols and isoclines for a shipshaped form. The isovols are for uniformly varying percentages of the total volume of the solid. The isoclines are for uniformly varying angles of inclination.

Curve of Flotation.—To each constant volume of displacement there will be a waterplane. Consecutive waterplanes intersect in their centres of gravity. The locus of centre of gravity of waterplane for constant volume for a given direction of inclination is called a Curve of Flotation.

Surface of Flotation, or Flotavol.—If the direction of inclination be varied infinitely a series of curves of flotation will be formed, which together will form a Surface of Flotation for constant volume of displacement. This surface will be the locus of all centres of gravity of waterplane cutting off constant volume.

6th. The tangents to the isocline will all pass through the point of the curve of flotation which corresponds to the centre of buoyancy, which is the touching point of the tangent, because each addition to the volume of displacement for constant angle of inclination is made by a small addition of volume at the waterline formed by a parallel layer whose centre of

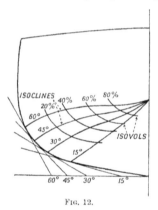

Fig. 12.

gravity is in the limit at that of the waterplane, and is therefore a point on the curve of flotation.

For each waterline of constant inclination there will be a centre of gravity of area which will be a point on the curve of flotation for one particular volume and inclination. Hence there will be a curve of flotation of constant inclination and varying volume, which may be called a Flotacline.* One end of this curve will coincide with the end A of the corresponding isocline (at the angle θ), which is normal to the midship section; the other end B will coincide with the corresponding end of the isocline at the angle $\theta + \pi$. This is shown in fig. 13.

This curve will be such that from any point of it, if a straight line be drawn to the corresponding C.B., this line will be a tangent to the isocline.

7th. Hence *the flotacline is a curve of pursuit to the corresponding isocline.*

* It may be noticed that there is the same flotacline for $(\theta + \pi)$ and v, as for θ and V.

The projection of the intersection of consecutive normals to the isovol will form the curve known as the metacentric evolute, which may perhaps be better called the Metavol. Such a curve is shown in fig. 9.

If we consider the consecutive metacentres for varying volume and constant inclination, we shall see that there will be a curve of metacentres for constant inclination. This curve may be called a Metacline.

8th. *A tangent to the metacline will always pass through the centre of curvature of the corresponding flotavol*, because the change in position of the metacentre is due to a small added volume at the corresponding waterline which acts for a small inclination through the intersection of consecutive verticals through consecutive C.G.'s of the waterplane, that is, through the intersection of consecutive normals to the flotavol. Hence the tangent to

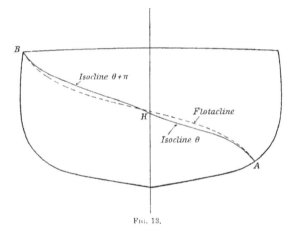

Fig. 13.

the curve of metaclines will pass through the corresponding point on centre of curvature of the flotavol.

For constant inclination and varying volume, the curve of centres of curvature of the consecutive flotavols will have its consecutive points on the tangents to corresponding consecutive points on the metacline. This curve thus forms a curve of pursuit to the metacline. Hence we have the two following statements :—

1. The flotacline is a curve of pursuit to the isocline.

2. The locus of the centre of curvature of the flotaclines is a curve of pursuit to the metacline.

Method of obtaining Isoclines and Isovols.—For any form isoclines can be drawn at convenient angles, say 15°, 30°, 45°, 60°, etc., and isovols are generally drawn at uniform percentages of the total volume from 20% to 80%.

In order to find the spots for an isocline, we have first to construct a stability body plan. It is better to leave out erections (so that the form may have no serious discontinuities), for purposes of comparison of forms independently of the variations in deck erections. A series of parallel waterplanes is then drawn at the required angle θ for the isocline.

At each waterplane we have to find—

(1) The displacement up to that waterline.

(2) The moment of the displacement about an axis perpendicular to the waterplanes.

(3) The moment of the displacement about an axis parallel to the waterplanes.

This is most conveniently done by the integrator. If possible, for working the integrator, the most suitable axis perpendicular to the waterline is taken through the keel. The axis parallel to the waterplane is taken at any convenient distance from the body plan.

Positions for axes are as shown in fig. 14. $K K_1$ is through the keel and is perpendicular to the waterplanes. $L L_1$ is outside the body plan and is parallel to waterplanes.

If we divide (2) by (1) we get the position of the centre of buoyancy with reference to the axis $K K_1$.

If we divide (3) by (1) we get the position of the centre of buoyancy with reference to the axis $L L_1$.

The actual position of C.B. can therefore be fixed, and thus a spot in the isocline obtained.

Obtaining a series of these spots by making the above calculations for each waterplane, we can get the isocline for all displacements for a constant angle of heel.

These operations for obtaining an isocline can be performed in the following order :—

(1) Draw a series of waterplanes at $\theta°$.

(2) Go over all the sections with the integrator up to each waterline, the axes being fixed :
      1st (a) perpendicular to the waterlines as at $K K_1$.
      2nd (b) parallel   „   „   „ $L L_1$.

(3) Set off the readings of the area and moment wheels for each section on a base representing the length. (There are thus for each $w l$ one curve of areas and two curves of moments.)

(4) Find the areas of (a) the area curves,
                              (b) the moment about $K K_1$ curves,
            and   (c) „   „   „ $L L_1$ „

(5) Apply the scales of the integrator and drawing to get the true volume and the true moment.

(6) Divide the moment results by the corresponding volume results.

(7) Set off the distances thus obtained for each waterline with reference to the axes $K K_1$ and $L L_1$ and we get the values of the offsets of B, which enable us to place the spots for the isocline.

Note.—This series of operations can be simplified by first spacing the body plan sections according to Tchebycheff's Rules, say, for instance, according to the three ordinate rule as used for displacement table in Vol. I., opposite page 82. The labour of plotting the integrator readings for each section is thereby saved, as the section spaced in this manner can be traced over in succession by the integrator, beginning at the keel and continuing, without stopping, to the end. It is only necessary to note the final readings of the area and moment wheels. There will be only one volume and two moment readings to record for each waterline, and we can now get the isocline by performing the operations (6) and (7) above described.

To find the spot in an Isocline corresponding to a given Waterplane.— Let $K K_1$ and $L L_1$ be the two axes as before, and let I H be the isocline obtained by setting off the ordinates obtained as described above. On a base line O A as shown, parallel to $K K_1$, set off as horizontal ordinates the displacements up to each waterplane. These form the curve O M. Thus at the waterline $w l$ the displacement is $a m$.

Let b_1 be the position on the isocline of the centre of buoyancy corresponding to waterline $w l$, which is assumed to be one for which the integrator readings have been taken. Set off along $a m$ the distance $a b$ equal to $a_1 b_1$, the distance of b_1 from O A. Doing this for all the waterplanes used for integrating we can get a new curve $B B_1$, from which can be obtained at any waterplane the distance of the centre of buoyancy in the isocline from

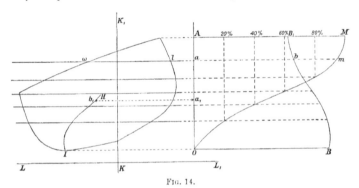

FIG. 14.

the line O A. By this means we can determine the spot giving the position of centre of buoyancy corresponding to *any* waterline parallel to $L L_1$.

To determine the Isovol Curves.—The above construction leads at once to the determination of the isovols.

If we have a series of isoclines, and know the point on each which corresponds to a chosen constant displacement which is a fixed percentage of the total bulk, we can draw a curve through these points. This curve will be the isovol for that displacement. It is convenient, therefore, to find first the waterlines giving certain percentages of displacement, say from 20% up to 80%. This is easily done by dividing the ordinate A M (fig. 14) into these percentage proportions. The vertical lines through these points cut the displacement curves at the required waterlines, and the ordinates of the B B_1 curve at these waterlines give the distances out from O A of the corresponding positions of C.B. on the isocline. Doing this for these percentages for the different angles of inclination we get spots on the isovol curves.

Isoclines are usually drawn for the following angles of inclination, 15°, 30°, 45°, 60°, 75°, and 90°. The isovols can then be found by the above method at 20%, 30%, 40%, 50%, 60%, 70%, 80% of total volume.

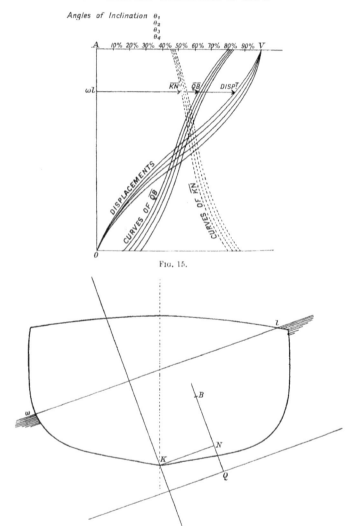

Fig. 15.

Fig. 16.

It is sometimes better to make a combined diagram giving the curves for each angle of inclination.

For each angle of inclination we have three curves (fig. 15), giving respectively—

      (1) Displacement.

      (2) Curve of K N's.   (See fig. 16.)

      (3) Curve of Q B's.   (do.   )

The values of these (displacement, K N, and Q B) are obtained for each waterline, and are set off in terms of the waterline interval.

Having a series of curves for the angles of inclination θ_1, θ_2, θ_3, θ_4, etc., we can draw the vertical lines at the required percentages of displacement for which the isovols are required.

Where these vertical lines cut the displacement curves, we get the positions of the waterlines cutting off the required volumes, and we also get the values of K N and Q B for these respective volumes. These values fix the positions of the centre of buoyancy of constant volume in the isoclines, and hence give points through which the isovol curve for each percentage of displacement can be drawn.

CHAPTER III.

DETERMINATION OF COORDINATES OF B FOR A GIVEN FORM FROM A SIMILAR FORM OF DIFFERENT DIMENSIONS.

It is sometimes useful to obtain the locus of centre of buoyancy of a known form of one set of dimensions from that of a similar form of different dimensions. If all the measurements defining a form are altered in the same proportion the coordinates of the centres of buoyancy will be similarly altered, but if the length, breadth, and depth measurements are altered respectively in different proportions, the changes in the coordinates of the centres of buoyancy are not so simple to determine. The following simple analysis enables us to obtain these :—

Suppose we have a form whose principal dimensions are L B D, and a new form is evolved by altering all the length, breadth, and depth measurements respectively in proportions such that L_1, B_1, and D_1 are the new principal dimensions.

The ratio of length dimension alteration will be $\dfrac{L_1}{L}$.

,,   breadth   ,,   ,,   ,, $\dfrac{B_1}{B}$.

,,   depth   ,,   ,,   ,, $\dfrac{D_1}{D}$.

For transverse inclinations the variation in length will produce no effect on the locus of B.

Let the breadth and depth be represented in section as shown at A O and A_1 O (fig. 17). Referring them to axis O Z, O Y, O X as shown, we see that the coordinates of a point P in A O are—

y the vertical height of P,
z the horizontal distance from Y O X,
x the longitudinal or fore and aft distance from Z O Y.

The coordinates of a corresponding point P_1 in A_1 O are therefore

$$z \times \frac{B_1}{B}.$$

$$y \times \frac{D_1}{D}.$$

$$x \times \frac{L_1}{L}.$$

At P the volume of an element $= dx.dy.dz = \delta V$.

At P the moment of an element about $OZ = y.dx.dy.dz = \delta M$.

Applying this formula to a corresponding element at P_1 in $A_1 O$ we have, by substituting the coordinates given above for P_1, the volume of an element

at $P_1 = \dfrac{B_1 D_1 L_1}{BDL}.dx.dy.dz = \delta V_1$, the moment of an element about OZ at P_1

$= \dfrac{D_1}{D}.\dfrac{B_1 D_1 L_1}{BDL} y.dx.dy.dz = \delta M_1$.

$$\therefore \quad \overline{Y}_1 = \int \frac{\delta M_1}{\delta V_1} = \frac{\dfrac{D_1}{D}.\dfrac{B_1 D_1 L_1}{BDL}\int y.dx.dy.dz}{\dfrac{B_1 D_1 L_1}{BDL}\int dx.dy.dz} = \frac{D_1}{D}\int \frac{\delta M}{\delta V}.$$

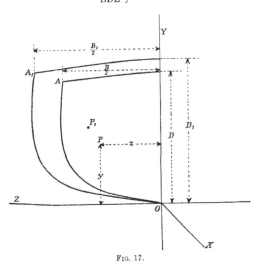

FIG. 17.

So that the alteration in a given form of the length and breadth dimensions alone do not affect $\overline{Y}$, the height of the C.B.   Only the alteration in depth affects the height of C.B.

Similarly, the alteration of length and depth alone do not affect $\overline{Z}$, the lateral position of C.B.

The total effect on C.B. of a change of length, breadth, and depth may therefore be seen to be for $\overline{Y}$ in proportion to the value $\dfrac{D_1}{D}$ and for $\overline{Z}$ to $\dfrac{B_1}{B}$.

Suppose that the waterplane of a form is inclined $\theta°$ to the horizontal, and that we enlarge all the breadth and depth dimensions, B and D being for the original form, and B_1 and D_1 for the enlarged form.

In fig. 18, W K L represents a section of the original form in which W L is the waterplane inclined at θ^0 to the horizontal O F. The dotted figure $W_1 K_1 L_1$ represents the corresponding section of the enlarged form. For clearness let the sections be so placed that the waterlines W L and $W_1 L_1$ intersect in O at the centre line. The inclination of $W_1 L_1$ to the horizontal is θ_1, and it is desired to find the relation between θ and θ_1.

If we take a point P in W L we can get the corresponding point P_1 in the

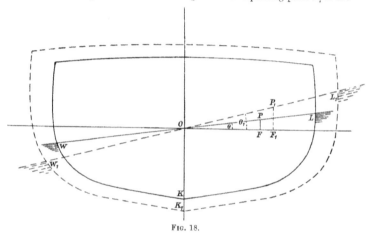

Fig. 18.

enlarged form by the method shown above, and the line O P_1 will be the waterline of enlarged form. Thus in the figure

$$P_1 F_1 = \frac{D_1}{D} P F.$$

$$O F_1 = \frac{B_1}{B} O F.$$

so that as $\tan \theta = \dfrac{PF}{OF},$

$$\tan \theta_1 = \frac{P_1 F_1}{O F_1} = \frac{\dfrac{D_1}{D} PF}{\dfrac{B_1}{B} OF} = \frac{D_1}{D} \cdot \frac{B}{B_1} \tan \theta.$$

∴ The relation between the angles of inclination of corresponding water-planes is expressed by the above formula or

$$\frac{\tan \theta_1}{\tan \theta} = \frac{D_1}{D} \cdot \frac{B}{B_1}.$$

The above consideration applies equally to any plane that is parallel to the floating waterplane ; and therefore if we have for a given form a series of waterplanes, we can at once get the angles of inclination of the corresponding waterplanes for any enlarged form of different dimensions. The actual position of the corresponding waterplane is got by setting up $KO_1 = \dfrac{D_1}{D} KO$, as in fig. 19, and drawing a straight line through O_1 inclined θ_1 to the horizontal, θ_1 being given by

$$\tan \theta_1 = \frac{D_1}{D} \frac{B}{B_1} . \tan \theta.$$

If we have an isovol of a form of known dimensions, we can easily deter-

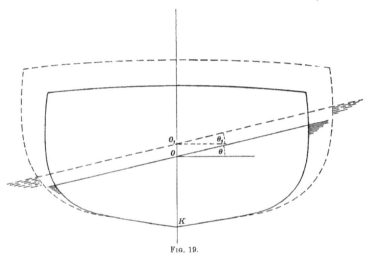

FIG. 19.

mine the corresponding isovol for the same form with the length, breadth, and depth measurements respectively. The same is true of an isocline.

Standardising.—We have seen how to find the corresponding points in a form similar to a given one, and also how to find the corresponding angles of inclination of the waterplanes.

$$\text{Ratio of breadths} = \frac{B_1}{B}.$$

$$\text{,,} \quad \text{depths} \quad = \frac{D_1}{D}.$$

$$\text{,,} \quad \text{angles} \quad = \frac{\tan \theta_1}{\tan \theta} = \frac{B}{B_1} \frac{D_1}{D}.$$

If we refer the results of a given form to a similar form of standard dimensions, we thereby standardise those results. That is, that whatever the dimensions of the forms we have been working upon may have been, if we plot the results as for the same forms to standard dimensions, we are then able to compare the results of different forms directly with each other, whatever may have been the absolute dimensions of the forms for which the results have been obtained.

The standard form chosen (for convenience) is one in which

$$D_1 = 10'',$$
$$B_1 = 20'',$$
or the half-breadth $= 10''.$

Therefore in the formulæ above,

$$\text{the ratio of breadth} = \frac{20}{B};$$
$$\text{,,} \quad \text{,,} \quad \text{depth} \quad = \frac{10}{D};$$

B and D being in inches;

$$\therefore \quad \frac{\tan \theta_1}{\tan \theta} = \frac{B}{2D}.$$

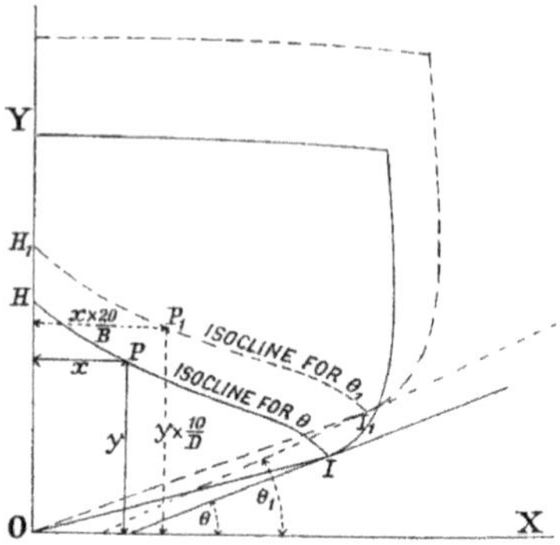

FIG. 20.

Standardising an Isocline.—Let I H (fig. 20) be the isocline of a given form of dimensions L, B, and D, and let the angle of inclination of the isocline be θ. We can plot the form to standard dimensions from the ratios of dimensions. This is shown dotted. H_1, the spot corresponding to H, is obtained from $OH : OH_1 : D : D_1$.

The angle which the tangent at I makes with the horizontal is θ. The tangent at I_1 will make θ_1, such that

$$\tan \theta_1 = \tan \theta \times \frac{B}{2D}.$$

$\therefore$ I_1, the spot corresponding to I, is found.

Take any other point P whose coordinates are x and y in inches on the isocline.   Then the coordinates of the corresponding point P_1 on the standardised isocline are

$$x \times \frac{20}{B} \text{ and } y \times \frac{10}{D}.$$

I_1 can also be found in this way, so that we can plot the standardised isocline from H_1 to I_1.

In order always to obtain isovols and isoclines of forms of standard dimensions at the same percentages of displacements and angles of inclination, it is more convenient to draw the waterlines on the actual form at angles corresponding to 15°, 30°, 45°, 60°, 75° on the standard form.   These can be obtained directly by substituting the above values in succession for θ_1 in the formula

$$\tan \theta_1 = \frac{B}{2D} \tan \theta.$$

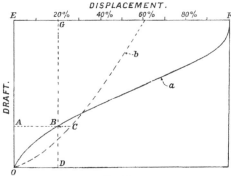

FIG. 21.

The values of θ obtained are those to which waterlines should be drawn in the actual form.

When the results are set off on a standardised form, as previously explained, they will then be for isovols at 20%, 40%, 60%, 80% of the total displacement, and for isoclines for 15°, 30°, 45°, 60°, and 75° inclination.

If all results for every form are so plotted, the curves so obtained will be directly comparable with each other, and will show directly the effect upon the isoclines and isovols of difference of form.

It is sometimes convenient to be able to carry out the standardising of stability curves direct from curves of K N, or "cross curves" as they are sometimes called.

To do this, first make a complete curve O F of displacement in the upright fig. 21.   Draw the locus of centre of buoyancy O b (fig. 21) by taking at a series of draughts, such as $\overline{O A}$, the value of

$$\frac{\text{area OBD in sq. inches}}{\text{AB in inches}}.$$

This value $\overline{A\,C}$, plotted at the corresponding draught, gives the height of B above the draught datum line when the vessel is floating at a draught $\overline{O\,A}$, and the curve $O\,b$ is obtained.

Divide the line $\overline{E\,F}$, representing the total displacement, by points at 20%, 30%, 40%, 50%, 60%, 70%, and 80% of the length $\overline{E\,F}$ from E; these points will represent corresponding percentages of total displacement. The heights of the C.B.'s for these displacements can be got from the curve $O\,b$ by drawing at any percentage of displacement, say 20%, a vertical, and where it cuts the curve O F drawing a horizontal line cutting the curve $O\,b$. The ordinate at this line will be the height above the draught datum line of the C.B. corresponding to 20% displacement.

Describe a (standardised) square of 10-inch side (fig. 22), in which place the half-breadth midship section of the vessel, using the following scales :—

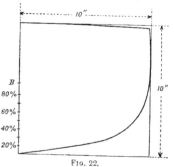

Fɪɢ. 22.

Horizontal scale

$$x_1 = \frac{x.n.20}{B} \qquad \cdot \qquad \cdot \qquad \cdot \qquad \cdot \qquad \cdot \quad \text{(i)}$$

Vertical scale

$$y_1 = \frac{y.n.10}{D} \qquad \cdot \qquad \cdot \qquad \cdot \qquad \cdot \qquad \cdot \quad \text{(ii)}$$

where x_1 and y_1 are the coordinates in inches of paper of a point on the standardised section, and x and y are the coordinates in inches of paper of the corresponding point on the ordinary section ; B and D the moulded breadth and depth respectively of the ship in feet; and $n \equiv$ the scale to which the ordinary section is drawn $\left(\dfrac{1^{\text{th}}}{n}\ \text{in.} \equiv 1\ \text{foot}\right)$

Using the vertical scale (ii), mark off the $\overline{K\,B}$'s on fig. 22 at the different percentages of displacement as found in fig. 21.

Take now the curves of $\overline{K\,N}$, sometimes called Cross Curves of Stability (fig. 23), for the vessel * and set up the different percentages of displacement.

* In view of standardising stability curves, it is advisable, when preparing $\overline{K\,N}$ curves for the ordinary stability calculations, to take the $\overline{K\,N}$'s for displacements ranging from 20% to 80% of the total displacement.

Set off horizontal lines (see fig. 23) $\overline{K\,B}$ sin C distant from the base, where C has the values 15°, 30°, 45°, 60°, and 75°, and $\overline{K\,B}$ is the distance of the centre of buoyancy above the datum line for draft.

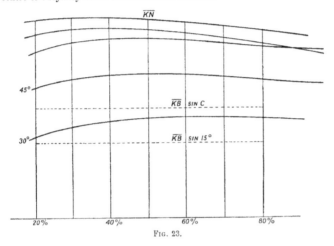

FIG. 23.

Since $B\,R = K\,N - K\,B$ sin C we have now a simple method of measuring $\overline{B\,R}$ at displacements 20%, 30%, etc., and angles of heel 15°, 30°, etc.

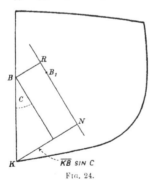

FIG. 24.

Plot curve of $\overline{B\,R}$ on a base of radians (fig. 25). Integrate these curves and we get the (dotted) curves of $\overline{B_1R}$, as $\overline{B_1R} = \int \overline{B\,R}.d\theta.$ See p. 10.

Next find the angles θ on the ordinary section which will correspond to the angles 15°, 30°, etc., on the standardised section from the formula

$$\tan \theta_1 = \frac{B}{2D} \tan \theta.$$

Set off the angles so found on fig. 25, then $\overline{BR}$ and $\overline{B_1R}$ can be measured

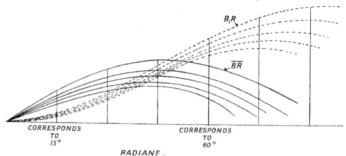

CORRESPONDS
TO
15°

CORRESPONDS
TO
60°

RADIANS.

Fig. 25.

for displacements 20%, 30%, etc., and angles corresponding to 15°, 30°, etc. . . . . (iii)

To find the values $\overline{br}$ and $\overline{b_1r}$ which correspond, on the standardised section, to $\overline{BR}$ and $\overline{B_1R}$ on the original section, proceed as follows :—

Fig. 26 shows the ordinary section, and fig. 27 the standardised section.

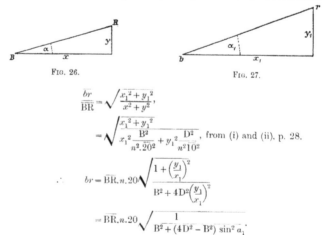

Fig. 26.   Fig. 27.

$$\frac{\overline{br}}{\overline{BR}} = \sqrt{\frac{x_1^2 + y_1^2}{x^2 + y^2}},$$

$$= \sqrt{\frac{x_1^2 + y_1^2}{x_1^2 \dfrac{B^2}{n^2.20^2} + y_1^2 \dfrac{D^2}{n^2 10^2}}}, \text{ from (i) and (ii), p. 28.}$$

$$\therefore \quad br = \overline{BR}.n.20 \sqrt{\frac{1 + \left(\dfrac{y_1}{x_1}\right)^2}{B^2 + 4D^2\left(\dfrac{y_1}{x_1}\right)^2}}$$

$$= \overline{BR}.n.20 \sqrt{\frac{1}{B^2 + (4D^2 - B^2)\sin^2 a_1}}.$$

a_1 has the values $15°$, $30°$, etc., and on substituting in this equation the corresponding values of $\overline{BR}$ from (iii) we get the values of $\overline{br}$ for the standardised section   The equation for $\overline{b_1r}$ is of the same form with B_1R substituted for $\overline{BR}$ and $(90° - a_1)$ for a_1, viz.,

$$b_1r = B_1R.n.20\sqrt{\dfrac{1}{B^2 + (4D^2 - B^2)\sin^2(90° - a_1)}}.$$

Having the values of br and b_1r we can now plot the curves giving the loci of B, viz. the isovols and isoclines, on the standardised form.

CHAPTER IV.

GEOMETRICAL PROPERTIES OF ISOVOLS, ETC.

THE curve of flotation has been defined as the locus of C.G.'s of waterplane cutting off constant volume for one direction of inclination. This is also called a Flotavol Curve. The locus of all flotavol curves has been called the Flotavol Surface.

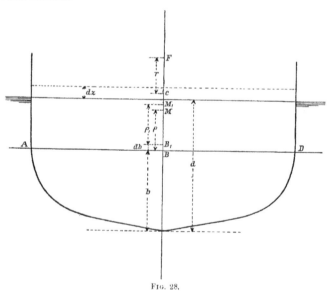

FIG. 28.

Leclert's Formula for the Radius of Curvature of the Flotavol.—F in fig. 28 is the centre of curvature of a flotavol curve, r is the radius of curvature, B and B_1 are C.B.'s at volumes V and V + dV and are at heights b and $b + db$ respectively. M and M_1 and ρ and ρ_1 are corresponding metacentric quantities.

32

Taking moments about $A\overline{D}$ of the volume V acting at M, and the volume dV acting at F, we have

$$\rho V + \left(r + \frac{dz}{2} + \overline{d} - b\right)dV. \qquad . \qquad . \qquad . \qquad (i)$$

By the principle of moments, this must be equal to the moment about $A\overline{D}$ of $V + dV$ (acting at M_1); or

$$(V + dV)(\rho_1 + db) \qquad . \qquad . \qquad . \qquad . \qquad (ii)$$

Equating (i) and (ii) we get

$$\rho V + r.dV + \left(\overline{d} - b + \frac{dz}{2}\right)dV = \rho_1 V + \rho_1.dV + db(V + dV) . \qquad . \qquad (iii)$$

Taking moments about $A\overline{D}$ of dV acting at C and $(V + dV)$ acting at B_1 we have,

$$\left(\overline{d} - b + \frac{dz}{2}\right)dV = db(V + dV),$$

equation (iii) becomes

$$\rho.V + r.dV = \rho_1(V + dV) \qquad . \qquad . \qquad . \qquad . \qquad (iv)$$

Now we know that

$$\rho = \frac{I}{V}$$

and $$\rho_1 = \frac{I + dI}{V + dV}.$$

Substituting these values for ρ and ρ_1 in (iv) we get

$$I + r.dV = I + dI,$$

whence $$r = \frac{dI}{dV} \qquad . \qquad . \qquad . \qquad . \qquad (v)$$

Another expression for the radius of curvature of the flotavol may be derived as follows:—

$$\rho = \frac{I}{V}$$

$$\therefore \quad \frac{d\rho}{dV} = \frac{1}{V}\frac{dI}{dV} - \frac{I}{V^2}$$

$$\therefore \quad \frac{dI}{dV} = \frac{I}{V} + V\frac{d\rho}{dV}$$

$$r = \rho + V\frac{d\rho}{dV}$$

which is known as "Leclert's formula."

It may be noticed that, in the case of a parabolic prism, floating with axis vertical and vertex downwards, for any inclination θ, ρ is independent of V and is given by $\rho = 2a \sec^3 \theta$, where $2a$ is equal to the semi latus-rectum of parabola. Thus, in this case $r = \rho$, since $\frac{d\rho}{dV} = 0$.

Properties of the Isocline.—Let I H be the isocline of a vessel inclined to the vertical at an angle θ (fig. 29).

Let X X be any vertical line.

Let B be the position of the centre of buoyancy corresponding to the waterline $w\,l$ which cuts off a volume V.

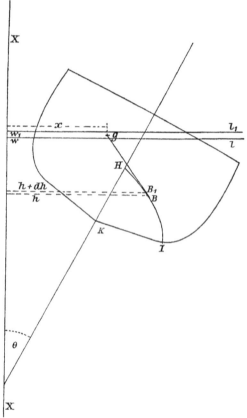

Fig. 29.

Let $w_1\,l_1$ be a waterline parallel, and- very close to $w\,l$, so that the volume cut off is $V + dV$. Let g be the centre of gravity of the layer between $w\,l$ and $w_1\,l_1$. Let g be distant x from X X and let B be distant h from X X. We can find the position of B_1 corresponding to the volume $V + dV$.

Let B_1 be distant $h + dh$ from X X.   Then, taking moments about X X we have

$$V.h + dV.x = (V + dV).(h + dh),$$

which, on neglecting quantities of the second order of infinitesimals, becomes

$$dV.x = h.dV + V.dh.$$

$$\therefore \qquad x = h + V.\frac{dh}{dV} \qquad . \qquad . \qquad . \qquad . \qquad (i)$$

Clearly the point B_1 will lie on the line g B, and $(V + dV).BB_1 - dV.gB = 0$:

$$\therefore \qquad BB_1 = \frac{gB.dV}{V + dV}.$$

In the limit B B_1 becomes zero when dV is infinitely small, and then the tangent to the isocline at B will be Bg and will pass through the centre of gravity of the corresponding plane of flotation.

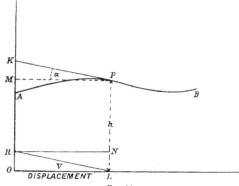

Fig. 30.

If we plot a curve of values of h in terms of V, we have a curve from which may be derived what is called a "cross curve." If X X passes through K, the keel, it will be a curve of K N's, fig. 16.   For a known position of G a cross curve can be at once obtained.

Let A B, fig. 30, be a cross curve giving values of h measured from a line such as X X in fig. 29.

Let P be the point h, V.   Draw the tangent at P, meeting the zero ordinate of displacement in K.   Draw P M parallel to O X.   Let K P M = α.

$$\text{Then} \qquad \tan \alpha = - \frac{dh}{dV}.$$

$$\therefore \qquad - PM \tan \alpha = V.\frac{dh}{dV}$$

$$\text{or} \qquad - KM = V\frac{dh}{dV} = x - h \text{ from (i), p. 35.}$$

$$\therefore \qquad x = h - K_1M.$$

Draw L R parallel to the tangent and R N parallel to O L. Then $x = $ P N.

Analogy of formula $x = h + V \dfrac{dh}{dV}$ **to Leclert's formula** $r = \rho + V \dfrac{d\rho}{dV}$.

Comparing the symbols we have :—

r is the radius of curvature of the surface of flotation.

x is the distance of the centre of gravity of waterplane from X X.

ρ is the radius of curvature of the surface of buoyancy.

h is the distance of the centre of buoyancy from X X.

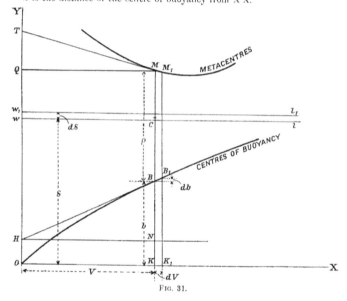

Fig. 31.

The following proposition explains the analogy $x = h + V \dfrac{dh}{dV}$.

Leclert's formula may be deduced from the equation as follows :—

The tangents to the isovol and to the flotavol at B and g respectively are horizontal.

Consider corresponding points whose coordinates are x_1 and h_1 for the same volume V, but at a new angle $(\theta + d\theta)$.

We have $\quad x_1 = h_1 + V \dfrac{dh_1}{dV}$.

But $\quad x_1 - x = r\, d\theta$ } since these are elements of arc

and $\quad h_1 - h = \rho\, d\theta,$ } corresponding to angle $d\theta$,

also $\quad x_1 - x = h_1 - h + V \dfrac{d}{dV}\,(h_1 - h)$.

$$\therefore \qquad r.d\theta = \rho.d\theta + V\frac{d\rho}{dV}.d\theta,$$

$$\text{or} \qquad r = \rho + V\frac{d\rho}{dV}.$$

Some properties of the locus of centre of buoyancy and metacentric curves.—Let the abscissæ of the curves be displacement V along O X, fig. 31. Let the height of the metacentres and centres of buoyancy be measured in the direction O Y.

We get curves of B and M as shown. At B draw the tangent B H meeting O Y in H. Draw H N, fig. 31, parallel to O X, meeting K B in N.

$$\text{Then} \qquad \tan BHN = \frac{db}{dV}$$

$$\text{and} \qquad HN \tan BHN = BN = V\frac{db}{dV} \qquad . \qquad . \qquad . \quad (\text{ii})$$

Let the draught to waterline $w\,l$ be δ.

It may be seen that this is a special case of $x = h + V\frac{dh}{dV}$ when X X, fig. 29, passes through K and is perpendicular to K H, then $x = \delta$, the distance of the centre of gravity of the waterplane from base,

and $b = h$, the distance of the centre of buoyancy of volume V from base. Hence we may write

$$\delta = b + V\frac{db}{dV} \qquad . \qquad . \qquad . \qquad . \qquad . \qquad . \quad (\text{iii})$$

$$i.e. \qquad KC = KB + HN \tan BHN$$

$$KC - KB = BN$$

$$CB = BN.$$

Draw tangent M T and draw Q M horizontal.

$$\text{Let} \qquad m = KM = b + \rho$$

$$dm = db + d\rho$$

$$V\frac{dm}{dV} = V\frac{db}{dV} + V\frac{d\rho}{dV}$$

$$= \delta - b + r - \rho \text{ from } \delta = b + V\frac{db}{dV}$$

$$\text{and } r = \rho + V\frac{d\rho}{dV}$$

$$= CB - \rho + r$$

$$\therefore \qquad V\frac{dm}{dV} + MC = r$$

$$\text{or} \qquad - QT + MC = r.$$

We have $\delta = b + V\dfrac{db}{dV}$ from (iii), p. 27.

$$\therefore \quad V\frac{db}{dV} = \delta - b$$

and $V\dfrac{dm}{dV} = \delta - b + r - \rho.$

If the tangent to the curve of M be parallel to the tangent to the curve of B where B corresponds to M,

Then $\dfrac{db}{dV} = \dfrac{dm}{dV}$

and $r - \rho = 0$

and $\therefore$ $r = \rho$ . . . . . . (iv)

The curve of B for ships is usually nearly straight, so that $\dfrac{db}{dV}$ is practically

constant, and where $\dfrac{dm}{dV}$ has about this value, r closely approximates to ρ.

Also when the tangent to the curve of m is horizontal, $\dfrac{dm}{dV} = 0$. See fig. 32.

$$\therefore \quad \delta - b + r - \rho = 0$$

i.e. $B C + r = \rho$

and the centre of curvature of the flotavol coincides with the metacentre.

If $\delta - b + r - \rho = 0$, one solution is $r = 0$, in which case M will be in the waterline and $\rho = \delta - b = V\dfrac{db}{dV}$. But $\rho + V\dfrac{d\rho}{dV} = 0$, and $\therefore \dfrac{d\rho}{dV} = -\dfrac{db}{dV}$ when

$r = 0$ and $\dfrac{dm}{dV} = 0.$

In fig. 33 we have a curve of ρ values set off to a base of volume Draw the tangent M T as before. Draw Q M parallel to O X.

Then $-QT = V\dfrac{d\rho}{dV}$ and $OQ = \rho.$

$$\therefore \quad OQ - QT = \rho + V\frac{d\rho}{dV}.$$

$$\therefore \quad = r.$$

Draw B R parallel to M T and R N parallel to O X.
Then $O Q - Q T = B M - B N = M N = r.$
This property is analogous to that shown for the isocline in fig. 30.
When the tangent to the curve of B M's is horizontal $r = \rho$, which is the same as in fig. 31 when the tangent to the B and M curves are parallel. When $r = 0$, $OQ - QT = 0$, fig. 33. The value of V, which fulfils this condition, can be transferred, if it exists, from fig. 33 to fig. 31, and it will give the draught at which M and F and C are in the waterline where F is the centre of curvature of the flotavol. As this point is one of no radius of curvature, it

will be a cusp in the flotavol. This will be a very exceptional combination, but when it does occur these two conditions must both exist for the same value of **V**.

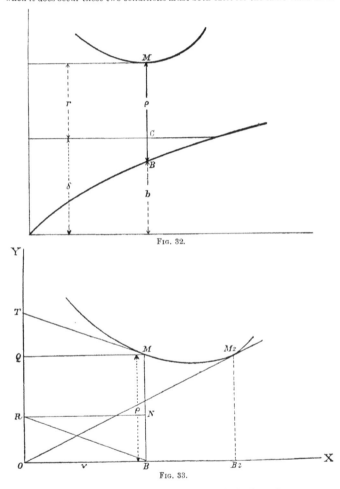

FIG. 32.

FIG. 33.

1. The tangent to the M curve in fig. 32 must be horizontal.
2. In fig. 33, M N must be zero.

Summary of the *properties* that have been proved in this chapter :—

$$\rho = \frac{I}{V}.$$

$$r = \frac{dI}{dV}.$$

$$x = h + V\frac{dh}{dV}.$$

$$r = \rho + V.\frac{d\rho}{dV}.$$

$$\delta = b + V\frac{db}{dV}.$$

$$\delta = b + \rho - r + V\frac{dm}{dV}.$$

And also—

(i) When the tangent to the curve of centre of buoyancy is parallel to the tangent to the curve of metacentres, the radius of curvature of the flotavol is equal to the radius of curvature of the surface of buoyancy.

(ii) When the tangent to the curve of metacentres is horizontal, the centre of curvature of the flotavol coincides with the metacentre.

In all the foregoing we have been dealing with the curves due to one direction of inclination, presumably the transverse. The results are true for any chosen direction of inclination. The curves of centres of buoyancy will be similar for all directions of inclination, but the metacentres and flotavol curves, which depend on the forms of the waterplanes, will differ with each direction of inclination, but the above relations hold notwithstanding.

The values of ρ and r for other directions of inclination can be found by direct calculation in each case from the calculated value of I, but it can be shown that it is only necessary to find two values of I in order to easily determine every other.

The following propositions show how this can be done.

Properties of the " Ellipse of Gyration " and of the " Indicatrix."
—When we consider the stability of any body, regular or irregular in form, floating in water, many questions relating to the shift of the centre of buoyancy may be conveniently solved by referring to the "ellipse of gyration" of the plane of flotation.

We shall see that this ellipse is similar to the "indicatrix" of the surface of buoyancy at the point corresponding to the plane of flotation.

Definition. The "ellipse of gyration" of a plane area is the ellipse that has the square of the perpendicular from the centre of the ellipse upon the tangent varying as the moment of inertia of the area about an axis through its centre of gravity and parallel to the tangent.

Definition.—The "indicatrix" of a point on a surface is the curve of intersection of the surface and a plane parallel and infinitely close to the tangent plane at that point.

This curve of intersection is a conic for any surface ; and if the curvature of the surface at that point is always of the same sign, then the curve will be an ellipse. The indicatrix of any point on an isovol is therefore an ellipse.

In a flotavol surface the curvature may change sign, and the indicatrix may be either an ellipse or a hyperbola.

The indicatrix has the property that the square of the radius vector to the centre varies as the radius of curvature of the normal section containing this radius vector.*

Let us first consider the properties of the ellipse of gyration for any given area.

Let the origin of the axes O X and O Y be taken at the centre of gravity of the area, fig. 34.

Consider an element of area $dx.dy$.

Definitions.—

The moment of inertia of $dx\ dy$ about O X $= y^2.dx.dy.$

     ,,   ,,   ,,   ,, O Y $= x^2.dx.dy.$

The rectangular moment of ,,   ,,   O Y and O X $= x.y.dx.dy.$

The moment of inertia of the whole area about O X $= \int\int y^2 dx.dy.$

$$\text{Call this I.}$$

,,   ,,   ,,   ,, O Y $= \int\int x^2 dx.dy.$

$$\text{Call this J.}$$

The rectangular moment   ,,   ,,   O X and O Y $= \int\int xy.dx.dy.$

$$\text{Call this K.}$$

We have then the functions I, J, and K for a given position of the axes.

We can find what these values become when the axes are turned through an angle θ.

Let O X_1 and O Y_1 (fig. 34) be the new axes.

Let $x_1 y_1$ represent the new coordinates of the point $x\,y$ referred to O X_1 and O Y_1.

Then the value I_1 for the moment of inertia about O $X_1 = \int\int y_1{}^2\,dx.dy,$

and   ,, J_1 ,,   ,,   ,, O $Y_1 = \int\int x_1{}^2\,dx.dy,$

,,   ,, K_1 for the rectangular moment $= \int\int x_1 y_1.dx.dy.$

But $x_1 = x\cos\theta + y\sin\theta.$

         $y_1 = y\cos\theta - x\sin\theta.$

$\therefore$ $I_1 = I\cos^2\theta + J\sin^2\theta - 2K\sin\theta\cos\theta,$

and $J_1 = J\cos^2\theta + I\sin^2\theta + 2K\sin\theta\cos\theta,$

and $K_1 = (I - J)\sin\theta\cos\theta + K(\cos^2\theta - \sin^2\theta).$

       $I_1 - J_1 = (I - J)(\cos^2\theta - \sin^2\theta) - 4K\sin\theta\cos\theta,$

            $= (I - J)\cos 2\theta - 2K\sin 2\theta.$

---

* In this case the principal radii of curvature of normal sections of the isovol are $\dfrac{I}{V}$ and $\dfrac{J}{V}$, and therefore the principal axes of the indicatrix are proportional to $\sqrt{I}$ and $\sqrt{J}$. Thus the indicatrix and ellipse of gyration are similar and similarly situated and will therefore have similar properties.

From the above equations we can deduce

$$I + J = I_1 + J_1 \qquad . \qquad . \qquad . \qquad . \qquad . \qquad \text{(i)}$$

and also $\qquad IJ - K^2 = I_1 J_1 - K_1{}^2 \qquad . \qquad . \qquad . \qquad . \qquad \text{(ii)}$

From these relations (i) and (ii) we can deduce that for every plane area there is a pair of rectangular axes, for one of which the moment of inertia is greater and for the other less than for any other axis. These axes are called the Principal Axes.

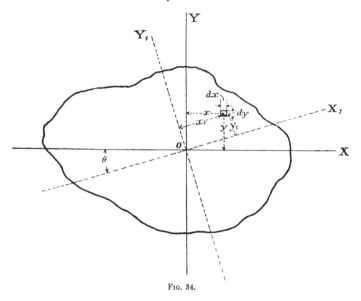

Fig. 34.

$(I + J)$ is constant for any axes.
$(I - J)$ is a maximum for the principal axes.
$(IJ - K^2)$ is constant for any axes.
K^2 is zero for the principal axes.

We can obtain the position of the principal axes when we know the position of the centre of gravity and the values I_1, J_1, and K_1 for any pair of rectangular axes.

Let β be the angle between the principal axis O X and the axis O X_1, for which we know I_1, J_1, and K_1.

Then K is zero for O X and O Y.

$$\therefore \qquad (I_1 - J_1) \cos \beta \sin \beta + K_1 (\cos^2 \beta - \sin^2 \beta) = 0.$$

$$\therefore \quad \tfrac{1}{2}(I_1 - J_1) \sin 2\beta = -K_1 \cos 2\beta,$$

$$\text{or} \quad \tan 2\beta = -\frac{2K_1}{(I_1 - J_1)}.$$

Let I be the maximum moment of inertia.
Let J   ,,   minimum   ,,   ,,
Let I_1, J_1, and K_1 be the functions, as before, for any other pair of axes of reference.

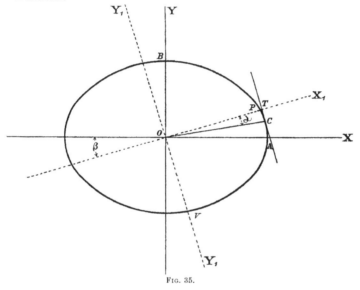

Fig. 35.

Then $I + J = I_1 + J_1$.

$$I J = I_1 J_1 - K_1{}^2.$$

$$I = \frac{I_1 + J_1}{2} + \sqrt{\left(\frac{(I_1 - J_1)^2}{4} + K_1{}^2\right)}.$$

$$J = \frac{I_1 + J_1}{2} - \sqrt{\left(\frac{(I_1 - J_1)^2}{4} + K_1{}^2\right)}.$$

Also, if I and J be known for the principal axes and β is the same angle as before,

Then $I_1 = I \cos^2 \beta + J \sin^2 \beta,$
and $J_1 = J \cos^2 \beta + I \sin^2 \beta,$
and $K_1 = (I - J) \sin \beta . \cos \beta.$

The above relations can be represented graphically by an ellipse, fig. 35.

Let A B be an ellipse, such that the semidiameter

$$OA = a = \sqrt{J},$$

and the semidiameter　　$OB = b = \sqrt{I}.$

Then from this ellipse we can obtain I_1, J_1, and K_1 for any pair of axes of reference other than O A and O B.

Let $A O X_1 = \beta$, and O A be the original axis O X. The equation to the ellipse will be

$$\frac{\cos^2 \beta}{a^2} + \frac{\sin^2 \beta}{b^2} = \frac{1}{r^2},$$

where $r = O P$.

Draw the tangent C T parallel to the axis $O Y_1$ touching the ellipse at C. Let O P meet the tangent in T.

Then O T is the perpendicular on this tangent.

If $O T = p$, the equation to the tangent is

$$x \cos \beta + y \sin \beta = p.$$

The condition that this line should touch the ellipse or be a tangent is

$$p^2 = a^2 \cos^2 \beta + b^2 \sin^2 \beta$$
$$= J \cos^2 \beta + I \sin^2 \beta.$$
$$\therefore \quad p^2 = J_1.$$

Again, if O V equals semidiameter of axis $O Y_1$,

$$\frac{1}{OV^2} = \frac{\cos^2 \left(\beta + \dfrac{3\pi}{2}\right)}{a^2} + \frac{\sin^2 \left(\beta + \dfrac{3\pi}{2}\right)}{b^2},$$

$$= \frac{\sin^2 \beta}{a^2} + \frac{\cos^2 \beta}{b^2}.$$

$$\therefore \quad \frac{a^2 b^2}{OV^2} = b^2 \sin^2 \beta + a^2 \cos^2 \beta,$$

$$= p^2.$$

$$\therefore \quad J_1 = p^2 = \frac{a^2 b^2}{OV^2}.$$

It is also a property of the tangent to the ellipse that

$$CT.OT = (a^2 - b^2) \cos \beta \sin \beta,$$

calling $CT = n$.

$$\therefore \quad p.n = (a^2 - b^2) \cos \beta \sin \beta,$$
$$= (I - J) \cos \beta \sin \beta,$$
$$= K_1.$$

$$\therefore \quad \tan a = \frac{pn}{p^2} = \frac{K_1}{J_1} = \frac{n}{p},$$

where $a = $ angle C O P.

Having discussed these properties of moment of inertia of a plane area, we can apply them to the area of the plane of flotation.

For any plane of flotation we have an ellipse of gyration which may be defined as follows :—

The ellipse of gyration for a plane of flotation is the ellipse having its centre at the C.G. of the waterplane, and having the property that the square of the perpendicular from the centre of gravity of the plane (this point being the centre of the ellipse) upon the tangent varies as the moment of inertia of the area about an axis through its centre of gravity and parallel to the tangent, and therefore it varies as B M.

Direction of Motion of the Centre of Buoyancy of a Floating Body as the Body is inclined.—Let B be the position of the centre of buoyancy (fig. 36) corresponding to a plane of flotation, and let C be the position of the centre of gravity of this plane.

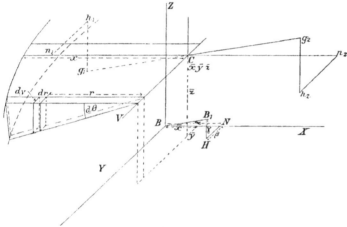

FIG. 36.

Let C V be parallel to the axis about which the body receives a small inclination, and therefore perpendicular to the plane of inclination.

Choose as axes B X, B Y, B Z, where B Y is parallel to C V and the plane X Z is parallel to the plane of inclination.

Let C have as coordinates $\bar{x}$, $\bar{y}$, $\bar{z}$, relatively to B.

Then the plane X Y is parallel to the plane of flotation.

Suppose the body has received a small inclination $d\theta$ about C V, and that the axes remain fixed relatively to the body. Then the centre of buoyancy will have moved from B to some position B_1, the coordinates of which are, say, a, β, and γ.

The ordinary method of calculating a transverse B M applies to the case of a body symmetrical about the line C V, which in a ship would be the middle line of the waterplane.

In this special case, for a very small inclination the transference of the volume of the wedge having its C.G. at y_1 on the emerged side takes place in a plane parallel to g_2 on the submerged side, i.e. $g_1 g_2$ is parallel to plane X Z and lies in the plane through C.

The moment of transference $v.g_1 g_2 = \text{V.B B}_1$,

where $v =$ volume of wedge of submersion or emersion,

    $\text{V} = $,, ,, displacement,

    $g_1 g_2 =$ shift of centre of gravity of wedge,

    $\text{B B}_1 =$ corresponding shift of the centre of buoyancy of V, which is the general case.

If the waterplane is not symmetrical about C V, then $g_1 g_2$ will not necessarily lie in a plane parallel to X Z, but in some plane inclined to it. The relation $\text{V.B B}_1 = v.g_1 g_2$ will still be true, and in the case of non-

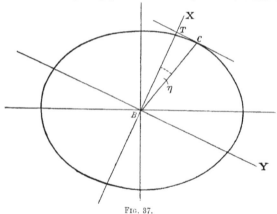

Fig. 37.

symmetry we can consider the projection of B B$_1$ and $g_1 g_2$ in the planes of reference.

$$\text{V}.a = v(n_1 c + c n_2) = \int\int r_1{}^2 \, d\theta \, dr \, dy + \int\int r_2{}^2 \, d\theta \, dr \, dy$$
$$= d\theta \text{J}.$$

$$\text{V}\beta = v(n_1 h_1 + n_2 h_2) = \int\int y r_1 \, d\theta . dr \, dy + \int\int y r_2 \, d\theta \, dr \, dy$$
$$= \text{K} d\theta.$$

For clearness, only the emerged side is shown in fig. 36.

The direction in the plane X Y in which the centre of buoyancy moves is therefore given by

$$\tan \eta = \frac{\beta}{a} = \frac{\text{K}}{\text{J}} \quad \text{where } \eta = \text{angle XBH}.$$

Again consider the ellipse of gyration (fig. 37).

Let B X Z be the plane of inclination, B Y the axis of inclination (fig. 36). Draw T C a tangent parallel to B Y (fig. 37).

$$\text{Then} \qquad \text{BT} = \sqrt{\text{J}}, \text{ see p. 44.}$$

$$\text{TC.BT} = \text{K}.$$

$$\therefore \ \tan \text{CBT} = \frac{\text{K}}{\text{J}} = \tan \eta. \qquad \therefore \ \text{CBT} = \eta.$$

Therefore the radius vector of the ellipse of gyration for the plane of flotation gives the direction of motion of the centre of buoyancy when the plane of inclination contains the perpendicular to the tangent of the radius vector.

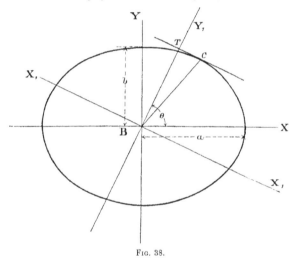

FIG. 38.

In the ellipse of gyration, fig. 38, let I be the moment of inertia about an axis B Y$_1$, let B T = p.
Then $\text{I} = p^2 k^2$ where k is a constant.
If we call I$_y$ and I$_x$ the principal moments of inertia about the axes B Y and B X respectively,

$$\text{Then} \qquad \text{I}_y = a^2.k^2,$$

$$\text{and} \qquad \text{I}_x = b^2 k^2,$$

$$\text{also} \qquad \text{I} = \text{I}_x \cos^2 \theta + \text{I}_y \sin^2 \theta.$$

$$\therefore \qquad \frac{\text{I}}{\text{V}} = \frac{\text{I}_x}{\text{V}} \cos^2 \theta + \frac{\text{I}_y}{\text{V}} \sin^2 \theta,$$

$$m = m_x \cos^2 \theta + m_y \sin^2 \theta,$$

$$\text{where} \qquad m = \frac{1}{V},$$

$$m_y = \frac{I_y}{V},$$

$$m_x = \frac{I_x}{V}.$$

This gives the value of m for a plane of inclination at θ to the principal axis B X.

Metacentre for any Direction of Inclination.—To incline a vessel in any direction such as B Y$_1$, fig. 38, it is necessary to apply a couple in a vertical plane parallel to B C. This is not parallel to the plane of inclination, and consequently two consecutive verticals, through consecutive centres of buoyancy, will not generally intersect.

The metacentre has been defined (Chapter IX., Vol. I.) as the projection, on the plane of inclination, of the line of shortest distance between consecutive verticals. This shortest distance will be β (fig. 36) $= \frac{K}{V} d\theta$. For the principal axes K is zero, so the corresponding metacentres are points actually in the plane of inclination, and not projections of the line of shortest distance.

The application of the metacentre, as defined above, has mostly been for positions of equilibrium and for directions of inclination corresponding to the principal axes of the ellipse of gyration, $i.e.$ of the transverse and longitudinal directions of inclination for a ship in the upright. For intermediate directions of inclination and for finite inclinations to the upright in a shipshaped form, the metacentre may better be defined as the projection of the shortest distance between consecutive verticals, through consecutive centres of buoyancy, upon the vertical plane passing through one of them and parallel to the plane of inclination. The locus of such metacentres will, in general, be a curve in three dimensions, and will always be a closed curve. Such a curve can, generally, only be shown by its projections upon planes of reference. For practical purposes it is sufficient to show its projection on a plane parallel to the plane of inclination. This projection has been called a "Metacentric Evolute," and sometimes a "Curve of Pro-Metacentres."

It is, however, necessary to bear in mind that the real curve of metacentres is a curve in three dimensions, and the curves of metacentres usually shown are only projections of the real curve.

CHAPTER V.

METHODS OF FINDING STABILITY.

In studying the stability of a vessel due to form, it is necessary to know the stability of the vessel at all angles of heel and all displacements. We have seen that a complete representation of the position of the C.B.'s of any form can be made by a series of isovols and isoclines. If we select one condition of the vessel, and determine for that condition the displacement and the corresponding position of centre of gravity, we can easily get from the isovols and isoclines the ordinary statical stability curve. If we consider the displacement variable and the centre of gravity fixed, we are able to get a series of cross curves of stability for a series of angles of inclination. Hence for a given position of C.G. we can obtain from the isovols and isoclines ordinary curves and cross curves of stability, or, what is the same thing, the surface of stability corresponding to that position of C.G. The work of obtaining a complete set of isovols and isoclines is laborious, and it is not necessary for ordinary cases of vessels, where the stability is only required to be known for a small number of special conditions and for a limited range of inclination.

The conditions of a vessel during service limit the range of displacement between the light and load draughts. At the commencement of a voyage the vessel is generally loaded to her deepest draught. The weights which she is carrying may be of such a nature that the centre of gravity of the loaded ship is dangerously high. A vessel with all her holds full of a light cargo and a quantity of timber stowed on her weather-deck ; or, a light draught passenger steamer crowded with a large number of passengers on the top-deck, are of this nature. The loaded conditions in these cases would most probably be less stable than the respective light conditions. During the voyage the condition of the ship varies : coal and stores become gradually consumed, so that the vertical position of the centre of gravity of the vessel may be altered. At the end of the voyage the stability of the vessel may be very different to that at the beginning.

Sometimes the stability of the vessel has to be calculated for conditions such as launching or dry-docking, which are lighter than the "light draught." In the launching condition the weight is made up generally only of the steel-work and a part of the wood-work. In the dry-docking condition the water is very often emptied out of the boilers, and other weights may have to be taken out of the lower parts of the ship.

We have seen that the metacentric height G M is a measure of the stability in the upright, and generally it is sufficient to know only G M for conditions when the vessel is in smooth water or in harbour ; but it is important to have curves of stability for a wide range of inclination for the conditions that the vessel is likely to be in at sea ; and in critical cases in harbour, it is desirable to know what is the stability at finite angles of heel, so as to be able to judge of the reserve of stability available for provision against loss of stability due to accidental change of position of the C.G. of the ship.

For an ordinary sea-going passenger and cargo steamer the following conditions should be examined :—

(1) Vessel in light condition.
(2) Vessel in load condition.
(3) Vessel fully loaded—coal burned out.
(4)   „   „   „   —coal and all consumable stores out.
(5) Vessel as in No. 4—water ballast in.
(6) Vessel with a light cargo completely filling the holds, and as in No. 4 (condition between light and load).

For each of these conditions the displacement and position of C.G. must be determined and recorded on the metacentric diagram as already described, Vol. I., Ch. X. p. 120.

It is usually sufficient to know the curve of G Z's in terms of θ for each condition.

The quickest and most accurate method of obtaining the curves of G Z's is to use an integrator and to, first, determine a series of cross curves of stability, from which may be deduced the ordinary curves of stability for the special conditions stated. An integrator is not always available, and the method known as Barnes's or some equivalent method of polar integration is adopted, whereby measured ordinates are integrated by Simpson's Rules. A third and more modern method is that of finding the cross curves by combining the use of Tchebycheff's Rules and the integrator or integraph. These methods will be described in the following order :—

(1) The method of obtaining a curve of G Z's directly from a prepared body-plan by the Barnes's process of polar integration.
(2) The method of obtaining a series of cross curves of stability from a prepared body-plan by the integrator, and from these the curves of G Z.
(3) The method of obtaining a series of cross curves, isovols, and isoclines by the application of Tchebycheff's Rules, combined with the use of the integrator or integraph.

Preparation of a Stability Body-Plan—see fig. 39.—In the body-plan for stability calculation by any of the methods, the sections are made to show the water-displacing portion of the hull. In an ordinary steel ship, with an "in" and "out" system of shell plating, it is usual to draw the sections at a distance of one and a half times the mean thickness of shell plating from the moulded sections. With the joggled system and with the flush system of plating the sections are drawn at a distance equal to the thickness of the plating. In sheathed ships the sections are made to the outside of the sheathing. The sections are sometimes made to show the outside form of the appendages, such as shaft bossing, keels and bilge kneels, but only if the volumes of these appendages are worth taking into account. These appendages may, however, be left out from the initial stages of the calculation, and included afterwards by making an approximate calculation of their effect. The sections are continued up to the weather-deck, and are made to include the round of the beam at the top of the wood or steel deck. On the weather-deck there are usually appendages in the shape of deckhouses, casings, forecastle, poop, bridgehouse, or other watertight deck erection. These have a considerable effect on the stability so soon as the angle of heel is great enough to submerge them. The effect they produce on the stability may be calculated separately as an appendage correction ; but if their volume is large in proportion to the displacement, or if it can be easily integrated, it is better to include them in the calculations at the preliminary stages. In any case they should be shown on the body-plan.

The ends of the deck erections, as far as possible, should be made stop-points in the longitudinal integration. This is arranged in fig. 39, which shows a stability body-plan for a shallow draught steamer.

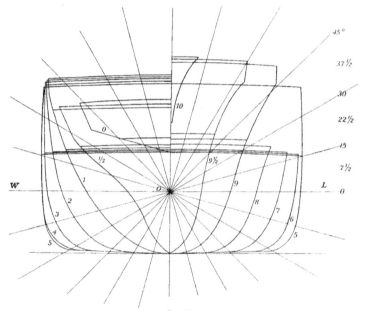

FIG. 39.

The deck erections of the vessel shown by this figure are a full forecastle, a bridgehouse, and a raised quarter-deck. These erections end on section Nos. 9, 5, and 1, which are stop-points in the longitudinal integration. The spacing of the sections is in accordance with Simpson's First Rule.

For methods (2) and (3) body-plans, as described, must be drawn, but for both sides of the vessel. It is convenient to draw both fore and after bodies on the same body-plan, and to make a distinction between them, either by the colouring or the dotting of the lines.

Many methods have been devised for obtaining G Z curves by polar integration, but they all more or less contain the principles involved in the following process, the differences consisting largely in the arrangements for tabling the figures and calculations.

The Barnes Process of Polar Integration.—The method of polar integration was first applied by Barnes, and consequently it is generally referred to as Barnes's Method.

The formulæ used in this method are the following :—

$$V.BR = v_1.oh_1 + v_2.oh_2 \pm (v_2 - v_1)\, O\, C \qquad . \qquad . \qquad . \quad (1)$$

$$V.B_1R = v_1.g_1h_1 + v_2.g_2h_2 - (v_2 - v_1)\, Cc \qquad . \qquad . \qquad . \quad (2)$$

These formulæ have been discussed in Vol. II., Ch. I. p. 4. The first equation gives the righting moment at the angle θ.

Righting moment $V.GZ = V.BR - V.BG \sin \theta$.

Equation (2) gives the dynamical stability $V.h$ where

$$V.h = V.B_1R - V.BG \text{ vers. } \theta.$$

The above equations may be expressed in words. See fig. 3, p. 5.

The righting moment $V.GZ$ is equal to the sum of the moments of the wedges of emersion and submersion about O *plus* or *minus* the moment of the correcting layer about O *minus* the expression $V.BG \sin \theta$.

The question whether the moment of the correcting layer in formula (1) is + or − may be decided from the following considerations. In formula (1), when the correction is an emerged excess with its C.G. on the emerged side, or a submerged excess with its C.G. on the submerged side, the correcting moment is negative. When the correction is an emerged excess C.G. on the submerged side, or a submerged excess C.G. on the emerged side, the correcting moment is positive.

The correcting layer moment is always *minus* in (2).

The dynamical stability $V.h$ is equal to the sum of the moments of the wedges about the new waterplane, *minus* the moment of the correcting layer about the new waterplane, *minus* the expression $V.BG \text{ vers. } \theta$.

Thus, to obtain the righting moment and the dynamical stability at any definite angle of heel, we have first to find the volumes v_1 and v_2 and the moments of the wedges of submersion and emersion.

These volumes and moments can be found by the polar method of integration.

Let us first examine the expressions for the volume and moment of a wedge such as is formed in a shipshape solid by two consecutive waterplanes W L and $W_1 L_1$, as in fig. 40.

Let O o be the axis of the wedge corresponding in the ship to the longitudinal middle line axis at O.

Let O A B and $o\, a\, b$ be two transverse sections distant x_1, and $O^1 A^1 B^1$ a section distant dx from O A B. Choose a small part like that shown shaded, between two radii very close together, at angles θ and $\theta + d\theta$ from O B.

Let the polar distance O P of the element from O be r.

The elemental area is therefore $dr \times rd\theta$.

Therefore the area between two consecutive radii $= d\theta \int r.dr$.

Therefore the area of the section OAB $= \int\int rd\theta.dr$.

The volume of an elemental layer made by the sections O A B and
$O^1 A^1 B^1 = \int\int r d\theta.dr.dx$, and therefore the total volume of the wedge

$$= \int\int\int r d\theta.dr.dx.$$

If a_1 = angle B O A and $x_1 = O\,o$, volume of wedge

$$= \int_0^{x_1} \left\{ \int_0^{a_1} \left(\int_0^{r_1} r dr \right) d\theta \right\} dx,$$

where r_1 represents the polar distance of any point on the side A B $b\,a$.

Then total volume of the wedge $= \frac{1}{2}\int_0^{a_1}\int_0^{x_1} r_1^2 d\theta.dx$ . . . . (1)

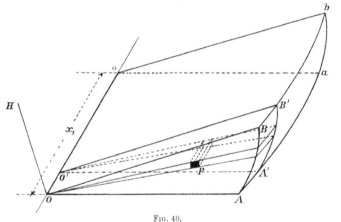

Fig. 40.

Draw a plane through O o perpendicular to the plane O B $b\,o$ cutting plane
O A B in O H.

The moment of the elemental layer about O H $= r^2.d\theta.dr.dx.\cos\theta$,
and ,, ,, ,, O B $= r^2.d\theta.dr.dx.\sin\theta$.

Therefore the total moment of wedge about O H $= \frac{1}{3}\int_0^{a_1}\int_0^{x_1} r_1^3\cos\theta\,d\theta\,dx$ (2)

and ,, ,, ,, O B $= \frac{1}{3}\int_0^{a_1}\int_0^{x_1} r_1^3\sin\theta\,d\theta\,dx$ (3)

Applying these formulæ (1), (2), and (3) to the wedges of fig. 3, and
calling r_1 the polar measurements of wedge v_1,
and r_2 ,, ,, ,, v_2,
the limits for x become O and L, the length of ship ;
,, ,, θ ,, O ,, a, the angle of inclination.

Therefore $\qquad v_1 . o h_1 = \frac{1}{3} \int_0^a \int_0^{1.} r_1^3 \cos \theta . d\theta . dx,$

and $\qquad v_3 . o h_2 = \frac{1}{3} \int_0^a \int_0^{1.} r_2^3 \cos \theta . d\theta . dx,$

also $\qquad v_1 = \frac{1}{2} \int_0^a \int_0^{1.} r_1^2 d\theta . dx,$

and $\qquad v_2 = \frac{1}{2} \int_0^a \int_0^{1.} r_2^2 d\theta . dx.$

The point c which is the *c.g.* of the correcting layer can be found when we know the areas and *c.g.*'s of the radial plane, and some planes parallel and near to it.

The moment about $O o$ of the plane $O B b o = \frac{1}{2} \int_0^{x_1} r_1^2 . dx.$

Moment for both planes $= \frac{1}{2} \int_0^{x_1} (r_1^2 - r_2^2) \, dx.$

Distance *c.g.* of whole plane is from $O = \dfrac{\frac{1}{2} \int_0^{x_1} (r_1^2 - r_2^2) dx}{\int_0^{x_1} (r_1 + r_2) dx}.$

The expression $\int_0^{a_1} \int_0^{1.} r_1^3 d\theta \cos \theta \, dx$

can be integrated by first integrating r_1^3 in the direction of x for a series of values of r_1 for values of a chosen to suit the spacing for Simpson's Rules.

These values of $\int r_1^3 . dx.$ can then be multiplied by $\cos \theta$, and integrated polarly to give the moment of the wedges.

This operation is the same for the emerged as for the submerged wedge.

Similar operations must be carried out for $\iint r_1^2 dx . d\theta$ for the volume of the wedges and $\int r_1^2 dx$ for the moment of the waterplane areas. The integral $\int r . dx.$ is also required to give the area of the radial plane.

To suit the polar integration the inclined waterplanes are chosen radiating from the point O as in fig. 39.

W O L in the figure is the horizontal waterplane cutting off the displacement corresponding to the condition for which we want a curve of righting arms. Through O a number of waterplanes are drawn at equal angular intervals. A waterplane must be drawn passing through the deck-edge at side. This waterplane forms a necessary stop-point in the integration, because the deck-edge forms a point of discontinuity in the radial waterplane area.

It is $15°$; and as it must be the third or fifth or so on ordinate in the polar integration to conform to continuity for the use of Simpson's First Rule, the angular interval must be $7\frac{1}{2}°$ or $3\frac{3}{4}°$, or such angle as divides the deck-edge into an even number of intervals. In the case given in fig. 39, $7\frac{1}{2}°$ is taken as the angular interval.

Modus Operandi of the Polar Method.

Two kinds of tables are used. The first, called the Preliminary Table, is arranged for finding the expressions $\int r_1 dx, \int r_1^2 dx$ and $\int r_1^3 dx$ for each waterplane. The other table is called the Combination Table, and completes the integrations of the expressions

$$\iint r^2 d\theta\, dx, \iint r^3 \cos\theta.d\theta.dx \text{ and } \iint r^3 \sin\theta.d\theta.dx.$$

Preliminary Tables.

It will be seen, p. 56, that each Preliminary Table is divided into two parts. The top part is for the submerged wedge, and the bottom part for the emerged wedge. To complete these tables, measure for each table and waterplane the distances r of the section along the radial plane from O, and tabulate for submerged and emerged sides the results under the heading ordinates, opposite to the number of the section. Fill in the column Simpson's Multipliers according to the longitudinal spacing. Fill in the subsequent columns by first squaring and then cubing the ordinates.

We have thus columns giving the values of r_1, r_1^2, and r_1^3 for submerged, and r_2, r_2^2, and r_2^3 for the emerged sides of the waterplane. Use Simpson's Multipliers, and add the results to obtain the functions of r_1, r_1^2, and r_1^3, and so get the expressions $\int r_1 dx, \int r_1^2 dx$, and $\int r_1^3 dx$ by dividing by 3 and multiplying by the common interval. To avoid large numbers in the Combination Tables, the values of r_1, r_1^2, r_1^3 are added and divided by 3 in the Preliminary Tables, and these numbers are then used in the Combination Tables, the whole being multiplied by the common interval afterwards.

The three function columns are not affected by Simpson's Multipliers until used in the Combination Tables. The functions of cubes for both sides are added together in the Preliminary Tables. *The Combination Table* is shown in Table, p. 58, and is arranged to complete the polar integration for one angle of heel, and to obtain G Z and the dynamical stability corresponding thereto.

Consider the Combination Table for the inclination 40°. Set down in the first column (A) 0°, 10°, 20°, 30°, 40°, and in the second (B) the functions of $\int r_1 dx$ from the corresponding Preliminary Tables. Put in a third column (C) the corresponding functions of $\int r_1^2 dx$ and integrate them by the Simpson Multipliers in column (D). We get in the column (E) the function of $\iint r_1^2\, dx\, d\theta$ which, when multiplied by half and the Simpson's intervals divided by three, gives v_1, the volume of the submerged wedge. Similarly, we find the value $\iint r_2^2\, dx\, d\theta$ for the volume v_2 of the emerged wedge. The difference of these two volumes $v_1 \sim v_2$ therefore represents the volume of the correcting layer, and if this be divided by the area of the waterplane, we can get its approximate thickness. The moments of the wedges $v_1.oh_1$ and $v_2.oh_2$ are obtained by integrating in the right-hand side of the Combination Table. The first column (F) is for the functions of $\left(\int r_1^3 dx + \int r_2^3 dx \right)$ which have been summed in the Preliminary Tables. The next column (G) contains products of the column (F) by Simpson's Multipliers. Column (H) gives the cosines of the angle of inclination of the respective radial planes to the angle of the waterplane up to which we are integrating, in this case 40°. Write down, in order from the top, cos 40° . . . . cos 0°, corresponding to the planes 0°, 10°, 20°, 30°, 40°. The next column (K) gives the product of columns (G) and (H), which, when added, give the value of the function of

$$ \left\{ \int\int r_1^3\, dx.d\theta.\cos\theta + \int\int r_2^3\, dx\, d\theta \cos\theta \right\} ; $$

if multiplied by one-third of the circular measure of angular interval and the longitudinal interval and divided by three, this gives $(v_1.oh_1 + v_2.oh_2)$, the moment of wedges uncorrected.

SPECIMEN OF PRELIMINARY TABLE.

WATERPLANE AT 40° (say) INCLINATION.

Submerged Wedge.

Number of Ordinates.	Lengths of Ordinates.	S.M.	Products of Ordinates.	Squares of Ordinates.	S.M.	Products of Squares.	Cubes of Ordinates.	S.M.	Products of Cubes.	
1	0·2	1	0·2	0·0	1	0·0	0·0	1	0·0	
2	4·0	4	16·0	16·0	4	64·0	64·0	4	256·0	
3	8·4	2	16·8	70·6	2	141·2	592·7	2	1185·4	
4	7·6	4	30·4	57·8	4	231·2	439·0	4	1756·0	
5	6·9	2	13·8	47·6	2	95·2	329·0	2	658·0	
6	6·1	4	24·4	37·2	4	148·8	227·0	4	908·0	
7	5·8	2	11·6	33·6	2	67·2	195·1	2	390·2	
8	5·4	4	21·6	29·2	4	116·8	157·5	4	630·0	
9	5·2	2	10·4	27·0	2	54·0	140·6	2	281·2	
10	5·6	4	22·4	31·4	4	125·6	175·6	4	702·4	
11	6·4	1	6·4	41·0	1	41·0	262·1	1	262·1	
			174·0			1085·0			7029·3	
Function of area of inclined W.P.		3 ⟶ 58·0		Function of moment of area		3 ⟶ 361·7		3 ⟶	2343·1	Sub. wedge
									1708·2	Em. wedge
									4051·3	Both wedges

Emerged Wedge.

Number of Ordinates.	Lengths of Ordinates.	S.M.	Products of Ordinates.	Squares of Ordinates.	S.M.	Products of Squares.	Cubes of Ordinates.	S.M.	Products of Cubes.	
1	0·2	1	0·2	0·0	1	0·0	0·0	1	0·0	
2	2·4	4	9·6	5·8	4	23·2	13·8	4	55·2	
3	4·5	2	9·0	20·3	2	40·6	91·1	2	182·2	
4	6·0	4	24·0	36·0	4	144·0	216·0	4	864·0	
etc.			etc.			etc.				
			144·7			830·8			5124·8	
Function of area		3 ⟶ 48·2		Function of moment of area		3 ⟶ 276·9		3 ⟶	1708·2	Em. wedge

The volume of the correcting layer $(v_1 \sim v_2)$ has been found.
The C.G. of the correcting layer can be found as follows :—
If the volume $(v_1 \sim v_2)$ is small, the C.G. of waterplane is obtained by
dividing the $\left(\int r_1 \, dx + \int r_2 \, dx \right)$ into $\frac{1}{2} \int (r_1{}^2 \, dx - r_2{}^2 \, dx)$, which will give the
C.G. of the correcting layer with sufficient accuracy.
The true thickness of the layer can be obtained as follows :—

If $(v_1 \sim v_2)$ is large the approximate thickness of the layer is $\dfrac{v_1 \sim v_2}{\int (r_1 + r_2) dx}$.

Draw a new waterplane M N (fig. 42) at the distance of this thickness
from O, and find the area and moment of this new plane about O P, a
perpendicular to it through O. If $(v_1 \sim v_2)$ is very large it may be necessary
to draw an intermediate waterplane and find its area and moment. Plot these
three moments, and find the area of this moment curve. This will be the

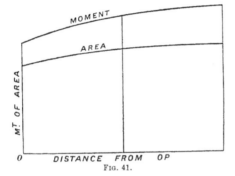

Fig. 41.

moment about O P of the layer bounded by the plane M N and W L. The
area of the area curve will give the volume of this layer, which will
generally be not quite equal to $(v_1 \sim v_2)$, so that a small further correction at
M N must be made, which offers no difficulty. Also, the area of the moment
curve, divided by the area of the area curve = distance of C G of layer from O P.
The corrected moment of wedges is V.BR ; from this we subtract V.BG
$\sin \theta$ and we get V.GZ, and dividing by V we get GZ.
V.h is got in a similar way to V.GZ, except that we have a new column
for $\sin \theta$ instead of $\cos \theta$, and a new column for $(v_1.g_1h_1 + v_2.g_2h_2)$, etc.
The sign of the correction for layer is determined from the formula
already given, and may shortly be remembered by the phrase "like sides
give a negative correction." Appendage corrections may have to be made
for bilge-keels, shaft-bosses, and propellers, rudders, partial or complete
deckhouses, but they are all simply corrections of the position of the centre
of gravity of the submerged volume, and their effect is determined in the
same way as the other corrections, viz. by taking moments about O P. It
must be remembered that the buoyancy added in underwater appendages must
be deducted at the waterline, so that the real volume of the layer correc-

SPECIMEN OF COMBINATION TABLE.

STABILITY AT 40° INCLINATION.

| Submerged Wedge. | | | | | Both Wedges. | | | | | | |
| A. | B. | C. | D. | E. | F. | | G. | Statical Stability. | | Dynamical Stability. | |
Angle of Inclination.	Products of Ordinates.	Products of Squares of Ordinates.	Multipliers.	Products.	Sums of the Products of Cubes of Ordinates, both Wedges.	S.M.	Products for Moments of Wedges.	H. Cosine of Angle of Inclination.	K. Product of Moments of Wedges × cosine θ.	L. Sine of Angle of Inclination.	Product of Moments of Wedges × sin θ.
0°	...	460·6	1	460·6	7456·4	1	7456·4	·766	5711·6	·6428	4793·0
10°	...	525·8	4	2103·2	7471·7	4	29886·8	·866	25882·0	·5	14943·4
20°	...	622·6	2	1245·2	7945·6	2	15891·2	·940	14937·7	·3420	5431·8
30°	...	491·1	4	1964·4	5749·3	4	22997·2	·985	22652·2	·1736	3992·3
40°	58·0	361·7	1	361·7	4051·3	1	4051·3	1·000	4051·3	0·0	0000·0

Submerged Wedge (calculations):

$\iint r_1^2\, dx\, d\theta$ 6135·1
$\iint r_2^2\, dx\, d\theta$ 4215·9
Difference   1919·2
              2
½ Angular interval   ·058
              959·6
              ·058
              7·6768
              47·980
              55·6568
Longitudinal interval   9
Volume of correcting layer } 501

Both Wedges — Statical Stability:

              73234·8
         3 ————
              24411·6
½ Angular interval   ·058
              195·29
              1220·58
              1415·87
Longitudinal interval   9
Moment of wedges uncor.   12742·83
Correction for Layer   200·40
              12542·43
÷ Displacement 5425
              2·312
BG = ·78   ·502
BG sin θ = ·78 × ·643 = ·502   GZ = 1·81

Dynamical Stability:

              29163·5
         3 ————
              9721·2
              ·058
              77·76
              486·06
              563·83
              9
              5074·47
            − 131·20
              4943·27
5425 |
              ·91
BG vers θ ·18
              h = ·73

Emerged Wedge.

0°	...	460·6	1	460·6
10°	...	399·0	4	1596·0
20°	...	341·2	2	682·4
30°	...	300·0	4	1200·0
40°	48·2	276·9	1	276·9

$\iint r_2^2\, dx\, d\theta$ 4215·9

Area of Inclined Waterplane.

Function of area, submerged side   58·0
   ,,   ,,   emerged   ,,   48·2
                        Total   106·2
Longitudinal interval   9
                        955·8 sq. ft.

Centre of Area of Inclined Waterplane.

Function of moment, sub. side 361·7
   ,,   ,,   em. ,,   276·9
Excess on submerged side   84·8
                        2
                        42·4
$\dfrac{42·4 \times 9}{955·8} = 0·4$ ft.
= Distance of centre of area from axis on sub. side.

Thickness of the correcting layer.

$\dfrac{501}{955·8} = \dfrac{\text{vol.}}{\text{area}} = ·524$

Correction for GZ.

Vol. × distance of C G. from O P
501 × ·4 = 200·4

Correction for h

$501 \times \dfrac{·524}{2}$(approx.)
= 501 × ·262
= 131·2

tion is not simply $(v_1 \sim v_2)$, but this with the volume of appendages subtracted or added according as $(v_1 - v_2)$ is positive or negative.

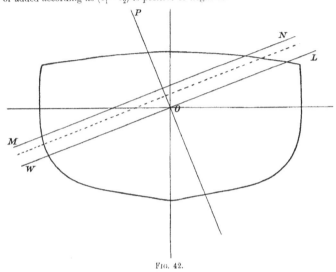

Fig. 42.

The dynamical stability, or rather $V.B_1R$, is found similarly to the $V.BR$, except in column (L) the sine is filled in, and the product of this column with column (G) integrated and multiplied by the same factors as for statical stability give the uncorrected $V.B_1R$. To correct for the layer, its

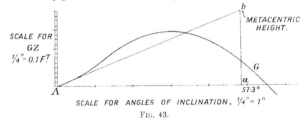

SCALE FOR
GZ
$\frac{1}{4}'' = 0.1 F^T$

METACENTRIC
HEIGHT.

A SCALE FOR ANGLES OF INCLINATION. $\frac{1}{4}'' = 1°$

G

a

$57.3°$

Fig. 43.

moments must be taken about the waterline W L and subtracted or added according as the sign of $(v_1 - v_2)$ is positive or negative.

To obtain G Z the value $V.BG \sin \theta$ is subtracted, and the remainder divided by V.

To obtain the dynamical arm $V.BG$ vers θ is subtracted, and the remainder divided by V.

The results of such a calculation are plotted in the usual manner to recognised standard scales.

The base line is used for degree measurements to a scale of $\frac{1}{4}$ in. $= 1°$. The ordinates are values of G Z or dynamical arm, and are set up to a scale of $\frac{1}{4}$ in. $= \frac{1}{10}$th of a foot.

In each case the ordinate to a scale of $\frac{1}{4}$ in. $\times \dfrac{V}{350}$ gives the statical or dynamical moment of stability in ft. tons.

At the abscissæ value of 1 radian, or 57·3°, an ordinate is usually drawn equal in length to G M in the upright. In figure 43 let A G be the statical curve of stability from the results of the calculation in the tables.

On this curve $ab = GM$.

Draw bA. Then bA is tangent to the curve at zero degrees.

We have already seen that
$$RM = \frac{dBR}{d\theta} \left.\begin{array}{c} \\ \\ \end{array}\right\} \text{ See p. 10.}$$
and
$$ZM = \frac{dGZ}{d\theta} ;$$

when θ approaches 0, Z approaches G, so that for zero value of θ, $\dfrac{dGZ}{d\theta} = GM$, so that the tangent of the angle which the tangent at A makes with the axis of x equals G M. If, therefore, we set off G M $= ab$ at $\theta = 1$ and join bA, we get the tangent to the curve of G Z at zero.

Similarly,
$$BR = \frac{dB_1R}{d\theta} = BG \sin\theta + GZ.$$

But
$$B_1R - BG \text{ vers } \theta = h \text{ (see p. 52).}$$

$$\therefore \quad \frac{d_1B_1R}{d_1\theta} - BG \sin\theta = \frac{dh}{d\theta}$$

Hence
$$GZ = \frac{dh}{d\theta}$$

GZ at 0° is zero,

hence
$$\frac{dh}{d\theta} \text{ at } 0° \text{ is } 0,$$

that is, a curve of dynamical arms has always a horizontal tangent at 0°, or at any other position where G Z is 0. Hence a condition of equilibrium is that the curve of dynamical arms shall have a horizontal tangent.

Determination of Cross Curves using the Integrator.—We have seen in the general treatment of the stability of a floating body (in the discussion of a surface of stability) that cross curves may be readily obtained from a series of ordinary curves of statical stability (G Z), and, conversely, a series of G Z curves may be obtained from the cross curves. Hence if we require curves of statical stability for several conditions of a vessel we can obtain them from a series of cross curves which have been constructed for a range of displacement varying between the lightest and the heaviest draughts for which the curves are required. A method of determining cross curves of a given vessel by means of the integrator may now be described. An ordinary stability body-plan with sections for both sides of the ship is first prepared in the manner described for the polar method. The limits of displacement must be determined within which the cross curves are to be made. In order to ensure accuracy within these limits it is important to make this range

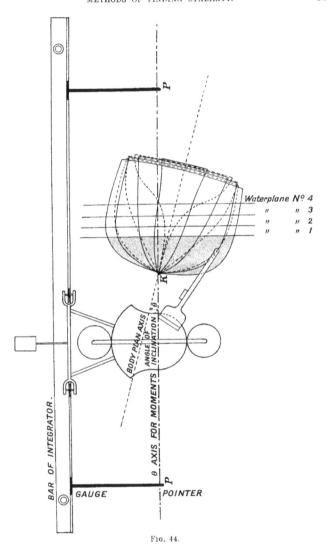

Fig. 44.

greater than that from the light to load conditions, as the form of the curves for the extreme conditions is more accurately determined by having points outside the limits. The cross curves are generally "fair" curves; and if the spots are determined at some displacement outside these limits, the curves themselves are more easily drawn, and consequently fewer spots require to be determined between the light and load displacements. On a separate tracing paper a series of parallel lines representing waterplanes is drawn. The number of these waterplanes is generally from four to six, according to the nature of the change of form of the vessel within the limits, and the distance apart is determined by placing the paper over the body-plan so that the lightest and deepest waterplanes are at a less and greater draught respectively than the light and load waterplanes. The position of the waterplanes has to be judged so that they contain the required range of displacement. On the body-plan axes for moments may be drawn, so as to radiate from a common point such as the top of the keel or any other fixed point in the middle line. The angles of inclination of the axes correspond to the angles of inclination for which we wish to determine the cross curves. Generally, the angular interval chosen is 15°, giving six cross curves, so that the maximum inclination considered will be 90°. Generally, for all practical purposes, 75° or 80° is a sufficient inclination.

The Calculation of the Moments and Areas of the Submerged Parts of the Sections.—It is found that the integrator is the most convenient and accurate instrument for this purpose. Suppose we want to determine the cross curve for an inclination, say 15°. The body-plan sheet is pinned down to a large level board. Over this is pinned the tracing with the waterplanes perpendicular to the 15° axis for moments. Fig. 44 shows how this is done. The waterplanes are Nos. 1, 2, 3, and 4, and the axis P P for moments passes through K, the top of keel. The angle between the body-plan middle line and P K P is therefore 15°. The fig. 44 also shows how the integrator is placed relatively to the body-plan. The bar is laid down parallel to P K P at a distance from it determined by the set pieces P and P, and the integrator is placed so as to run in the groove of the bar. The moment wheel will give a moment reading about the axis P K P. A starting-point is selected, and the tracing point of the integrator is guided clockwise over the whole of the submerged part of one of the sections up to one waterplane. When the pointer comes back to the starting-point the readings of the area and moment wheel are taken. The pointer is then guided over the other sections in order, and similar readings are taken for each. The readings thus obtained should be put in a table of the form shown opposite.

We have thus one table of results for one inclination 15° and for each waterplane. Each reading recorded corresponds to one section, one inclination, and one waterplane, and consists of an area reading and a moment reading. Instead of taking absolute readings for each observation, it is better to subtract the previous reading from each new reading and record the difference. This can be done in the table in the column headed "differences" after each column headed "readings." This method avoids setting the wheels to zero at the end of each observation, and so avoids wearing the instrument always in the same place. The difference column therefore gives the readings for the actual areas and moments of the sections. If the sections are spaced to Simpson's Rules the figures in the difference column can be multiplied by the corresponding factors which are put in a column at the left-hand side. We thus get the functions which can be added up for integration.

TABLE I.

TABLE FOR CROSS CURVE AT ANGLE OF INCLINATION θ_1.

Number of Section.	Simpson's Multipliers.	Waterplane No. 1. Areas. Reading.	Differ-ence.	Func-tions.	Moments. Read-ing.	Differ-ence.	Func-tions.	Waterplane No. 2. Areas. Differ-ence.	Func-tions.	Read-ing.	Moments. Read-ing.	Differ-ence.	Func-tions.	Waterplane No. 3. Areas. Differ-ence.	Func-tions.	Moments. Read-ing.	Differ-ence.	Func-tions.	Waterplane No. 4. Areas. Read-ing.	Differ-ence.	Func-tions.	Moments. Read-ing.	Differ-ence.	Func-tions.
0	½																							
½	2																							
1	1¼																							
2	4																							
3	2																							
4	4																							
5	2																							
6	4																							
7	2																							
8	4																							
9	1¼																							
9¼	2																							
10	½																							
		Σa_1		Σm_1				Σa_2		Σm_2				Σa_3		Σm_3				Σa_4		Σm_4		

$$KN_1 \text{ in ft.} = \frac{\Sigma m_1}{\Sigma a_1} \times 2n =$$

$$KN_2 \quad ,, \quad = \frac{\Sigma m_2}{\Sigma a_2} \times 2n =$$

$$KN_3 \quad ,, \quad = \frac{\Sigma m_3}{\Sigma a_3} \times 2n =$$

$$KN_4 \quad ,, \quad = \frac{\Sigma m_4}{\Sigma a_4} \times 2n =$$

$$\Delta_1 = \left(\Sigma a_1 \times 20 \times n^3 \times \frac{l}{3} \times \frac{1}{35}\right) \text{ tons.}$$

$$\Delta_2 = \left(\Sigma a_2 \times 20 \times n^3 \times \frac{l}{3} \times \frac{1}{35}\right) \quad ,,$$

$$\Delta_3 = \left(\Sigma a_3 \times 20 \times n^3 \times \frac{l}{3} \times \frac{1}{35}\right) \quad ,,$$

$$\Delta_4 = \left(\Sigma a_4 \times 20 \times n^3 \times \frac{l}{3} \times \frac{1}{35}\right) \quad ,,$$

Scale for true moments $= 40 \times n^3 \times \frac{l}{3}$ }

,, ,, areas $= 20 \times n^2 \times \frac{l}{3}$ } Scale $= 2n$ for KN.

The sum of the area column gives the function of the volume for the corresponding waterplane, and the sum of the moment column gives the function of the moment of that volume about the axis P K P at 15° inclination. These functions are given by Σa_1 and Σm_1, etc. in the table.

The righting lever is found by dividing the moment of the volume by the volume, which is the same as $\dfrac{\Sigma m_1}{\Sigma a_1} \times$ factor for scale.

In order to determine this factor,
Let 20 = scale of integrator for area,
Let 40 = ,, ,, ,, moment.

Let the body-plan be drawn to a scale of n,—i.e. $\dfrac{1''}{n} = 1$ foot, — and let longitudinal interval of sections be l feet.

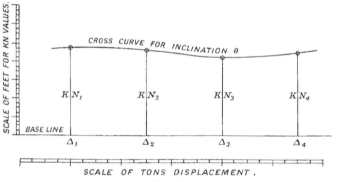

SCALE OF TONS DISPLACEMENT .

FIG. 45.

Then the volume in cubic feet $= \Sigma a_1 \times n^2 \times 20 \times \dfrac{l}{3}$,

and the moment in (feet)^4 $= \Sigma m_1 \times n^3 \times 40 \times \dfrac{l}{3}$.

Therefore distance of C.B. of volume from axis P K P

$$= K N_1 = \cfrac{\Sigma m_1 \times n^3 \times 40 \times \dfrac{l}{3}}{\Sigma a_1 \times n^2 \times 20 \times \dfrac{l}{3}}$$

$$= 2n\frac{\Sigma m_1}{\Sigma a_1}.$$

After the readings have been filled in the table for the first cross curve, the results should be worked out before the integrator is adjusted to a new inclination. An error in the readings can be sometimes detected at this stage, and can be rectified before the calculation for another cross curve is proceeded with. The process for a new curve is exactly the same.

We have now a series of K N's and displacements for each inclination. These may be set off in curves of K N's to a base of displacements. Where

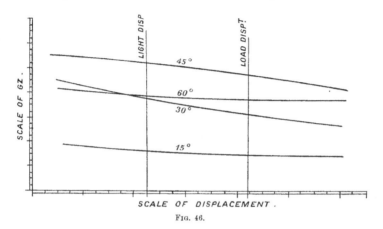

FIG. 46.

practicable the scale of K N's should be the same as that of G Z's, viz. ¼ inch = ·1 foot. This will give a large ordinate, but the base need not be a zero value. The manner in which this is done is shown in fig. 45. Only one

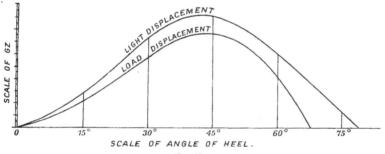

FIG. 47.

curve has been drawn, for the sake of clearness. This figure contains the results of only one table, viz. table for the inclination 15°.

The actual diagram of cross curves contains a series of curves corresponding to a series of inclinations.

It will now be seen that it is important to have the range of displacement at any inclination given by that between waterplanes 1 and 5 greater than that between the light and load conditions.

Figs. 46 and 47 give the cross curves and ordinary curves for a vessel.

The conditions for which ordinary curves have been drawn are fully noted.

In order to obtain an ordinary curve from the given cross curves, it is necessary to know the condition of the vessel. A list is made describing the various conditions for which ordinary curves are required, and giving also for each condition the corresponding displacement and height of centre of gravity.

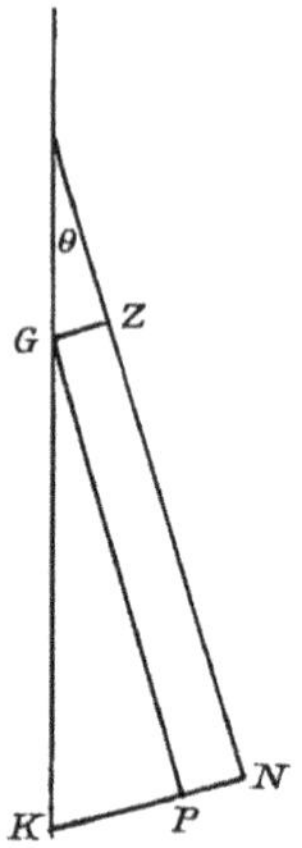

Let Δ be the displacement of any condition of the vessel for which the height of G is given by K G. We mark on the base line the displacement Δ, set up an ordinate to intersect the cross curves which give the corresponding values of K N.

Let K N be the value of the ordinate at inclination θ.

Then $KN = KG \sin \theta + GZ$,

or $GZ = KN - KG \sin \theta$.   Fig. 48.

Therefore we get G Z values by subtracting the corresponding value of KG sin θ.

Fig. 48.

Table II. gives a list of the conditions and the corresponding heights of G.

TABLE II.

Condition No.   . $\Delta =$ (   ).   K G =

Inclination.	Sin θ.	K N.	K G sin θ.	K N − K G sin θ or G Z.
θ_1	$\sin \theta_1$			
θ_2	$\sin \theta_2$			
θ_3	$\sin \theta_3$			
θ_4	$\sin \theta_4$			
θ_5	$\sin \theta_5$			

Application of Tchebycheff's Rules to Stability Calculations.—

The method of obtaining cross curves that has just been described is much simplified by using Tchebycheff's Rules for the spacing of the sections. The rule that is most convenient to use for a stability calculation is the three-ordinate Rule. The application of this Rule to ship calculations has been fully treated in Chapter XI., Part II., Vol. I.

If, instead of the ordinary spacing of sections, we use the three-ordinate Rule for Tchebycheff's spacing to give fifteen sections and make a stability body-plan, the subsequent process of determining cross curves or the process of any stability calculation is much simplified. To do this set off from each ordinate at $\frac{1}{13}$th of the length a section $\frac{1}{30} \sqrt{2}$ from this ordinate.

The labour of this calculation by Simpson's Rule by the integrator method partly consists in observing and recording readings for each section after the pointer has gone round the perimeter of the section. On looking at the table we see that the readings have each to be subtracted in succession and multiplied by the corresponding Simpson's Multipliers before they can be added for the integration. If the sections have been spaced according to Tchebycheff's Rules, the readings themselves are functions, and therefore each reading does not require to be noted separately. The pointer of the integrator may therefore be towed in succession round all the sections up to one water-line, and only the final readings need to be taken.

The final readings correspond to the values Σa and Σm in Table, p. 63.

The whole calculation can be made in a table of the following form :—

RESULTS OF INTEGRATOR READINGS ON SECTIONS SPACED TO TCHEBYCHEFF'S RULE.

Water Planes.	Inclinations.							
	θ_1.		θ_2.		θ_3.		θ_4.	
	Area Reading.	Moment Reading.	Area Reading.	Moment Reading.	Area Reading.	Moment Reading.	Area Reading.	Moment Reading.
1								
2								
3								
4								
Totals	Σa_1	Σm_1	Σa_2	Σm_2	Σa_3	Σm_3	Σa_4	Σm_4

If the three-ordinate Rule has been used and there are fifteen sections, the multiplier, after adding the function, is $\frac{L}{15}$, where L is the length of the vessel.

Let the scale of body-plan be $\frac{1''}{n} = 1$ foot. Then the multiplier for displacement is

$$\left(20 \times n^2 \times \frac{L}{15} \right) = \frac{4Ln^2}{3} \text{ cubic feet.}$$

The multiplier for moments is

$$\left(40 \times n^3 \times \frac{L}{15} \right) = \frac{8Ln^3}{3}.$$

The multiplier for K N is $\dfrac{8Ln^3}{3} \div \dfrac{4Ln^2}{3} = 2n.$

$\therefore$ The multiplier for K N is $2n$ as before.

The table shown merely arranges columns for the readings of the area and moment wheels at each inclination, and each waterplane for each inclination.

All that has to be done is to multiply the Σa values by $\dfrac{4Ln^2}{3 \times 35}$ to obtain displacement in tons, and the K N values by $2n$ to obtain values of K N in feet, and the information for setting up the cross curves is complete.

In order to shorten the work, and as a means of affording a valuable check on the correctness of the work, the volumes of the parts between the water-planes are treated separately. Supposing the body-plan sections to be to Tchebycheff's spacing, we can deal with the volume up to the first waterplane and find Σa and Σm. The values of Σa and Σm for layer between water-planes Nos. 1 and 2 can be found. The layer between Nos. 2 and 3, 3 and 4, etc., may be similarly treated. All that has to be done is to go round the parts of the sections and between the waterplanes. The last operation is to go over the whole sections up to waterplane No. 5.

Let Δ_1 and M_1 be the displacement in tons and the moment of the displacement of the part up to the first waterplane.

Let d_1 and m_1 be the corresponding quantities for the layer between waterplanes 1 and 2, d_2 and m_2 the quantities for the layer between 2 and 3, and so on.

Let Δ_4 and M_4 be the values for the whole volume up to the last waterplane. Then we have

$$\Delta_4 = \Delta_1 + d_1 + d_2 + d_3$$
$$M_4 = M_1 + m_1 + m_2 + m_3.$$

This gives a useful check on the intermediate steps of finding the displacement and moments of the volume up to the intermediate waterplane.

$$KN_1 = \dfrac{M_1}{\Delta_1},$$

$$KN_2 = \dfrac{M_1 + m_1}{\Delta_1 + d_1},$$

$$KN_3 = \dfrac{M_1 + m_1 + m_2}{\Delta_1 + d_1 + d_2},$$

$$KN_4 = \dfrac{M_4}{\Delta_4} = \dfrac{M_1 + m_1 + m_2 + m_3}{\Delta_1 + d_1 + d_2 + d_3}.$$

Stability by the Integraph.—If the sections are spaced for Tchebycheff's two-ordinate Rule, it is convenient to divide the length of the ship into, say, ten equal intervals, then to space off Tchebycheff's abscissæ $\left(\dfrac{1}{\sqrt{3}} \times \dfrac{L}{20} \right)$ on either side of each of these divisions.

Sections are drawn where the Tchebycheff ordinates come giving twenty sections in the body-plan.

The rule for three ordinates can be conveniently worked by dividing the length into ten divisions as before, and spacing off the Tchebycheff abscissæ

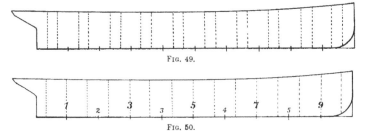

FIG. 49.

FIG. 50.

$\left(\dfrac{1}{\sqrt{2}} \cdot \dfrac{L}{10} \right)$ from divisions Nos. 1, 3, 5, 7, 9. This method gives fifteen ordinates.

It is necessary to make a stability body-plan of complete sections.

Vessel in the Upright.—We can draw the displacement curve by means of the integraph in two ways.

BODY PLAN. *INTEGRAPHED* *BODY-PLAN.*

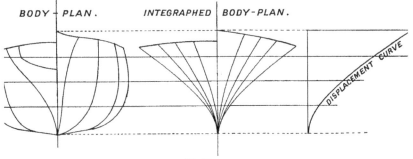

FIG. 51.

(1) By integraphing the areas of body-plan sections, and then summing up the intersections of these integraphs with the waterline (fig. 51).

(2) By summing up the waterline ordinates so as to make a curve of areas of waterplanes, and then integrating this curve (fig. 52).

The second method is the easier.

To obtain from displacement curve the C.B. curve (fig. 53) :—

Let O D be the displacement curve in terms of draughts O X. Integraphing this curve along O X we get a moment curve O C. From the moment curve we can get the centre of buoyancy corresponding to any waterline ac by drawing the tangent at c to intersect O X in B. As there often is a practical difficulty in drawing the tangent, we may use the method described

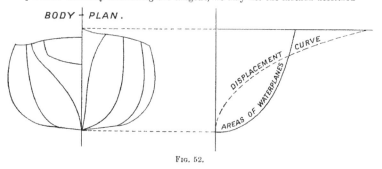

FIG. 52.

at p. 163, Vol. I. Let d be the intersection of the waterline with the displacement curve.

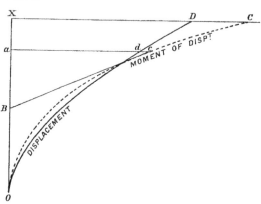

FIG. 53.

ad represents displacement to draught O a, and ac represents the moment of that displacement about the waterline at a.

$\therefore \dfrac{ac}{ad}$ gives the distance below ac of the centre of buoyancy corresponding to that waterline.

In this way the centre of buoyancy heights can be obtained by finding ratios ac to ad, and setting them off in terms of draught in the usual manner.

Passing now to the consideration of the vessel in the inclined condition. See fig. 54.

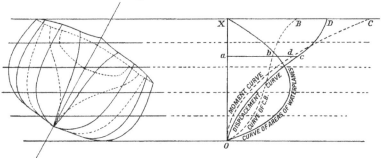

FIG. 54.

Angle of inclination θ.

(1) Set off a curve of areas of waterplanes on O X as described for the case in the upright. Where any obvious irregularity occurs, such

CURVES OF
WATERPLANE AREAS.

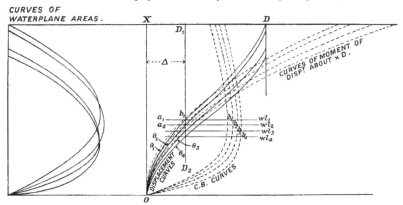

FIG. 55.

as at the deck-edge amidships, a waterline should be drawn there.

(2) Integraph this curve along O X, thus getting the displacement curve O D.

(3) Integraph the curve O D to get the moment curve O C.

(4) By drawing tangents to the moment curve, or by taking the ratios $\dfrac{ad}{ac}$

we get the positions of B, and hence a curve OB can be drawn giving the depth of B at any draught below the corresponding waterline.

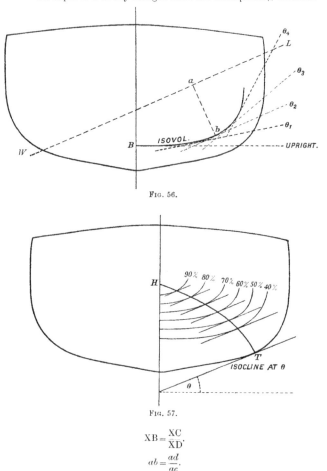

FIG. 56.

FIG. 57.

$$XB = \frac{XC}{XD}.$$

$$ab = \frac{ad}{ac}.$$

To get an Isovol Curve for Displacement Δ.—Suppose we have a series of waterplane curves at different angles of inclination θ_1, θ_2, θ_3, etc. (fig. 55).

(1) Integraph these waterline area curves to get the displacement curves.
(2) Integraph the displacement curves to get moment curves.
(3) From the moment and displacement curves construct C.B. curves.

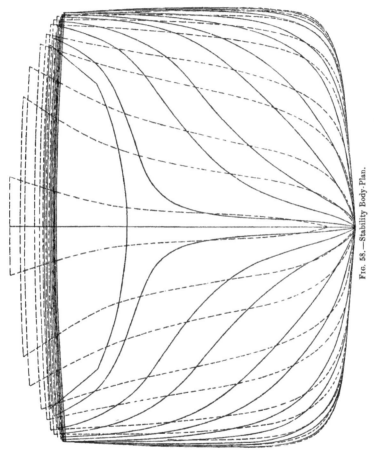

FIG. 58.—Stability Body-Plan.

(4) At the required displacement Δ draw a line $D_1 D_2$ parallel to O X. This line intersects the displacement curves at the heights of the waterplane $w l_1$, $w l_2$, $w l_3$, $w l_4$, giving the constant displacement Δ for the angles of inclination.

(5) The intersection of these waterlines with the C.B. curves gives the depth of C.B. for each inclination and constant displacement Δ.

(6) Draw the waterline W L (inclined at the corresponding angle of heel), and set off the distance $a\,b$ to this W L on the body-plan (fig. 56), where $a\,b$ is the depth of C.B. found for this inclination. A line through b parallel to W L gives a tangent to the isovol. Draw a series of these tangents for the different angles of heel for the constant displacement. An enveloping curve to these tangents will be the isovol for Δ. A series of these isovols may be drawn for varying values of Δ.

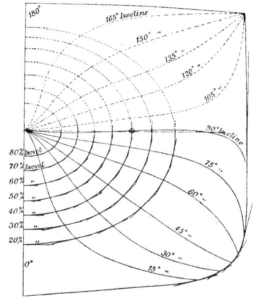

FIG. 61.—" Isoclines " and " Isovols."

The values of Δ chosen are percentages of the total displacement of the whole total, usually 10%, 20%, to 90%.

From a series of Isovols to construct an Isocline Curve for a chosen value of θ.—Draw tangent to the isovols at θ (fig. 57). Tangents parallel to the waterplanes touch the isovols at the corresponding C.B.'s. The points of contact lie on the isocline. The endings of the isocline (the points H and T) can be determined. H is the same for all isoclines. T is the point of contact of the tangent at an angle θ to the midship section.

Examples of Stability Calculations.— The calculations which have been appended are examples of the methods that have been described in this chapter. The following method is by the integraph.

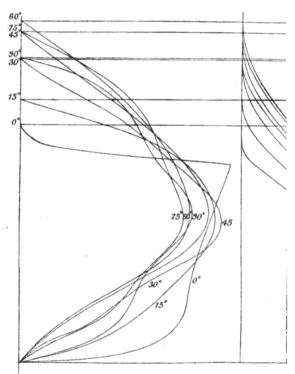

Fig. 59.—Areas of Waterplane Curves.

[PLATE I.

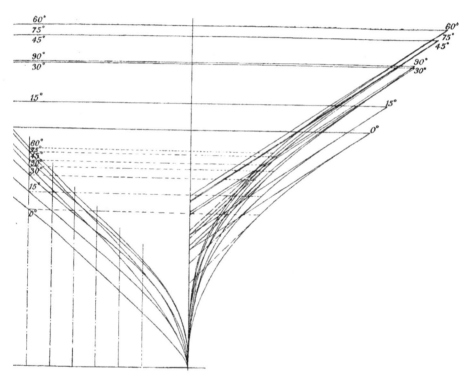

FIG. 60.—Displacement Curves.   Moment of Displacement Curves.

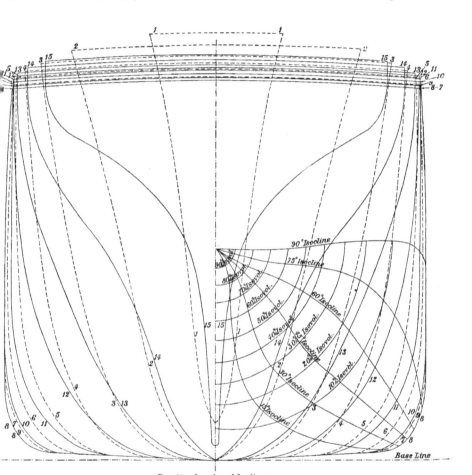

Fig. 62.—Isovols and Isoclines.

Dimensions—350′ × 45′ × 37′.

Load displacement = 6880 tons = 54%.
Light   ,,   = 2920 ,,   = 23%.
Bulk   ,,   = 12730 ,,   = 100%.

Sections spaced according to Tchebycheff's Rule for three ordinates.

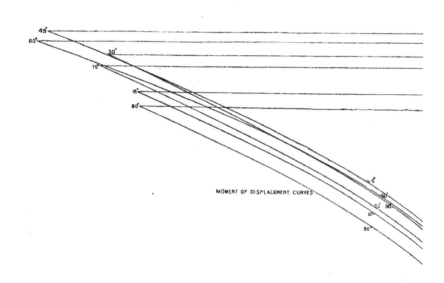

MOMENT OF DISPLACEMENT CURVES

CURVES OF DISPLACEMENT IN TERMS OF DRAUGHT
AT DIFFERENT ANGLES OF INCLINATION AND CORRESPONDING
CURVES FOR POSITIONS OF THE CENTRE OF BUOYANCY

[PLATE III.

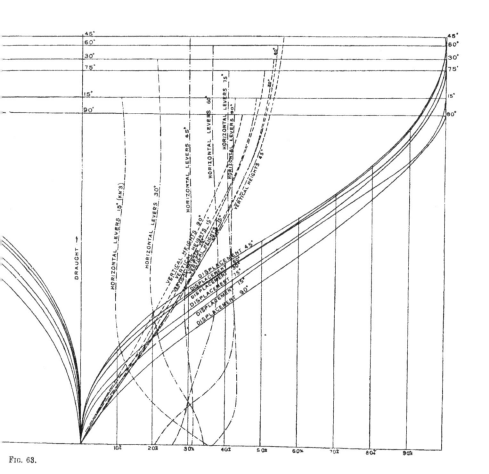

FIG. 63.

Fig. 58 shows the body-plan. The sections have been spaced according to Tchebycheff's Rule for two ordinates. Fig. 59, Plate I., shows the "area of waterplane curves" which when integrated give the displacement curves shown

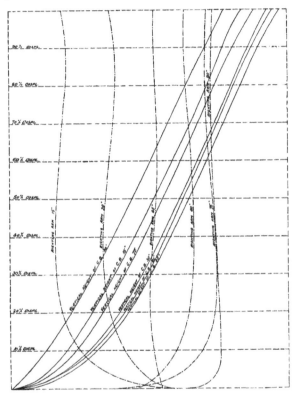

FIG. 64.—Curves of Righting Arms and Vertical Heights of C. B. in terms of Displacement.

Vertical scale of displacement, $\frac{1}{2}'' = 10\%$.
Horizontal scale of righting arms and heights of C.B., $\frac{1}{8}'' = 1$ ft.

in the same diagram. The integrals of the displacement curves are given in fig. 60, Plate I., and from these and the displacement curves the heights of the centre of buoyancy can be determined. The waterplane area curves have been drawn for angles of inclination 0°, 15°, 30°, 45°, 60°, 75°, 90°, and the heights of the centres of buoyancy have been determined for 20%, 30%, 40%, 50%,

60%, 70%, and 80% of the total volume. Drawing lines parallel to the corresponding waterplane for any of the above percentages of total volume, the corresponding isovol can be drawn. The complete set of isovols and isoclines are shown in fig. 61.

A more correct method for drawing the isovols and isoclines is as follows. It necessitates the use of the integrator. The body-plan is given in fig. 62, Plate II. As in finding cross curves, the moments and areas of the submerged sections are obtained by the integrator about a horizontal axis, and also about a vertical axis. Dividing the moment readings by the corresponding area readings, we get the distances of the centres of buoyancy from those axes.

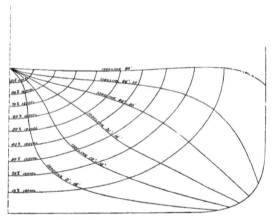

Fig. 65.—Standardised Isovols and Isoclines.

Vertical scale—depth $= \frac{1}{3}0'' \therefore \frac{1}{3}'' = \frac{9}{10}$ ft.
Horizontal scale—breadth $= \frac{2}{3}0'' \therefore \frac{1}{3}'' = \frac{4}{3}0$ ft.

These distances have been plotted in fig. 63, Plate III., as it is more convenient to obtain the vertical heights of the centre of buoyancy in the same way as described in the previous method by the integraph. Hence it is only necessary to record the moments and areas about a vertical axis giving the positions of centre of buoyancy from the vertical axis at each inclination. If the area readings be plotted, we have the displacement curves, and by integraphing these curves we can get the curves giving the vertical heights of the centre of buoyancy.

In standardising the isoclines and isovols it is better to first plot the above two sets of curves in terms of percentage of displacement. This has been done in fig. 64. The isovols and isoclines curves have been drawn on the body-plan of fig. 62, Plate II., and the standardised isovols and isoclines are shown in fig. 65.

Examples of statical stability curves have been appended.

Case A, p. 78, is a fast Atlantic passenger steamer. It will be seen that

CASE A.

Conditions.	No.	Cargo Stowage.	W.T.	Coal.	Stores, Fresh-water, Passengers and Baggage.	Water Ballast Tanks Filled.	W.T.	Dis-placement.	Mean Draught.	G M.	Remarks.
Light	1	...	...	...	...	...	...	10295	19' 4"	·4	This includes 100 tons refrigerating fittings and 46 tons steward's furnishing.
Boilers and condensers empty, donkey boilers full	2	...	...	...	...	...	...	9920	18' 9"	·05	Same as No. 1.
Docking	3	...	...	...	...	Fore peak No. 1 to orlop-deck Nos. 2, 3, 4, and 75 tons iron in No. 2	510	10430	19' 7½"	·75	Ship on even keel.
Loaded with cargo to lower-deck	4	To lower-deck 2, 3, 4, 10, H, 13 to orlop-deck 12	900 at 150 ft. per ton.	2650	420	...	...	14220	25' 3"		
Crossing the bar	5	,,	900	100	283	Fore peak No. 1 to orlop-deck Nos. 2, 3, 7 tanks	506	12038	21' 11¾"	1·46	Draught (extreme) 22' 0¾".
Loaded, coal out	6	To lower-deck same as No. 4, between main and upper- decks 2, lower- & upper- decks 3, 12, 13	900	...	283	...	...	11432	21' 1"	·7	
Deep load, cargo to upper-deck	7	,,	1798	2650	421	...	...	15118	26' 7"	·52	
Crossing the bar	8	To lower-deck 2, 3, 12, 13	1798	100	283	Fore peak No. 1 to orlop-deck Nos. 2, 3, 4, 5, 7	766	13196	23' 9¼"	1·39	Draught (extreme) 23' 10½".
Deep load, coal out	9	,,	1798	...	283	No. 7	...	12330	22' 6"	·16	
	9A	...	1798	...	283	...	190	12520	22' 9½"	·5	

curves have been drawn for ten different conditions of the vessel. These conditions are fully described in the Table A. The most stable condition is

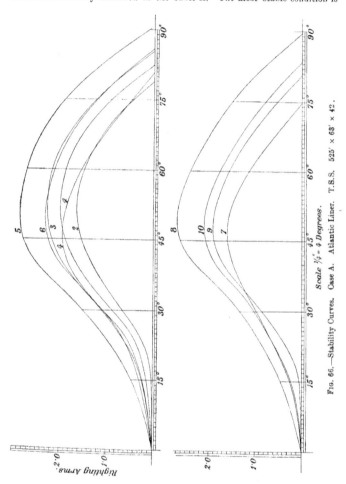

FIG. 66.—Stability Curves. Case A. Atlantic Liner. T.S.S. 525′ × 63′ × 42′.

No. 5, which is the condition at the end of a voyage, the G M being 1·46 feet. The most unstable condition is the docking condition, No. 2, which has only a G M of ·05 foot. None of the conditions give a negative G M. Sometimes vessels of this kind are in a condition when the G M is negative ; and if such a

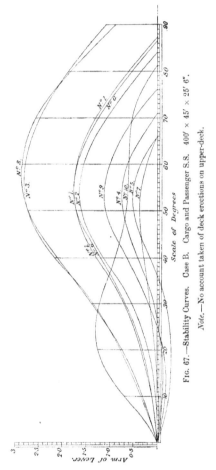

FIG. 67.—Stability Curves. Case B. Cargo and Passenger S.S. 400' × 45' × 25' 6". *Note.*—No account taken of deck erections on upper-deck.

condition occurs while the vessel is at sea, means can be adopted to make the vessel stable.

Case B, fig. 67, is a vessel which in some conditions has a negative

CASE B.—CARGO AND PASSENGER.

No.	Conditions.	Mean Draught.	Displacement.	C.G. above Keel.	G.M.
1	3900 tons cargo to main-deck and with 1000 tons coal aboard .	24' 0"	10350	21·64	·24
2	3900 tons cargo to main-deck (coal burnt out) . . .	22' 1"	9350	21·97	– ·32
3	3900 tons cargo to main-deck (coal burnt out) (850 tons water ballast) .	23' 8"	10200	20·37	1·45
4	3900 tons cargo to upper-deck and with 1000 tons coal aboard	24' 0"	10350	22·9	– 1·0
5	3900 tons cargo to upper-deck (coal burnt out) . .	22' 1"	9350	23·4	– 1·77
6	3900 tons cargo to upper-deck (coal burnt out) (850 tons water ballast) .	23' 8"	10200	21·7	·12
7	Light condition	13' 7"	5250	24	– ·8
8	Light condition (with 850 tons water ballast) . .	15' 4"	6100	21	1·3
9	Bunkers full (no cargo aboard) . . .	16' 6"	6635	23·1	1·18
10	Launching condition (95 tons water ballast aboard) .	10' 9"	3830	23	2·65

G M, as will be seen from condition No. 5, in which the vessel is very
unfavourably loaded, and with all the coal burned out the G M is

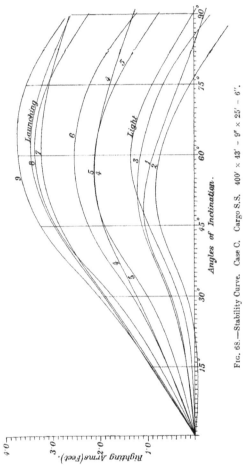

FIG. 68.—Stability Curve. Case C. Cargo S.S. 400′ × 43′ - 9″ × 25′ - 6″.

1·77ft. negative. The best condition for this vessel, with the exception
of the launching condition, is No. 3, where 850 tons of water ballast are
in. The effect of adding this amount of water ballast to the worst condi-

tion when the vessel has 1·77 negative G M is to give her a positive G M of ·12.

Case C is another cargo vessel about the same size as B. In all her conditions she has a positive G M except in No. 2 condition, where it is 3 ft. negative, which will cause the vessel to heel to 22° before acquiring positive stability. In the light condition it is least, and equals ·194 ft., and in the

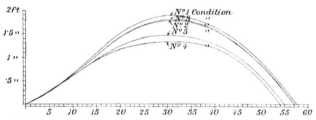

Fig. 69.—Stability Curve. Case D. T.S. Channel Steamer. 310′ × 42′ × 18′.
Ship intact to upper-deck.

Case D.—Channel Steamer, 310 × 42 × 18.

No.	Condition.	Displ. Tons.	Draught. Mean.	G M. Feet.	Max. righting arm.
1	Light: Vessel complete with water in boilers	1921	10′ 10¼″	2·85′	1·87
2	Light: with coal, passengers, stores, fresh-water, reserve feed, on board. Cattle spaces filled	2265	12′ 3½″	3·0′	1·79
3	As in No. 2, with coal bunkers and reserve feed tanks empty	2142	11′ 9¾″	2·84′	1·8
4	Load condition as in No. 2, with all cargo holds full	2901	14′ 8¼″	3·2′	1·32
5	As in No. 4, with coal, fresh-water and reserve feed, and stores finished . .	2725	13′ 11″	3·07′	1·46

load condition, with coal out and water ballast in, the G M is greatest except for the launching condition, and is 3·48 ft.

Case D, fig. 69, gives the curves for a fast Channel steamer of 310 ft. in length for five different conditions. This vessel is very stable even in the light condition, when the G M is 2·85 feet. The most stable condition is the load No. 4, when the G M is 3·2 feet. This type of vessel has generally no double bottom ; and as she only carries about 90 tons of coal, the centre of gravity is not much altered, so that there is no necessity for having ballast tanks. From the curves of these four types may be obtained the range of stability and the maximum righting arm in each case.

CASE C.—400' × 43' - 9" × 25' - 6".

No.	Conditions.	Mean Draught.	Displacement.	Weight of Cargo.	Weight of Coal.	C.G. above Keel.	G.M.	Free-board.	Density of Cargo.
1	Cargo stowed homogeneously to spar-deck, coal in	25' 0"	9010	3598	890	19·37	·6	9' 0½"	78·7
2	Cargo stowed homogeneously to spar-deck, coal out	22' 11"	8120	"	Ballast 307	19·83	-3·0	11' 1½"	"
3	Cargo stowed homogeneously to spar-deck, {coal in ballast in}	23' 8"	8427	"	890	19·2	·46	10' 4½"	"
4	Cargo stowed homogeneously to main-deck, coal in	25' 0"	9010	"	890	17·86	2·13	9' 0½"	58
5	Cargo stowed homogeneously to main-deck, coal out	22' 11"	8120	"	Ballast 307	18·16	1·38	11' 1½"	"
6	Cargo stowed homogeneously to main-deck, {coal out ballast in}	23' 8"	8427	"	Ballast 307	17·59	2·08	10' 4½"	"
7	Cargo stowed homogeneously to lower-deck, {coal in cattle in lower- & main-dk.}	25' 0"	9010	{Cattle in 3426}	890	16·54	3·43	9' 0½"	40·9
8	Cargo stowed homogeneously to lower-deck, coal out	22' 11"	8120	"		16·7	2·8	11' 1½"	"
9	Cargo stowed homogeneously to lower-deck, {coal out ballast in}	23' 8"	8427	"	Ballast 307	16·18	3·48	10' 4½"	"
	Light condition	13' 10"	4354	Nil	Nil	18·81	·194	20' 2½"	
	As launched	12' 2"	3675	"	"	17·34	3·63	21' 10½"	

Note.—No account taken of deck erections above upper-deck.

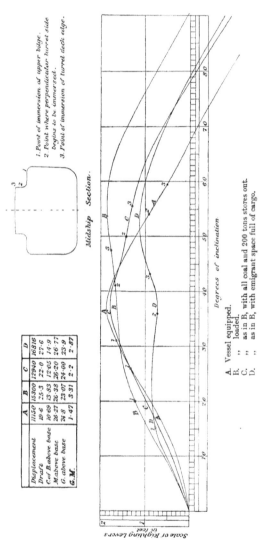

1. Point of immersion at upper bilge.
2. Point where perpendicular turret side begins to be immersed.
3. Point of immersion of turret deck edge.

Midship Section.

	A	B	C	D
Displacement	11150	15300	12940	16816
Draft	19·6	25·3	22·0	27·6
Cel. B above base	10·69	13·83	12·05	14·9
M. above base	26·27	26·38	26·20	26·77
G. above base	24·8	23·07	24·00	23·9
G.M.	1·47	3·31	2·2	2·87

Degrees of inclination

A. Vessel equipped.
B.   ,,   loaded.
C.   ,,   as in B, with all coal and 200 tons stores out.
D.   ,,   as in B, with emigrant space full of cargo.

FIG. 70.—Turret Steamer.   Curves of Statical Stability.

Scale or Righting Levers in feet

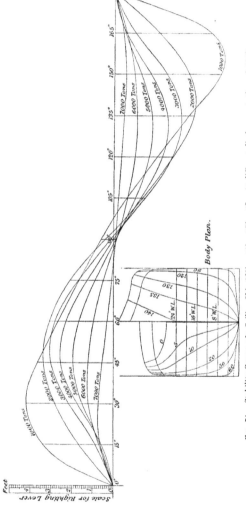

Fig. 71.—Stability Curves of a Sailing-Ship 283′ × 42′ × 27′ – 6″. At different displacements through 180°.

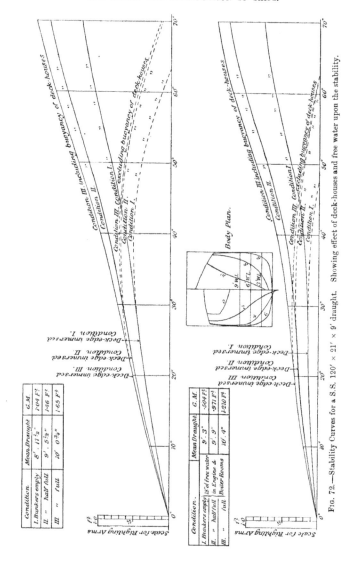

FIG. 72.—Stability Curves for a S.S. 120′ × 21′ × 9′ draught. Showing effect of deck-houses and free water upon the stability.

In considering the effect of altering the dimensions in designing similar types, the following points should be noted.

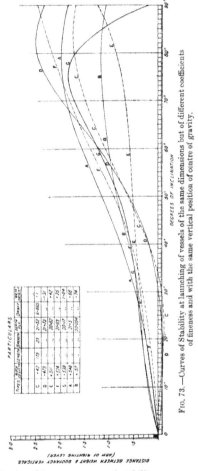

FIG. 73.—Curves of Stability at launching of vessels of the same dimensions but of different coefficients of fineness and with the same vertical position of centre of gravity.

Increase of freeboard increases range of stability.

Increase of beam proportion increases G M and increases the righting arm, but may decrease the range of stability.

With the alteration of the depth proportion the relative height of the centre of gravity to depth may alter, so that this has to be taken into account.

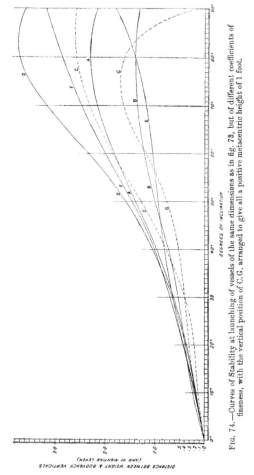

FIG. 74.—Curves of Stability at launching of vessels of the same dimensions as in fig. 73, but of different coefficients of fineness, with the vertical position of C.G. arranged to give all a positive metacentric height of 1 foot.

It is therefore of importance in the design of a new vessel to have the isovol and isocline curves which give the stability due to form only, and to consider separately the calculation for the position of centre of gravity.

Fig. 70 shows curves of stability for a turret steamer, the shape of the

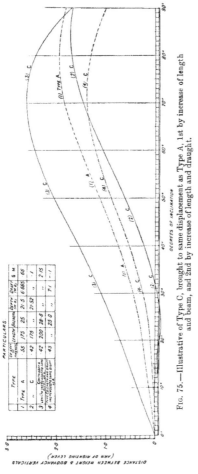

FIG. 75.—Illustrative of Type C, brought to same displacement as Type A, 1st by increase of length and beam, and 2nd by increase of length and draught.

midship section being shown. It is instructive to note the effect in the curves, of the points marked 1, 2, and 3.

Fig. 71 shows curves of stability for a sailing-ship, as the vessel is heeled through 180°. These are drawn for seven different displacements, rising from 1000 tons by equal increments to 7000 tons. In this case it is seen that as the displacement increases, both the range of stability and maximum righting arm decreases.

Fig. 72 shows the effect upon stability of the presence of free water in a vessel, and also the great effect of deck erections, when watertight. With bunkers empty and 18 inches of free water in boiler and engine rooms, neglecting effect of deck erections the maximum righting lever is ·15 ft., and range 47·5°. If the deck erections are watertight the range is enormously increased, and the value of the lever at 70° is ·8 ft.

Stability of Ships at Launching.—This problem differs from that of the stability when the ship is actually at rest in still water. This is due to the following causes :—

(1) The disturbance which the ship herself creates by her sudden intrusion into the comparatively small quantity of water in the vicinity of most shipbuilding yards.

(2) The pressure of wind upon the side of the vessel.

(3) The unequal effect of the buoyancy of the bilgeways caused by the release of a larger quantity on one side than on the other.

(4) Shifting of loose weights on board.

(5) Heeling action due to the checking of one drag chain before the other.

Fig. 73 shows curves of stability at launching, of vessels of the same dimensions but of different block coefficients and the same vertical position of centre of gravity.

Fig. 74 shows curves of stability for the same vessels as in fig. 73, but with the C.G. arranged to give all a positive G M of 1 foot.

Fig. 75 shows curves of stability for types A and C, and also for type C brought to the same displacement as A—

(1) By increase of length and beam.

(2) By increase of length and draught.

Stability required.—The amount of stability required for any particular circumstance of wind and water for any particular type of vessel can only be a matter of opinion based upon experience. It is possible to determine how much righting arm and range any vessel will have under any assumed condition. The amount which she ought to have for any condition of wind and weather can best be determined by reference to the corresponding data of ships which have successfully withstood similar conditions.

PART V.

RESISTANCE.

CHAPTER VI.

PRELIMINARY.

THE subject of resistance of ships has had a fascination for many at all times. The form of least resistance has been a subject which has had as much charm for some as the philosopher's stone has had for the alchemists. Newton evolved a form of least resistance, not necessarily for a ship only. Lord Kelvin has determined forms of least resistance for bodies moving on the surface of the water. Every naval architect who has designed a ship has attempted to produce the form of least resistance consistently with all the other conditions to be fulfilled. The problem has so far proved to be too difficult for mathematical solution from *a priori* considerations. The only solution which even in an approximate degree can be considered reliable is the experimental one.

Beaufoy's Experiments.—Until the end of the eighteenth century the only experimental solution of the question was on the forms of full-sized ships. In 1791 a Society for the improvement of Naval Architecture undertook experiments on comparatively small-sized forms to determine the variation in resistance associated with variation of form. The Society resolved to make a series of experiments on the resistance of bodies moving through water upon a scale much more extensive than any which had yet been made in this or any other country. A portion of the Greenland dock at Deptford, of about 400 feet long and 11 feet depth of water, was selected as being suitable for carrying out the experiments. The Society, soon after its formation, fell into decay, and the experiments were for a considerable period conducted and brought to a conclusion by the only remaining member, Colonel Beaufoy. The experiments were carried out under his supervision in each successive year from 1793 to 1798, but it was not until 1834 that the results were published. It cannot be said that the results contributed much to the science of naval architecture, though they afforded data for later experiments.

The early experiments of the series referred to were all conducted with a pendulum apparatus which was made to carry through a tank of water the solid whose resistance was to be estimated. A wooden vessel or trough 7 feet by 1 foot by 20 inches deep was filled with water, and into it the lower part of the pendulum was immersed. The pendulum was $5\frac{1}{2}$ feet long. The different solids on which experiments were intended to be made were arranged so that they could be easily attached to the bottom of the pendulum, and bob weights of different masses could also be attached to the pendulum rod. The momentum of the pendulum could thus be altered by altering the mass of the bob.

The following are the general conclusions of Colonel Beaufoy on these experiments.

Increasing the length of a solid of almost any form, by the addition of a

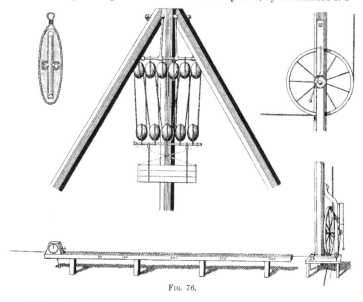

FIG. 76.

cylinder in the middle, exceedingly diminishes the resistance with which it moves, provided the displacement remains unaltered.

A cone will move through water with less resistance with its apex foremost than with its base,—a conclusion which is opposed to the current opinion.

The greatest breadth of the moving body should be placed at two-fifths the length from the bow. There are some exceptions to this general rule. Thus, in the double parabolic body, the greatest breadth should be given to the middle, and in the double cone it should be placed farther aft.

The bottom of a floating solid should be made triangular, as in that case it will meet with the least resistance when moving in the direction of its longest axis, and with the greatest resistance when moving with its broadside foremost.

In 1793 the resistance experiments on bodies towed through the water were commenced. Some were made upon floating logs, others upon submerged.

The towing apparatus, which was said to have proved satisfactory, was arranged as follows :—A tripod, the apex of which was about 60 feet above the ground, was made to support on a horizontal bar a system of six blocks corresponding to another system of five similar blocks also attached to another horizontal bar, upon which was hung a weight, the fall of which gave the motive power to the forms which were towed by means of a rope running round the system of blocks. The running end of the rope which passed through the blocks was led round the circumference of a large wheel about $4\frac{1}{2}$ feet in diameter, from which it passed horizontally to the body on trial. The tension in the rope was one-twelfth of the suspended weight, since there were twelve ropes, each taking an equal share of the weight (fig. 76). The friction of the apparatus was determined independently. In order that the body might rapidly attain the required constant velocity, the motion was started by an additional weight

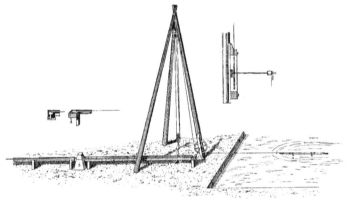

Fig. 77.

in the form of a chain in a box attached to the lower horizontal bar. This chain had its upper end fixed so that the weight of it gradually left the box containing it as the bar descended until it was ultimately released. The amount of the weight first described determined the uniform velocity ultimately obtained. It will be seen that the whole apparatus was in principle the same as Atwood's machine for measuring acceleration. In order to measure the velocity of the body on trial, a batten constructed as lightly as possible was allowed to be drawn over a trough by means of a silken thread which passed over a pulley on the axis of the large wheel. This was so arranged that the batten moved 1 inch for every foot moved by the model. A clock was arranged to mark intervals of time on this moving batten, thus giving sufficient data for measuring fairly accurately the velocity at which the body moved for the given motive weight. The early experiments were attended with great trouble and disappointment.

The later experiments, which were begun in 1793, and conducted each successive year thereafter, gave more trustworthy results.

The first series, 1793, was made up of experiments on the towing resistance of a parallelepipedon. Different lengths were tried, and geometrically shaped ends were fitted first at the bow, second at the stern, third at both ends. The shapes of the end pieces were semicircular, semielliptical, and triangular. In 1795 these experiments were extended. Sixteen of them have been selected, and the results plotted in curves (fig. 78).

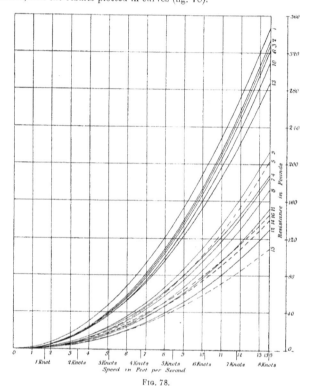

FIG. 78.

The shapes tried were as shown in figs. 79 and 80.

The results taken from the tables and plotted in terms of speeds show consistency up to 13·5 feet per second. At that speed the resistance in lbs. for the different types ranged from 109·2 to 345·8. In the following table the resistances at the speed of 13·5 feet per second are compared with the resistances at the speed of 4 feet per second. The results are tabulated in the order of the resistances.

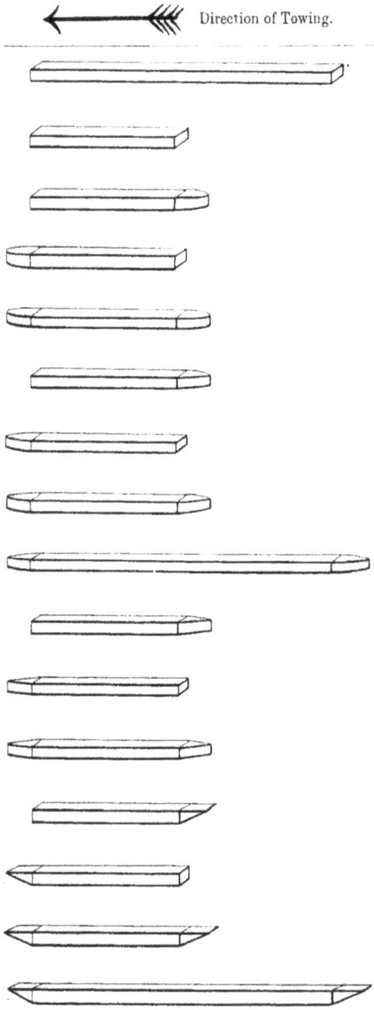

	← Direction of Towing.	Length.	Breadth.	Depth.	
		Feet.	Feet.	Feet.	
1		42·198	1·219	1·219	
2		21·099	,,	,,	
3		,,	,,	,,	Shape a aft
4		,,	,,	,,	,, c forward
5		,,	,,	,,	,, a for'd and aft
6		,,	,,	,,	,, b aft
7		,,	,,	,,	,, b forward
8		,,	,,	,,	,, b for'd and aft
9		42·198	,,	,,	,, b for'd and aft
10		21·099	,,	,,	,, c aft
11		,,	,,	,,	,, c forward
12		,,	,,	,,	,, c for'd and aft
13		,,	,,	,,	,, d aft
14		,,	,,	,,	,, d forward
15		,,	,,	,,	,, d for'd and aft
16		42·198	,,	,,	,, d for'd and aft

FIG. 79.

was the discoverer of the relation which existed between the resistance of the vessel and the waves produced by it. His theory of the resistance of a ship was stated in the Report of a Committee of the British Association in 1869 as follows : —

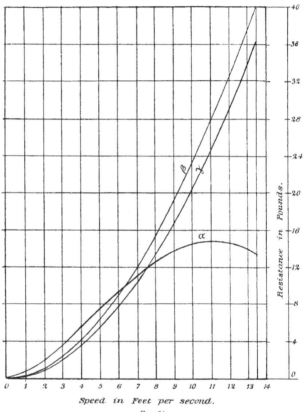

Speed in Feet per second.

Fig. 81.

Viscosity is resistance to change of shape. A perfect fluid offers no resistance to change of shape.

Water offers resistance to change of shape, but if time be neglected it offers no resistance ; neither do tar, treacle, nor even sealing-wax substances, which are classed as fluids.

Large waves have very little viscosity in relation to energy. Small waves have much. The former go on for days, the latter for very short periods. The velocity of a wave in a canal whose length is many times the depth of the canal $= \sqrt{gk}$, where k is the depth of the canal and g is the acceleration due to gravity.

If the boat on the canal is made to travel at a velocity less than $\sqrt{gk}$ it leaves a long train of waves behind it.

If the boat is made to travel faster than the velocity $\sqrt{gk}$ it only forms one wave, which travels as fast or faster than the boat, and no procession has to be formed.

The viscosity of the water causes the waves to die out in the canal at from 50 to 60 wave-lengths astern.

If the canal has a depth of from three-quarters to once the wave-length, the system moves at half the speed of the wave.

On the basis of the above, he proposed his wave-line theory of forms of ships.

The following are the chief points of this principle :—

A vessel may be divided longitudinally into three portions : bow, straight middle-body (if any), and after-body. The midship section may be of any shape whatever, the resistance due to it depending on its area and wet girth only.

The fore-body must have for its level sections curves of versed sines, the maximum ordinate of which is half the greatest breadth at the waterline. Its length must be the same as that of a wave of translation, moving at the same speed as the ship is intended to have, in order that the resistance may be the least possible.

The after-body must have trochoids for its level lines. Its length is not to be less than one-half—preferably two-thirds—the length of an oscillating wave moving at the same speed as the ship, its maximum ordinate being half the greatest breadth of the waterline.

The straight middle-body may be of any length, to suit the necessary requirements of stability, etc.

Subject to these conditions, the resistance of the ship will be expressed by

$$(K \oplus + K'S) V^2$$

where $\oplus$ represents the area of the midship section and S the wetted surface. K and K' are coefficients, the former of which is roughly one-tenth that due to a flat plane drawn flatwise through the water, and the latter depending upon the condition of the surface.

The general formula for the length of the ship given by this theory is—

Fore-body in feet $= \dfrac{2\pi V^2}{g}$, where V is in feet per second.

After-body in feet $= \dfrac{4}{3} \dfrac{\pi V^2}{g}$,,   ,,   ,,

Professor Rankine states, as the results of his own investigations, that it is possible to shorten the bow to two-thirds the length given in the above formula without materially increasing the resistance, but that it is very disadvantageous to shorten the after-body.

The following is an example of the application of this method :—

Suppose we have fixed the form of the midship section of a ship, so that B is the beam, D the draught, and the half ordinates of a series of water-lines at the midship section are r_0, r_1, r_2, etc.

Let V be the speed required in feet per second, l_f and l_a the lengths of fore- and after-bodies respectively.

Then $$l_f = \frac{2\pi V^2}{g} \qquad l_a = \frac{4}{3}\frac{\pi V^2}{g}.$$

Suppose we take the waterline at r_0 as an example. In fig. 82 set off l_a and l_f according to the above formulæ, and l_m the length of parallel middle-body desired.

Set up A B and C D perpendicular to B F and D E, each being equal to r_0. Upon A B and C D describe semicircles, and divide their circumferences into a number of equal parts, say four.

Divide B F and D E into the same number of equal parts. The rest of the construction is obvious from the figure.

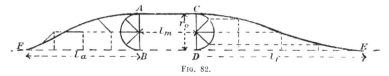

FIG. 82.

Similarly for the other waterlines.

Scott-Russell's theory, underlying this mode of construction, is that at the bow of a ship moving through the water a wave of translation is formed, and at the stern a series of oscillating waves are formed. These waves, in each case, move with the velocity of the ship. The water, when acted upon by natural forces only, assumes these forms at the bow and stern. When water at rest is moved from its equilibrium position to make way for the passage of a ship through it, the path of least resistance of a particle would be, at the bow, the shape of a wave of translation, and at the stern, the shape of a wave of oscillation, the sizes of these waves being such that their natural velocity of propagation is the speed of the ship. He further mentions that, while in all cases the shape of the bow should be such that the waterlines are curves of versed sines, in some cases the shape of the after-body may be such that the buttock-lines may be trochoids. He advises making the waterlines of this shape in boats that are to be used in shallow water, and the buttock-lines of this shape in boats designed for deep water. In most cases a combination of these two systems is the best.

It should be noticed that this is of historical interest only.

CHAPTER VII.

RESISTANCE TO BEING SET IN MOTION.

A VESSEL floating freely in water is free to move in a straight line if force is exerted upon it. The resistance to change of motion which the inertia of the body offers will absorb some of the force, while the remainder will be absorbed by the resistance which the fluid offers to motion through it. The force which overcomes the inertia of the body will produce a velocity which would continually and uniformly increase as long as the force is applied if there were no resistance to motion from the fluid or other external medium. With the increase of velocity, however, will inevitably ensue an increase of resistance of the fluid, which in time will be so great as to balance the total operating force and leave none available for overcoming the inertia of the body. When this point is reached the velocity of the body will cease to change, or, in other words, will become uniform, and the total force will be absorbed in overcoming the resistance of the fluid. It is this resistance which is usually called the resistance of a ship, and it is the determination of this quantity which constitutes the study known as the Resistance of Ships. The force which balances the resistance in uniform motion is known as the propelling force, and it is the determination of this which constitutes the study known as the Propulsion of Ships. This propelling force may be created outside the ship, such as in the case of a ship being towed, or in a sailing ship ; or it may be created inside the ship, as in the case of rowing, the screw propeller, the paddle, or the jet, or hydraulic propeller. It may be a combination of external and internal forces, as in the case of a river barge with sails up and the crew rowing, or as in the case of an auxiliary yacht steaming with sails set.

Considering first the question of the force necessary to overcome the inertia of a vessel, we can treat the problem as one of the time required to overcome the inertia in changing the body's motion from rest to that of the maximum velocity she is likely to attain in a resisting medium such as water.

Take a simple case of a vessel of 1000 tons displacement or weight, having engines of 600 horse-power, capable of driving it at a speed of 10 knots. A horse-power is a unit of energy or work given off in a unit of time—the unit of energy being 33,000 foot lbs., and the unit of time being one minute. The speed of 1 knot is a speed of 6080 feet (one nautical mile) per hour. Hence engines of 600 horse-power are capable of giving off $600 \times 33,000$ foot lbs. $= 19,800,000$ foot lbs. of energy or work per minute ; and if this work be employed in overcoming a resistance or force at 10 knots (or 60,800 feet per hour, or 1013·3 feet per minute), the force will be $\dfrac{19,800,000}{1013\cdot3}$ lbs. $= 19,540$ lbs. $= 8\cdot72$ tons.

All the energy of a steam engine in a ship is not available for overcoming resistance, and it will be seen later that often not more than one-half is available.

Suppose we consider a force of 5 tons to be constantly available. We have then a force of 5 tons to apply to a weight of 1000 tons, and we can determine how long this force will have to act before the vessel is moving at 1013·3 feet per minute. We know that if the body were falling freely under the action of gravity, *i.e.* if it were being acted upon by a force of 1000 tons, it would increase its velocity in one second by g, or 32·2 feet per second. A force of 5 tons would only increase its velocity $\frac{5}{1000}$ths of 32·2 feet per second in one second. If this force acted for one minute it would change the velocity $\frac{5}{1000} \times 32\cdot2 \times 60$ feet per second, or $\frac{5}{1000} \times 32\cdot2 \times 60 \times 60$ feet per minute $= 579\cdot6$ feet per minute. To increase it from 0 to 1013·3 feet per minute would take $\frac{1013\cdot3}{579\cdot6}$ minutes $= 1\frac{3}{4}$ minutes. Hence if there were no resistance other than the inertia of the body, it would only take $1\frac{3}{4}$ minutes to attain the speed of 10 knots with a propelling force of 5 tons. But as the speed increases the resistance increases, so that the force available to overcome the inertia of the body gradually diminishes. When the vessel has arrived at 5 knots speed the resistance will be about one-fourth what it is at full speed, *i.e.* about $1\frac{1}{4}$ tons, so that there will be only $3\frac{3}{4}$ tons left for overcoming inertia. At 8 knots it will be about 3·2 tons, leaving only 1·8 tons.

On the assumption that the resistance varies as the square of the speed, and assuming also that the propelling force is constantly 5 tons, we can find the propelling force available for overcoming the inertia of the vessel's motion at any speed up to 10 knots, assuming the resistance at 10 knots to be 5 tons.

The curves in figs. 83 and 84 show how the time taken by the vessel to reach the full speed of 10 knots can be calculated.

The equation $R = kv^2$ gives the value of the resistance R of the vessel at the speed v. $k = \dfrac{R}{v^2}$ is a constant, and is found by substituting 5 tons for R at the full speed of 10 knots, $k = \frac{1}{20}$. We are thus able to find at any speed between 0 and 10 knots the amount of force available for overcoming the inertia of the ship's motion. From this we get the acceleration of the vessel by the equation

$$\frac{W}{g}a = T - R$$

or $$a = \frac{g}{W}(T - kv^2)$$

where W = weight of vessel in tons,
T = total propelling force in tons,
R = resistance of vessel in tons at speed v,
a = acceleration.

The curve a (fig. 83) gives the acceleration so found in terms of the speed v. From this curve we can get the curve showing the distance traversed and the curve of time elapsed in terms of the speed v by applying the ordinary equations

$$\frac{dv}{dt} = a.$$

$$\therefore \quad t = \int \frac{1}{a}\,dv.$$

This equation enables us to find the time velocity curve.

The best way to apply this equation is to plot the curve of values of $\dfrac{1}{a}$ in

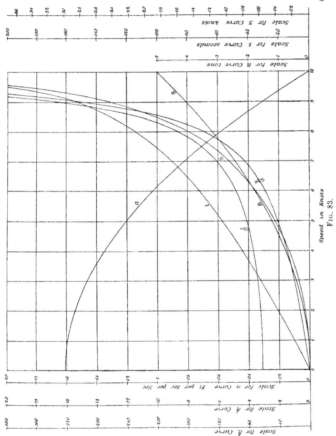

Fig. 83.

terms of v, and then to integrate this curve. The $\dfrac{1}{a}$ curve and the t curve

are shown in fig. 83. The $\dfrac{1}{a}$ curve may be quickly and conveniently inte-

grated by using the integraph. It will be seen that the final ordinate of the

$\frac{1}{a}$ curve is infinite, so that $\int_0^V \frac{1}{a}.dv$ is ∞, since $a = 0$ when $v = V$.

This means that, *if resistance varies consistently as the square of the speed, the vessel never reaches the speed V, but it approaches indefinitely close to it, like the asymptote to the hyperbola.*

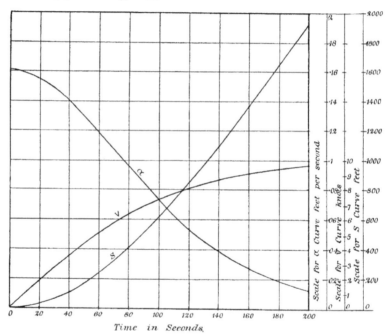

Time   in   Seconds.

Fig. 84.

From the relation $\dfrac{v}{a} = \dfrac{v \cdot \dfrac{ds}{dt}}{\dfrac{dv}{dt}}$

we get $\dfrac{v}{a} = \dfrac{ds}{dv}$ $\therefore$ $s = \int \dfrac{v}{a} dv$

which enables us to get the distance traversed in terms of the velocity.

This curve is obtained by integrating the curve of values of $\frac{v}{a}$ in terms of v.

These curves are also shown in fig. 83.

The final ordinate of the S curve is $\int_0^V \frac{v}{a} dv$ and is ∞.

It is more usual to have curves of v, S, and a plotted on a time base. This can be easily done by measuring the ordinates of S and a and the abscissæ value at convenient values of the t ordinate. Curves of v, S, and a in terms of t are shown in fig. 84.

The acceleration curve becomes asymptotic to the base line. The velocity curve is asymptotic to the horizontal line $v = V$, and the space curve is asymptotic to a line parallel to $y = Vt$, where y is the ordinate corresponding to the time t and V is the final velocity (10 knots).

Similar curves for other assumed relations between resistance and speed may be worked out in a similar manner. If the actual curve of resistance of a vessel is known, the value of the ordinates of the a curve can be obtained.

It should, however, be noted that the force available for acceleration has to act upon a mass of water, whose velocity is changing, as well as upon the mass of the vessel. This will be dealt with in a later chapter, see page 154.

CHAPTER VIII.

PRESENT THEORY OF RESISTANCE.

WE have seen that the resistance of a vessel moving at a uniform velocity may be a very small force in relation to the weight of the body moved. The force propelling a 35-knot torpedo vessel is about 1/10th of its weight. In an ordinary tramp steamer carrying 4000 tons dead weight and moving at 10 knots it is about 1/400th. Though the latter force is comparatively small, yet it is of enormous national importance, and should not be despised on account of its relative smallness to the weight of the ship. When we consider the enormous number of ships, we can see that even a small saving in the economy of propulsion will mean a large saving of coal in the total amount of coal burnt by vessels. It is therefore of importance to study closely and accurately the subject of resistance. The present theory of resistance, which may be called the Froude theory, may be stated as follows :—

The resistance of a ship is made up of three parts :—

    (1) Surface friction.
    (2) Eddymaking resistance.
    (3) Wavemaking resistance.

We shall deal with these three parts separately in the above order, but before discussing them it is necessary to give a short account of the researches of the late Dr Froude. It is to the work of the Froudes, father and son, that the present position of the science is due. The experiments which formed the basis of the late Dr Froude's research were mostly carried out at Chelston Cross, Torquay. At the Admiralty experimental works, Haslar, Portsmouth, they have been continued by his son, Dr R. E. Froude, who had most ably seconded him during his lifetime. As already stated, in 1869 a committee of the British Association recommended that experiments should be carried out on a steamer of known form by towing her at various speeds by means of an apparatus which would register the towing force. It was also proposed that further experiments should be made with the vessel under her own steam-power at a similar range of speed, so that the relation between the force exerted by the engine and that necessary for towing the vessel should be determined. Mr W. Froude, as a member of the committee, approved of these recommendations, but further suggested that towing experiments on small models of about 12 feet in length should be carried out so as to properly investigate the subject. Mr Froude's view was : "So great a variety of forms ought to be tried that it would be impossible, alike on the score of time and expenditure, to perform the experiments with full-sized ships." The

Admiralty (acting upon the advice of Sir E. J. Reed, when asked to carry out the proposals of the committee) declined to do so, but agreed to carry out Mr Froude's proposal to try models.

The basis of the application of model experiments to the determination of the total resistance of full-sized ships is dependent on two things :—

(1) Resistance due to surface denoted by R_f.
(2) ,,   ,, form ,, ,, R_m.

Both are dependent on the speed. The first is also dependent on the extent and nature of the surface. Its amount is determinable by applying the results of experiments upon planes of various dimensions and character of surface.

The second is determinable by model experiments. The resistance of a model like that of a ship is dependent on surface-friction, and form. The first can be calculated from data available. If the total resistance of the model can be determined, the resistance due to friction can be deducted, and the remainder will be that due to form. If the form be exactly to scale it represents the full-sized ship ; and if we can determine the relation between the resistance of two forms differing only in scale, we can determine the resistance due to form in the full-sized ships. This, added to the determined resistance due to surface friction, will give the total resistance of the full-sized ship. Mr Froude discovered the method of finding the relation between the resistance of forms which differed only in scale. It had been discovered before, but its discovery had been lost sight of and had produced no practical result. It is generally known as Froude's Law of Comparison, and may be stated as follows :—

If the linear dimensions of a vessel be l times those of the model, and the resistances, due to form, of the model at speeds V_1, V_2, V_3 . . . . are R_1, R_2, R_3, etc., respectively, then at speeds $V_1 \sqrt{l}$, $V_2 \sqrt{l}$, $V_3 \sqrt{l}$, etc., in the ship, the resistances due to the form of the vessel will be $R_1 l^3$, $R_2 l^3$, $R_3 l^3$, respectively. The speeds $V_1 \sqrt{l}$, $V_2 \sqrt{l}$, $V_3 \sqrt{l}$, etc., are called the corresponding speeds to V_1, V_2, V_3.

From this it may be seen that the resistance of a ship can be determined from that of a model.

It was necessary first to determine the surface friction of planes of kinds similar to the surfaces of models and ships.

In 1872 Mr Froude made his report to the British Association on this subject, and determined the law of variation of frictional resistance in terms of speed, length, and nature of surface of the plane. From these results he was able to determine the amount of the other resistances which his models encountered, and thereby establish a law for the determination of these resistances in terms of the speed and size of the vessel of the same form as the model. To these resistances he added that due to the surface friction of the vessel, based on the results of his experiments on surface friction of planes, and so was able to calculate the total resistance of the full-sized vessel.

In 1874 Mr Froude published the results of towing experiments on H.M.S. "Greyhound," in which he showed that, with a properly selected coefficient of friction, the resistance obtained by model experiments was practically identical with that measured on the actual ship. He also showed that the force necessary to tow the vessel was only 45 per cent. of the equivalent force developed in the cylinder of the steam engine, and that in consequence 55 per cent. of the total power developed at the engines went in non-effective work.

By these experiments he established the value of model experiments for determining the resistance of ships, and gave the initiative to the whole field of investigation of the problem of the best form of vessel for a given set of conditions. The science of resistance was established on an experimental basis, and nothing has happened since to shake the faith of naval architects in the soundness of that foundation. The practical value of the "Greyhound" experiments was twofold : the accuracy of the Froude method of determining resistance was established, and the inefficiency of the apparatus then used to develop and utilise the power to overcome the resistance was demonstrated. Improvement became possible in both directions—in the form of the ship, and in the efficiency of propulsion. In both directions the elder Froude rapidly extended knowledge, and before his death, which occurred in 1880, had determined qualitatively and quantitatively the causes of the loss of work between the engine and the overcoming of the resistance of the vessel, and had laid the foundation of the first and only satisfactory theory of the efficiency of propellers.

Dr R. E. Froude took up his father's work, and has continued it till the present time. Practically, the whole of the scientific development of the subject since his father's death is due to him ; and though others have carried out experimental work in similar tanks, it has been largely done for the solution of definite practical problems, and to only a very small extent has it been done for systematic research.

Having outlined the work of research conducted by the Froudes, we can now consider the investigations and experiments which have been made on resistance in the light of the present theory.

1. **Surface Friction, or Frictional Resistance.**—Let us first consider the nature of surface friction.

The frictional resistance of a body moving through water is due to the friction of the water rubbing on the surface of the body. The friction is caused by the viscosity of the water and the roughness of the surface. In a perfect fluid there could be no frictional resistance, as also would be the case if the surface were perfectly smooth. The nature of the surface to a large extent governs the amount of the frictional resistance, and for a given kind of surface the frictional resistance depends upon the area of the surface and the relative speed of the body through the water. Frictional resistance is thus clearly distinguishable from wavemaking and eddymaking resistances, which depend upon the shape, size, and speed of the body through the water. A thin plane board moving through the water will experience a resistance which is almost entirely due to the friction of the water on its surface. The wavemaking and eddymaking resistances will be negligible in amount if the ends of the board are pointed. When a body is moving through the water the particles in immediate contact with the surface are set in motion by being partially dragged along with the surface by the friction between the water and the surface. This motion will also be partly conveyed to the adjacent layer of particles. The motion of the particles near the surface cannot be a purely forward one. There will most likely be also a rotary motion, and in the rougher kinds of surfaces minute eddies will exist at the surface. There will thus be a region of disturbed particles of water ; and if we imagine a line bounding this region, and separating the disturbed from undisturbed water, we have what is called the "zone of frictional disturbance." It is impossible to determine accurately the motion of the particles in the disturbed zone, but from practical experiments on ship models or on thin boards observations can easily be made to find the speed of the following wake. In every case of a body being towed through the water a definite forward current is observed astern of the body. To this current the name of "frictional wake" is given.

In the Chapter on Propellers it will be seen that the speed of this wake in a vessel may range from 5 per cent. to 15 per cent. of the speed of the ship, and the efficiency of the propeller is thereby increased.

If we knew exactly the mass of water acted upon per second by the friction of the surface, and the velocity at all points in this wake, we could estimate the frictional resistance of the body. When a thin board is towed through the water, the friction per unit area is greatest at the entrance, and this value decreases slowly as the distances from the forward end increase. This fact has been clearly demonstrated by Froude's experiments on surface friction of planes, but it may be briefly explained by referring to fig. 85, which roughly represents the zone of frictional disturbance around a thin board B A.

At the forward end, A, the relative speed of the surface and the contiguous particles will be V, the velocity of the board. As the distance aft increases, the particles have a definite forward velocity, so that the relative speed will be less than V. The breadth of the zone increases gradually with the distance aft, because the motion imparted to the particles at the forward end is gradu-

Fig. 85.

ally transmitted to a wider and wider zone as the plane passes it. The friction is governed by the relative motion of the particles to the surface. The friction per unit of area consequently decreases gradually as the distance aft increases.

The experiments conducted by Dr Froude senior to determine the law of variation of resistance are described later.

The late Dr Froude, in the report to the British Association for 1874, gave a method of determining the breadth of the zone of the frictional disturbance, which is interesting as showing the approximate mechanical construction of the frictional wake, but from which little practical result can be obtained. The frictional resistance must be equal to the momentum imparted to the particles of water in the frictional wake per unit of time when the speed is uniform.

Let F = force in pounds, or the frictional resistance.

W = weight of water operated on in lbs.

V = velocity of surface in feet per second relatively to the surrounding still water.

t = time during which F acts.

Then Ft = change of momentum in this time.

Therefore there must be left behind the body, in each second of time, new momentum as expressed above, in the shape of a following current.

In considering how this momentum is generated, take at any point an elemental layer parallel to the surface of unit depth and thickness dh. At any instant let the velocity of the water in this layer be v feet per second. We then see that the quantity of water put into motion per second will at that point be $(V - v)$ in length, dh in thickness, and of unit depth. Its length is $(V - v)$, since that is the length left behind by the surface. Its weight is therefore

$$= \rho(V - v)\, dh, \text{ where } \rho = \text{weight of water per cubic foot.}$$
$$\therefore \quad dw = \rho(V - v)dh.$$

Now if we assume that the current possesses a velocity V at the surface, and that this velocity decreases uniformly as the distance from the surface decreases, we have

$$v = \frac{V(H - h)}{H},$$

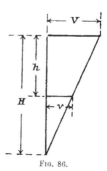

Fig. 86.

where H is the breadth of the zone, and h is the distance of the layer dh from the surface (fig. 86).

$$\text{Then} \quad dw = \rho\ (V - v)dh$$
$$= \rho \frac{Vh}{H}dh.$$

If M be the momentum,

$$dM = v\, dw = \frac{\rho}{g} \frac{Vh}{H} \frac{V(H - h)dh}{H}$$
$$= \frac{\rho}{g} \frac{V^2}{H^2}(H - h)h\, dh.$$
$$\therefore \quad M = \frac{\rho}{g} \int_0^H \frac{V^2(H - h)h}{H^2}dh.$$
$$\therefore \quad M = \frac{\rho V^2 H}{g6},$$

and this must be equal to Ft.

If t is unity,

$$F = \frac{\rho V^2 H}{g6} \qquad\qquad \rho = 64,$$

$$= \frac{V^2 H}{3} \qquad\qquad g = 32\cdot2,$$

or $\qquad H = \dfrac{3F}{V^2}.$

It is shown later that the resistance in lbs. per square foot on a plane 50 feet long is ·25 lb. at 5·92 knots or 10 feet per second on a varnished surface. Counting both sides of a plane 50 feet long and 1 foot wide, the total resistance is 25 lbs. Substituting in $H = \dfrac{3\,F}{V^2}$ we get $H = \dfrac{3 \times 25}{100} = \cdot75$ feet $= 9$ inches. In a plane 500 feet long moving at 20 knots, H is about 6 feet. This result does not appear to be probable, and it seems as if the assumptions are not correct.

Among the earlier experimenters on this subject may be mentioned Coulomb and Beaufoy. The former conducted experiments on bodies suspended so as to swing in water, and measured the resistance by the decrease in each amplitude of the swing. His results are of little practical importance, but he stated, as one of the deductions from the experiments, that the frictional resistance was independent of the pressure of the liquid, and therefore independent of the depth of the body in the water.

Colonel Beaufoy's experiments on resistance have already been described. He also conducted a series of pendulum experiments. From his towing experiments, however, it was possible to deduce the amount of frictional resistance offered by certain areas. His results were not of great practical importance. By far the greatest contribution to the science of frictional resistance has been made by the late Dr Froude. His experiments have become classical.

Full reports of these experiments will be found in the Report of the British Association for 1872 and 1874. The experiments were conducted in a tank about 280 feet long and 36 feet broad at the top. The water was 9 feet deep. The investigations were carried out on thin boards which were towed lengthwise through the water. They were ballasted by a lead strip fixed along one long edge so that the plane of the board was always vertical in the water. When the boards were towed in this manner the resistance was almost entirely due to the surface friction of the water on the sides of the board. The towing and the dynamometer apparatus were designed by Dr Froude ; and as the main principles in its design have been carried out in the construction of similar apparatus for experimental tanks that have since been built, it may be of interest to describe its main features here. The towing truck carrying the apparatus ran on a light suspension railway which was about 20 inches above the water. It was moved by a wire rope which was coiled round a spiral groove on a drum. This drum could be driven so as to tow the truck at any desired steady speed between 100 and 1000 feet per minute. Fig. 87 shows the arrangement in detail.

The attachment of the board B to the apparatus was designed so as to have as little friction as possible in the connections. The horizontal driving force is wholly delivered by a helical spring H, one end of which is fixed to the frame of the truck, and the other end is fixed to the light woodwork frame C C supporting

the board.   The extensions of the spring are measured by the movements of
an index arm K K, which are automatically recorded by a pen S which follows
the motion of the end of the index arm and traces a line on the sheet of paper
wound round the cylinder U.   The cylinder is geared to one of the truck wheel
axles so that the circumferential travel of the paper represents the forward
motion.   Another pen V, actuated by clockwork, marks intervals of time on
the paper.   For one experiment or one run the lines on the paper give the
necessary records, and we are able to get the resistance of the plane at a
particular speed.

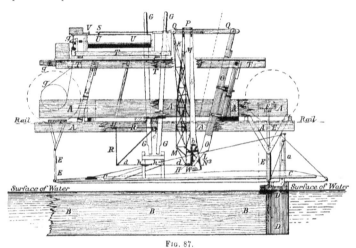

FIG. 87.

A A	Bed of carriage.
E E	Parallel motion supporting beam C C.
F	Counterbalance to beam C C, etc.
G G	Lever arrangement for steadying the apparatus (taking the strain off the spring) while uniform speed is being obtained.
W	Counterbalance to index arm.
L	Fulcrum of index arm carried by bar b b.
M M	Lever communicating extension of spring to index arm.
N	Connecting link, medium of communication of extension of spring to index arm.
O O	Towing beam, holding fore end of spring.
P	Brass cap, about which b b and M M hinge.
Q Q	Bar uniting head of towing beam and cap P to frame carrying cylinder.
R R	Bell crank for extending spring by known weights hung on at e, thereby testing scale.
d d	Connection of bell crank with spring.
e	Weight giving initial extension to spring, forming zero of scale.
T T	Frame carrying cylinder, etc., capable of vertical adjustment.
g g	Gear for transferring motion of carriage to cylinder U U.

The truck can be run at any desired speed between the limits of 100 and
1000 feet per minute, so that a curve of resistance in terms of speed for the
plane or body which is towed can be obtained.
    The planes upon which Dr Froude first experimented were about $\frac{5}{16}$

inch thick. The length varied from 1 to 50 feet, but they were all 19 inches deep. When fitted to the towing apparatus the upper edge was 1½ inch

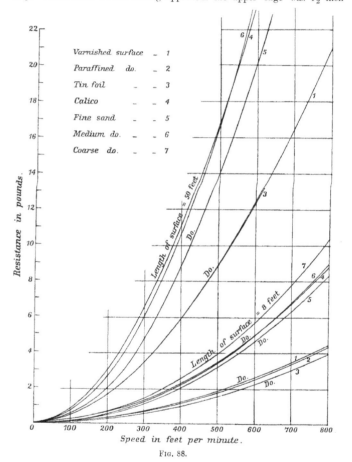

Varnished surface _ 1
Paraffined do. _ 2
Tin foil _ _ 3
Calico _ _ 4
Fine sand _ _ 5
Medium do. _ _ 6
Coarse do. _ _ 7

Speed in feet per minute.

FIG. 88.

below the surface of the water. The framework supporting the board was of special design. Part of it, the forward support D, formed a cutwater to the board, and was like a sheath, so that it could be easily detached and secured to the frame by pins or bolts.

The investigation on surface friction was separated into the following divisions :—

(1) To determine the law of variation of resistance with the velocity.

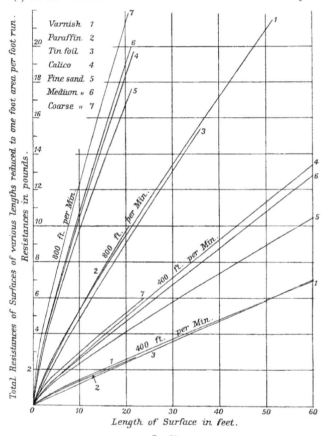

Length of Surface in feet.

FIG. 89.

(2) To determine the differences in resistance due to the quality of the surface.

(3) To determine the variation of resistance per unit of surface at different points of the length of the surface.

The results of the experiments were plotted in curves, which are shown in figs. 88 and 89. In fig. 88 the base line measures speed and the ordinates measure resistance. The curves of this diagram therefore establish the (1) law of variation of resistance with the velocity.

In fig. 89 the base line measures length of plane and the ordinates measure resistance. These curves show that the resistance per unit of surface varies at different points of the length of the surface. Had the resistance per unit of surface been uniform throughout the length, the curves in this diagram would have been straight lines. The fact that they are concave towards the base shows that the resistance per unit surface becomes less as the length from the forward end increases.

Corrections were made in the results for the air resistance of the supporting frame, and for the resistance of the cutwater support and the shape of the tail edge. The latter correction was determined by experimenting on very short planes with ends varying from square to sharp.

Experiments were also conducted on planes with different qualities of surface to determine (2), but later and more complete investigations were made, the results of which were published in the 1874 Report of the British Association

The surfaces tried were—

(1) Varnish.
(2) Paraffin.
(3) Tinfoil.
(4) Calico.
(5) Fine sand.
(6) Medium sand.
(7) Coarse sand.

The results are shown in figs. 88 and 89, but are summarised in the following table, which was included in the report.

In the headings of the columns—

m is the power of the speed to which the resistance is proportional.

f_m is the mean resistance in lbs. per square foot of surface on the length of plane specified in the heading.

f_u is the resistance per square foot on the last foot of the length which is specified in the heading.

The results are all given for a speed of 600 feet per minute = 10 feet per second = 5·92 knots.

It will be seen that the power of the speed is two, or nearly two, in all cases, and that there is a tendency for the power to decrease as the length of plane increases.

It will be found from the curves that the power of the speed, although given in the tables for a particular speed of 600 feet per minute, is practically constant throughout the range of speed in the diagram.

The formula for the total frictional resistance may be expressed—

$$R_f = fSV^m,$$

where R_f is the total frictional resistance,
  S is the submerged area of the surface,
  V is the speed of the surface relatively to still water,
  m is the power of the speed according to which the resistance varies,
  f is a coefficient depending upon the nature or roughness of the surface.

m and f are values which can be obtained from the following table.

Froude's Experiments on Surface Friction.

m —Power of speed to which resistance is approximately proportional.
f_m—Resistance in lbs./ft.^{2} of surface, taken as a mean over the length specified in heading.
f_n—Resistance in lbs./ft.^{2} on unit at a distance from the cutwater specified in heading.

		Length of surface, or distance from cutwater, in feet.										
		2 feet.			8 feet.			20 feet.			50 feet.		
		$m.$	$f_m.$	$f_n.$	$m.$	$f_m.$	$f_n.$	$m.$	$f_m.$	$f_n.$	$m.$	$f_m.$	$f_n.$
Varnish . .		2·00	·41	·390	1·85	·325	·264	1·85	·278	·240	1·83	·250	·226
Paraffin . .		1·95	·38	·370	1·94	·311	·260	1·93	·271	·237	...	...	...
Tinfoil . .		2·16	·30	·295	1·99	·278	·263	1·90	·262	·244	1·83	·246	·232
Calico . .		1·93	·87	·725	1·92	·626	·504	1·89	·531	·447	1·87	·474	·423
Fine Sand .		2·00	·81	·690	2·00	·583	·450	2·00	·480	·384	2·06	·405	·337
Medium Sand.		2·00	·90	·730	2·00	·625	·488	2·00	·534	·465	2·00	·488	·456
Coarse Sand .		2·00	1·10	·880	2·00	·714	·520	2·00	·588	·490	...	...	...

All run at constant speed of 10 ft./sec.
= 600 ft./min.
= 5·92 knots.

It is a matter of great importance to determine the values of m and f that should be taken for a vessel with a painted hull, as nearly all steamers have a painted surface in the water. The condition of the skin of a vessel varies very much. When the skin is in a foul condition there is a marked decrease in the speed from what it would be were the skin clean.

The following are the results of trials of the same vessels, made, in each case, with the same kind and quality of coal, and under the same conditions of wind and sea, the same number of boilers being used in each case.

For comparison, a measure of the efficiency is taken in the form of cube of speed divided by the coal consumed per day.

Name of Ship.	Condition of bottom.	Knots.	Revolutions per minute.	Revolutions per knot.	Nautical miles per day.	Tons of coal per day.	Efficiency value = $\frac{V^3}{coal}$	Rates of efficiencies.	Displacement of ship in tons.	Months out of dock.
U.S.S. "Charleston".	Foul	6·8	50·9	449	163	35·3	8·9	1	3730	5
,, ,, .	Clean	8·7	49·4	341	208	33·1	20·0	2·25		1
U.S.S. "Baltimore"	Foul	10·0	55·2	331	239	45·0	22·2	1	4400	4
,, ,, .	Clean	11·3	60·5	321	271	46·7	30·8	1·4		$\frac{1}{2}$
U.S.S. "San Francisco"	Foul	9·1	61·8	405	219	40·3	18·7	1	4088	$7\frac{1}{2}$
,, ,,	Clean	9·6	58·8	367	235	34·8	25·4	1·36		1

It should be pointed out that foulness has an indirect effect upon the speed as well as a direct one. Owing to the increased resistance, it is impossible, with a given effective pressure, to obtain the same number of revolutions with a foul bottom as when the bottom is clean and the resistance less. Thus, unless the mean effective pressure can be increased when fouling ensues, the revolutions and I.H.P. will fall off when the ship becomes foul, and there will be a double loss of speed.

In making an estimate for the necessary power to overcome frictional resistance, it is assumed that the vessel's bottom is clean and newly painted. We can thus assign values to m and f that can be used in nearly all estimates of this kind. For large vessels the value of m is taken as 1·83 and of f_m ·25 lb., which when multiplied by $\dfrac{1}{(5·92)^{1·83}}$ gives ·009 $= f$. The formula, therefore, for the frictional resistance of a vessel is

$$R_f = ·009 \; SV^{1·83},$$

where R_f is the frictional resistance in lbs.,
  S is the expanded area of the wetted skin (sq. ft.),
  V is the speed of the vessel in knots.

The horse-power necessary to overcome the frictional resistance will be

$$= \frac{R_f \times V \times 101·33}{33000} \qquad \text{\small (101·33 being 6080, the number of feet in a nautical mile, divided by 60, the minutes in an hour.)}$$

$$= \frac{·009 \times 101·33}{33000} \times S \times V^{2·83}$$

$$= ·00002763 \times S \times V^{2·83}.$$

The most accurate method of obtaining S is to expand the girths of the sections and the waterlines and find the developed area, but a close enough approximation to S can be made by using the following formula : --

$$S = 1·7 \; LD + \frac{V}{D} \; \Big(\text{published by Mr A. Denny}\Big)$$

where   L = length of vessel in feet,
    D = draught in feet,
    V = volume of displacement in cubic feet.

In this formula L D roughly represents the area of one side and $\dfrac{V}{D}$ is the mean waterline area.

The following are values of f that may be taken for the frictional resistance of a vessel moving at 5·92 knots:--

Length of vessel	50	100	150	200	250	300	350	400	450	500
f = lbs. per sq. ft. $_{m}$	·256	·242	·235	·232	·229	·228	·227	·226	·225	·225
$f = f_m \times \left(\dfrac{1}{5·92}\right)^{1·83}$		·00988	·00934	·00907	·00896	·00884	·00880	·00876	·00872	·00869	·00869

A series of values of $\left(\dfrac{V}{5·92}\right)^{1·83}$ is given in the following table :--

V.	$\left(\dfrac{V}{5\cdot92}\right)^{1\cdot83}$	V.	$\left(\dfrac{V}{5\cdot92}\right)^{1\cdot83}$
1	·0386	21	10·146
2	·1373	22	11·048
3	·2883	23	11·985
4	·4882	24	12·955
5	·7341	25	13·961
6	1·025	26	14·999
7	1·359	27	16·071
8	1·735	28	17·177
9	2·152	29	18·317
10	2·610	30	19·489
11	3·107	31	20·694
12	3·644	32	21·932
13	4·219	33	23·202
14	4·831	34	24·505
15	5·482	35	25·841
16	6·169	36	27·207
17	6·893	37	28·606
18	7·652	38	30·037
19	8·448	39	31·499
20	9·280	40	32·993

These values are shown in a curve in fig. 90, so that any intermediate values can be read.

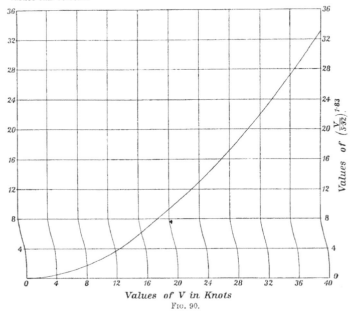

Values of V in Knots

Fig. 90.

Take as an example a vessel of 2200 tons displacement and dimensions 330 ft. length, 42 ft. breadth, 12 ft. draught.

$$S = 1\cdot7LD + \frac{V}{D} = 13150 \text{ square feet.}$$

The frictional resistance at 22 knots is

$$R_f = \cdot227 \times 11\cdot048 \times 13150 = 33000 \text{ lbs. about.}$$

(2) **Eddymaking resistance.** — Eddymaking resistance is due to abruptness of change of form, and is comparatively small in modern ships. It is so small that in all questions affecting resistance it is left out of account. A square-ended stern-post causes eddymaking resistance, but it is seldom of an appreciable amount, and may be easily obviated. It will be shown later that it can be included in the wavemaking resistance. See p. 168.

CHAPTER IX.

WAVES.

Wave of Translation.—Before entering on the subject of wavemaking resistance proper we shall look briefly at the commonly accepted theories of wave motion.

Lord Kelvin defines a wave as "the progression through matter of a state of motion," or as "the progression of a displacement." Taking the case of water waves, the motion which travels and forms the wave is an elevation called the crest and a depression called the hollow. Thus the water itself does not travel, although the *wave form* does. The simplest way of seeing this is to take a piece of rope 6 to 10 yards in length, fix one end of it, and

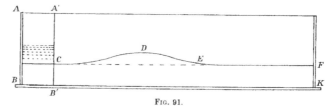

FIG. 91.

then to shake the other end. The *wave form* will be seen to travel along the rope, but the rope itself only swings to and fro.

Let us take, in the first place, a *solitary wave*, or *wave of translation*. This wave represents the result of a local disturbance, as opposed to those which we will consider later, which occur naturally in definite series, and are produced by some widely-spread disturbance.

Suppose we have a canal such as B K (fig. 91), and at one end of canal, say A B, we can bank up water as shown at A B B' A'. Now if we suddenly remove A' B' the heaped-up water will travel along the free level surface as a heap of water, and will continue to so travel until, through viscous forces and air resistance, the energy is entirely dissipated. This wave is a wave of translation, and there is a natural speed = $\sqrt{y(d+h)}$ for this wave, where d is the depth of the canal and h the height of the wave.

The form of the wave surface, for small waves, is sensibly a curve of versed sines, the horizontal ordinates of which vary as the arc of a circle of radius d, and the vertical ordinates are the versed sines of a circle of radius $\dfrac{h}{2}$.

Thus $x = d\theta$,

$$y = \tfrac{1}{2}h \text{ versin } \theta = \frac{h}{2}(1 - \cos \theta).$$

The wave-length $l = 2\pi d$ when h is small. If h is very small compared with d, as in the case of a long wave, $v = \sqrt{gd}$—nearly, the same as that required by a body falling freely from a height equal to half the depth of the canal. Hence the *natural* speed of a *long* wave in a canal d feet deep is $\sqrt{gd}$ feet per second, *i.e.* in a canal 8 feet deep it would be 16 feet per second, or about 11 miles per hour. Scott Russell, in a series of experiments carried out on the Forth and Clyde Canal, observed that if the speed of the boat was less than this *natural* velocity a train of waves

Bottom of Canal.

FIG. 92.

was left behind the boat, and the length of these waves was such that their velocity of propagation was equal to the velocity of the boat, the boat taking up a position just on the rear slope of the leading wave (fig. 92).

The length of this stern procession of waves, if the fluid is perfect, depends on the time the boat has been running. The water is, however, of a viscous nature and stops the procession of stern waves at a certain distance from the boat. In a canal this effect is very noticeable, owing to the water having to flow up and down the banks and across the bottom.

The rear of the procession of waves travels at *half* the speed of the boat when the water is at least one wave-length in depth, or, without any very serious error, a depth of at least three-quarters wave-length. Now the work

Bottom of Canal.

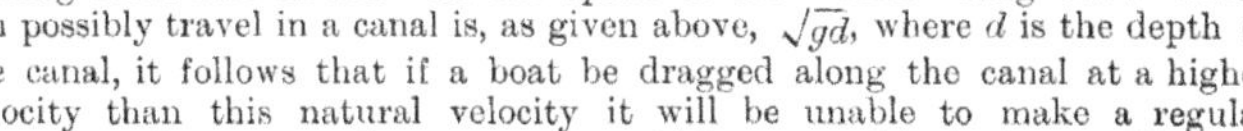

FIG. 93.

done in dragging along this boat is equal to the energy required to generate the procession of waves astern. The work so done per minute in foot lbs. divided by the distance travelled per minute by the boat gives the wave-making resistance in lbs. As the speed of the fastest "long wave" which can possibly travel in a canal is, as given above, $\sqrt{gd}$, where d is the depth of the canal, it follows that if a boat be dragged along the canal at a higher velocity than this natural velocity it will be unable to make a regular procession of waves at all, as no wave could keep up with the boat. The boat can only make a *hump* travelling along with it, as shown in fig. 93.

Consequently since there is no continual production of waves above this natural velocity, no energy will be expended, *i.e.* there is no wavemaking resistance. The discovery of this critical speed resulted in the introduction of canal boats known as "fly boats," which were made of sheet iron and drawn by a pair of horses. "The boat starts at a low velocity behind the wave, and at a given signal it is pulled up with a sudden jerk on the top of the wave, where it moves with diminished resistance at the rate of from 7 to 9 miles per hour."

If the speed of the boat be equal to or less than that of the natural velocity of the wave system, the procession of waves formed astern can only keep up with the boat by a continuous generation of waves formed at a rate sufficient to make up for the natural lagging behind of the system at the stern. The rate at which this lagging behind takes place is one-half the speed of the boat, because the system will, as already stated, naturally travel at one-half the speed of the boat. Hence the amount of energy consumed in overcoming the wavemaking resistance through the distance between the bow of the boat and the rear of the procession of waves is one-half the total amount of energy in the system.

It is therefore necessary to be able to determine the amount of energy in a wave system in order to determine the wavemaking resistance.

The same considerations apply to a ship in the open ocean, but with some modifications due to the circumstances.

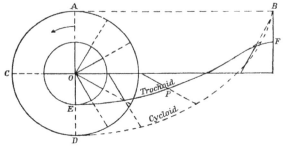

FIG. 94.

Trochoidal Wave.—The exact form of the waves of the ocean is not regular or easily determined, but it can be shown that a trochoidal wave, which is approximately of the character of a sea wave, is hydrodynamically possible, and is capable of forming a regular series. If this can be proved, it makes calculations as to distribution of pressure in a wave quite definite and simple, and makes possible the solution of some problems.

A trochoid is the curve traced out by a point on a radius of a circle, this circle being rolled on the underside of a given line (fig. 94). The limits of the curve are a cycloid and a straight line.

To establish the fact that such a trochoidal form of wave is one that is possible, we must prove that these conditions of motion are consistent with all the necessary hydrodynamic conditions of fluid motion.

The formation of a trochoidal wave has been outlined in Vol. I., Chapter XXIV., fig. 195, and the basis of the Trochoidal Wave Theory has been given at p. 319. The proof of the Theory is given here.

In order to construct a trochoidal wave the following conditions must be assumed :—

(i) A series of horizontal planes or layers of smooth water assume a trochoidal form in wave water.

(ii) Particles of water in the wave all move in vertical planes in circular orbits with the same uniform angular velocity.

(iii) Particles in an originally horizontal plane take up the orbital motion in uniform succession.

(iv) The radii of the orbits of the particles originally in the same horizontal plane are equal.

(v) The radii of the orbits of particles decrease as the depth of the original horizontal plane increases.

(vi) Surfaces of equal pressure in still water, *i.e.* horizontal planes, will be surfaces of equal pressure in the wave, *i.e.* trochoidal surfaces.

(vii) Trochoidal surfaces and subsurfaces are of the same length and have their crests in one vertical plane which is perpendicular to the vertical plane of the orbital motion. The hollows are necessarily in a parallel vertical plane.

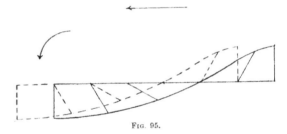

FIG. 95.

Let us first deal with a single layer which in still water is horizontal. We have to show that if the particles take up the motion in uniform succession in vertical circles with the same uniform angular velocity, the pressure on all the particles will be the same. If we consider all the particles at any time after they have all taken up the orbital motion, it will be seen that they will at any instant lie in a trochoid. This can be seen from fig. 95.

If we consider the position of the particles when they have rotated through a further small angle anticlockwise, we see that the crest of the trochoid will have moved to the left, and if a continuous uniform circular orbital anti-clockwise motion be given to the particles the crest will move uniformly from right to left. It will pass through a length from crest to crest in one complete revolution of the particles. Suppose the number of revolutions per minute to be n, then if the trochoid be generated by the revolution of a circle 2R in diameter the distance the crest will move through will be $2\pi Rn$ per minute. The movement of the crest or any other point of the wave surface is a wave motion. No particle moves through more than $2\pi r$ per revolution, where r is the radius of the small orbit of the particle, but the form of the trochoid moves through $2\pi R$ in the same time. If we call V the velocity of the wave it will be equal to $2\pi Rn$. If, now, we impose on every particle a horizontal velocity V from left to right, the form of the wave will be reduced to a zero velocity, and the particles of water will flow in the trochoidal stream of the form of the trochoidal wave. The forces on the particles will not be different to what they were before the uniform horizontal velocity V was imposed on them.

We will first show that *in a trochoidal stream the pressure is uniform throughout for a definite relation between the radius R and the angular velocity of the orbit.*

For such a stream Bernoulli's equation* will hold, viz.:—

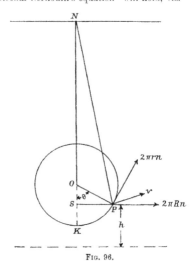

FIG. 96.

* *Proof of Bernoulli's Theorem.*—Let A B, fig. 97, be an elementary stream tube in a steadily flowing liquid mass. In a short interval of time, t, let A B come to $A_1 B_1$. The work done by gravity due to the fall of A B to $A_1 B_1$ is the same as that done in transferring A A_1 to B B_1. Let the cross section area of tube at A be a_1, the velocity v_1, the unital pressure p_1 and the height above datum line h_1, and let a_2, v_2, p_2 and h_2 be the corresponding quantities for the cross section at B. Since the fluid is incompressible, the quantity $Qt = a_1 v_1 t =$ volume A A_1 flowing in at A must equal the volume flowing out at B, *i.e.* volume B $B_1 = a_2 v_2 t$, or we have $Q = a_1 v_1 = a_2 v_2$. The work done by gravity, therefore, in the fall from A A_1 to B $B_1 = wQt[h_1 - h_2]$ ($w =$ weight per unit volume). The work done by the pressure over the ends during the motion of the stream line from A B to $A_1 B_1$ is $p_1 a_1 v_1 t - p_2 a_2 v_2 t$

$$= Qt(p_1 - p_2).$$

If the motion of the stream line A B be not widely different from that of the surrounding stream lines, then the frictional and viscous resistances will be negligible. The work done, therefore, by gravity and pressure is spent in accelerating the motion of A B, and therefore $wQt(h_1 - h_2) - Qt(p_1 - p_2) =$ difference of kinetic energies of B B_1 and A A_1

$$= Qtw\left(\frac{v_2^2}{2g} - \frac{v_1^2}{2g}\right).$$

$$\therefore \quad \frac{v_1^2}{2g} + \frac{p_1}{w} + h_1 = \frac{v_2^2}{2g} + \frac{p_2}{w} + h_2 = \text{constant.}$$

$\dfrac{V^2}{2g} + \dfrac{p}{w} + h = \text{const.}$ where V is velocity,[*]

               p is pressure,

               h is the vertical distance from a datum straight line.

If the pressure is uniform throughout, $\dfrac{p}{w}$ will be constant and

$$\dfrac{V^2}{2g} + h = \text{constant.}$$

A B, fig. 94, is the straight line under which the circle A C D is rolled. The full line represents the form of a trochoid, the dotted line that of a cycloid, which would represent a wave just on the point of breaking. A B is half a wave-length.

The particle P has a velocity v which is the resultant of the orbital velocity $2\pi r n$ and the impressed velocity $2\pi R n$. The triangle P O N, fig. 96,

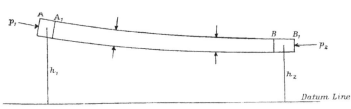

FIG. 97.

where O N and O P are perpendicular to the directions of these velocities, will represent them. P N will therefore represent the velocity v and be perpendicular to it. It can be shown that if $O N = R$, P N is perpendicular to the trochoid.[†] Hence P N will represent the velocity v on the same scale that

---

    [*] Since the motion is supposed to be steady, the friction between the particles of the liquid and the viscosity are small enough to be neglected, and the liquid being incompressible, we can proceed to apply Bernoulli's Theorem to the stream-line systems.

    [†] P N is normal to the surface of the wave, or, what is the same thing, the tangent to the trochoid at P is at right angles to P N in fig. 98. Take the coordinates of P with reference to axes through H the point of contact of the rolling circle, at which point $\theta = 0$,

        then $\tan a = -\dfrac{dy}{dx}.$

Where a is the angle the tangent to the trochoid at P makes with the horizontal,

$$x = HN + KP$$
$$= R\theta + r\sin\theta$$

   and $y = ON - OK$
$$= R + r\cos\theta.$$

   $\therefore$ $\dfrac{dy}{d\theta} = -r\sin\theta$

   and $\dfrac{dx}{d\theta} = R + r\cos\theta.$

O P and O N represent $2\pi rn$ and $2\pi \mathrm{R}n$ respectively. Call P N, ρ and $2\pi n = \omega$. Then the orbital velocity of P $= r\omega$, the impressed velocity is $\mathrm{R}\omega$ and v, the resultant of the two is $\rho\omega$.

The values of ρ corresponding to v_1 and v_2, the velocities at hollow and crest, will be $(\mathrm{R} + r)$ and $(\mathrm{R} - r)$ respectively. Hence

$$v_1{}^2 = (\mathrm{R} + r)^2\omega^2.$$

From Bernoulli's equation

$$\frac{v^2}{2g} + \frac{p}{w} + h = \text{constant}.$$

$$\therefore \quad \frac{v_1{}^2}{2g} + \frac{p_1}{w} + h_1 = \frac{v^2}{2g} + \frac{p}{w} + h.$$

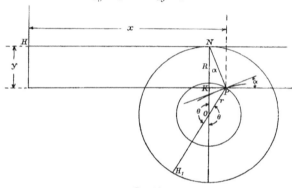

Fig. 98.

If p is constant throughout the stream tube then, see fig. 96,

$$v_1{}^2 - v^2 = 2g\mathrm{SK} = 2gr(1 - \cos\theta)$$

hence $\quad (\mathrm{R} + r)^2\omega^2 - \rho^2\omega^2 = 2gr(1 - \cos\theta)$ . . . (a)

From the triangle P O N

$$\rho^2 = \mathrm{R}^2 + r^2 + 2\mathrm{R}r\cos\theta.$$

Substituting in (a) we get $2\mathrm{R}r\omega^2(1 - \cos\theta) = 2gr(1 - \cos\theta)$ which will be true if $\mathrm{R} = \dfrac{g}{\omega^2}$.

$$\therefore \quad \frac{dy}{dx} = \frac{-r\sin\theta}{\mathrm{R} + r\cos\theta}$$

$$= -\frac{\mathrm{KP}}{\mathrm{KN}}$$

But $\quad \dfrac{dy}{dx} = -\tan a.$

$\therefore$ the angle $\mathrm{KNP} = a$

and NP is normal to the trochoid.

Hence we have established a relation between the speed of orbital motion and the radius of the rolling circle of the trochoid which will satisfy the condition of $\frac{p}{w}$ being constant. That is to say, that a trochoidal stream of rolling radius $\frac{g}{\omega^2}$ which has been generated by the orbital motion and the reversed velocity assumed will have uniform pressure throughout. It may therefore be a free surface or a subsurface of uniform pressure.

Period of Wave.—The period T of the wave from hollow to crest $= \frac{\pi}{\omega}$.

But $\quad$ R $= \frac{g}{\omega^2}$.

Hence $\quad$ T $= \pi \sqrt{\frac{R}{g}}$.

The period T of a conical pendulum for a half revolution is $\pi \sqrt{\frac{l}{g}}$ where l is the length of the cord.

Therefore *the period of the wave is the same as that of a simple conical pendulum whose length of cord is equal to the radius of the rolling circle of the wave.*

Length of Wave.—If λ is the length, from crest to crest, $\lambda = 2\pi R$

$$= \frac{2\pi g}{\omega^2}.$$

Having shown that a trochoidal stream is one of uniform pressure if $R = \frac{g}{\omega^2}$ we may now consider what relations must exist between successive trochoidal streams generated from successive horizontal layers. It is seen that any value of r less than R is consistent with uniformity of pressure. We can therefore draw another trochoid P_1 (fig. 99) at a distance $N N_1 = O O_1$ below the trochoid P, but with a value of r, $O_1 P_1$ not equal to O P. If the surfaces are of uniform pressure they may be considered as boundaries of a pipe $P P_1$ through which may run all the water originally between the horizontal layers which ultimately became the trochoids P and P_1. If there are no empty spaces in this pipe the pressure in the lower trochoid will support the water in the pipe. If there were empty spaces it would be necessary to have a material boundary which would not change form under the varying pressure. It is evident that if the trochoidal boundaries are not to be distorted in form, so that a confused mass without wave form would result, the pipe must run full.

If, as before, v be the velocity, fig. 99, $v = \rho \omega$, v P Q measures the flow of water in the trochoidal pipe. For continuity v P Q must be constant, *i.e.* $\rho \omega$P Q and therefore ρ P Q must be constant.

$$\rho + PQ = \rho_1 + NN_1 \cos \phi.$$

Let $\quad \rho_1 - \rho = d\rho \quad$ and $\quad NN_1 = dY$.

Then $\quad PQ = d\rho + dY \cos \phi$

$\quad\quad \rho PQ = \rho d\rho + \rho dY \cos \phi,$

but $\quad\quad \rho^2 = R^2 + r^2 + 2Rr \cos \theta.$

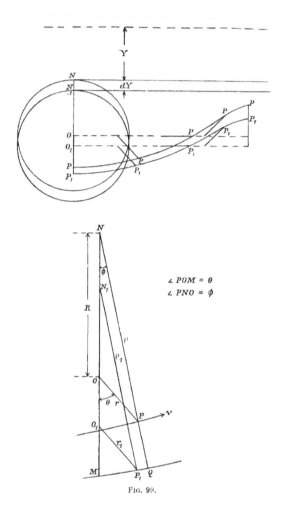

FIG. 99.

Differentiating for the same value of θ, we have $\rho d\rho = rdr + R \cos \theta dr$.

By inspection we have $\rho \cos \phi = R + r \cos \theta$.

Substituting we have $\rho PQ = rdr + RdY + (Rdr + rdY) \cos \theta$.

In order that ρPQ shall be the same for all values of θ,

$$Rdr + rdY = 0$$

$$i.e. \quad \frac{dr}{r} = -\frac{dY}{R}.$$

Integrating we have

$$\log r = -\frac{Y}{R} + \text{const.}$$

If $Y = 0$ when $r = r_0$ the radius of the tracing circle of the surface trochoid, then the const. $= \log r_0$ and

$$\log r - \log r_0 = -\frac{Y}{R}, \quad \text{and}$$

$$r = r_0 \epsilon^{-\frac{Y}{R}}.$$

This relation of r in terms of the depth of the corresponding line of orbit centres below the surface line of centres enables us to determine *a trochoidal surface which in stream-line motion has a uniform pressure and is capable of forming the boundary of a stream of continuous flow.*

To determine the position of this trochoid it is only necessary to notice that the same amount of water must lie between the trochoidal surfaces as lay between the corresponding horizontal layers.

The time during which the particles have moved through $d\theta$ of their orbital motion will be $\dfrac{d\theta}{\omega}$ and the volume swept through will be $\dfrac{vd\theta}{\omega}PQ = \rho d\theta PQ$ per unit of length of wave, measured along its crest.

Summing this up between $\theta = 0$ and $\theta = 2\pi$ we get volume between trochoids $= \displaystyle\int_0^{2\pi} \rho PQ d\theta$.

But $\rho . PQ = rdr + RdY + (Rdr + rdY) \cos \theta$.

Since $Rdr + rdY = 0$, $\rho . PQ = rdr + RdY$.

$$\begin{aligned}
\text{Vol.} &= \int_0^{2\pi} (rdr + RdY)d\theta \\
&= \int_0^{2\pi} \left(-\frac{r^2}{R}dY + RdY \right)d\theta \\
&= 2\pi \left(\frac{R^2 - r^2}{R} \right)dY.
\end{aligned}$$

If dY_0 be the distance between the layers in still water, $2\pi RdY_0 = $ total volume.

Hence

$$2\pi RdY_0 = 2\pi \frac{R^2 - r^2}{R}dY,$$

$$dY_0 = \left(1 - \frac{r^2}{R^2} \right)dY,$$

or

$$dY = \frac{R^2}{R^2 - r^2}dY_0.$$

This expression gives *the relation of the distance between consecutive horizontal layers to that between the centres of the trochoids, which in this position will contain between them the same amount of water as was between the horizontal layers.*

Hence from uniformly spaced waterlines we can get the corresponding spaces between the rolling lines of the trochoids.

It should be noticed that the surface trochoid must be placed at such a position that it includes the same amount of water as in still water. To do this *the rolling centre must be raised* $\dfrac{r^2}{2R}$ *above the still waterline.*

With E (fig. 100) as origin, $x = (HN + KP) = R\theta + r \sin \theta$,
$$y = SK = O_1S - O_1K = r(1 - \cos \theta).$$

Area of trochoid $EFX = \displaystyle\int_0^{\pi R} y.dx$,
$$dx = (R + r \cos \theta).d\theta.$$

Substituting for y we get $ydx = r(1 - \cos \theta)(R + r \cos \theta).d\theta$.

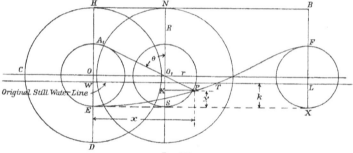

FIG. 100.

If we integrate the right-hand side of this for all values of θ from 0 to π we shall get the area E F X,
$$\int_0^\pi r(1 - \cos \theta)(R + r \cos \theta)d\theta = EFX$$
$$\pi r(R - \frac{r}{2}) = EFX.$$

What we have to find is the position of the waterline W L which shall be such that the areas W T E and F T L are equal. This W L will occupy to the trochoid E F the position which the original horizontal still waterlevel will occupy to the trochoidal wave surface. If k be the distance W E then $k \times \pi R = E F X$.

$$\therefore \qquad k\pi R = \pi r(R - \frac{r}{2})$$
$$k = r - \frac{r^2}{2R}$$

but $k = OE - OW = r - OW$.

$$\therefore \qquad OW = \frac{r^2}{2R}.$$

That is, the rolling centre must be raised $\dfrac{r^2}{2R}$ above the still waterline.

We can now construct a series of trochoidal surfaces in which the pressure in each trochoid is uniform thoughout, and between which there are no void spaces.

Pressures in Trochoidal Surfaces.—To determine the pressure in each trochoid, let us consider the orbital condition between two consecutive trochoids.

In fig. 101 any element P Q of unit section between consecutive trochoidal surfaces has a centrifugal force acting on it $\frac{mv^2}{r}$.PQ (m being the unit of mass), and the force of gravity mg.PQ. The resultant f.PQ of these forces acts along P N.

Hence $\qquad r : \mathrm{R} : \rho : : \dfrac{mv^2}{r} : mg : f$

$\qquad \therefore \quad f = \dfrac{mg\rho}{\mathrm{R}}, \text{ or } f.\mathrm{PQ} = \dfrac{mg\rho}{\mathrm{R}}\mathrm{PQ}.$

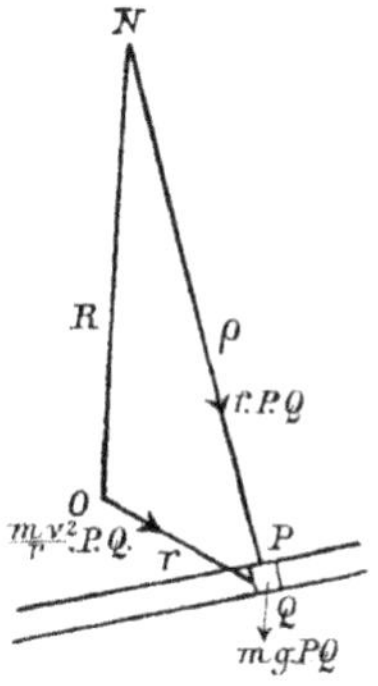

FIG. 101.

This force causes a difference of pressure in the two consecutive layers which may be called dp. Hence $dp = \dfrac{mg\rho}{\mathrm{R}}.\mathrm{PQ}$. But $\rho\mathrm{PQ}$ is constant throughout the stream; therefore dp is constant. *Hence if we have a surface trochoid of uniform pressure, the next surface below will have a pressure increased throughout by a constant amount, and therefore will also be uniform.* This being so, the next and all others will be uniform. Hence, in the assumed construction of a trochoid, all the surfaces have uniform pressure. To find the pressure we have

$$dp = \frac{mg}{\mathrm{R}}.\rho.\mathrm{PQ}$$
$$= \frac{mg}{\mathrm{R}}\left(\frac{\mathrm{R}^2 - r^2}{\mathrm{R}}\right)d\mathrm{Y}$$
$$= mg.d\mathrm{Y}_0.$$

Hence the increment of pressure in passing from one trochoidal surface to another is the same as the difference between the corresponding horizontal layers. Since the pressure at the free surface is the same in both cases it is evident that—

The pressure at any point in a trochoidal wave is the same as that on the particle in its corresponding position in still water.

Construction of Wave.—Hence, summarising, we are able for a wave of known height and length to determine the exact position of every particle in the wave, so that there are no void spaces ; and the pressure at every point.

(1) Knowing the value of r_0, the half height of the wave, we can find the value of r for any trochoid whose rolling line is Y below the rolling line of the surface trochoid, from the formula—

$$r = r_0 \epsilon^{-\frac{Y}{R}}.$$

(2) The rolling line will be $\dfrac{r^2}{2R}$ above the corresponding still-water horizontal line.

(3) The pressure in any trochoid will be that of the still-water horizontal line from which it has been evolved.

This particular mechanical arrangement of wave may not have the exact form and distribution of a sea wave, but it is one which cannot differ very much from it, and is one which is hydrodynamically possible and stable, and we may determine the forces which act upon a ship in a seaway with a fair degree of approximation.

Any deviation from this assumed form will cause a change of forces, which will be small and comparatively the same between different ships. This is the assumption on which our strength and rolling calculations are based.

The Energy of the Wave.—When the particles in the wave are at rest those in any layer are $\dfrac{r^2}{2R}$ below their mean position when in orbital motion. Hence there must be an expenditure of energy to raise the particles this amount. Further, there is the accumulated energy of orbital motion.

In any one particle of mass m and velocity v the total energy will therefore be

$$mg\frac{r^2}{2R} + m\frac{v^2}{2}.$$

But $v = \omega r$

$$= r\sqrt{\frac{g}{R}}.$$

$$\therefore \quad \text{Energy} = \frac{mgr^2}{2R} + \frac{mgr^2}{2R} = \frac{mgr^2}{R}.$$

Hence the total energy in a trochoidal layer equals the weight of the layer multiplied by $\dfrac{r^2}{R}$.

It will be seen that the energy due to raising the particles is the same as that of the accumulated energy. In other words, the total energy is one-half accumulated and one-half due to position, sometimes called "potential energy."

We have now to sum up the total energy of all the particles to obtain the energy of the wave.

Earlier in this chapter we saw that the area between two consecutive layers, whose rolling lines were a distance dY apart, is

$$\int_0^{2\pi} \rho.\text{PQ}.d\theta = \frac{2\pi}{R}(R^2 - r^2).dY.$$

Hence the weight of water between these two consecutive layers, supposing a unit width, is

$$\frac{2\pi w}{R}(R^2 - r^2) \cdot dY,$$

where w is weight per unit volume. This gives the total energy of this layer of unit width as

$$\frac{r^2}{R} \cdot \frac{2\pi w}{R}(R^2 - r^2)dY,$$

or

$$2\pi r^2 w\left(1 - \frac{r^2}{R^2}\right)dY \quad . \qquad . \qquad . \qquad . \qquad . \qquad (1)$$

We have already seen that

$$R dr + r dY = 0.$$

Hence

$$dY = -\frac{R}{r} \cdot dr.$$

Substitute this in (i) above and we get total energy of volume between layers and of unit width as

$$= -2\pi R r w\left(1 - \frac{r^2}{R^2}\right) \cdot dr.$$

So that the total energy of the wave of unit width, $i.e.$ the total energy of all the layers from $r = 0$ to $r = r_0$, is

$$= -2\pi \int_0^{r_0} w\left(rR - \frac{r^3}{R}\right) \cdot dr$$

$$= \pi w\left(\frac{r_0^4}{2R} - r_0^2 R\right).$$

Hence, if we have a wave of height h, breadth b, and length l,

so that

$$h = 2r_0$$

$$l = 2\pi R,$$

the total energy is

$$b\pi w\left(\frac{h}{32l}2\pi - \frac{h^2}{4}\frac{l}{2\pi}\right)$$

or, changing sign, as energy is positive,

$$\text{energy} = \frac{bwh^2}{8}\left(l - \frac{\pi^2 h^2}{2l}\right)$$

$$= \frac{bwh^2 l}{8}\left(1 - \frac{\pi^2 h^2}{2l^2}\right).$$

Usually $\frac{h}{l}$ is small, and energy may be taken to be $\frac{bwh^2 l}{8}$, that is, it varies as the square of the height of the wave and directly as its length.

Shallow-water Waves.—In shallow water of uniform depth the paths of the particles become oval in form, the height of the orbit being less than the breadth. The ovals are very nearly ellipses.

On the assumption that they are true ellipses, that the angular velocity of the particle is uniform, and that the pressures at the crest and trough are equal, we are led to the following conclusions :—

Let a, b be the semi-major and semi-minor axes respectively of the orbit of the surface particles; ω the angular velocity of the particle about the centre of its orbit, and R the radius of the rolling circle.

Draw any radius O A, fig. 102, making an angle θ with the vertical O N, and cutting the auxiliary circles at A and B. Draw A P parallel to N O and B P parallel to H N. Then P is a point on the wave surface.

Take as axis of x the horizontal line H N along which the rolling circle rolls, and as axis of y the vertical line H K through the trough of the wave, i.e. when $\theta = 0$.

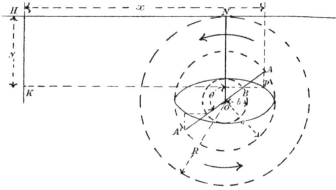

FIG. 102.

Then the coordinates of P are given by

$$x = R\theta + a \sin \theta$$
$$y = R + b \cos \theta$$

and $\therefore$

$$\frac{dx}{dt} = (R + a \cos \theta)\frac{d\theta}{dt}$$
$$= (R + a \cos \theta)\omega,$$

and $\therefore$ at the crest, velocity $= (R - a)\omega$,
and at the trough, velocity $= (R + a)\omega$.

At the crest $\theta = \pi$ and at the trough $\theta = 0$. And therefore, on the assumption of equal pressures at crest and trough,

$$(R + a)^2\omega^2 - (R - a)^2\omega^2 = 2g \cdot 2b.$$

$$\therefore \quad \omega^2 = \frac{b}{a} \cdot \frac{g}{R}.$$

If v is the velocity of propagation and $l = 2\pi R$ is the wave-length,

$$v = \omega R = \sqrt{\frac{b}{a} \cdot gR}$$

$$= \sqrt{\frac{gl}{2\pi} \cdot \frac{b}{a}}.$$

If $b = a$ we get the ordinary trochoidal wave. This equation can be reduced to the form

$$v^2 = \frac{gl}{2\pi} \tanh \frac{2\pi d}{l},$$

where d is the depth of water and $\tanh \dfrac{2\pi d}{l}$ is the hyperbolic tangent given by the formula

$$\tanh \frac{2\pi d}{l} = \frac{\epsilon^{\frac{2\pi d}{l}} - \epsilon^{-\frac{2\pi d}{l}}}{\epsilon^{\frac{2\pi d}{l}} + \epsilon^{-\frac{2\pi d}{l}}}.$$

If d is very small compared with l

$$\tanh \frac{2\pi d}{l} = \frac{2\pi d}{l},$$

and $\therefore$ $v^2 = gd$,

which is the formula already shown to apply to waves of small ratio of height to length in a canal.

Thus, as waves in deep water approach a shelving beach, the orbits at first become flatter, and the waves become of the nature of shallow-water waves. Afterwards, as the water shoals more and more, these are transformed to waves of translation, which break and roll upon the beach, carrying with them any floating bodies and heaping up the shingle.

Ripples or Capillary Waves.—In the theory of wave motion so far considered, gravity has been the sole motive power assumed. When, however, the disturbing forces are very small, surface tension plays a great part in the phenomena. If the velocity of the wind, or a body drawn through the water, is less than half a mile per hour, no disturbance of the surface of the water is noticeable, but at about that speed the surface becomes coated with a series of capillary waves, which die away almost at the same instant as the disturbing force is removed.

Formation of Waves at Sea.—Suppose the sea to be initially calm and quiescent, and to be then exposed to an increasing wind. At first, while the velocity of the wind is less than half a mile per hour, there is no sensible disturbance of the smoothness of the surface. When the velocity is about one mile per hour, the surface is coated with ripples. This stage has this distinguishing circumstance, that the phenomena on the surface cease almost simultaneously with the removal of the disturbing cause. When the velocity is about two miles per hour, small waves begin to rise uniformly over the whole surface of the water. Capillary waves disappear from the ridges of these waves, but are to be found upon the anterior surfaces and in the troughs. As the velocity of the wind increases, the length of the waves created also increases. The longer ones outstrip the shorter ones, and are less speedily worn down by fluid friction. Thus the long ones survive and absorb the smaller ones.

There are, on the sea, frequently three or four series of coexisting waves, each series having a different direction from the other, the individual waves of each series remaining parallel to one another.

CHAPTER X.

WAVEMAKING RESISTANCE OF SHIPS.

HAVING thus given a short discussion on particular properties of the trochoidal wave as the one most nearly corresponding to deep-sea waves, and yet allowing of simple calculations, we shall proceed with the study of wavemaking resistance proper.

When a ship is in motion there is a disturbance of the "still-water and at-

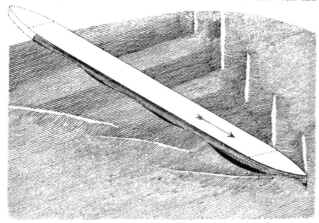

FIG. 103.

rest" distribution of forces. This disturbance of the forces is such as to give an increase of pressure at some parts and a diminution at others, but the pressure at the surface must remain constant, being that of the atmosphere. At the surface, instead of changes of pressure, changes in the level of the water make their appearance, or, in other words, waves are produced.

Figs. 103, 104, 105, 106, 107, and 108 show wave-forms as observed by Mr R. E. Froude for the cases mentioned. These figures show two quite distinct varieties of wave form and distribution :—

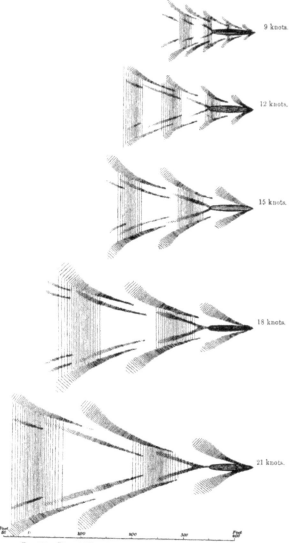

9 knots.

12 knots.

15 knots.

18 knots.

21 knots.

Fig. 104. —**Plan of Wave System** made by 83-foot Launch at various speeds. Position of wave-crests indicated by shading.

(1) Waves with crests perpendicular to line of motion, forming the transverse series.

(2) Waves with crests oblique to line of motion, forming the oblique or divergent series.

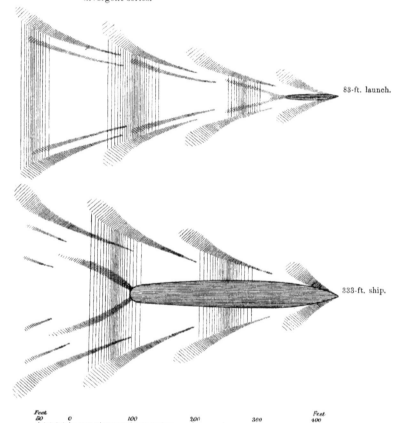

83-ft. launch.

333-ft. ship.

Feet
50   0   100   200   300   Feet
400

FIG. 105.—**Plan of Wave Systems** made by different ships at 18 knots, showing the similarity of the systems. Position of wave-crests indicated by shading.

The bow and stern each form separate systems of transverse and diverging waves similar in form and character, but the transverse are much less marked in the stern system than in that of the bow.

The profiles of the transverse waves are distributed along the line of motion, and may be seen where the wave-form is cut by the ship, and can be looked on as a group of waves somewhat similar to trochoidal waves, but not of uniform height. The speed of the individual waves is the same as that of the ship, and so their length, crest to crest, corresponds closely to that of a deep-water trochoidal wave travelling at the speed of the ship. A crest is always formed at, or close to, the bow ; this crest may be taken as the first visible result of the disturbance of the pressure equilibrium, i.e. the wave-forming tendency. The energy of this bow wave is dissipated in a sternward direction relatively to the ship, and this forms a second series of waves or "echoes." The primary and its echoes form one series as a whole. These series of diverging waves show pronounced crests spreading away from the

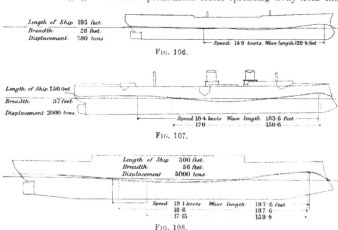

Length of Ship 195 feet.
Breadth   26 feet.
Displacement   780 tons
Speed 14·8 knots. Wave length 120·4 feet
FIG. 106.

Length of Ship 250 feet
Breadth   37 feet
Displacement 2000 tons
Speed 18·4 knots   Wave length 183·5 feet
17·0   156·6
FIG. 107.

Length of Ship   300 feet.
Breadth   56 feet.
Displacement   5000 tons.
Speed 19·1 knots   Wave length   197·6 feet.
18·6   187·6
17·15   159·4
FIG. 108.

ship. The diverging crests are parallel to one another. The inclination of each crest to the line of advance of the ship is about double that of the "line of divergence," or the line separating the disturbed from the undisturbed water. It will also be noticed that each of the diverging crests appears to form the end of the transverse waves already mentioned, whose crests appear against the side of the ship.

The diverging waves have a definite length : they advance in echelon. The angle that a line drawn through the crests makes with the line of advance has been calculated upon limited assumption, and it is found that it is constant for all forms and all speeds, and is about 19 degrees 28 minutes. The diverging series formed by the passage of the stern has the same angle. But Professor Hovgaard has shown from observations on ships that it decreases as the speed increases. The value of this angle is generally about half that of the angle that the individual waves make with the line of advance. In many cases it is somewhat greater than this. The diverging waves at the stern have an angle about equal to that of the bow series, but in many cases it is less than this.

The waves of a diverging series are curved in a section along their length, coming to a crest and sometimes breaking. The distance between the crests of the transverse waves varies as the square of the actual speed. Whatever the length of the vessels, when run at the same speed the crests of the diverging series of waves would be absolutely coincident if placed the one above the other; also the crests of the transverse waves should be exactly coincident. Lord Kelvin gave the equation and form of these as in figs. 109 and 110.

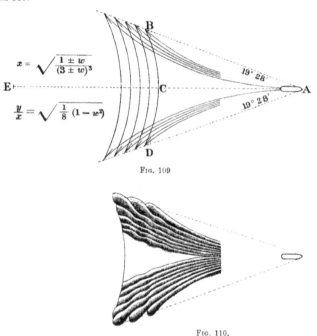

$$x = \sqrt{\frac{1 \pm w}{(3 \pm w)^3}}$$

$$\frac{y}{x} = \sqrt{\frac{1}{8}(1 - w^2)}$$

FIG. 109

FIG. 110.

We have seen that the energy of the waves is, relatively to the vessel, constantly passing away sternwards, but at the same time the energy of the wave system as a whole requires to be kept up. The only place from which the energy can be supplied is from the ship, and hence we have a constant drain on the power of the ship which gives rise to this part of wavemaking resistance. As to the amount of energy which is lost astern with each wave, this will depend on the form of the wave, but it is generally considered that approximately one-half of the energy of each wave is lost astern. So that the work a ship has to do is to maintain a system of waves unchanged in character and position relatively to herself at half her rate of advance.

Thus if we suppose E to be the energy of the wave, L the wave-length, and R the resistance due to its maintenance, we get

$$R = \frac{E}{2L} \quad \text{or} \quad R \propto \frac{E}{L}.$$

A similar expression would hold for the divergent waves. From this it will be seen that the work necessary is to create one new wave for each system for every two wave-lengths travelled.

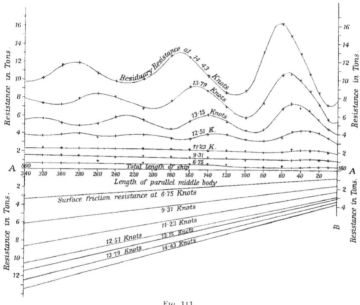

Fig. 111.

At low and moderate speeds wavemaking resistance in well-designed vessels is practically negligible, but as the speed is increased we reach a point where the wavemaking resistance forms an important part of the total resistance. The growth of the wavemaking resistance is not uniform, but follows a somewhat harmonic law.

Influence of Parallel Middle Body.—Fig. 111 shows the influence of parallel middle body on wavemaking resistance, as determined by experiment with a model representing a ship which without any middle body was 160 feet long. Into this model, successive 20-foot lengths of parallel middle body were inserted until the total length represented was 500 feet. The breadth and draught remain the same for all lengths of middle body. These models were tried at various speeds and their resistance measured. Of course the total resistance was measured, but the frictional resistance could be calculated and then subtracted from the total, leaving the residuary resistance, which at high speeds is practically all wavemaking resistance. These two values were, for simplicity, plotted one on each side of a given base line. Each set represents the resistance at a definite speed for varying length of middle body. The speeds range from 14·43 to 6·75 knots. The features of the wavemaking resistance are very marked, especially at the higher speeds, where the maxima and minima values of this resistance are clearly defined. The crests of the curves show much higher resistances than the hollows, though the displacement gradually increases with the length of the middle body.

An inspection of this figure reveals one or two points which may be regarded as criteria of wavemaking resistance.

(1) The spacing or length from crest to crest appears uniform throughout each curve.

(2) The spacing is more open in the curves of higher speed, the length apparently varying as the square of the speed.

(3) The amplitude of the variation increases as the speed increases.

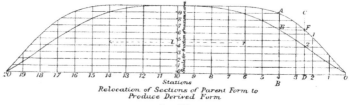

Relocation of Sections of Parent Form to
Produce Derived Form

FIG. 112.

(4) The amplitude of the variation in each curve diminishes as the length of the vessel increases.

These variations in residuary resistance for varying lengths are supposed to be caused by the interference of the bow and stern transverse system of waves; thus we should have a *maximum* for the residuary resistance when the crests of the bow-wave system coincide with the crests of the stern-wave system, and a *minimum* when the crests of the bow-wave system coincide with the troughs of the stern-wave system.

Mr D. W. Taylor, of the United States Navy, has recently made a series of experiments concerning the effects upon resistance, in full vessels, of varying percentages of length of parallel middle-body, to determine if there was a best length of parallel middle-body in a given case.

All the models tested had the same midship section coefficient, ·96 ; ratio of beam to draught, 2·5. Variations were made in the prismatic coefficient, and in size and shape of the curves of sectional area. They were derived from a parent form, whose prismatic coefficient is ·68.

Let curve 1, fig. 112, be the curve of sectional areas desired, having a length of parallel middle-body l and ends of the same cross sections as parent form but more closely spaced. Let curve 2 be the curve of sectional areas of the parent form. Both are drawn to the same maximum ordinate. To determine the section of derived model at C D, square F across to E. Then section B E of parent form is the shape of section F D in derived model.

Three series of models were tested ; each series contained twenty, there being four sizes, and for each size five curves of sectional area. The

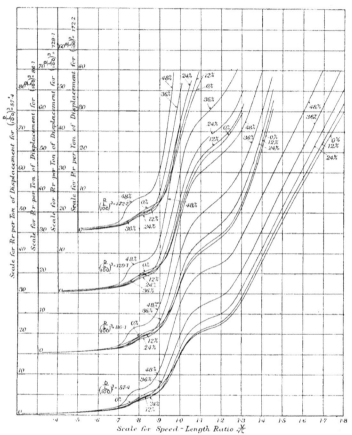

Fig. 113.—Curves of residuary resistance per ton of displacement for four displacement-length ratios. Each with definite per cent. of parallel middle-body as indicated, all for prismatic coefficient of ·74. Block coefficient ·71.

prismatic coefficients were ·68, ·74, and ·80. There were varying percentages of parallel middle-body from 0 to 60.

Resistance being partly due to the surface friction, this was separately estimated. It was found that practicable variations in the length of parallel middle-body in a given case will have hardly any effect upon the skin resistance.

Concerning the residuary resistance, fig. 113 shows the curves of

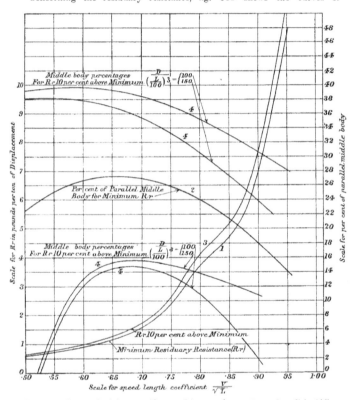

FIG. 114.—Curves of minimum residuary resistance and percentages of parallel middle body for series of prismatic coefficient = ·74.

residuary resistance per ton of displacement for the series whose prismatic coefficient is ·74. The abscissæ are values of the speed length ratio $\frac{V}{\sqrt{L}}$, and the ordinates are values of residuary resistance per ton of displacement. The four sizes are indicated by the four values 57·4, 86·1, 129·1, and 172·2 of the displacement length ratio $\left(\dfrac{L}{100}\right)3$. Each set is drawn for percentages of parallel middle-body, 0, 12, 24, 36, and 48.

It is seen that, at the very high speeds, the resistance increases as the percentage of parallel middle-body increases.

The results, for series of prismatic coefficient ·74, are summarised in fig. 114. The results are plotted upon values of $\dfrac{V}{\sqrt{L}}$ and consist of—

(1) A curve showing the minimum residuary resistance.

(2) A curve showing the percentage of parallel middle-body corresponding to the minimum resistance.

(3) A curve of residuary resistance 10 per cent. above the minimum.

(4) Curves of percentages of parallel middle-body, above and below the minimum percentage, for which the residuary resistance is 10 per cent. above the minimum resistance. These curves vary slightly with displacement-length coefficient, and may be taken as indicating the boundaries within which the length of parallel middle-body may be varied without appreciable effect upon the resistance.

For the range of speeds attained in practice by full vessels, the best length of parallel middle-body is, for a prismatic coefficient ·68, from 12 to 16 per cent., but may be 25 per cent. without material increase in resistance.

For a prismatic coefficient ·74, the best length is from 24 to 27 per cent., but may be 36 to 40 per cent. without material increase in resistance.

For a prismatic coefficient ·80, it is from 32 to 35 per cent., but may be 44 to 48 per cent. without material increase in resistance.

These conclusions apply to values of $\dfrac{V}{\sqrt{L}}$ above ·50. For very low values of $\dfrac{V}{\sqrt{L}}$ the above limits may be materially exceeded.

Professor Sadler of Michigan University has recently conducted a series of experiments upon *the influence of the position of the midship section upon resistance.* The two series of models tried were of the ordinary form, and in each series the length, breadth, draught, displacement, sections and curves of sectional area were kept constant; the only variation in the form being that due to expanding or contracting the forward- and after-body, due to placing the midship section at various positions in the length.

When the midship section is at the centre of the length, the curves of sectional area in both models are the same for both forward- and after-bodies.

The following table gives the particulars of the models :—

Model.	$\dfrac{L}{B}$	$\dfrac{B}{d}$	$\dfrac{L}{D}$	Coefficients.		
				Block.	Prism.	Mid. sect.
A	8	2·143	17·14	·503	·538	·935
B	8	2·143	17·14	·567	·606	·936

In each case the midship section was placed in four positions :—

(1) At the centre of the length.
(2) At 5 per cent. of the length, aft of the centre.
(3) At 10 per cent. of the length, aft of the centre.
(4) At 10 per cent. of the length, forward of the centre.

The curves of sectional areas for the two models are shown in fig. 115. The curve for 2 is omitted, and that for 4 is simply 3 reversed.

The curves of residuary resistance for model A are shown in fig. 116, the abscissæ representing the position of the midship section with respect to the length, and the ordinates the residuary resistance for a constant value of $\dfrac{V}{\sqrt{L}}$ for each curve.

Similar curves for model B are shown in fig. 117.

It is seen that, at low values of $\dfrac{V}{\sqrt{L}}$ —·7 in A and ·5 in B—the position of the midship section has little or no influence upon the resistance, but as

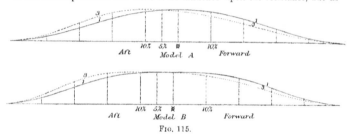

Fig. 115.

the speed increases there is a certain position for each speed where the resistance is a minimum. This position travels aft as the speed increases. With the midship section 10 per cent. aft, or forward, of the middle of the length, the resistance shows a marked increase at the higher values of $\dfrac{V}{\sqrt{L}}$. The "cod's head and mackerel's tail" is wrong for high speeds.

In the fuller form, B, the effect of the position of the midship section is noticeable at a smaller value of $\dfrac{V}{\sqrt{L}}$ than in the finer form A.

In A, for values of $\dfrac{V}{\sqrt{L}} = 1$, the resistance is a minimum when the maximum section is amidships. At $\dfrac{V}{\sqrt{L}} = 1\cdot25$, it is a minimum at 5 per cent. abaft amidships.

In B, for values of $\dfrac{V}{\sqrt{L}} = \cdot8$, the resistance is a minimum when the maximum section is amidships, and when $\dfrac{V}{\sqrt{L}} = 1\cdot15$, it is a minimum when this section is 5 per cent. abaft amidships.

Interference of the Bow- and Stern-wave Systems.—As stated above, the variations in the wavemaking resistance are due to the interference of the bow and stern transverse systems of waves. In order to make clear the principles involved, the following mechanical explanation, suggested by Dr Froude, is of some value :—

Imagine a pendulum fastened to a ring which travels along a frictionless

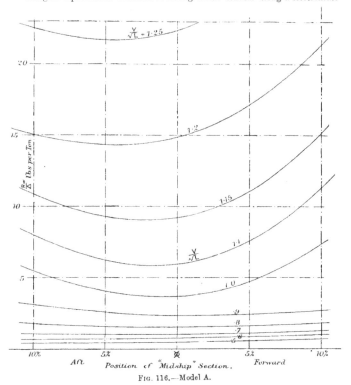

FIG. 116.—Model A.

rod at a uniform speed. Let the rod be bent transversely in two places by S curves, as at A A, B B, fig. 118, the two straight parts at each end being in the same straight line, and the middle straight part A B parallel to them.

When the ring travels on the part A A, B B, it will be first displaced sideways in one direction. This will set up a lateral swing in the pendulum, which will remain unaltered as long as the ring remains on the middle straight part. This swing represents the transverse wave series left by the bow, which shows unaltered all along the parallel side, except so far as it diminishes by spreading sideways.

If the pendulum be artificially stopped swinging before the second curve is reached, the replacement on to the part beyond B B will likewise generate a swing which will remain unaltered throughout this succeeding straight part, and will represent the train of independent transverse waves left by the stern in a vessel with long parallel sides.

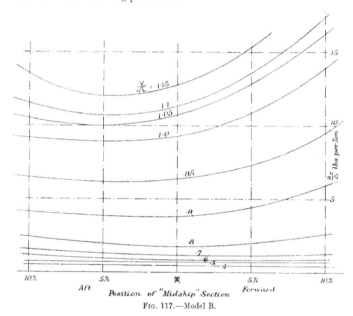

FIG. 117.—Model B.

If, however, the pendulum remains swinging when the ring reaches the second curve, the behaviour of the pendulum on it, and the magnitude of the resulting swing, will depend entirely upon the point in its vibration which it has reached at the moment of commencing the second curve.

If the curves A A, B B are exactly symmetrical with one another, and the length of the middle straight is so chosen that the pendulum enters the second curve in the attitude and state of motion symmetrical to that in which it left the first, then the behaviour of the pendulum over the second curve will be symmetrical to its behaviour on the first, and it must therefore leave the former as it entered the latter, namely, in a state of rest.

If A A A in fig. 119 represents the actual path of the pendulum bob in reference to the rod, B B B what would be the continuation of this path if the straight continued, and C C C the path it would acquire in passing over the second curve if it entered without swing, then the actual resulting path will be such that the ordinate to it, at any distance from D D, will equal the sum of the ordinates to the paths B B and C C ; the ordinates being measured from the middle lines of the vibrations, and reckoned positive in one direction and negative in the other.

When the two components are simultaneous in the same direction, the resulting vibration will be at its largest, and will be the sum of the two, the energy being proportional to the square of that swing. When the two components are opposite to one another, the resultant will be at its smallest, being equal to their difference.

It has been pointed out that the height of the waves made, and the resistance caused, will be at a maximum or minimum according as the

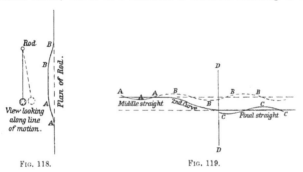

FIG. 118.   FIG. 119.

crests of the bow-wave series coincide with the crests or troughs of the natural stern-wave series. The wave sections observed in the wake of the models used by Dr Froude, at the speed corresponding to 13·15 knots for the ship (see fig. 111), are shown in fig. 122. They are drawn above one another, so that the vertical intervals between their base lines are proportional to the differences in length of parallel side ; the points in each, A_1, B_1, etc., representing the position of the stern, being vertically over one another, so that the points representing the bow, fig. 123, fall naturally into a diagonal line. Parallel lines G G_1, H H_1, etc., represent the position, as measured from the bow, of the successive crests of the bow-wave series as they show against the parallel side in the longer ships.

In fig. 122 a curve of residuary resistance is also shown, and it will be seen that the maximum resistance and largest waves are about where the crest positions of the components coincide ; and the minimum resist- ance and smallest waves, where the crest of one falls in the trough of the other. Fig. 124 shows lines of parent ship and wave profile at 14·43 knots.

Principal effects of interference of the Bow and Stern transverse Wave Systems.—We must at first consider the problem of the combination of waves of equal lengths, but of different amplitudes.

Consider two waves, of same length and different amplitudes, moving in the same direction.

Let $h_1 h_2$ be the heights of the waves, λ the wave-length, and S the phase difference.

Let O be the orbital centre of the surface particles, fig. 120, and A O B the constant difference of phase angle.

If we draw A C parallel to O B, and B C parallel to O A, the resultant wave is that traced out by O C.

And therefore, if h is the height of the resultant wave,

$$h^2 = h_1^2 + h_2^2 + 2h_1 h_2 \cos \psi,$$

or, in terms of phase difference S,

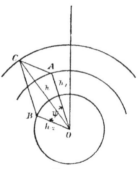

FIG. 120.

since $\psi = \dfrac{S}{\lambda} 2\pi$

$\therefore$ $h^2 = h_1^2 + h_2^2 + 2h_1 h_2 \cos \dfrac{2\pi S}{\lambda}.$

To apply this to the bow and stern transverse wave systems, assume these waves to be simple waves of height h_1 and h_2. Their wave-lengths are the same, being that due to the speed of the ship.

Let the height of the bow wave, when it has reached the stern, be kh_1; k will be a number less than unity.

Let S be the distance between the primary crests of the natural bow and stern systems, and let S' be the distance between the primary crest of the stern system and the next crest of the bow series. Fig. 121.

Then the resulting series will have a height h given by

$$h^2 = k^2 h_1^2 + h_2^2 + 2k h_1 h_2 \cos \dfrac{2\pi S'}{\lambda}.$$

Now, $S + S'$ is the distance between two of the crests of the bow series, and therefore $S + S' = n\lambda$ where n is a whole number.

$$\therefore \quad S' = n\lambda - S$$

$$\text{and} \quad \cos\frac{2\pi S'}{\lambda} = \cos\frac{2\pi(n\lambda - S)}{\lambda}$$

$$= \cos\left(2n\pi - \frac{2\pi S}{\lambda}\right)$$

$$= \cos\frac{2\pi S}{\lambda}.$$

$$\therefore \quad h^2 = k^2 h_1{}^2 + h_2{}^2 + 2k h_1 h_2 \cos\frac{2\pi S}{\lambda}.$$

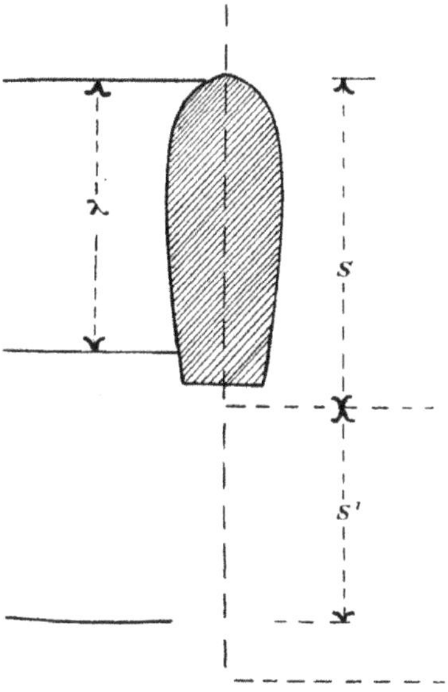

Fig. 121.

Let $S = m\mathrm{L}$ where L is length of ship and m is a number very nearly equal to unity.

Let v be the velocity of the ship in feet per second.

$$\text{Then} \quad \lambda = \frac{2\pi v^2}{g}.$$

$$\therefore \quad h^2 = k^2 h_1{}^2 + h_2{}^2 + 2k h_1 h_2 \cos\frac{g m \mathrm{L}}{v^2}.$$

Now the energy of a unit breadth of a wave is proportional to its length and to the square of its height (see p. 133). The wavemaking resistance is due to the amount of energy that is drained away from the ship due to the creation of these waves.

Thus, the energy lost due to the degradation of the bow wave as it passes aft is proportional to

$$h_1{}^2 - k^2 h_1{}^2$$

and the energy lost in the resultant stern-wave system is proportional to

$$k^2 h_1{}^2 + h_2{}^2 + 2k h_1 h_2 \cos \frac{gm\mathrm{L}}{v^2}.$$

and therefore the total loss of energy is proportional to

$$h_1{}^2 + h_2{}^2 + 2k h_1 h_2 \cos \frac{gm\mathrm{L}}{v^2}.$$

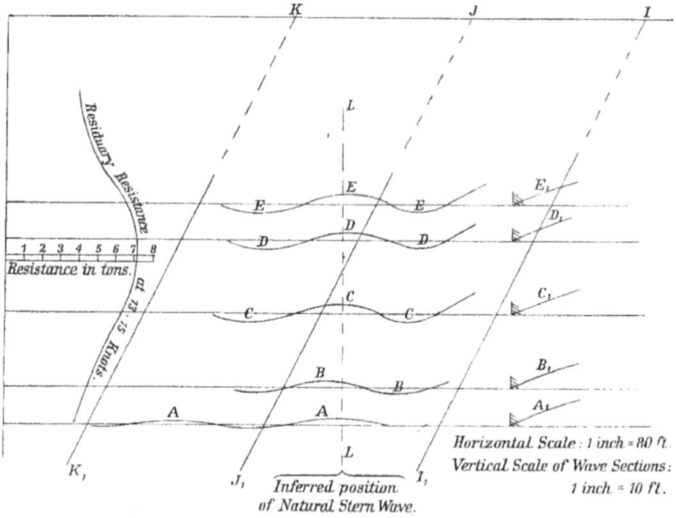

Horizontal Scale : 1 inch = 80 ft.
Vertical Scale of Wave Sections:
1 inch = 10 ft.

Inferred position
of Natural Stern Wave.

FIG. 122.

Consider a ship run at gradually increasing speeds. L is constant, m is practically constant. h_1 and h_2 and the coefficient k will increase with speed. The value of $\frac{gm\mathrm{L}}{v^2}$ will continually decrease. Thus the resistance will fluctuate about an ever-increasing mean value, the spacing of the fluctuations depending upon successive increments of $\frac{gm\mathrm{L}}{v^2}$, each equal to 2π. Thus the speeds corresponding to successive humps and hollows are such that their squares are in harmonical progression.

With a given entrance and run, and at a given speed, h_1 and h_2 are constant, but k will decrease as L increases. Thus the resistance will not be constant but will fluctuate about a mean value, the amplitudes of the fluctuations decreasing as L increases ; and the spacings such that successive values of $\frac{gmL}{v^2}$ differ by 2π. Hence the spacing at the same speed is constant, and at different speeds it varies as v^2.

Effect of Density of Liquid on Resistance.—The density of the liquid in which the vessel is floating will affect the energy of the wave, and consequently the wavemaking resistance. The energy varies directly as the density. Frictional resistance also varies directly as the density. In passing from fresh to salt

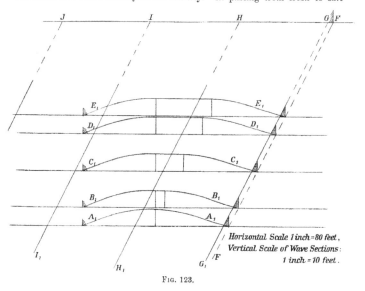

/ Horizontal Scale 1 inch = 80 feet ,
Vertical Scale of Wave Sections:
1 inch = 10 feet .

FIG. 123.

water, or *vice versâ*, any change is, in a large measure, counteracted by the variation in the amount of immersed volume of ship.

Effect of Form on Resistance.—In 1876 Mr Wm. Froude published in a paper the results of a series of experiments on the comparative resistances of models of four ships of the same displacement, but of known differences of form. The corresponding dimensions of ships varied from a length of 369' to 294', beam from 49·4' to 37·2', and draughts from 19·32' to 16·25'; the common displacement was 3980 tons. The conclusion arrived at from these experiments showed that in general the resistance will be decreased if, instead of a parallel middle-body, the fore and after bodies are expanded so as to obtain a ship of the same displacement as that with parallel middle-body, although the ratio of B to L be somewhat increased. The results are shown in fig. 125, and are deserving of careful study, as showing the effect of form on resistance for varying speeds.

Another cause of the variation in the resistance is that of irregular movement. All bodies moving in a frictional fluid have a certain amount of water moved with them. There is also a mass of water in motion relatively to the vessel, some moving ahead and some astern. This must be taken into consideration in any rapid changes of velocity involving acceleration or the opposite, as it practically takes part in the motion of the vessel. This amount is generally from 15 per cent. to 20 per cent. of the displacement.

The resistance of a ship in a seaway is considerably greater than the resistance in smooth water for the same speed, the chief causes tending to produce this result being as follows :—

   (i) The wave disturbance of the water produces in the regular streamline motion a confusion and disturbance, thus entailing an increased amount of energy required to sustain the wave system above that necessary in smooth water at the same speed.

   (ii) Pitching and rolling, especially the former, place the ship in positions which, relatively to the propulsion, are most unfavourable, thus causing an increase in the mean resistance.

   (iii) The waves and the action of pitching and rolling tend to make irregularities of speed, and so increase the resistance on account of the energy lost in overcoming the inertia of the body.

   (iv) The frictional resistance is increased as larger volumes of water have to be set in motion.

It is, of course, impossible to estimate the exact effect of these irregular modifications, but they may be counteracted to a certain extent by increase of length and good freeboard, large size, and the resultant large weight.

Mr R. E. Froude contributed to the Institution of Naval Architects in 1905 the results of a series of tank experiments made upon the resistance of models in artificially created waves, to determine the effect upon the resistance due to the pitching caused by the waves. The sea condition of the ship, which is thus represented by the model, is that of steaming against a regular head sea. The models were fully decked in, and in some cases were fitted with a forecastle. They were ballasted to float at the desired trim, and so that the longitudinal moment of inertia about the C.G. should be proportional to that of the ship. The period of pitching was thus proportioned to the period of the wave in the same ratio as in full-sized ships and waves. The results of augment of resistance were plotted for a given speed, and longitudinal radius of gyration to a base of wave period. The resistance has a very marked maximum. A difference in wave period of 15 per cent. either way reduces the increase of resistance over that in still water by 50 per cent. The period of the wave corresponding to greatest resistance exceeded that of the pitching period of the ship. The largest series of waves used caused a pitching of 6° from out to out, and increased the resistance by over 100 per cent. above that for smooth water. Under these conditions water is shipped forward with nearly every wave. Resistances with varying longitudinal moments of inertia were measured, with the result that the maximum resistance and pitching angle increased with the radius of gyration. Differences in resistance against waves due to small variation in forms were obtained, but they are much less than the differences due to variation in longitudinal radius of gyration. The effect of straightening the lines of a hollow lined form was to increase smooth water resistance but to make the difference between smooth and wave water resistance greater in the hollow than the straight lined ship.

CHAPTER XI.

DETERMINATION OF THE RESISTANCE OF SHIPS FROM MODEL EXPERIMENTS.

EXPERIMENTS on resistance have been made in a few cases on the actual vessels, but generally such experiments have been limited to models not exceeding 20 feet in length. In trying a model of a ship in order to determine its resistance, we have already seen that there must be some speed for the model which will correspond to the speed of the ship, and the law used is that of "corresponding speeds." *In comparing similar ships with one another, or ships with models, the speeds must be proportional to the square roots of their linear dimensions.* Take as an example a ship of 500 feet which we wish to drive at 23 knots, and for which we have made a model 12 feet long. Then the ratio of the linear dimensions is

$$\frac{500}{12} = 41\cdot66 \, ;$$

then the speed for the model corresponding to 23 knots for the ship is

$$\frac{23}{\sqrt{41\cdot66}} = 3\cdot56 \text{ knots.}$$

We have now obtained the speed at which the model has to be run. To determine the resistance of the ship from the resistance of the model we must—

(1) Determine the total resistance of the model.
(2) Calculate the frictional resistance of the model.
(3) Deduct the frictional from the total, and obtain thereby the wave-making resistance of the model at the "corresponding speed."

By means of Froude's law of comparison we can determine the wave-making resistance of the ship. The law is as follows : If the linear dimensions of a vessel be l times the dimensions of the model, and the resistances of the latter at the speeds V_1, V_2, V_3, etc., are R_1, R_2, R_3, etc., then at the "corresponding speeds" of the ship $V_1 \sqrt{l}$, $V_2\sqrt{l}$, $V_3 \sqrt{l}$, etc., the resistance of the ship will be $R_1 l^3$, $R_2 l^3$, $R_3 l^3$, etc.

The total resistance of the vessel can now be found by—

(1) Calculating the frictional resistances of the ship at the various speeds.
(2) Calculating the wavemaking resistance of the ship from that of the model at the various speeds.
(3) Adding the results of (1) and (2) together for the respective speeds.

The results may now be set off in a curve to a base of speed. The curve is usually called a "curve of resistance."

It will be seen from the foregoing that in order to determine the resistance of a ship of known form, it is necessary to determine the resistance of a model

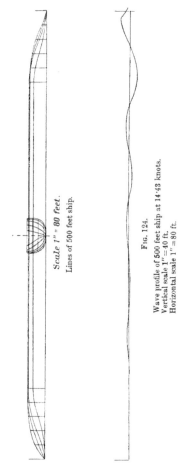

Scale 1" = 80 feet.
Lines of 500 feet ship.

Fig. 124.

Wave profile of 500 feet ship at 14·43 knots.
Vertical scale 1" = 40 ft.
Horizontal scale 1" = 80 ft.

of the ship on a convenient scale. From this may be deduced the wave-making resistance (r_w) for the model by deducting the value of the frictional resistance (r_f). Then applying the law of comparison we may obtain the value R_{sc} at the corresponding speed for the ship, then add to it the calculated value of R_f and so obtain the total resistance at the chosen speed. The determination of model resistance is therefore the foundation of accurate determination of ship resistance. This work is done in what is known as an experimental tank, but it would be better named a resistance tank. The following is a description of one of the most recently constructed of these tanks, namely, that at the shipyard of Messrs John Brown & Company of Clydebank.

RESISTANCE CURVES "MERKARA," ETC.

		L.	B.	d.	Disp.	Area of Skin.	$\sqrt{E+R}$
A	"Merkara" .	369	37·2	16·25	3980	18600	17·03
B	Similar to model .	368	45·88	18·0	,,	19130	18·95
C	,, ,, .	318	49·4	19·32	,,	17810	17·58
D	,, ,, .	294	45·56	17·89	,,	16950	13·78

Note.—$\sqrt{E+R}$ limit of economical speed—Knots.

$E \equiv$ length of entrance (ft.).

$R \equiv$,. ,, run ,,

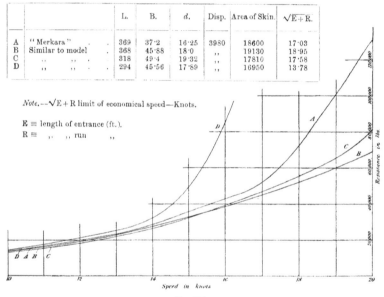

FIG. 125.

It should be noted that all experimental tanks are not only used for the purposes of determining the resistance of the model, but for the study of the problems of propulsion by screws and paddles, both alone and in conjunction with the ship models. This latter use of the experimental tank will be treated fully under the head of Propulsion. The following description includes that for the whole apparatus, part of which is used for the subject of propulsion.

The experimental tank at Clydebank is very similar to the Haslar tank except in details in which experience has shown that the latter could be improved. The length of the actual tank is 400 feet, although the water extends to a distance of 445 feet to allow of docking facilities for the models.

The depth of the tank varies uniformly from 9 feet to 10 feet, the slope being given for the purpose of draining and cleaning the tank. There is a uniform breadth of 20 feet of water, and at the one end there are wet and dry docks, the wet docks being used for the storage of models, and also for the purposes of ballasting previous to a trial run. The dry dock is so placed that the towing truck can be run over it, and so allow of an examination of the gears for the dynamometer and propellers. At the other end of the tank there is a sloping concrete beach, which helps to break up the waves caused by the

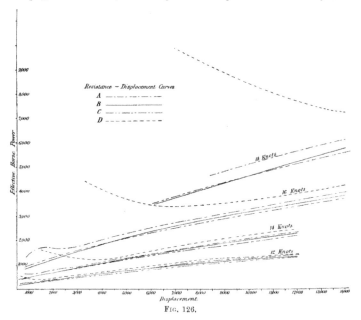

Fig. 126.

travelling of the model through the water, a recess being left up the middle to prevent damage to models or screws. The cross section of the tank is rectangular, and the basin is made of concrete, backed with puddled clay, as shown in fig. 127. The building is of brick and contains, besides the tank proper, a large drawing-office, tracers' room, and superintendent's office, with the necessary safes, etc. In connection with the tank there is a staff of model-makers, who assist by making cores for the castings of the paraffin-wax models, and who, after the model leaves the shaping machine, help to fair up its form. In order to keep the temperature of the tank constant, a complete system of hot-water piping is installed, which is under perfect control.

The models used are generally about 15 feet long, except in the case of high-speed torpedo boats, when the length is about 11 feet. During the trials, the models are run at speeds corresponding to greater and less than the trial speed, and at several displacements.

When the wax casting of the model is sufficiently hard it is levelled up on the top and taken to the shaping machine, where it is placed on a wheel carriage. It is secured at the middle line, keel upwards. In front of this carriage there is a table on which the half-breadth plan of the ship is fixed.

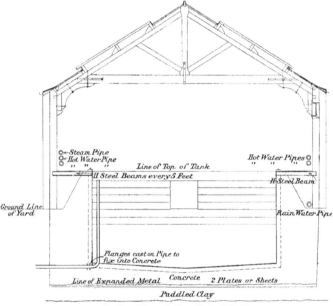

Section Through Deep End of Tank.

Fig. 127.

There are two cutters, which rotate at about 2500 revolutions per minute. These cutters are adjustable about the centre line of the carriage, and also in a vertical direction. The cutters are driven through belt and rope gearing by a $2\frac{1}{2}$ B.H.P. electric motor. The cutter is traversed backwards and forwards and in and out. A 3-inch copper pipe runs underneath the carriage for its whole length. Through this tube runs a piano wire, and attached to this wire are two leather hydraulic pistons. The wire is led through packing glands at each end of this cylinder, and is carried over horizontal guide wheels fixed at each end of the carriage. The ends of the wire are ultimately fixed on the carriage centre. From a valve box, with which are in connection a rotary paddle pump and reservoir, connections are made to each end of the cylinder. The cylinder, pump, and connections are filled with paraffin oil, and the pump forces this oil at a pressure of about 15 lbs. per square inch into either end of the cylinder, thus causing the carriage, through the wire, to move. By suitably working the valves in the valve box the carriage, and consequently the model, can be run in either direction. The travel of the carriage is uniform, and there is no backlash to take up. Waterlines are cut from midships to the ends in order to prevent hollows being cut into the model. Should it happen that the cutters are run into the wax to such an extent as to offer a resistance greater than the oil pressure could overcome, the carriage will stop, and so prevent the cutter spindles from being overstrained. The table with the half-breadth plan is in gear with this carriage, and by using suitable change wheels any degree of relative motion can be got. One hand-wheel controls the up-and-down motion of the cutters, and a similar wheel controls the in-and-out motion. This second wheel imparts, through a pantograph (to the tracing point at the drawing), a similar motion to the cutters. It is possible by adjusting the fulcrum of the pantograph to cut models from one set of lines to any proportions of length, breadth, and draught. On coming out of the shaping machine the model is not smooth, but the surface has the appearance of a series of ridges one behind the other. The model-makers now take it in hand and finish it off to the waterlines cut on. It is then accurately weighed and launched. When a test is to be made with a model, it is correctly loaded to the designed draught and trim. The models when not in use are kept submerged, to prevent alteration in shape from taking place. The dynamometers and screw trucks are shown in fig. 128. The structure is of wood boxing, giving a maximum stiffness for weight. This is the only electrically-driven tank truck in this country so far, all the others being rope-driven. The current is supplied from the power station, but, owing to the constant change in the voltage, the current is first passed through a motor generator into accumulators, from which it is again discharged through the generator at a suitable and regular voltage. Due to this arrangement, and to the particular way in which the trolley wiring is carried out, it is possible to maintain uniformity of speed on a run down the tank. Two 6 B.H.P. motors drive the truck, and also, through counter-shafts and cord-leads, (1) the resistance recording drums, (2) trim cylinders on the main truck (for measuring the change of trim of the model), (3) the screw propellers, and (4) the recording drum on the screw truck. Automatic cut-offs and brakes prevent the truck running too far either way. The recording drums and trim cylinders are so geared as to make one revolution in the length of the tank, no matter at what speed the carriage may be travelling. By using differently proportioned sets of pulleys it is possible to give the propellers almost any desired number of revolutions in conjunction with a particular speed of model. The method of measuring resistance is the same as that used by Dr Froude, viz. to record graphically the extension of an accurately made spiral spring. The magnification used in this instance is twelve, and each spring is standardised before using. A diagrammatic representation of the apparatus for recording resistance is shown in fig. 129. The drag of the model pulls horizontally at B and produces at D a parallel, equal, and opposite motion to that at B. This motion extends the spring S to such an extent as to produce equilibrium. F is moved proportionately to its distance from the fulcrum (A), and this motion produces a magnified and opposite movement of G. The bearings at B, C,

FIG. 128.

and D are all at the same distance from A. These bearings are all knife-edges, and a weight w hung on at C will produce the same extension of the pen rod along the drum as if there were a horizontal pull of value w at B. It is thus possible by hanging known weights on at C to get a scale for evaluating the resistance diagrams.

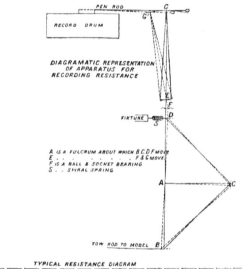

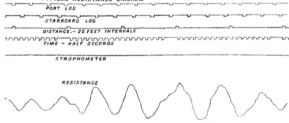

FIG. 129.

On the resistance drum the following are recorded : (1) resistance in lbs. ; (2) the distance traversed, in multiples of 25 feet, there being small electric contact-makers alongside the rail 25 feet apart ; (3) time in half-seconds ; (4) measure of the current in the water (this is measured by means of two log screws running in advance of the model) ; (5) a graphic record of the speed, to show any want of uniformity of motion. Thus for a certain model at known draughts and displacements the resistance in lbs. and speeds in

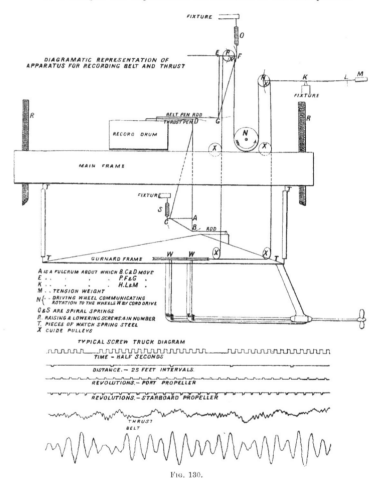

FIG. 130.

feet per minute are obtained. It is also possible to note the trim of the model under the various conditions of loading. On the screw truck, time, distance, and revolutions are recorded on one drum, while thrust and belt pull or turning moment are recorded automatically, these latter being measured by spiral springs, as in resistance. The above diagram (fig. 130) gives a rough idea of this arrangement.

. The wheel N is driven off the main driving-wheels of the carriage, and by using appropriate gearing any chosen number of revolutions can be given to N. This wheel is always driven in the direction shown, whether right- or left-handed screws are used, so that the spring O may always be in tension and not compression. Now if T be the tension in the cord on the driving side and t that in the slack side, then the effective driving force is T − t, which acts on the rims of wheels W. The downward pull on P is 2T, which causes an elongation in the spring O, which extension is recorded by the movement of the pen rod G. The slack portion of the cord passes over the pulley H, which is consequently pulled down with a force 2t, the value of this force being determined by the weight M on the lever H L.

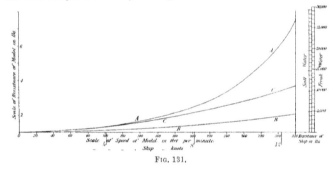

FIG. 131.

The gurnard frame which carries the propellers is swung from the main frame by steel spring suspensions, thus allowing the propellers, as they exert a thrust, to carry forward the gurnard frame, whose motion, through a bell crank lever pivoted at A, is recorded on the drum by the pen rod D. Thrust and belt with the propellers off are recorded under the same conditions as held with the propellers on, and so the nett value of these due to the presence of the propellers is obtained. It is thus possible by using the screw truck alone, the main truck alone, or the two in combination, to get propeller efficiencies, thrusts, wake factors, thrust deduction, hull efficiency, and resistance for any model, in conjunction with any chosen screw or screws. The results of all model experiments are first plotted in terms of lbs. of resistance on a base of speed in feet per minute. Afterwards the results are reduced to the "constant" system of Mr Froude, which is described later. This system is a method of standardising results. A standard length of form is used, and values of (C) (resistance) in terms of K (speed) are plotted. Iso (K) curves are also made. Curves showing E.H.P. (effective horse-power) in terms of speed in knots are also plotted.

The propellers used are of a white metal, and are made and finished by the staff of the tank.

The tank experiments give on the recording machine a record of the total resistance, and not of the wavemaking resistance alone ; it is, however, quite a simple matter to separate the resistance into frictional and residuary resistances.

In the above fig. 131 A A represents the curve of total resistance for model, as obtained from the tank experiments. We have now to calculate the resistance due to the skin friction of the model by the formula $R_f = fSV^n$, where R_f is the frictional resistance in lbs., f is a coefficient obtained by Froude for planes of paraffin wax of a length the same as the model, S is the wetted surface, and V is the speed ; n is the power of the speed, and is obtained from the experiments on planes, p. 117. From the base set up, the values so obtained at the different speeds of the model and through the points draw the curve C C. The difference of the ordinates of the curves A A and C C gives the residuary resistance for the model, or, to the proper scale, that of the ship. Now, knowing the length of the ship and the wetted

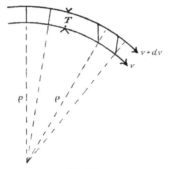

FIG. 132.

surface, we can choose a coefficient value of f and a value of n in the formula $R_f = fSV^n$. These will give us the frictional resistance of the ship at various speeds. Set down the values from the curve C C and we shall get the curve B B ; the difference of the ordinates between the curves A A and B B will give the total resistance of the ship at various speeds. Now the model has been tried in fresh water ; and as the resistance in various liquids vary as the densities of the liquids, it will be necessary to multiply the resistances so obtained by (in this case) 1·026, which is the ratio between the density of fresh and salt water. This gives the resistance of the ship under the ordinary salt-water conditions. Very full results of investigation made by Dr R. E. Froude upon the resistance due to forms having block coefficients of ·5 to ·6 have been published in the *Transactions of the Institution of Naval Architects* for 1904. Professor Sadler, of Michigan University, U.S.A., has recently published in the *Transactions of the American Society of Naval Architects* for 1907 and 1908 the results of experiments on models having block coefficients of about ·7 to ·85.

Proof of Froude's Law of Comparison.—Consider a stream-line motion in a perfect fluid. No rotation can be imparted to any element of the fluid, since an interface can only have pressure across it, and no tangential stress along it.   Therefore any rotation which an element seemingly possesses due to its motion in a curved path, must be equal and opposite to the rotation due to the difference in velocity of the stream lines.

Thus, for an irrotational motion we have

$$\frac{v}{\rho} + \frac{dv}{\tau} = 0 \qquad . \qquad . \qquad . \qquad . \qquad (1)$$

See fig. 132.

Where τ is the thickness of the path across which the difference of velocity is dv, ρ is the radius of curvature of the path.

$\therefore \dfrac{v}{\rho}$ is the angular velocity supposing the water solid.

$\dfrac{dv}{\tau}$ is the necessary opposite rotation for irrotationality.

Also for continuity, $\qquad v\tau = \text{constant} \qquad . \qquad . \qquad . \qquad . \qquad (2)$

$$\therefore \qquad v\,d\tau + \tau\,dv = 0,$$

$$\text{or} \qquad d\tau = -\,\tau\frac{dv}{v}$$

$$= \frac{\tau^{2}}{\rho} \text{ from (1).}$$

This shows the increase of thickness of the stream tubes as we pass from one to another.   Hence, given two stream lines, we can get a third, and so on.   In motion round a solid, the boundaries must be stream lines if the motion is steady.   If a body be totally submerged and moving through a perfect fluid, with true stream-line motion, the excess of pressure on its forward part is exactly balanced by the defect on its after part, and hence the body experiences no resistance to motion.   This is on the assumption of an infinite fluid, stretching away in all directions from the body.   When, however, as in the case of a ship, the body is not wholly submerged, the modifications of the pressures caused by the discontinuity of the fluid, i.e. by the surface of the fluid which is a boundary, cause a resistance to motion. Waves are created, which are due to the differences of hydrodynamical pressure inherent in the system of stream lines which the passage of the ship creates.

We have seen that between successive stream lines the equation $d\tau = \dfrac{\tau^{2}}{\rho}$ holds.   Now τ and ρ are linear quantities, and therefore their absolute dimensions depend upon the scale.

Thus, for one ship form a stream-line form can be derived, and from this form the next, and so on, until a complete system is obtained which will be, in actual dimensions, dependent upon the scale, and one drawing will represent many forms of varying scales.   Hence the stream-line motion round one ship's form will be exactly the same as for the same ship's form on another scale.   There must be a variation of velocity between the different dimensions at the corresponding points in the form, but we need not attempt to evaluate the exact velocities.   We only need to find the relationship between them.

Suppose A and B, fig. 133, are stream lines for the same form, but on different scales.   Let dimensions of A be m times those of B.

Let symbols with suffix A refer to tube A.

,, ,, ,, B ,, ,, B.

Then, by Bernoulli's equation, taking the datum line at still water level, where p_A and p_B are the super-atmospheric pressures,

$$\frac{v_A^2}{2g} + \frac{p_A}{w_A} + z_A = h_A$$

$$\frac{v_B^2}{2g} + \frac{p_B}{w_B} + z_B = h_B$$

Now $h_A = m h_B,$

and $z_A = m z_B.$

Hence $\dfrac{v_A^2}{2g} + \dfrac{p_A}{w_A} = m\left(\dfrac{v_B^2}{2g} + \dfrac{p_B}{w_B}\right).$

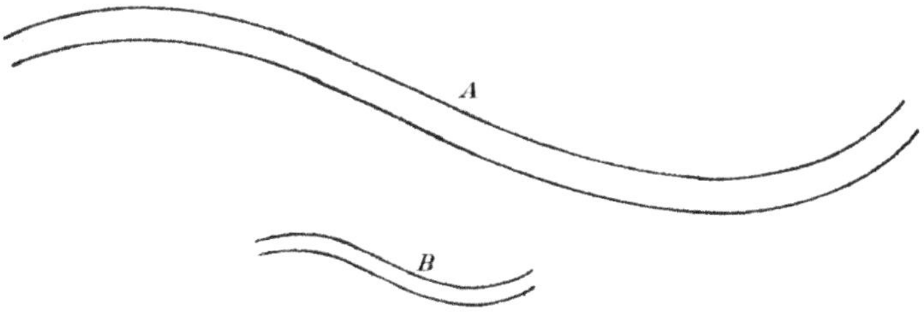

FIG. 133.

If $v_A^2 = m v_B^2,$

then $\dfrac{p_A}{w_A} = m\dfrac{p_B}{w_B}.$

The resistance is the total net resolved values of p, in a fore and aft direction, over the whole surface of ship.

Let dA and dB represent elements of area of surface of forms A and B.

Let θ be the inclination of the normal to the element with the middle line of waterplane.

Then, $\dfrac{\text{Resistance of A}}{\text{Resistance of B}} = \dfrac{\displaystyle\iint p_A dA \cos\theta \text{ all over A}}{\displaystyle\iint p_B dB \cos\theta \text{ all over B}}$

$$= m^3 \frac{w_A}{w_B}$$

$$= \frac{\text{cubic displacement of A} \times w_A}{\text{cubic displacement of B} \times w_B}$$

where w_A and w_B are the weights per cubic unit of the fluids in which A and B respectively are moving

$$= \frac{\text{displacement of A in tons}}{\text{displacement of B in tons}},$$

i.e. at speeds v_A and v_B where $v_A^2 = m v_B^2.$

We see from the above that the wavemaking resistance of similar ships at velocities related as $\sqrt{m}$ will vary as the displacement. This is Froude's law of comparison.

$$\text{Suppose} \qquad R_w = kD^{\alpha}V^{\beta}$$

in which D is the displacement, V the velocity, and k a coefficient which is constant for the same form.

For a smaller ship of same form,

$$r_w = kd^{\alpha}v^{\beta}$$

$$\text{and therefore} \qquad \frac{R_w}{r_w} = \left(\frac{D}{d}\right)^{\alpha}\left(\frac{V}{v}\right)^{\beta}.$$

From the law of comparison, if V and v be corresponding speeds,

$$\frac{V}{v} = \left(\frac{D}{d}\right)^{\frac{1}{6}}$$

$$\text{and} \qquad \frac{R_w}{r_w} = \frac{D}{d}.$$

And therefore, if the ships move in water of the same density,

$$\frac{D}{d} = \left(\frac{D}{d}\right)^{\alpha}\left(\frac{D}{d}\right)^{\frac{\beta}{6}}$$

$$\text{or} \qquad \left(\frac{D}{d}\right)^{\alpha+\frac{\beta}{6}-1} = 1,$$

$$\text{therefore} \qquad \alpha + \frac{\beta}{6} - 1 = 0.$$

Thus, if the wavemaking resistance can be expressed in such a manner, the above relationship must hold between α and β.

The following table gives the law for various values of α and β. For any value of β deduced from a curve of resistance of a given vessel, then the value of α which must satisfy the above equation is shown in the same column.

α	1	$\frac{5}{6}$	$\frac{2}{3}$	$\frac{1}{2}$	$\frac{1}{3}$	$\frac{1}{6}$	0
β	0	1	2	3	4	5	6
R_w	kD	$kD^{\frac{5}{6}}V$	$kD^{\frac{2}{3}}V^2$	$kD^{\frac{1}{2}}V^3$	$kD^{\frac{1}{3}}V^4$	$kD^{\frac{1}{6}}V^5$	kV^6

Hence, if the resistance for a given ship varies as the 6th power of speed, at a given speed, the displacement may be increased or decreased indefinitely by proportional enlargement or reduction without change of wavemaking resistance, at that speed.

The resistance due to eddy motion is found to vary as the square of the velocity and also as the cross-sectional area, and therefore follows a law $R = D^{\frac{2}{3}}V^2$; that is, it follows the law of comparison. It may therefore be included in the wavemaking resistance.

The skin resistance follows the law

$$R_f = \int SV^{1\cdot83},$$

and cannot, therefore, be included in the law of comparison.

Effect of Size on Economical Propulsion.—Let D_1, D_2 be the displacements of similarly shaped ships, R_1 the wavemaking resistance of D_1 at speed V_1. Then the wavemaking resistance of D_2 is, by Froude's law,

$$R_2 = \frac{D_2}{D_1}R_1 \text{ at speed } V_1\left(\frac{D_2}{D_1}\right)^{\frac{1}{6}} = V_2.$$

If we assume, in the neighbourhood of V_1 and V_2, that R_1 varies as V^n, the residuary resistance of the first at speed V_2 is

$$R_1\left(\frac{D_2}{D_1}\right)^{\frac{n}{6}},$$

so that the ratio of the resistance of the second to that of the first

$$\text{at speed } V_2 \text{ is } \quad \left(\frac{D_2}{D_1}\right)^{1-\frac{n}{6}},$$

and therefore the ratio of the resistance per ton of displacement, of the second to the first, is

$$\left(\frac{D_2}{D_1}\right)^{-\frac{n}{6}} = \left(\frac{D_1}{D_2}\right)^{\frac{n}{6}}.$$

Thus, if $D_2 > D_1$ and n is positive, the resistance per ton of displacement is smaller in the larger ship. At corresponding speeds the resistance varies as the displacement, and therefore the resistance per ton of displacement is the same in each.

Surface of Resistance.—We have seen that the wavemaking resistance of a ship is a function of the displacement and speed. Hence with these three variables we may form a surface. If we have a curve of resistances of a known form at different speeds, we can deduce the resistance of any sized vessel of similar form at any desired speed.

Thus we may draw a series of resistance curves for the same form at different displacements. We can thus obtain a "surface of resistance" such that the coordinates of any point on that surface represent the displacement, speed, and resistance at that speed and displacement. Such a surface is shown in fig. 134.

If we consider the plane $X O Y$ we see that, at corresponding speeds, the speed varies as (Displacement)$^{\frac{1}{6}}$. If therefore we draw curves like $A B C D$ and $A E F$ in the plane $X O Y$, so that, for these curves, $y^{\frac{1}{6}}$ varies as x where x and y are measured from the point of zero displacement parallel to $O X$ and $O Y$ respectively, these curves pass through points of corresponding speeds, and the resistance at any point is proportional to the displacement corresponding to that point. The standard curve is shown drawn in the plane $X O Z$. Knowing the displacement, 57·4 tons, corresponding to this curve, we can find the resistance at all points of corresponding speed. Thus if we make $O G$ equal to the resistance of the standard form at 13 knots and join $A G$, then, to find the resistance of a vessel of 40 tons at the speed represented by point H, we draw $L M$ and $H K$ parallel to $O Z$, where M is a point on the line $A G$, and make $H K = L M$. Then K is a point on the resistance surface. Thus we get curves shown by the full line $A K P$ corresponding to 13 knots for the standard form and A Q R which corresponds to 7 knots for the standard. These curves therefore project into straight lines A G and A S in the plane Y O Z. Intermediate spots, corresponding to any particular displacement, can be obtained from the law of corresponding speeds, and thus

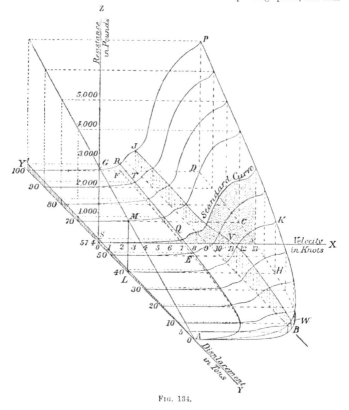

FIG. 134.

the whole series of curves shown can be drawn in. If we now draw any line B T parallel to Y O Y¹, and where it intersects the base line of each resistance curve we draw lines, as shown, parallel to O Z to meet the curves, we can draw a curve J V W showing the resistance of vessels of the same form but varying displacement, at a constant speed. In this case it is 9 knots. We notice in this case that it is easier to drive a ship of this form of 100 tons displacement at 9 knots, than one of 40 tons at the same speed.

Instead of plotting the resistance curves on a base of displacements, we can plot them, as in fig. 135, on a base of lengths.

In this case the curves A B D and A E F, in plane X O Y, at corresponding speeds, will be of the form y varies as x^2. Also, the resistances at corresponding speeds are proportional to the cube of the length, and therefore the projection of the curves A K P and A Q R in the plane Y O Z are curves of the form z varies as y^3.

Curve J V W shows a resistance curve, for various lengths of vessels, at a constant speed of 10 knots. It is seen that, at this speed, the value of R_{io} for a vessel of this form 130 feet long is less than for one 100 feet long, and therefore of less displacement.

The standard curve in these figures is taken from fig. 113, p. 143, and

$$\text{D corresponds to } \left(\frac{L}{100}\right)3 = 57\cdot4, \text{ with a parallel middle-body of 48 per cent.}$$

Fig. 126 shows curves of effective horse-power and displacement for the vessels A, B, C, and D, whose resistance curves are given in fig. 125. These curves have been calculated for speeds 12, 14, 16, and 18 knots, Froude's law having been applied. These are equivalent to the section J V W of fig. 134.

The " Greyhound" Experiments.—These were the first and most important experiments made in this country on a full-sized ship, and were carried out by Mr W. Froude. The primary object of the experiments was to verify the law of comparison.

In order to obtain definite results, the "Greyhound" was towed by another ship called the "Active," and the speed, force exerted, and time were automatically measured.

The arrangements of towing, in order to avoid the wake effect of the towing ship, are shown in fig. 136. No trouble was experienced in keeping the "Active" on a straight course.

Measurement of Speed.—The speed was registered by paying out a continuous length of twine attached to a log-ship consisting of a board 2½ feet square, and ballasted to sink 4 feet, and to set itself square to the motion. The twine was saturated with tallow, which improved its buoyancy and prevented contraction when wet. As the twine ran out it caused a drum to rotate. Time was marked upon this drum at equal intervals by means of a clock. To keep the log-ship clear of the wake, the line was run out over a 20-foot spar. The tension in the twine was kept constant, and caused a constant slip of about 0·3 knot.

A check on the log was given by the "Active's" screw, the number of revolutions very correctly indicating the speed.

Measurement of Towing Force.—This was measured by means of a dynamometer, in which the full force was brought to a piston of 14 inches diameter, and the magnitude of the pressure measured by means of the deflection of a spring attached to a piston of 1⅛-inch diameter. This deflection was reproduced on an enlarged scale on the recording drum previously mentioned, the recording apparatus being similar to that used in the plank experiments, and described at fig. 87. The force to be measured was the horizontal component of the tension in the tow-rope. This was effected by attaching the rope to a truck resting on a small length of railway on the "Greyhound's" deck, the after-end of the truck being linked to the dynamometer.

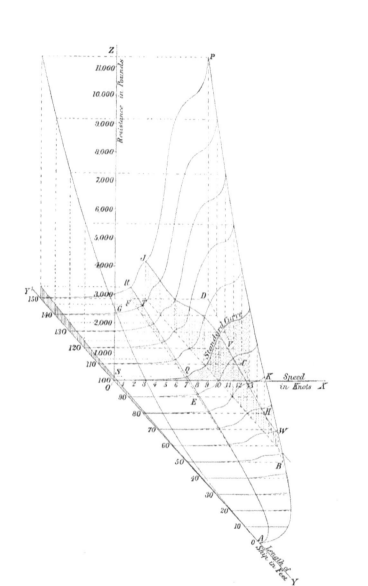

Fig. 135.

Wind Effect.—The resistance of the atmosphere had to be eliminated. The velocity and direction of the wind were determined by means of wind gauges. The tow-rope strain was measured when the ship moved with and against the wind with the same velocity, and also when the velocity of the wind varied.

Acceleration or Retardation Effect.—When the ship is being towed, the

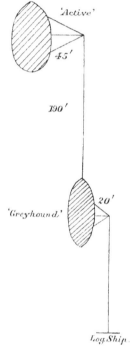

'Active'

45'

190'

'Greyhound'   *20'*

Log.Ship.

FIG. 136.

total registered strain on the rope is resistance of the water + or − the force necessary to accelerate or retard the mass of the ship and the water surrounding her.

If the speed is uniform, the second term on the right-hand side is zero. Any variation of speed would be at once shown on the automatic record, and from that record the acceleration or retardation can be calculated. If the velocity of the ship increase, so also, on account of the stream-line action, does the velocity of every part of the system, and the force thus necessary must be derived from the ship. The virtual mass of the ship is, in other words, greater than its actual mass.

The virtual mass was experimentally determined by slipping the tow-rope when the ship was going at a high rate of speed, and observing from the automatic record the rate at which the speed of the ship was destroyed by her resistance. From this record a curve of travel-time was obtained, and, by graphic differentiation, a curve of speed-time was deduced. A further graphic differentiation gave a curve of retardation-time.

At any speed let the water resistance be R (previously observed), and let f^{1} be the observed retardation at that speed. Let m_s be the mass of the ship and m_w the mass of the accompanying water, so that the virtual mass is $m_w + m_s$.

$$\text{Then} \qquad (m_w + m_s)f^{1} = \text{R}.$$

Thus m_w is deduced.

Acceleration experiments were also carried out, but were not very successful, owing to the alternate slackening and tightening of the rope.

For value of $\dfrac{m_w}{m_s}$ Mr Froude gave 0·2 for deep draughts and 0·16 for lighter draughts.

Results of Trials.—The ship was tested under different draughts, and under different trims for each draught. The particulars were :

Draught	13′ 9″	13′ 0″	12′ 1″
Surface in square feet . . .	7540	7260	6940
Displacement in tons . . .	1160	1050	938
Length	172′ 6″		
Beam	33′ 2″		
Trim	Varied from 1′ 6″ by the head to 4′ 6″ by the stern		

The speeds varied from 3 to 12½ knots. The normal displacement was 1160 tons, and the normal draught 13′ 6″ forward and 14′ 0″ aft. The ship was tried in this condition with and without bilge keels. The change of trim for each displacement did not alter the wetted surface.

Effect of Speed on Resistance.—Up to 6 knots R varies as V². Above 6 knots it increases at a greater rate. The tow-rope strain at different speeds was—

Speed in feet per minute . .	400	560	720	880	1,040	1,200	1,230
Tow-rope strain in pounds . .	1,001	1,940	3,420	5,900	10,100	17,400	23,300

Effect of Alteration in Trim.—This did not affect the resistance to any great extent. From 8 to 10 knots there was no appreciable difference under extreme trims. Generally, as the ship is down by the head, the resistance is increased at the higher and diminished at the lower speeds. With bilge keels, the advantage of the ship at high speeds when trimmed greatly by the stern was not maintained.

Effect of Draught.—The resistance was less at light than at normal draught. Increased displacement did not cause the total resistance to

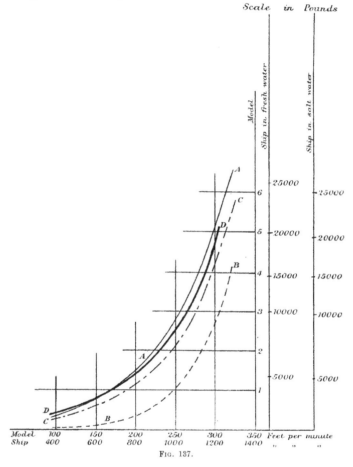

FIG. 137.

increase at anything like the same rate for the same speed. This indicates the economy of deep-draught vessels.

Bilge Keels.—The extra resistance, when these were fitted, was less than that caused by the skin friction alone. This would indicate that the surface changed slightly for the better. Possibly some of the bilge keel was in the frictional wake, where its resistance would be less than that of the average surface of the ship.

Test of Law of Comparison.—The curves for the " Greyhound " are shown in fig. 137. The curve A A represents the total resistance of the model, curve B B represents the wavemaking resistance of the model. On a different scale, B B will represent the wavemaking resistance of ship, and C C the total resistance of the ship. The curve D D represents the actual curve of resistance obtained from the towing experiments. The coefficient of friction of the " Greyhound " was assumed to be that of a varnished surface, which was less than it actually was. The test of the law is whether the ratio of the vertical distances between the curves D and B, and C and B, is a constant ratio, *i.e.* whether curves C and D can be made to coincide by a change in *f*. The following table gives the ratio at different speeds :—

Speed in feet per minute . .	700	800	900	1000	1100	1200
Ratio.	1·36	1·39	1·36	1·30	1·33	1·30

Thus the ratio is practically constant, and so the "law of corresponding speeds" is verified. In other words, by choosing a value of *f* which would give D D as the estimated total resistance instead of C C, we get a complete verification of the law of comparison and the modern theory of resistance. The value of *f* necessary to arrive at this result is a reasonable one, a little higher than that due to a varnished surface.

CHAPTER XII.

RESISTANCE RESULTS AND METHOD OF STANDARDISING.

It is desirable to eliminate the element of absolute size from the comparison of resistances of various forms; in other words, to standardise resistance results in a similar way to that which has been attempted in strength and stability. The method of standardising form has been explained in Vol. I., Chapter XI., and in this volume in Chapter III. All forms are reduced to the same length and set off as 40″ long, so that if L be the length of a ship in feet the scale upon which waterlines and body-plans are set off is 1 in. = $\frac{L}{40}$ ft., or $\frac{40}{L}$ ins. = 1 ft. For a vessel 320 feet long the scale would be ⅛th of an inch to the foot.

Mr Froude has devised a method which is based upon the three variables —displacement, resistance, and speed. The underlying assumption in this case is that the results should be plotted to variables which give the most serviceable *available* criterion of performance, and that these are given if we know the degree of resistance at a given speed for a given displacement.

The standardised values of speed are called K, and the standardised value of resistance C. To standardise speed it is related to $\Delta^{\frac{1}{6}}$, and resistance is related directly to the displacement Δ.

For similar forms of different displacements (neglecting " the skin-friction correction " due to the true friction not following the law of comparison), we have—

(1) At corresponding speeds, K and C are constant. From this follows—

(2) *For dissimilar forms of the same given displacement and speed*, K should be constant and C proportional to the resistance.

Corresponding speeds are expressed by the relation $K = \dfrac{V}{\Delta^{\frac{1}{6}}} = \text{constant}$

(Δ being the displacement and V the speed).

C can be expressed in the form of $\dfrac{R}{\Delta}$, and when plotted to a base of K would give a measure of the *degree* or intensity of resistance, which would be independent of size in so far as displacement measures size. But this gives inconvenient values for diagram purposes. To obviate this, the values of C are plotted so that $C = \dfrac{R}{\Delta K^2}$, which is merely an alteration of scale, as K is constant.

Substituting for K its value $\dfrac{V}{\Delta^{\frac{1}{6}}}$ we have

$$C = \frac{R}{\Delta^{\frac{2}{3}} V^2},$$

This can be made similar to the inverse of the well-known Admiralty co-efficient if we further modify it by multiplying numerator and denominator by V, so that

$$C = \frac{RV}{\Delta^{\frac{2}{3}} V^3} = \frac{E.H.P.}{\Delta^{\frac{2}{3}} V^3},$$

expressing E.H.P. not in the usual units, but in the same units in which R and V are expressed:

The unit for dimensions of hull is the value $U = \Delta^{\frac{1}{3}}$, and the unit of K is chosen from the speed of the wave, having a length $= \frac{U}{2}$, which expressed in feet, seconds, and cubic feet units gives one unit of $K = \sqrt{\frac{g}{4\pi}}$, so that K for any speed V expressed in ft. per sec. will be in these units,

$$K = \frac{V}{\Delta^{\frac{1}{6}}} \sqrt{\frac{4\pi}{g}} \text{ (where } \Delta \text{ is in cubic feet).}$$

The region of speed which corresponds to a value 1 of K is 7 knots for a 5000 tons ship. When K is unity the value of R is about $\frac{1}{1000}$th of the displacement in a cruiser or Channel steamer form, so that the ratio $C = \frac{R}{\Delta K^2}$ is more conveniently expressed as

$$C = \frac{R}{\Delta K^2} \times 1000, \text{ and these are the values actually used.}$$

There is no real constancy in C for all dimensions or displacements, even in similar forms, as surface friction does not follow the law of comparison. The method of taking account of this is to set off the proper value of C for a standard length of, say, 300 feet, and then to calculate the difference in surface friction due to the altered dimensions, having length x. This correction is added to the C value if x is less than 300 feet, and subtracted from it if x is greater than 300 feet. This has been fully worked out, and the results are shown by curves on the Iso-K diagrams, see fig. 141. Thus we at first assume that the whole of the resistance conforms to the law of comparison, and finally make a correction for skin friction.

It has been shown, p. 168, that when resistance varies as the square of the speed for a form of standard dimensions, it will vary as the wetted surface S for other dimensions at the same speed. Further, if the resistance varies as S and as the square of the speed, it will vary as Sn at corresponding speeds, $i.e.$ it will vary as n^3, which is the same as by the law of comparison. Hence we can introduce a friction resistance correction by making a deduction of

$$Sf(V^2 - V^{1\cdot83}).$$

If f varies with alteration of size, this has to be allowed for; but for ships above 200 feet long there is not sufficient reliable data to say that it does. S expressed in standard units above would be $\frac{S}{U^2}$, where S is the wetted surface in square feet and U^2 is $\Delta^{\frac{2}{3}}$ in square feet. This is expressed as a "skin constant" or skin coefficient, and is analogous to a midship area or waterplane area coefficient.

The length constant or coefficient is called M, and is $\frac{L}{U}$, where L is length between perpendiculars. This gives us a measure of the length for a given displacement. It is evident that the greater the displacement in a given length, the smaller M will be.

As the wavemaking features depend on the ratio of the length to the speed, a further constant or coefficient called L, the length-speed constant or coefficient, is introduced. The unit selected for L is that which is obtained from a wave of length $=\frac{l}{2}$ (L.B.P.) instead of as in unit K, which is obtained from a wave-length $\frac{U}{2}$.

In the same units as before, one unit of $L = \sqrt{\dfrac{g}{4\pi}}$, and $\therefore$ for speed V,

$$L = \frac{V}{\sqrt{L}} \times \sqrt{\frac{4\pi}{g}}$$

$$= \frac{K}{\sqrt{M}} \quad \text{since} \quad M = \frac{L}{\Delta^{\frac{1}{3}}} \quad \text{and} \quad K = \frac{V}{\Delta^{\frac{1}{6}}}\sqrt{\frac{4\pi}{g}}.$$

L is of value in comparing the results of forms which differ only in longitudinal scale, since in such cases it is at the common value of L that wavemaking conditions correspond.*

If we plot the results of a resistance (C) intensity curve for a given *form* of ship to a base of K, it will be a C K curve to a constant M value. $C = \frac{R}{\Delta^{\frac{2}{3}}V^2} \times 2938$. Therefore for a given value of $\frac{V}{\Delta^{\frac{1}{6}}}$, *i.e.* for $\frac{V^2}{\Delta^{\frac{1}{3}}}$ constant, C gives a value of $\frac{R}{\Delta}$.

If we have different forms, each will have a C K curve, and generally each curve will have a different value for M. If we set off a series of these curves, each for a definite value of M, we can get cross curves of M and C for constant values of K. But these curves will not necessarily be fair or continuous unless the variations in Δ and L which determine M are made on some systematic basis which represents a gradual and systematic variation in these

---

* Where V is speed in knots, Δ is displacement in tons in salt water, L is length in feet between perpendiculars, and S is wetted skin area in square feet.

(1) The speed constant $\qquad K = \dfrac{V}{\Delta^{\frac{1}{6}}} \times \cdot 5834.$

(2) The resistance constant $\qquad C = \dfrac{\text{E.H.P.}}{\Delta^{\frac{2}{3}}V^3} \times 427 \cdot 1.$

(3) The length-speed constant $\qquad L = \dfrac{V}{\sqrt{L}} \times 1 \cdot 0552.$

(4) The length constant $\qquad M = \dfrac{L}{\Delta^{\frac{1}{3}}} \times \cdot 3057.$

(5) The linear dimensions constant $= \dfrac{\text{Dimensions}}{\Delta^{\frac{1}{3}}} \times \cdot 3057.$

(6) The skin constant $\qquad S = \dfrac{S}{\Delta^{\frac{2}{3}}} \times \cdot 09346.$

quantities. Such a systematic variation, for instance, would be made if length and draught remained unchanged while Δ was changed by reducing all breadth measurements in the *same* proportion.

A series made by *varying the proportion* would give systematic variation of M, which if C were plotted to the base of M for constant K value would give a fair curve showing the modification of C in terms of variation of the breadth proportion.

Other systematic variations might be adopted, such as altering the draught proportion without altering breadth ; or by retaining the ratio of breadth to draught, but altering both in the same proportion.

All these variations could be made on *one parent form*. Several parent forms differing from each other may be taken, and the same systematic variations be made in these. The results will enable us to see the relative effect of the same variation on different forms.

Mr Froude published in the *Transactions I.N.A.* in 1904 the result of an investigation of the change in C which accompanied systematic variations, most of which were of a purely proportional character. He took a vessel of the cruiser form, $350 \times 57 \times 22'$ draught, from which he formed five other distinct forms, making six in all. The modifications in form were made entirely in the last 6 per cent. of the length at the fore end, and the same per cent. at the after end. The dimensions and other particulars are given in the following table :—

SERIES A.

Type.	Length.	Beam.	Draught.	Dis-place-ment.	Block Co-efficient.	Prismatic Co-efficients.		Mid Sec. Coefficient.	Snubbing from type 1.
	Feet.	Feet.	Feet.			F.B.	A.B.		
1	350	57	22	6100	·486	·538	·570	·877	
2	340	,,	,,	6083	·500	·538	·601	,,	A.B. 10 ft.
3	330	,,	,,	6056	·514	·538	·634	,.	A.B. 20 ft.
4	325	,,	,,	6048	·521	·553	·634	,,	F.B. 5 ft. / A.B. 20 ft.
5	320	,,	,,	6037	·528	·567	·634	,,	F.B. 10 ft. / A.B. 20 ft.
6	310	,,	,,	6008	·541	·598	·634	,,	F.B. 20 ft. / A.B. 20 ft.

The changes made from type 1 are indicated in the right-hand column. 2 to 6 were produced from 1 by snubbing the ends of the lines as in fig. 138.

Hence there are six distinct forms, differing in length, fulness, and proportions of length and breadth. Each of these forms has a distinct C K curve, which (neglecting skin-friction correction) will give the resistance for all speeds and displacements within the limits upon which the experiments were carried out. To each form there will be a definite M value ; and as the variation in M is due to a systematic variation in the amount of snubbing, it is possible to plot M in terms of amount snubbed at each end separately.

Similar variations were made on another set of proportions of the same type of lines. The following table gives similar particulars to those for Series A :—

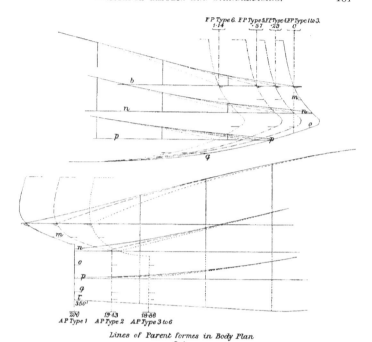

Lines of Parent formes in Body Plan

Fig. 138.

SERIES B.

Type.	Length.	Beam.	Draught.	Dis-placement.	Block Co-efficient.	Prismatic Co-efficients.		Mid Sec. Coefficient.	Snubbing from type 1.
	Feet.	Feet.	Feet.			F.B.	A.B.		
1	350	66	19	6100	·486	·538	·570	·877	
2	340	,,	,,	6083	·500	·538	·601	,,	A.B. 10 ft.
3	330	,,	,,	6056	·514	·538	·634	,,	A.B. 20 ft.
4	325	,,	,,	6048	·521	·553	·634	,,	{ F.B. 5 ft. { A.B. 20 ft.
5	320	,,	,,	6037	·528	·567	·634	,,	{ F.B. 10 ft. { A.B. 20 ft.
6	310	,,	,,	6008	·541	·598	·634	,,	{ F.B. 20 ft. { A.B. 20 ft.

Further variations from these two series were made by altering the scale of the cross-sectional area curve, the proportions of beam to draught remaining unaltered. The following tables show the method by which this variation was effected in type 1, and the consequent changes in dimensions :—

TYPE 1.

A.

2,500 tons $350 \times 36\cdot50 \times 14\cdot10$
3,500 ,, $350 \times 43\cdot20 \times 16\cdot68$
4,750 ,, $350 \times 50\cdot3 \times 19\cdot41$
6,100 ,, $350 \times 57\cdot00 \times 22\cdot00$
8,000 ,, $350 \times 65\cdot25 \times 25\cdot20$
10,500 ,, $350 \times 74\cdot80 \times 28\cdot88$

B.

1,250 tons $350 \times 29\cdot88 \times 8\cdot60$
1,750 ,, $350 \times 35\cdot35 \times 10\cdot18$
2,500 ,, $350 \times 42\cdot26 \times 12\cdot17$
3,500 ,, $350 \times 50\cdot00 \times 14\cdot40$
4,750 ,, $350 \times 58\cdot25 \times 16\cdot77$
6,100 ,, $350 \times 66\cdot00 \times 19\cdot00$
7,750 ,, $350 \times 74\cdot40 \times 21\cdot42$

Similar models were made for each of the other five types, with one or two exceptions in which results appeared not to be necessary or desirable to be obtained, the only variation in the other types being in that of length and snubbing, the cross-sectional dimensions being the same as in this variation for type 1.

The results of all the experiments are standardised in the manner already described, *i.e.* C values are recorded in terms of M for constant values of K. These are called iso-K curves, and are really C M curves, each for a fixed value of K. The whole of the results of the A and B series, with the proportion variations as described, were given by Mr Froude in the *Transactions I.N.A.* One set of C M curves for a K value of 2·8 was given. The other results were given in tabular form.

The C and M values given by Mr Froude in tabular form, as well as the one set in diagram form, are, however, all given here in iso-K diagrams for K values of 2·0, 2·4, 2·8, 3·2, 3·6, 4·0, 4·4, and 4·8. See figs. 139–146.*

* The skin friction correction curves in figs. 139–146 are rather faint except in fig. 141. As, however, this correction is precisely the same for all values of K and M, reference may be always made to fig. 141 for the necessary correction.

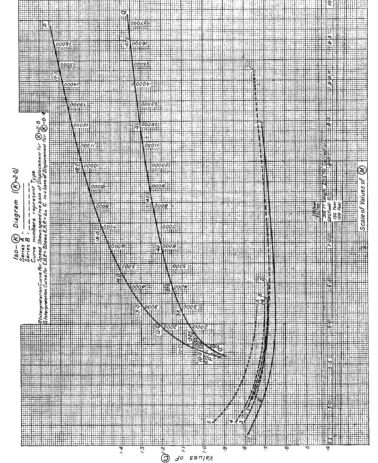

FIG. 139.

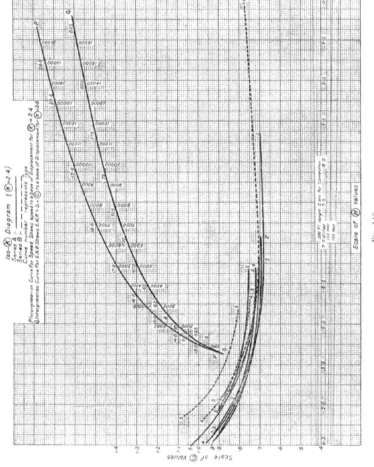

Fig. 140.

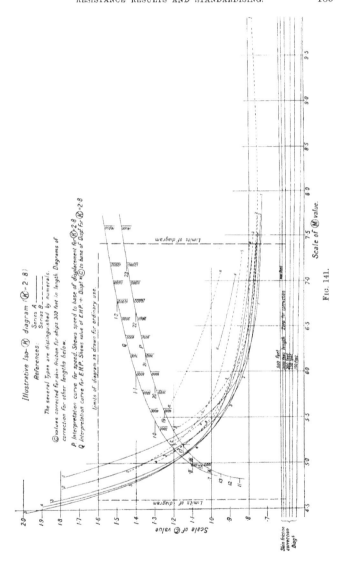

FIG. 141.

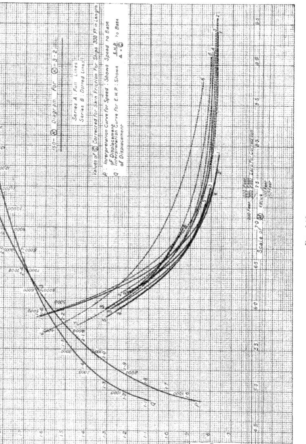

FIG. 142.

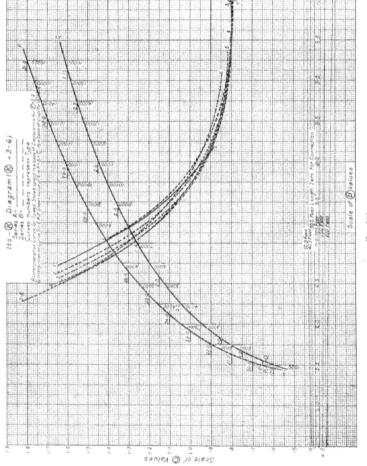

Fig. 143.

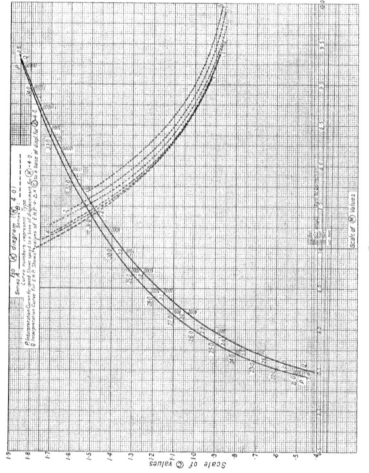

Fig. 144.

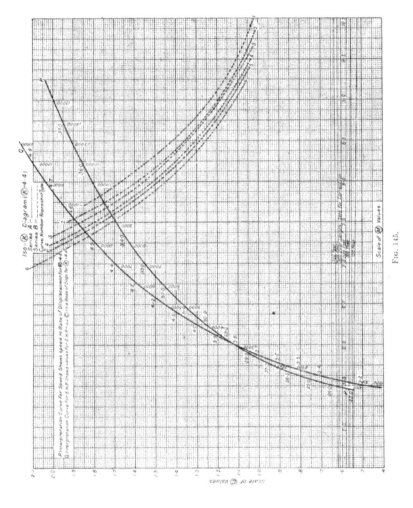

Fig. 145.

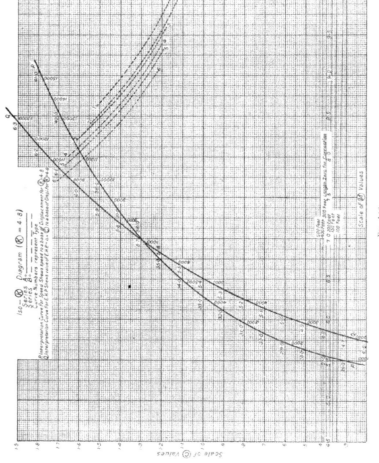

Fig. 146.

The results under series A are directly applicable to designs where the ratio of draught to breadth is ·386, and series B to designs where the ratio of draught to breadth is ·288, and the mid-area form coincides with the one given, viz. having a coefficient of ·8775.

For ratios of draught to beam between these two and slightly beyond their range the nature of the variation of C may be taken as arithmetical, i.e. for any variation in the draught to breadth ratio between ·288 and ·386

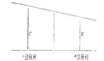

·288   ·386

Fig. 147.

the value of C is the ordinate at the value of the ratio on the straight line joining the C values at ·288 and ·386 respectively. See fig. 147.

Mr Froude goes further, however, and states that the ratio of draught to beam in either of the two series can be modified, and the mid-area coefficient correspondingly, within certain limits, without altering the resistance provided the mid-area and the longitudinal distribution of displacement are maintained (see fig. 148). This enables one to use the given data directly

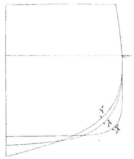

Fig. 148.

for a design with a slightly different form of section such as is given by a different rise of floor to that for which the data were made.

Generally stated, Mr Froude's conclusions are *that the resistance of a form is determined solely by the curve of the cross-section areas, together with the extreme beam and the surface waterline of the forebody*, provided that the lines are fair, and that no features are introduced which may cause serious eddymaking.

From the above statements it will be seen that, as a guide to the estimation of resistance, the prismatic is better than the block coefficient.

It should be noted that in applying these data to a cruiser form with extended bow and stern the waterline length is not the length over which the block and prismatic coefficients and the M values have been calculated, whereas in a merchant-steamer design that would generally be the case ; the displacements of the immersed counter and ram have been taken into account, however, in obtaining these coefficients and M values.

It will best serve the purpose of explaining these curves if we take an illustration of their application to a particular case. Suppose that it is required to find the E.H.P. for a vessel $330' \times 42' \times 12.096'$ draught, of a displacement of 2395 tons and speed of 25 knots. The ratio of draught to beam is ·288, and the block coefficient is ·5 ; hence the vessel is of type 2 series B as regards the ratio and the coefficient mentioned. The M value is $\frac{L}{\Delta^{\frac{1}{3}}}$·3057, which is equal to 7·53 ; and the K value, corresponding to 25 knots, is $\frac{V}{\Delta^{\frac{1}{6}}}$·5834, which is equal to 4·0. At the M value of 7·53, the C value for curve 2, series B, should now be read off on the sheet marked iso-K 4·0 (fig. 144) : the value for C so obtained is 1·550 for a vessel of length 300 feet. As the vessel under consideration has a length of 330 feet, a skin-friction correction in this C value has to be made. This can be read off from fig. 141, and the correction will be found to be ·005. As the length of 330 feet is an increase over the standard 300 feet, the "rate of power" will be diminished from 1·550, by ·005, to 1·545. From the formula $\text{E.H.P.} = \frac{\Delta^{\frac{2}{3}} \times V^3 C}{427 \cdot 1}$ we get, by substituting $\Delta = 2395$, $V = 25$, and $C = 1.545$, the value for E.H.P. is 8300.

If the lines for type 2 be proportioned to the above dimensions of length, breadth, and draught, the vessel obtained will require 8300 E.H.P. to steam 25 knots. This vessel would have an immersed piece aft of the 330 feet from the fore perpendicular, as in the cruiser type for which these data were compiled. If the new design had been a merchant ship with the load line terminating at the after perpendicular, in order to use these tank results a correction for the immersed counter would have to be made ; taking the counter as 4·6 per cent. of the length between perpendiculars, the design, instead of being considered as having an L value of length between perpendiculars of 330 feet, could have been considered as having L = 316 feet, and an immersed part thereafter for 14 feet. The block coefficient over this shortened length would have been ·522 instead of ·50 over the 330 feet, and the M value $\left(\frac{L}{\Delta^{\frac{1}{3}}} \times .3057 \right) = 7 \cdot 2$ instead of 7·53. To obtain the E.H.P. for this vessel necessitates interpolating between the types 4 and 5 ; the C values for this type at M = 7·21 is 1·655 for the standard length of 300 feet ; correcting for the length of 316 feet, this becomes 1·652, and the E.H.P. is 8800. Thus, by shortening the waterline by the length of the immersed counter, and carrying the same displacement, on the same breadth and draught, for a speed of 25 knots, the E.H.P. is increased from 8300 to 8800.

Reverting to the cruiser type, let us, as a further illustration, find the E.H.P. required to propel the same displacement on the same length and co-efficient, but with a different ratio of draught to beam, say of ·386, the dimensions will then be $330 \times 36 \cdot 29 \times 14$ feet draught, and the displacement and block coefficient will be as before for the cruiser type, and correspond to type 2 series A.

It is not possible to obtain the power for this vessel at 25 knots, as the range of the curves is not sufficient in this type to reach this speed. At 20·2 knots, corresponding to a K value of 3·2, a comparison of the powers can be made, as series B and A are both extended to this speed.

For the former vessel, type 2, ratio of draught to beam ·288, dimensions 330′ × 42′ × 12·096′ and 2395 tons displacement, the C value at 20·2 knots is ·818 and the E.H.P. 2830 ; for the latter vessel, same type, ratio of draught to beam ·386, dimensions 330 × 36·29 × 14 feet and 2395 tons displacement, the C value is ·780 and the E.H.P. 2700.

For the same vessel with any ratio of draught to beam between ·288 and ·386, and slightly beyond these limits, the variation in C value (and consequent E.H.P.) is inversely proportionate to the variation of this ratio for this speed. Thus for a vessel 330 × 40 × 12·7′ draught, and 2395 tons displacement at 20·2 knots, the C value is obtained as follows : the ratio of draught to beam is ·318 and the C value is $\left\{ ·818 - \left(\dfrac{·03 \times ·038}{·098}\right) \right\} = ·806$; the E.H.P. corresponding is 2790.

In a similar manner the E.H.P. for any vessel within the range of these data can be determined.

Applying Froude's Table of C.—From the foregoing it may be seen that the resistance of a form of given displacement and speed may be found if the choice of dimensions is quite free. The form must necessarily be one of the types 1 to 6 of the series A or B, varied only by varying the scale of the cross-sectional areas of the parent curves. This fixes the type of cross section to that of either A or B, and consequently fixes the ratio of beam to draught to that one of these two forms, i.e. to 57 : 22 = 2·59 or 66 : 19 = 3·47. Neither section may suit the circumstances of the case, and it may be necessary to make two variations on the type of section, and to adopt—

(1) some other proportion of beam to draught than 2·59 or 3·47 ;
(2) some other form of section.

(1) If for a given displacement and length, and therefore M value, it is decided that a particular type number of A or B will give the best results as to C value, but that a different ratio of beam to draught is necessary, it is easy to produce a form fulfilling this further condition. The breadth and draught corresponding to the given value of displacement and L can be determined from fig. 149, the type number and the letter A or B fixing them exactly. If the ratio of beam to draught that is required or the actual beam or the actual draught be fixed, we shall get a corresponding draught or beam respectively from the condition that the product of the altered beam and draught must be the same as the product of the beam and draught determined from fig. 149.

Thus suppose L, B and D to be length, beam, and draught respectively as determined from the given displacement from the chosen type, say 6 A, and suppose, for instance, that it is necessary to have a beam B_1, the draught D_1 of the altered form will have to be

$$D_1 = \frac{BD}{B_1}.$$

If now all the waterline spacings be altered on the type 6 A in the ratio of $\dfrac{D_1}{22}$, and the half-breadth ordinates in the ratio of $\dfrac{B_1}{57}$, we shall have the ordinates for a form fulfilling the required conditions.

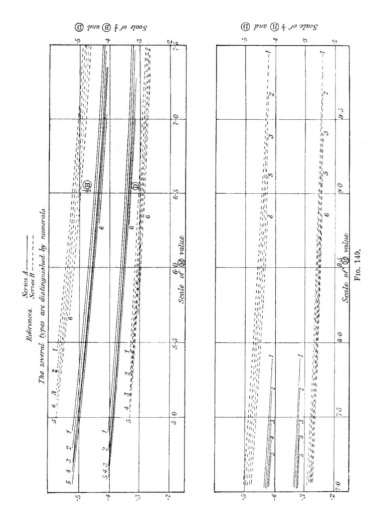

Fig. 149.

To determine the C value for such a form it is necessary to know the variation of C in terms of variation of $\dfrac{\text{beam}}{\text{draught}}$ between 2·59 and 3·47. This has been determined, and it is found that between these limits and a little beyond, the variation varies directly as the ratio $\dfrac{B}{D}$.

Suppose, for instance, for $\dfrac{B}{D}$ value of 2·59 and 3·47 the C values are known, then for any intermediate value of $\dfrac{B}{D}$ the value of C can be measured directly from a diagram such as fig. 147.

(2) It is evident, however, that while this method of variation of form adds greatly to the range of form which can be adopted with known results, it does not include all forms of the given displacement and length. It only includes forms of one parent type of section, the modifications all being made by altering the length, breadth, and draught ratios proportionately throughout.

Sections A and B, fig. 150, represent the midship sections of the parent

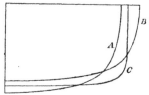

Fig. 150.

types having ratios $\dfrac{B}{D}$ of 2·59 and 3·47 respectively. Suppose it is desired to have for a given displacement and length a midship section of form C such as is now common in nearly all ships. To determine from the parent forms types 1 to 6 a form having such a midship section, it is necessary to determine the effect upon the resistance of a change of cross section from A or B other than dealt with.

It has been found by experiment that the resistance of form of about the character of types 1 to 6 having other types of cross sections depends on—

(1) the curve of cross-sectional areas ;
(2) the beam of the ship ;
(3) the form of the waterline forward ; and that if these three are unaltered, considerable shipshape variations in cross sections can be made without affecting resistance.

Suppose it is desired to adopt a section of form C having an area co-efficient of say ·95. It is necessary to show how to get the complete form so that the curves of cross-sectional areas shall be unaltered. For a form X, see fig. 151, having the same characteristics and sectional area as A or B we can determine the actual resistance as already explained. One condition must be that $Oa : Ox : Ob :: \dfrac{1}{Oc} : \dfrac{1}{Oy} : \dfrac{1}{Od}$.

Also the area coefficient must be the same in all cases, viz. ·877.

Suppose that we want to find the resistance of a form having the same prismatic coefficient as A or B, viz. ·598 in the fore-body and ·634 in the after-body, but with a midship area coefficient of ·95. It is to be remembered that if the beam, the waterline form, and the curve of cross-sectional areas are all the same the resistance will be the same ; and we may assume that if we retain the curve of cross-sectional areas and reduce the waterline areas the necessary amount to get the same displacement, we shall not increase the resistance. First find the value of Ob and Od, the half beam and draught that will give the required displacement. Suppose B and d to be the values of beam and draught of the form C which will be satisfactory and will give the

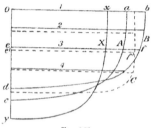

Fig. 151.

same displacement and therefore midship section area as in the form B. The resistance of the form C may be taken as not more than that of form B.

To obtain the actual form which the sections other than the midship one will have, it is necessary to divide up C vertically by the same number of equally spaced waterlines as B. All ordinates of each corresponding waterline of B must be altered in the proportion of the ordinate of the midship section of the same waterline. For instance, all the ordinates of No. 3 water-line of the B form, if multiplied by the ratio $\frac{e'f'}{ef}$, will give the corresponding waterlines of C. In this way a form can be produced whose midship section will have a coefficient of ·95 and whose resistance will be not more than that of B.

We may also apply this method to find the resistance of forms having ends similar to C, but having a parallel middle body.

CHAPTER XIII.

SADLER'S RESISTANCE RESULTS.

PROFESSOR SADLER of Michigan University carried out a series of experiments upon forms which were varied systematically from a parent form much fuller than that upon which Dr Froude's experiments, described in the last chapter, were based. The experiments upon the effect of varying lengths of midship body, or straight of breadth as it is technically called, which were published by the elder Froude in 1877, were made with ends the same in all cases.

The experiments published by Professor Sadler were made to determine the effect upon resistance of variation in the longitudinal distribution of buoyancy. Starting with a form of about the Atlantic intermediate type of steamer of about 500 feet long and 16 knots speed, he modified the distribution of buoyancy longitudinally by—

(a) putting as much as was practicable in the parallel middle, and

(b) by putting as little as practicable.

The forms as represented by curves of cross-sectional area are as in fig. 152 (over).

Body Plan Forms I & III

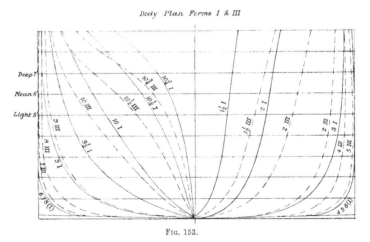

FIG. 153.

The body-plan forms of I. and III. are shown above in fig. 153.

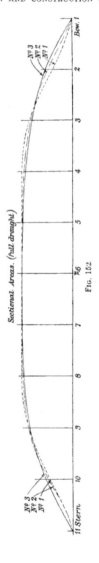

FIG. 152

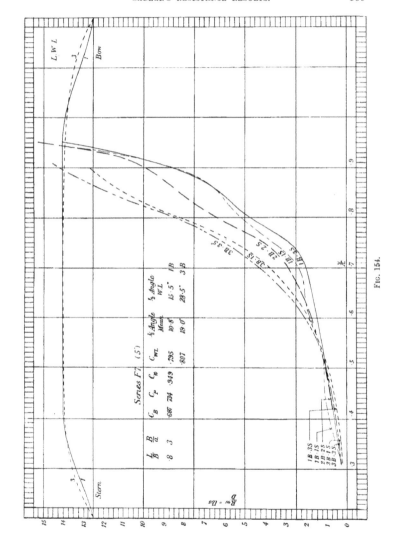

FIG. 154.

Each of these forms was tried at three different draughts, corresponding to ballast, intermediate, and load trim.

Given in ratios they are as follows :—

$\dfrac{L}{B}$.	$\dfrac{B}{D}$.	$\dfrac{L}{D}$.	Coefficients.		
			Block.	Prism.	Midship.
8	3·0	24	·697	·734	·949
8	2·5	20	·715	·747	·956
8	2·143	17·143	·733	·760	·964

In addition to the results from these forms, the stern of No. 3 was run with the bow of No. 1, and *vice versa*. Hence five models in all were tried, each at three draughts, giving fifteen resistance curves in all. The wetted surface being practically the same in all forms at the same draught, the results are plotted in terms of wave-making resistance only, one set of curves for each draught.

The abscissæ of the curves are $\dfrac{V}{\sqrt{L}}$ (V in knots and L in feet), ranging in value from ·2 to ·9, which values correspond to about $4\frac{1}{2}$ knots to 20 knots in a 500-feet ship.

The ordinates are resistances in lbs. per ton of displacement in salt water. Hence the results may be said to be standardised, though not in the same way as Dr Froude has standardised by the method already described.

The general character of a curve of resistance is the same at all draughts for a given model. The value of $\dfrac{V}{\sqrt{L}} = ·55$ (12·22 knots in a 500-feet ship) gives approximately the same results for all forms at the two deeper draughts, and a minimum of difference even in the lightest draught.

From this value of $\dfrac{V}{\sqrt{L}}$ to the practical limit of speed at which such ships would be run, viz. at ·7, there is a very rapid variation in resistance, the fine bow with the full stern giving the best results except in the lightest draughts for values between ·55 and ·65. For lower speeds than ·55 the worst form is

COMPARATIVE WAVE-MAKING RESISTANCE.

$\dfrac{V}{\sqrt{L}}$.	Light Draft.	Medium Draft.	Deep Draft.
·6	1·0 : 1·448	1·0 : 1·24	1·0 : 1·457
·65	1·0 : 1·715	1·0 : 1·57	1·0 : 1·545
·7	1·0 : 2·150	1·0 : 1·945	1·0 : 1·75
·75	1·0 : 2·130	1·0 : 1·925	1·0 : 1·68

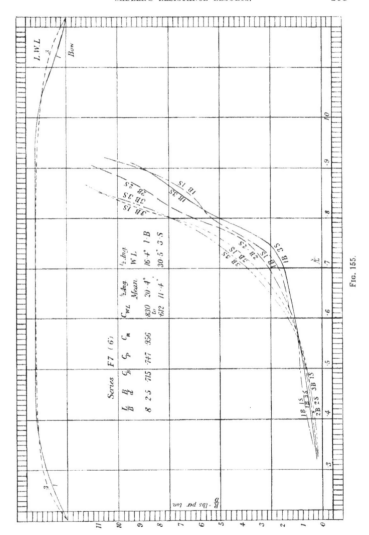

FIG. 155.

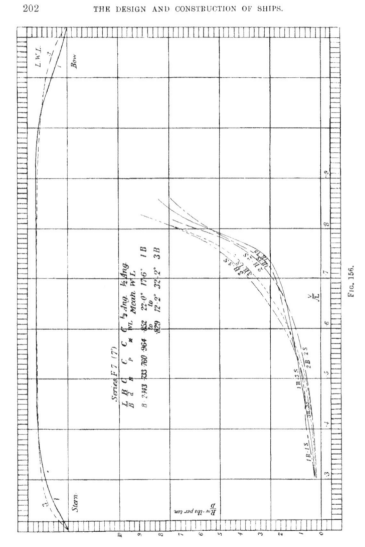

FIG. 156.

generally that with the finest bow and stern, the best being that with the full
bow and stern except at the lightest draught, where the usual ship form is
slightly better. Altogether it seems that the least resistance at practical
speeds for the given fineness of form is given by a vessel with full stern
and fine bow. The results in tabular form are given in the preceding and
following tables :—

COMPARATIVE TOTAL RESISTANCE.

$\dfrac{V}{\sqrt{L}}$.	Light Draft.	Medium Draft.	Deep Draft.
·6	1·0 : 1·075	1·0 : 1·053	1·0 : 1·055
·65	1·0 : 1·16	1·0 : 1·14	1·0 : 1·13
·7	1·0 : 1·26	1·0 : 1·222	1·0 : 1·20
·75	1·0 : 1·305	1·0 : 1·262	1·0 : 1·20

These figures indicate the ratio between the resistance of a vessel with
fine bow and full stern to one with full bow and stern.

Further experiments were undertaken on the same lines as the preceding
with models of finer and fuller block coefficients than the ·733 of the foregoing. They were then all compared. The particulars of the models are
given below.

Series No.	$\dfrac{L}{B}$.	$\dfrac{B}{d}$.	$\dfrac{L}{d}$.	Coefficients.		
				Block.	Prism.	Midship.
F 6 (1)	8	2·142	17·142	·6533	·6778	·9638
F 7	8	2·142	17·142	·733	·760	·964
F 8	8	2·142	17·142	·855	·869	·984

The curves of sectional areas of F 8 and F 6 are shown in fig. 157 and the
body-plan in figs. 160, 161. In each case the dimensions, displacement, and
coefficients have been kept constant for each series, and the displacement
distributed longitudinally by altering the curve of sectional areas. The
general shape of the section was kept constant, and parallel middle body
was actually parallel, not virtually so. The results of trials are given for
maximum draught only. The fine bow and stern are marked 1 B, 1 S, and
the fuller bow and stern with no middle body, or in the case of the fullest
type a reduced middle body, 2 B, 2 S, and combinations of the two, such as
fine bow with the full stern, 1 B, 2 S.

With the fullest form, F 8, there is not much scope for variation in form
of the ends on account of their shortness, and here the form with the fine

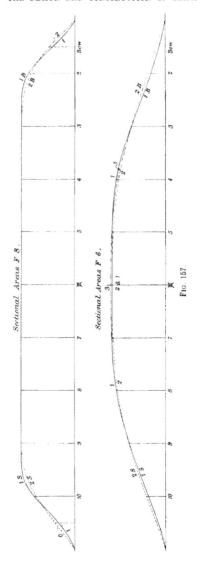

Fig. 157.

ends and long middle body is decidedly the worst, while that with the shorter
middle body and fuller ends is the best: this is shown in the accompanying
diagram of residuary resistance per ton of displacement, fig. 158, and in
the table of comparisons as follows:—

$\dfrac{V}{\sqrt{L}}$	1 B, 1 S.	1 B, 2 S.	2 B, 1 S.	2 B, 2 S.
·5	100	80·0	84·5	56·0
·55	100	77·7	79·0	50·6
·6	100	74·0	72·0	53·0

The results for this full form (·855 block coefficient) are the reverse of those
obtained for the finer forms, and the explanation is probably that in fining
the short ends a rather abrupt shoulder is formed. In the finer form,
F 6 (1) (·6533 block coefficient), the curves of residuary resistance are shown
in fig. 159, and the comparative residuary resistances are as follows:—

$\dfrac{V}{\sqrt{L}}$·	2 B, 1 S.	2 B, 2 S.	1 B, 1 S.	1 B, 2 S.
·75	100	86·5	62·6	64·5
·80	100	87·6	61·7	63·5
·85	100	91·2	71·7	69·5

In this case, as in the intermediate case, F 7 (with block coefficient ·733),
the combination of the fine bow with the full stern gives the best result
within the limits of practical speed-length ratios. At higher values of $\dfrac{V}{\sqrt{L}}$ the
somewhat easier form represented by 2 B, 2 S showed it to be slightly better
than the one with the finer bow: at these speeds the fuller after-body also
seems better than the finer form.

A further set of experiments was conducted with the F 6 (1) model and
two others related to it in the following manner: The beam was increased
by the same amount in the two new models, which were numbered F 6 (2)
and F 6 (3); F 6 (2) had exactly the same curve of sectional areas as F 6 (1),
the beam being changed and increased rise of floor being given; F 6 (3)
had the same beam as F 6 (2), but the area of the midship section was
increased to compensate for the reduction of displacement due to cutting
away the form between sections 3 and 5 (fig. 157). The midship sections
are shown in fig. 162. Nos. F 6 (1) and F 6 (2) have therefore the same
prismatic but different block coefficients, while F 6 (2) and F 6 (3) have
the same block but different prismatic coefficients. The lines at the extreme
ends are in all cases the same. The particulars of these three models are
as under:—

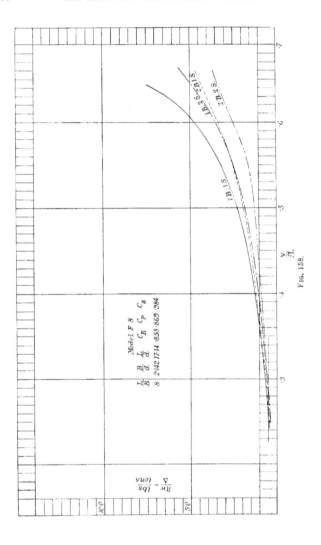

FIG. 158.

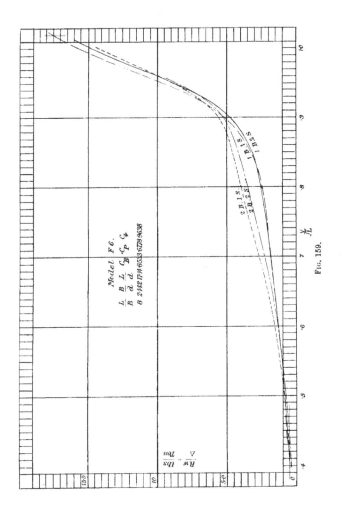

Fig. 159.

Model F. 6

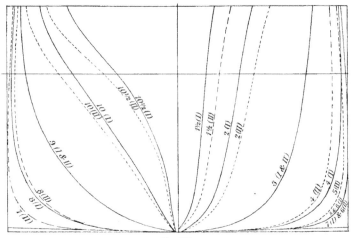

Fig. 160.

Model F 8.

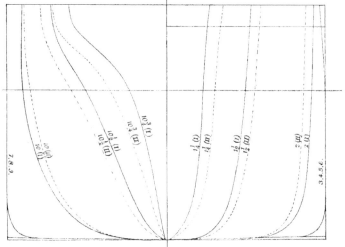

Fig. 161.

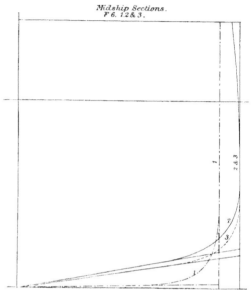

Midship Sections.
F 6. 1 2 & 3.

FIG. 162.

No.	$\frac{L}{B}$	$\frac{B}{d}$	$\frac{L}{d}$	Block.	Prism.	Midship.
F 6 (1)	8	2·142	17·142	·6533	·6778	·9638
F 6 (2)	7·272	2·358	17·142	·594	·6778	·874
F 6 (3)	7·272	2·358	17·142	·594	·664	·895

The curves of residuary resistance are shown in fig. 163, and the comparative residuary resistances are as in the following table :—

$\frac{V}{\sqrt{L}}$.	F 6 (1).	F 6 (2).	F 6 (3).
·8	100	96	96
·85	100	95·4	92·3
·9	100	92·3	81·2

Up to ·8 speed-length ratio there is very little to choose between the

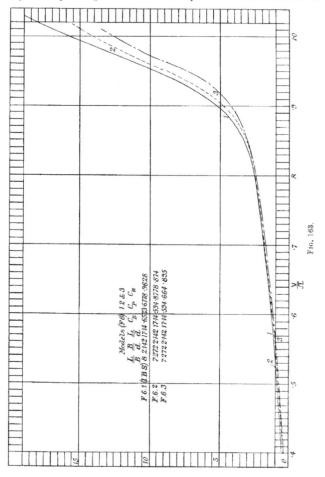

FIG. 163.

three models, but above that the improvement is well defined, F 6 (3) showing it to be better than either of the other two.

CHAPTER XIV.

OTHER RESISTANCE RESULTS.

The two preceding chapters give actual resistance results which are applicable to fine ships of the cruiser or Channel steamer type and to the full commercial steamer type respectively. They are each based upon very good parent forms, and, within the limits of fulness to which they are applicable, they enable the actual resistances of forms suitable for practical designing to be obtained. The methods of standardising are the same in principle, viz. the intensity of resistance measured as a ratio to displacement is plotted to a base of speed measured as a ratio to the square root of the length. In this chapter a third method of plotting results is given, in which, for displacements of a given form varied by proportional increase of all dimensions, the corresponding E.H.P. is plotted for constant speed.

Diagrams 164 to 180 have been prepared from the resistances of twelve models of actual ships as obtained in an experimental tank. These are all of good form and proportions, and the diagrams are deduced from results obtained at one draught of each of the parent types. The diagrams are ordinates of E.H.P. plotted in terms of displacement at a constant speed, and diagrams are given at speeds from 15 to 26 knots at intervals of 1 knot, and from 26 to 36 knots at intervals of 2 knots. A second series of curves is drawn on each diagram, giving the length of ship corresponding to each displacement in the different types.

Each sheet therefore gives the E.H.P. required to drive a given displacement at the speed for which the sheet is prepared, and the length of ship corresponding, and the designer can select the number of the ship requiring the least horse-power at that displacement and speed. The number indicates the parent ship ; and if her dimensions of length, breadth, and draught are all multiplied by the same factor as that by which the length has been altered from the parent type, the dimensions and displacement of the ship required will be given, and the form will be the same as that of the parent ship.

This is simply a graphic method of comparing the forms of the twelve ships enlarged or diminished to any desired displacement to see which of the forms will at a required speed be driven for the least power. The power is correctly proportioned from the parent ship, and not approximated to, as is the case where the Admiralty coefficient method is used ; that is to say, the E.H.P. is proportioned in the ratio of speed$^{2\cdot83}$ for friction as against speed^3 in the Admiralty coefficient method, and the actual wavemaking resistance is calculated.

Some of the types do not occur in all the seventeen sheets, either because

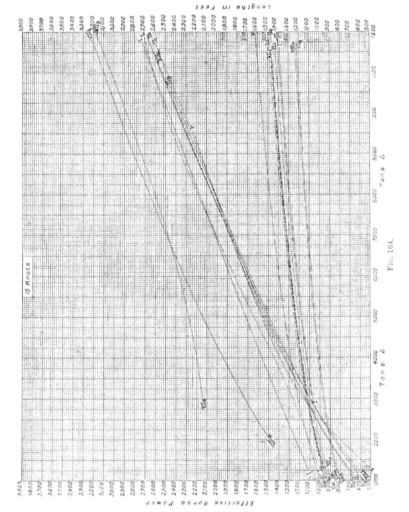

Fig. 164.

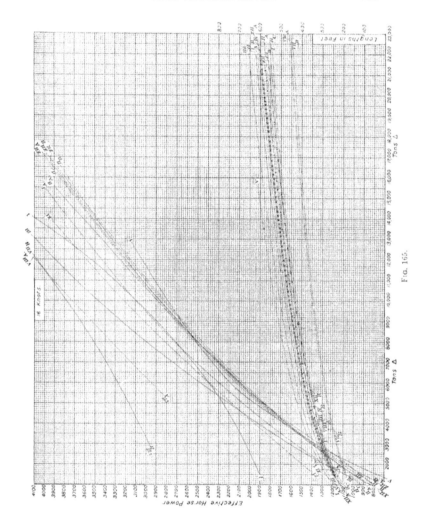

FIG. 165.

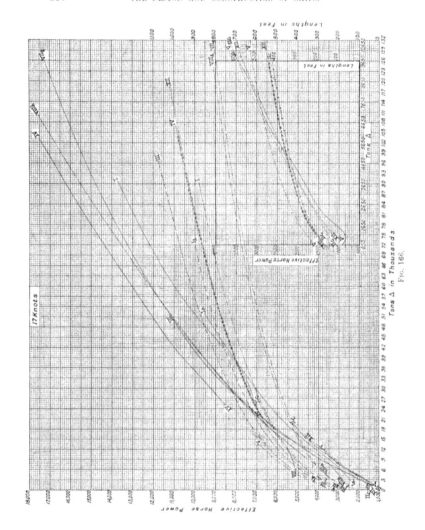

Fig. 166.

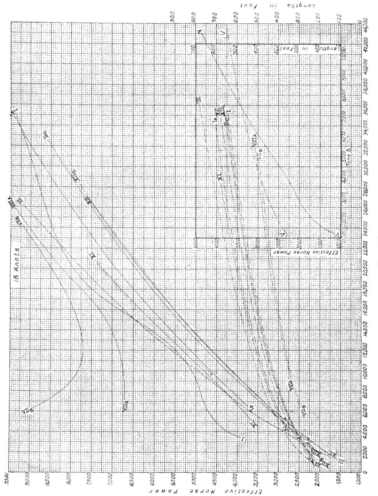

Fig. 167.

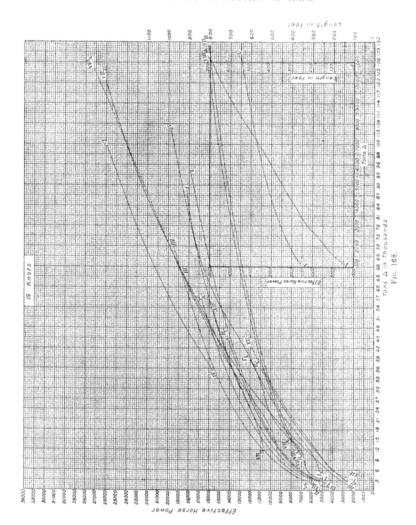

Fig. 168.

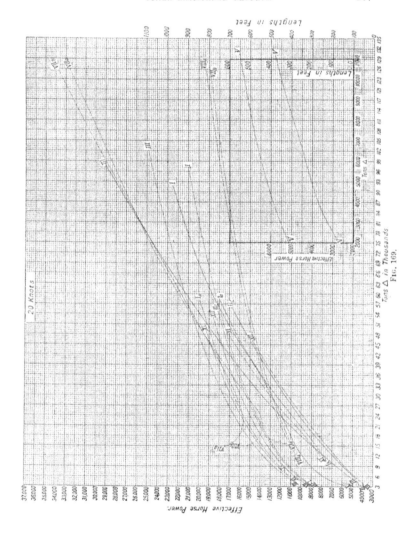

Fig. 169.

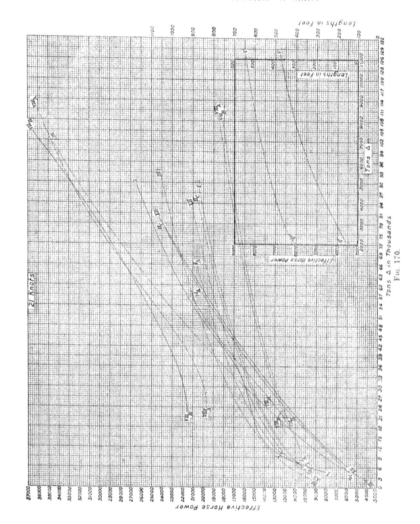

Fig. 170.

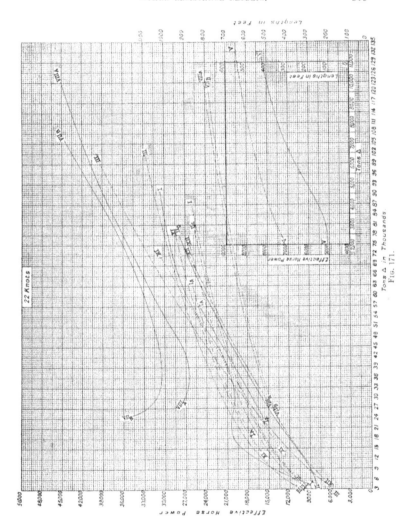

Fig. 171.

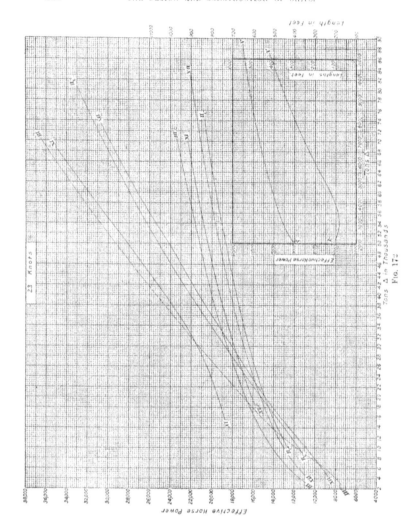

FIG. 172

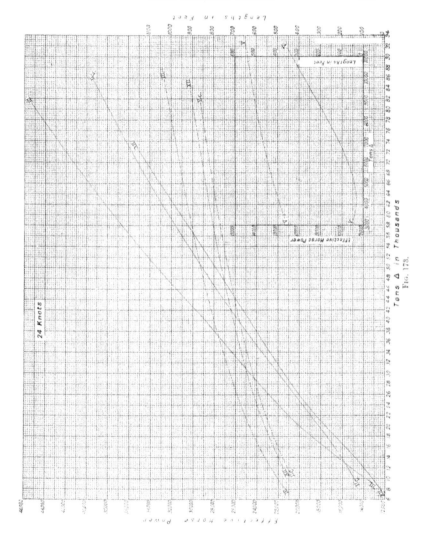

FIG. 178.

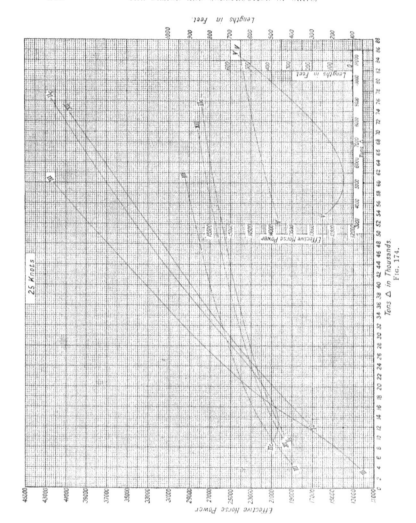

Fig. 174.

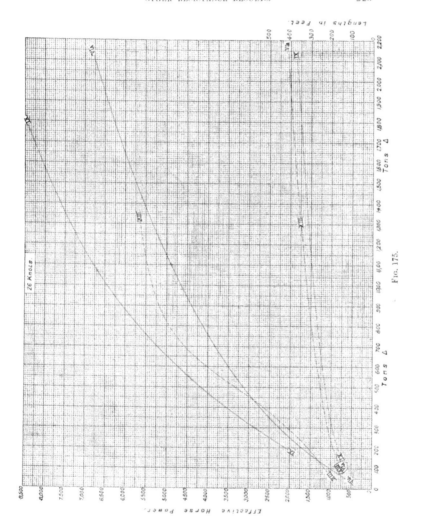

Fig. 175.

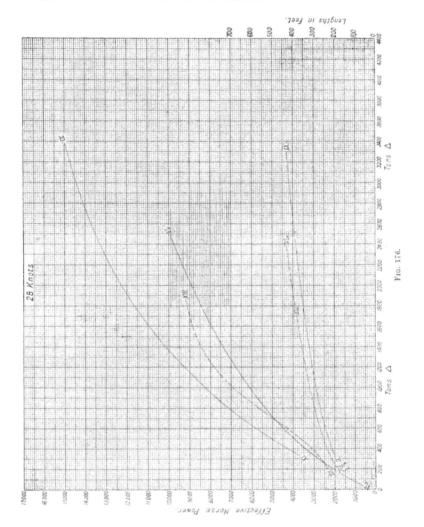

Fig. 176.

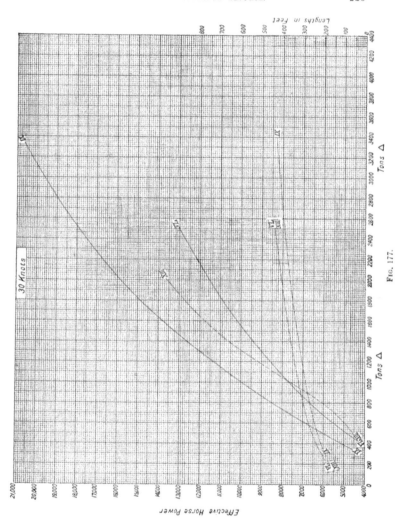

FIG. 177.

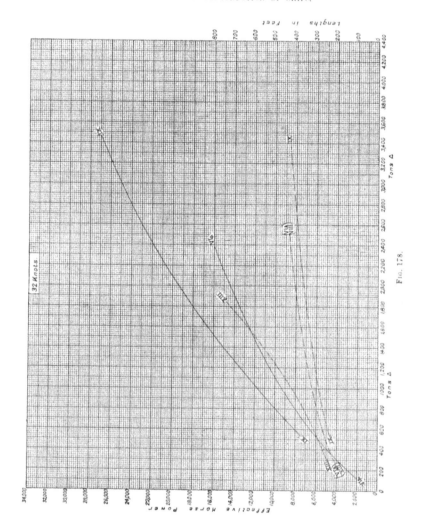

Fig. 178.

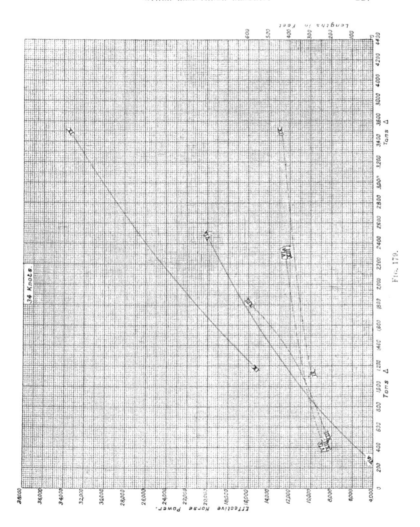

Fig. 179.

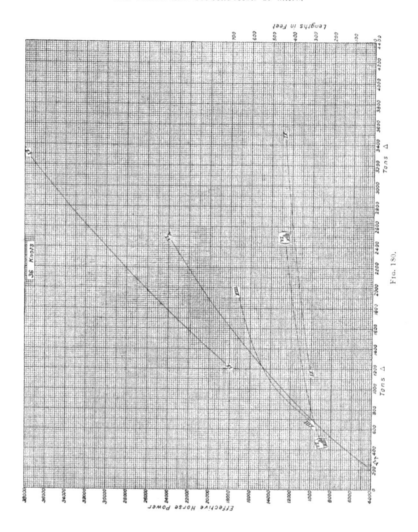

Fig. 180.

the range of speeds over which their original was tried will not proportion to that extent without introducing too high or too low displacements, or because the E.H.P.'s obtained were so high in comparison with those given as not to be worth recording.

The ordinates of the E.H.P. curves, as obtained from the experimental tank results, were subdivided into E.H.P. ordinates corresponding to frictional and wavemaking resistances. The frictional resistances were calculated directly, and from these the frictional E.H.P. obtained, and the difference between the total E.H.P. and the frictional E.H.P. gave wavemaking E.H.P. The frictional resistance in lbs. of any ship is equal to $f\mathrm{A}V^{1\cdot83}$, where f is the frictional coefficient or average resistance in lbs. per square foot at unit velocity over her whole length, A is the wetted surface in square feet, and V is the speed in knots : in these units f for a painted steel surface of 300 feet length in sea water is $\cdot00892$ lb., and greater for shorter lengths : this is deduced from the classical experiments of Froude and Tideman ; it is taken as constant, however, over the range of lengths in these results.

The frictional E.H.P. $=$ R.V. in proper units, R being the resistance due to friction at speed V : frictional E.H.P. $= \mathrm{R}V = \dfrac{(f\mathrm{A}V^{1\cdot83})V \times 101\cdot33}{33000} =$

$\dfrac{\cdot00892 \times \mathrm{A} \times V^{2\cdot83} \times 101\cdot33}{33000} = \dfrac{\mathrm{A}V^{2\cdot83}}{36510}.$ Thus from the total E.H.P. the frictional E.H.P. can be deducted, and curves of E.H.P. residuary and E.H.P. frictional can be plotted on the base of speeds.

If the ship's dimensions be altered to $n\mathrm{L}$, $n\mathrm{B}$, and nd, the wetted surface will become $n^2\mathrm{A}$ and the displacement $n^3\Delta$; if the speed be altered to n^1V the E.H.P. frictional will become $\dfrac{(n^2\mathrm{A})(n^1V)^{2\cdot83}}{36510} = \dfrac{\mathrm{A}V^{2\cdot83}n^{3\cdot45}}{36510}$, i.e. the E.H.P. frictional will be altered by multiplying the original E.H.P. frictional by $n^{3\cdot45}$. In this

PARTICULARS OF VESSELS.

No. of Curve.	Dimensions of Vessel. Length × Extreme Beam × Draught.	Displacement Tons.	Prismatic Coefficient.	Mid Sec. Coefficient.	Block Coefficient.
I.	430 × 51 × 28	10430	·624	·952	·594
Iᴀ.	430 × 51 × 21·9	7650	·599	·93	·557
IIᴀ.	440 × 66 × 24·5	9800	·554	·871	·482
IIʙ.	440 × 66 × 22·7	8800	·545	·861	·468
IIᴄ.	440 × 66 × 26·2	10800	·564	·879	·497
III.	529 × 63 × 21·25	11550	·611	·935	·571
IV.	480 × 57 × 21·4	12250	·759	·96	·730
V.	272 × 34 × 9·9	1350	·551	·934	·515
VIᴀ.	208 × 19·8 × 5·7	270	...	...	·408
VIIʙ.	390 × 75 × 27·5	14840	·685	·942	·645
VIIIᴀ.	400 × 75 × 26·7	15000	·702	·932	·654
IX.	212 × 21·2 × 9·8	400	·537	·592	·318
XI.	600 × 65 × 27·0	19600	·675	·963	·650
XII.	500 × 71 × 26	14000	·576	·924	·532
XIIᴀ.	500 × 71 × 24	12600	·564	·918	·518
XIIʙ.	500 × 71 × 28	15400	·585	·929	·543
XIII.	200 × 19·5 × 4·9	240	·627	·712	·441

way, and by taking series of values of n, new E.H.P. frictional curves can be obtained for series of speeds, lengths, and displacements.

Similarly, the E.H.P. wavemaking can be altered to suit these altered dimensions. Froude's law of comparison holds in this case, and it states that if the linear dimensions be altered to nL, nB, and nd (when the Δ will become $n^3\Delta$), at speeds of $n^{\frac{1}{2}}$V the wavemaking resistance will be n^3 times the original wavemaking resistance. E.H.P. wavemaking $=$ RV where R is the wavemaking resistance at speed V. For linear dimensions altered in the ratio of n, and V altered in the ratio of $n^{\frac{1}{2}}$, E.H.P. will be altered to R$n^3 \times$ V$n^{\frac{1}{2}}$, which is the original E.H.P. wavemaking altered in the ratio of $n^{3\cdot5}$.

The general formulæ for all values of n thus become

$$\text{E.H.P.}_{f}@\text{V}n^{\frac{1}{2}} = \frac{\text{A.V.}^{2\cdot83}n^{3\cdot415}}{36510} = (\text{E.H.P.}_{f}@\text{V})n^{3\cdot415}$$

and $\quad$ E.H.P.$_{w}@$V$n^{\frac{1}{2}}$ $\quad = (\text{E.H.P.}_{w}@\text{V})n^{3\cdot5}$.

The particulars of the parent ships from which these diagrams have been prepared are given on p. 229.

CHAPTER XV.

DETERMINATION OF MACHINERY HORSE-POWER FROM RESISTANCE HORSE-POWER.

WHEN the resistance R necessary to maintain the given speed V is known, the power expended in overcoming this resistance will be = RV. When, as in the case of sailing-ships or in vessels being towed, the force necessary to balance the resistance is obtained from outside the vessel, the total power expended upon the vessel will be RV, but when the force is developed from inside the vessel, such as in the case of steamers propelled by paddles, screw propellers, or hydraulic propulsion, the total power expended on the vessel is much more than RV, but in all cases the useful power is RV. In the case of vessels internally propelled, the source of energy is a machine which is capable of delivering so many units of work per unit of time. The rate of energy developed or the energy developed per unit of time is spoken of as power, and the unit most commonly applied in steamship work is a horse-power which is 33,000 foot-lbs. per minute. Hence, if R be in lbs. and V in feet per minute, $\dfrac{RV}{33000} =$ the horse-power required to overcome R at speed V. This is usually called effective horse-power, or E.H.P. The actual work done or energy developed in the cylinder of the steam engine is spoken of as indicated horse-power because it is measured by indicators which continuously record the pressure of the steam from point to point throughout the stroke of the engine. The indicated horse-power is the work done by the steam, and is the asset which the designer has to work upon in obtaining his speed. The useful effect produced is measured by the E.H.P., so that the ratio $\dfrac{\text{E.H.P.}}{\text{I.H.P.}}$ is the measure of the efficiency of the method of propelling, and is usually called the propulsive coefficient. The difference between the E.H.P. and the I.H.P. represents the losses of power, avoidable and unavoidable, between the steam cylinder and the result produced in power necessary to maintain the speed of ship. They may be summed up as follows :—

1. Engine friction due to tightness of glands and bearings. This absorbs some of the forces in the steam cylinder before the engine can be moved, and therefore before any power can be obtained.

2. Engine friction due to load, or the additional friction brought on the engine when it begins to overcome the resistance to motion, and develops a reaction from the thrust of propeller back again on the engine. These reactions or pressures cause increased friction, which increases as the thrust increases.

3. Work taken off the main shaft for other purposes than turning the

propeller, such as air pumps, feed pumps, and bilge pumps, when they are connected to the main engine.

4. In a screw ship there is an edgewise resistance of the blades of the propeller—the blades having an appreciable thickness and form, and having surfaces which develop frictional resistance with the water — so that the turning of the propeller causes resistance to be developed which produces no thrust, and therefore no useful work.

5. Augment of resistance or thrust deduction. The stream-line motions which are round a model when it is being towed have a head pressure in them at the stern which partially balances the pressures at the bow. When the screw propeller revolves it disturbs the stream-line motion, so that these pressures do not act so effectively as when there is no propeller. The propeller thereby increases the resistance of the ship. We shall see later that this may be also considered alternatively as a deduction of the thrust of the propeller.

6. Slip of propeller. The method of propelling a vessel by an internally-driven propeller necessitates that the propeller should drive water astern in order that the resistance of the ship to motion ahead shall be balanced. The motion imparted to this water is the slip, and is usually related to the speed of advance which the propeller would make if there were no slip. The work spent on setting the water in motion, thereby developing thrust in the propeller, can never be totally recovered, and therefore is to a greater or less extent an unavoidable loss.

These losses for a good modern screw steamship may be summed up and evaluated as follows :—

1. Engine friction dead load .	·05 I.H.P.	
2. ,, light ,, .	·05 ,,	
3. Auxiliaries	·02 ,,	
4. Augment of resistance (this varies with the fulness of the ship)		·15 E.H.P.
5. Edgwise resistance of screw .		·15 to ·25 ,,
6. Slip	·10 ,,	
	·22 I.H.P.	·30 to ·40 E.H.P.

These together make the total losses which are the difference between the E.H.P. and the I.H.P., so that I.H.P. − E.H.P. = ·22 I.H.P. + ·30 to ·40 E.H.P. ·78 I.H.P. = 1·3 to 1·4 E.H.P.

$$\frac{\text{E.H.P.}}{\text{I.H.P.}} = ·6 \text{ to } ·557.$$

The following is a list of values of the coefficient for different types :—

Twin screws.	Battleships and cruisers .	·5 to ·55
,,	Channel steamer . .	·5 ,, ·55
,,	Destroyers with twin screws .	·6 ,, ·65
,,	,, and Channel steamers with turbines	·48 ,, ·54
,,	Atlantic liners, high speed . .	·5 ,, ·55
,,	Intermediate type . .	·55 ,, ·6
Single screws.	Atlantic liners . . .	·6 ,, ·65
Twin screws.	Full cargo steamers . .	·55 ,, ·6
Single screws.	,, ,, . .	·6 ,, ·65

In the cases of paddle vessels the losses are greater than in screws generally, and are of a somewhat different character. The first three are naturally similar, and the sixth is of a similar character, but generally greater in amount. No. 4 does not exist, and No. 5 may be replaced by the losses due to shock on the paddle-wheel.

On account of the arrangement of a paddle engine, and the fact that it is much slower running, the frictional resistance in proportion to I.H.P. is probably higher than in a screw vessel, and is about 8 per cent. to 10 per cent. of the I.H.P. The live load friction will probably be about the same per cent.

The following may therefore be taken as an average distribution of the losses :—

$$
\begin{array}{ll}
1. & \cdot 09 \ \text{I.H.P.} \\
2. & \cdot 06 \quad ,, \\
3. & \cdot 02 \quad ,, \\
5. & \cdot 15 \quad ,, \\
6. & \cdot 20 \quad ,, \\
\hline
& \cdot 52 \ \text{I.H.P.} = \text{I.H.P.} - \text{E.H.P.} \\
& \text{E.H.P.} = \cdot 48 \ \text{I.H.P.}
\end{array}
$$

With these values of propulsive coefficients the power of the machinery can be found when the resistance and the E.H.P. are determined.

CHAPTER XVI.

INFLUENCE OF DEPTH OF WATER ON SPEED.

In shallow water and confined channels we get an alteration in the wave system generated by a ship, and hence a change in the resistance. This is also accompanied by a difference in trim.

This alteration in the resistance was, as stated in Chapter IX., noticed by Scott Russell while experimenting on wave forms in canals by towing a boat. On one occasion a spirited horse attached to the boat took fright and ran off, dragging the boat with it, and it was then observed that the vessel was carried along through comparatively smooth water with greatly diminished resistance.

Since then various experiments have been made to determine the exact influence of the depth of water upon the speed of a ship moving through it. Some of the experiments were made upon models and some upon actual ships. The following are amongst the most important of these :—

Captain Rasmussen's Experiments on Torpedo-Boats.—Captain Rasmussen, of the Imperial Danish Navy, made a series of trials on torpedo-boats in shallow water of varying depths.

Fig. 181, p. 235, gives the results for the same boat at two different draughts. The principal dimensions are :—

Length, 140 feet ; breadth, 14 feet 3 inches ; draught, when fully equipped, 7 feet 4 inches ; and corresponding displacement, 127 tons.

The particulars of the curves are—

	Depth of water in feet.	Displacement in tons.
Curve A	51	105
,, B	37$\frac{1}{2}$	105
,, C	19$\frac{1}{2}$	105
,, D	12	105
,, E	51	118
,, F	37$\frac{1}{2}$	118
,, G	19$\frac{1}{2}$	118
,, H	12	118

Curves d and e show the change of trim of the boat, in reference to the trim in still water, corresponding to the H.P. curves D and E.

The most important deductions from these trials are—

(1) The H.P. curve for the greatest depth is free from humps.

(2) A hump occurs on the H.P. curve, in a given depth, when the speed is given by $v = \sqrt{g \times \text{depth}}$, where v is in feet per second and depth is in feet.

(3) The less the depth the more marked is the hump in the curve, and from (2) the lower the speed at which it is formed.

(4) The speed at which the hump is formed is independent of the displacement for the same vessel.   The H.P. increases with the displacement.

(5) At the speed v, corresponding to the hump, the boat goes along on the top of a wave of translation which travels with the speed of the boat ; and

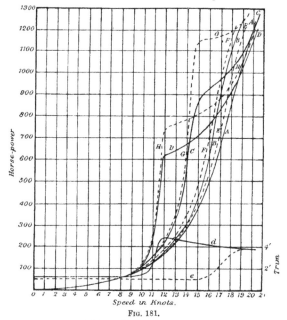

FIG. 181.

Full lines, displacement 105 tons.
Dotted lines, displacement 118 tons.

hence, at about this speed, the resistance increases at a much lower rate for an increase of speed than before.

It has already been pointed out in Chapter IX. p. 121, that if d is the depth of the channel, the speed of a wave of translation is given by $v = \sqrt{gd}$, where v is in feet per second and d in feet.   This speed will be found to agree with the points corresponding to the humps on the H.P. curves.

The system of waves which follows the boat is very unstable at speeds near v.   If, for example, the rudder is put hard over, the speed may fall below v ; but, on the contrary, the speed may become much greater at the same power if the boat has been running for some time on the same course.

Major Rota's Experiments.—Major Rota, of the Royal Italian Navy, has conducted a series of experiments upon models in the experimental tank at Spezia.

Figs. 182, p. 236, and 183, p. 237, show the results obtained for a model of the following dimensions :—

Length, 12·33 feet ; breadth, 1·35 feet ; mean draught, 0·32 feet ; displacement, 145·2 lbs. ; block coefficient, 0·43.

Fig. 183 shows curves of resistance at constant speeds for varying depths of water. These are equivalent to curves of E.H.P. on a base of depths at a different scale. The dotted curve shows the depths for the various speeds at

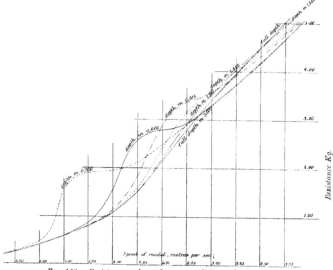

Fig. 182.—Resistance and speed curves at different depths of water.

which any increase in depth will not affect the resistance, but any slight decrease of depth will increase the resistance. This may be regarded as a " Critical Depth " for the particular speed at which the resistance curve is drawn. At very shallow depths, however, the resistance at the highest speed is seen to be less than in deep water. It is also to be noticed that the minimum resistance occurs at the same depth for all speeds. This depth appears to be about $\frac{1}{10}$th of the length of the boat. This is borne out by the results of all the trials.

Mr A. Denny's Experiments.—These were carried out in his experimental tank. Fig. 184, p. 238, shows the results obtained from the model of a barge, the particulars of which are given in the Table, p. 238.

The model was run at one depth, 1·252 feet ; and this was compared with the results at a depth of 10 feet. The rise of bow and fall of stern are also given for the same speeds. As a result of the investigation, Mr Denny came to the conclusion that he could not guarantee for shallow river boats any definite speed. The shaded portion of the diagram denotes a region of instability of motion similar to that to which reference has been made above.

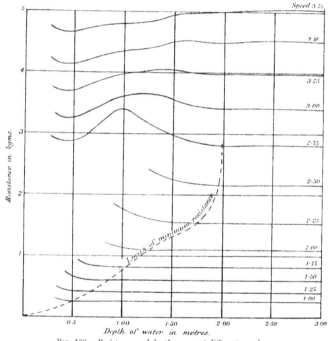

FIG. 183.—Resistance and depth curves at different speeds.
Speeds are in metres per second.

Sir Philip Watts' Results.—Sir Philip Watts contributed a paper to the Institution of Naval Architects, 1909, upon the speed trials of a Torpedo-Boat Destroyer at Skelmorlie and the Maplin Sands, which was run at speeds varying up to about 35 knots.

At Skelmorlie the depth of water is 40 fathoms, while at the Maplins it is only 7·5.

The dimensions of the vessel are—

Length, 270 feet; breadth, 26 feet; mean draught, during trial, 8 feet 2 inches; displacement, 836 tons.

The trim at the different speeds was measured. The wave profiles were also obtained by measuring the distances down from the gunwale at various points along the length of the vessel. Fig. 185, p. 239, shows the results obtained. The figure shows the shaft horse-power, total torque, mean revs. per minute, and change of trim by the stern, plotted on a base of speeds. The curves for the deep condition are all smooth, and continuously rise with the speed. *In the shallow water*, however, a hump occurs on each curve at the same speed—22 knots—which is the critical speed for this depth, viz. $\sqrt{gd}$.

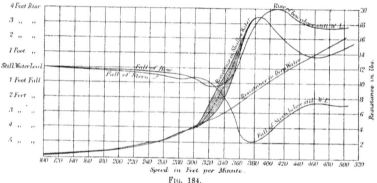

Fig. 184.

COMPARISON OF RESISTANCES IN DEEP AND SHALLOW WATER AS OBTAINED AT MESSRS DENNY BROS.' EXPERIMENTAL TANK, DUMBARTON, WITH A MODEL OF A BARGE 200′ × 27′.

PARTICULARS OF MODEL.

Length.	Breadth.	Moulded Draught.	Displacement in Fresh Water.	Coefficients.			
				Pris.	⊗ Area.	Block.	Depth of Deep Water = 10′. Depth of Shallow Water = 1·252′. The shaded parts show the extreme variation caused by instability.
12′	1·62′	·27′	274 lbs.	·846	·980	·837	

At speeds above 27 knots in the shallow water, we notice that the H.P., torque, and revs. are much less than for the deep water. The change of trim is also much less. Above 30 knots this difference seems to be constant, and may be appreciated by noticing that the H.P. is about 2000 less in the shallow than in the deep water. This is equivalent to a difference of speed of 1½ knots. Judging by Rota's experiments given above, it may be supposed that had the depth of water been only one-tenth of the length of the vessel, viz. 27 feet, the resistance would have been 2 to 3 per cent. less.

Mr Yarrow had a series of experiments made upon models at the North German Lloyd tank at Bremerhaven. The results of these experiments are

shown in fig. 186, p. 240, and contain the same characteristics as those
of the preceding experimenters.

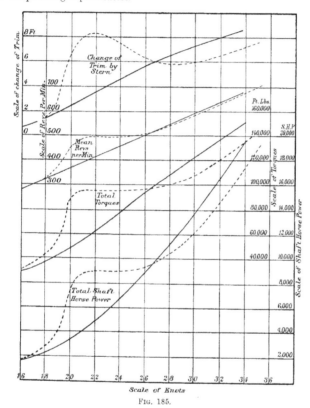

Fig. 185.

Displacement, 836 tons.
Maplin, 7·5 fathoms—shown dotted.
Skelmorlie, 40 fathoms, shown full lines.

Mr Marriner gave an analysis of these trials, supplemented by the
actual results obtained from the trials of full-sized vessels. He came to
the conclusion that at each depth of water there is a speed above which
—for that depth—there is no wave. He calls this the "critical speed" for
this depth.

Also, for a given speed there is certain depth below which there is no wave—for that speed.   This is called the " critical depth " for this speed.

It is found that the relation between the critical depth and the critical speed can be expressed in the form $v^2 = gd$, where v and d are in ft. sec. units,

$$\text{or} \qquad V^2 = 11\cdot 3d,$$

where V is in knots and d in feet.

When we have a combination of "critical depth" and "critical speed" we get augmented resistance.

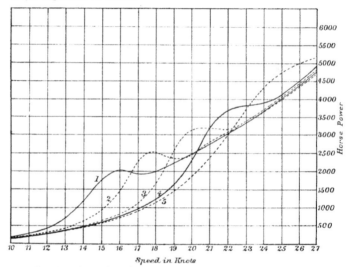

Fig. 186.—Curves of effective horse-power and speed in various depths of water.

No. 1.	Depth of water	= 20 ft.			No. 4.	Depth of water	= 60 ft.
,, 2.	,,	,,	= 30 ,,		,, 5.	,,	,,	= 90 ,,
,, 3.	,,	,,	= 45 ,,				

His main conclusions are—

(1) The critical combinations of depth and speed do not depend upon the size of the vessel.

(2) There is, for every vessel, one combination of critical depth and speed that is more serious than the others, and this depends largely upon the length of the vessel.

(3) The depth to be avoided is given by about $d = \dfrac{V^2}{10}$, where d is in feet and V in knots.   The resistance is less in both greater and smaller depths.

These conclusions indicate that as a vessel runs into gradually shoaling water, or increases her speed in the same depth of water, the system of oscillating waves formed by the vessel is gradually changed into a system of shallow-water waves; and, as has been shown on p. 135, these are again changed into the wave of translation. For the same depth there is only one velocity for a wave of translation; and if the velocity of the boat exceeds that, there will be no wave system formed, and hence the resistance will be diminished.

In order, however, to reach this speed, the critical point has to be passed, which calls for a large increase of power. Once this point has been passed, the H.P. decreases for a slightly increased rise of speed, and then increases as the speed increases, but at a much slower rate than before.

Dr Froude states that the phenomenon may be divided into three principal elements :—

1. As the water shallows, the stream lines become more and more two-dimensional in character instead of three-dimensional. This tends to accentuate the stream-line variations of speed and pressure, and hence increases the resistance.

2. The intensification of the stream-line variation of speed which increases the eddymaking.

3. The resistance due to wavemaking. This depends upon the relation between the speed of the boat and that of a wave of translation for the same depth of the channel.

When the depth of water is so small that the wave of translation cannot keep pace with the boat there is no wavemaking, and hence there is a reduction in the resistance.

From the results given it will be seen that it is possible, within fairly wide limits, to determine the difference in resistance between that obtained on the assumption of deep water and that at any shallower depth. It is also seen that the resistance in shallow water may be greater or less than in deep water according as the speed is near $\sqrt{gd}$ or much above it.

PART VI.

PROPULSION.

CHAPTER XVII.

ELEMENTARY CONSIDERATION OF PROPULSION.

CONSIDER two floating bodies. If one of the bodies acts on the other which is free to move in a fixed straight line, there must of necessity be a reaction from that other. This reaction can only be provided by the resistance of the body to change of motion in virtue of its inertia, or by the resistance of the fluid to the motion of the body through it. If the other body's motion becomes uniform, the resistance of the fluid will then be equal to the force with which the first body acts on the other.

The first body we may consider as a propeller. The pictures of the screws on the stern of a vessel show what kind of instrument a screw propeller is. In most cases each blade is a piece of a surface which is swept out by a straight line revolving uniformly about a fixed axis, and moving at a uniform speed along that axis,—in which case the propeller is said to have constant pitch. The part of the surface appropriated for the form of a propeller blade is frequently elliptic in form, so that it is practically an elliptic plane slightly twisted and placed obliquely to the shaft axis. Every square inch of the blade in rotating meets with resistance, due to the inertia of the water. This is usually considered as being of two separate kinds—one due to rubbing the particles of water out of the way, the other due to pushing them. We generally call these two kinds of resistance frictional and head resistance, respectively. For a given speed of blade through the water, the more oblique the blade is the more will be the normal pressure; and the less oblique, the greater will be the frictional resistance. Also, generally, the greater the area of the part of the blade moving at the given speed, the greater will be these resistances. If the blade be square to the shaft there will be no push in it, it will be all rubbing resistance. If it be in the line of the shaft, it will be all push and no rub. But in both these cases we shall have no reaction in the direction of motion, and there will be no force to cause propulsion. For positions of the blade between these two there will be both rubbing and pushing resistances, and there will be a resultant reactional push in the direction of motion, which will vary from zero to a maximum and back again

242

to zero between the two extreme positions of blade considered. What we have to find out is : where is this maximum, and what is it ?

Stream-lines.—We will first try to see what goes on in the vicinity of a propeller when a ship is being driven by it. Fig. 187 shows the results of observations made by Mr Calvert upon the direction of the flow of water as a ship passes through it. The thick lines represent floating thin radial feathers which indicate the line of motion of the water relatively to the ship. This kind of change of relative motion is called stream-line motion, and its effect may be seen in actual forms round which flows a coloured fluid. This shows the same kind of view which one would have in looking over the stern or bow of a ship if the water were parti-coloured in a similar way.

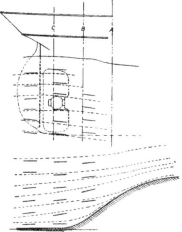

Fig. 187.—Showing the positions taken up by the stream lines at the stern of a moving vessel.

Suppose in this stream at the stern we put a revolving screw propeller. There will be a disturbance of these stream lines. The rubbing and pushing action of the propeller sends the water in many directions, and the action of rubbing and pushing will react on the propeller and tend to resist the rotation of the propeller, and will push the ship ahead. The more push the reaction gives to the ship for a given turning effort of the propeller, the more efficient will be the result We have seen that there is a zero of push ahead in two directions of the blade relatively to the shaft, and a maximum somewhere between. This will be so in the case of the propeller acting under the stern of the ship ; but inasmuch as the direction of the water to the axis of the shaft and to the line of motion of the ship is itself varying and slightly oblique, the position of zero push will not necessarily be either at right angles to each other or at the positions square to and along the shaft, as in the simpler case already dealt with.

Relation between Propeller and Engine.—Let us consider the simpler case first. Suppose a propeller to be carried by a phantom ship having no form, but only a capability of (1) delivering a turning effort to a propeller and (2) receiving a push from the propeller. Suppose the turning effort on the shaft to be always the same, and such as might be delivered by the steady pull of a rope on a drum attached to the shaft. If the blade of the propeller is placed in a plane square to the line of shaft, the resistance which the turning effort will meet with will be a rubbing or frictional resistance, and there will be no forward push given to the propeller by the reaction of the water. The shaft will run very fast, and its limit of speed will only be reached when the total rubbing resistances balance the turning effort due to the rope in the drum. A large amount of work will be done by the force in the rope moving at a great speed. But the useful effect in propelling the vessel will be zero. If, for a rope, we were to substitute an engine, we might have a very efficient engine so far as work delivered in relation to weight of machine or in relation to steam used, but the whole combination of screw and engine would be a useless machine. If we place the propeller blade in a plane along the shaft we should get a large head resistance to the propeller, but it would all be in a direction square to the shaft, and no forward push due to the reaction of the water would be caused. As before, the limit of speed would be reached when the resistance to pushing the blade through the water balanced the pull in the rope. This would be at a much lower speed than in the former case, and the work done would be less in proportion to the lowering speed. If the work were done by the same engine as before, it would not be so efficient an engine in relation to its weight nor to that of the steam used. We might be able to make it as efficient in relation to steam used by making it larger and heavier, but this would still more sacrifice its efficiency in relation to its weight. Whatever was done to improve the efficiency of the engine in one respect or the other would not make the propeller drive the ship, and, as before, the efficiency of the apparatus would be zero. If, however, we put the propeller blade in some oblique intermediate position we shall get less rubbing and pushing resistances than in the respective first and second cases, but we shall get some effective push or thrust in the propeller. Suppose, by a process of trial, we can get the exact obliquity which will give a maximum push forward for a given pull on the rope at a given speed, that is, for a given amount of work done per unit of time (usually called a given amount of H.P.), we should then have the best propeller result as far as the obliquity of the particular blades of the propeller are concerned. But we should only then have one best result. Consider how many things have been given or assumed for the whole installation. First, we assume a certain work done per unit of time called horse-power. Next we assume a given speed of the rope and a given force. These two multiplied together give the H.P., but it is evident that one-half the speed and twice the force would give the same H.P. In fact, there is a great variety of speeds and forces whose product is the H.P., and each one of these will have a different effect on the propeller. It will also probably reduce the efficiency of both weight and steam consumption if the H.P. is derived from an engine instead of a rope and drum. Increase of speed will increase forward push, but the obliquity of the blades may not be the best for this increased speed. The engine would probably be increased in efficiency by the increased speed. But even with this set of conditions it may not be that the particular propeller, even if at its best obliquity, would be the best propeller for that particular speed of turning. Its blade area may be capable of improvement. It may be that the increased speed would cause too much to be done in rubbing and not enough in push, so that it will be seen that though a propeller may be the best for a given set of conditions, it may be that it is not the best best, but that a change of conditions may make a better best. Thus it is seen that, for the highest efficiency, not only is the best best propeller the best for its own engine, but it must also have the best engine. Sometimes it is possible to combine these excellences, but generally it is not, and the sacrifice of one or other bests has to be made.

It is certain that we must study the engine efficiency in terms of speed of rotation and H.P., and the propeller in the same terms, and also in that of speed of ship.

The subject is wide and difficult to deal with in detail, and later it will be seen that it has been treated experimentally by model propellers as large as 16 inches in diameter, having varying areas of blades, diameters, obliquities (usually called pitch), revolutions, and speed of ship. These five variables all cause varying efficiencies, so that, treating efficiency as the result of any of these five variables, we have six in all. It is to be noticed that efficiency of

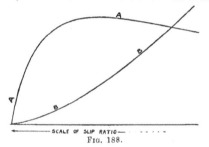

SCALE OF SLIP RATIO—

Fig. 188.

propeller is the ratio of push forward to turning effort, and these are capable of varying independently. It will therefore be necessary to permutate all these combinations by finding how some vary, while others remain fixed. For instance, for a given speed of ship, and a given H.P., and given propeller, we may trace the change of efficiency in terms of revolutions or slip-ratio. This is shown in such a curve as fig. 188, in which B B is the thrust curve and A A the efficiency curve.

Elementary Plane Propeller.—Let us first consider the simplest kind of propeller—a plane attached to the floating body in such a manner that when acted on by a force it only moves a small distance, while the floating body moves a comparatively large distance. We can examine the conditions of thrust by resolving the forces or the reactions in the direction of motion of the floating body, and thereby arrive at a determination of the efficiency of the propeller.

As viewed from this standpoint, the action of a screw propeller is the same as that of a series of planes rigidly fixed to a revolving shaft, the planes being inclined to a transverse plane perpendicular to the shaft.

In the case of the paddle or stern wheel, the planes swing in vertical circles about a horizontal transverse axis, and are perpendicular to the fore and aft vertical plane.

We can apply Newton's second law to determine the available thrust for overcoming the ship's resistance when moving at a uniform speed if we make certain assumptions as to the speed of the water in the region of the propeller. If we look upon the ship as provided with means whereby it can act on a certain volume of water so as to change the momentum of the water in a certain direction, we know that in order to produce this change a force is necessary, and that there must have been a reaction to this force, such reaction being provided by the resistance of the water to the motion of the ship. The efficiency of the screw propeller and of the paddle-wheel can be considered from this point of view.

In some ships the agent for acting on the water is constructed inside the ship, and the water led to and away from it by means of guide passages. This means of propulsion is called the jet propeller, and the action is almost the same as that of the centrifugal pump.

Efficiency of the Jet Propeller.—

Let $m =$ mass of unit volume of water,

        $A =$ area of passage to pumps,

        $V =$ velocity of feed,

        $v =$ velocity of water after it leaves the pumps.

We can simplify the consideration by supposing the ship to be stationary, and the water to flow past the ship with a speed V.

Then the mass of water entering the passage per second $= mAV$.

Energy in mass of water entering passage per second $= \left(\dfrac{mAV}{2}\right)V^2,$

,,   ,,   leaving   ,, $= \left(\dfrac{mAV}{2}\right)v^2.$

Therefore, total work done, supposing no work is done on the friction of the passages, $= \dfrac{mAV}{2}(v^2 - V^2).$

Let the resistance of the water to the motion of the ship through it be R. Then when V is uniform,

R $=$ change of momentum in the water per second,

    $= mAV\,(v - V)\,;$

i.e. the thrust available for overcoming the resistance being equal to the change of momentum per second, is balanced by the resistance R, or overcomes the resistance R at the speed V.

The useful work is the work done in overcoming the ship's resistance R at speed V,

i.e. useful work done per second $= RV,$

       $= mAV(v - V)V.$

$\therefore$ Efficiency $= \epsilon = \dfrac{\text{Useful work}}{\text{Total work}},$

or $\epsilon = \dfrac{mAV(v - V)V}{\frac{1}{2}mAV(v^2 - V^2)} = \dfrac{2V}{v + V} = \dfrac{2}{\dfrac{v}{V} + 1}.$

It may be noted here that the lost work is equal to the energy lost in the race,

$$= \tfrac{1}{2}mAV(v^2 - V^2) - mAV(v - V)V$$
$$= \tfrac{1}{2}mAV(v - V)^2.$$

In estimating this value for the efficiency, the assumption has been made that there is no loss by friction either in the passages or pumps. We may estimate the loss due to friction as being a function of the velocity $(v + V)$, so that the formula for the efficiency will take the form

$$\epsilon = \frac{2V}{(v + V)(1 + c)},$$

where c is a coefficient depending on the amount of friction.

Looking at the above expressions for useful and for lost work, we see that in order to make ϵ as large as possible $\left(\dfrac{v}{V}\right)$ should be small and A should be large. Theoretically this is the direction to go in order to increase the efficiency, but in practice a limit to the size A is very soon reached. There are also other questions which arise, but these will be discussed later on. The efficiency of a jet propeller is therefore not large, and in actual cases it has been found that the best forms of this means of propulsion only give something like 35 to 40 per cent. efficiency.

The above method of treating the efficiency of a jet propeller applies directly to the case of the screw propeller.

We see that in the jet propeller the water leaves the ship with a greater velocity than it enters. The difference of these two velocities, i.e. $(v - V)$, is called the speed of slip.

If there were no slip the speed of water leaving the ship would be equal to the speed of the water entering the ship, and there would be no change of momentum and no reaction. There could therefore be no propelling force.

Sometimes slip is defined as the theoretical speed of propeller minus the actual speed of ship. Care must be taken to see that we relate these two velocities to the same thing. The speed of slip, therefore, is the speed of the water in the race relatively to the surrounding water through which the ship is moving.

Efficiency of Screw.—Passing to the screw, we see that here there are no guide passages. The screw works in open water, and is fed without any directing surfaces.

We may imagine, however, a certain stream of water to be acted upon, and apply the same formulæ as for the jet propeller, and so get $\epsilon = \dfrac{2V}{v + V}$. The defect in this application lies in the assumption as to the stream of water acted upon (see also p. 271). If we do not take into consideration the disturbed motion of the stream lines in the wake of the ship and about the screw, the efficiency of the latter should be greater than that of the jet propeller, for the reason that there are no passages to cause friction. The efficiency of a good working screw propeller is generally about 60 to 70 per cent. The jet form, however, can claim the advantages of all the machinery being inside the ship, easily accessible, and better under control, and therefore less liable to damage from the outside, but on account of its low efficiency it is seldom used. It is employed in some steam lifeboats where moderate speed is sufficient, and loss of efficiency not so important a factor. It is important to make the orifices for the passages in a jet propeller of suitable size, and not too large. The shape and position of the orifices also require careful consideration, and it is best to make the largest dimension horizontal.

Efficiency of Paddle.—The efficiency of the paddle can be examined in the same way. The ordinary form of paddle consists of a number of floats fixed on a circular frame. The floats are placed so that at the instant when one of them is vertically under the axis it is a little more than submerged below the load waterplane. The inclination or feather of the floats does not affect the question at present. The action of any float in the water while the paddle-wheel is revolving is to pile up the water on the after side, and by the defect of pressure on the forward side to cause the water to flow in to follow it on the forward side. At any instant there is, say, an area of stream equivalent to the area of two floats submerged, one on each side of the ship. The assumption as to the race, which it is necessary to make here, is that the speed of the race relatively to the ship is equal to the linear speed of the floats. The cross-sectional area of the race is equal to the area of two floats.

These assumptions would be nearly true for a paddle-wheel whose floats were always vertical, and entered and left the water without disturbing the stream-line flow of the race.

Let the linear velocity of float $= v$.

,,   ,,   ship $= V$.

V must be less than v before a forward thrust can be developed.

∴ Velocity of race relatively to still water $= v - V$.

Let the cross-sectional area of stream affected be A. Then, as before, the useful work $= RV$.

The total work $= Rv$.

This assumes the condition of the water to be solid, yet penetrable without effort.

$$\text{The efficiency is therefore} = \frac{RV}{Rv} = \frac{V}{v}.$$

The mass of water acted on per second $= mAV$.

Change of momentum per second $= mAV(v - V)$.

Thrust or resistance $R = mAV(v - V)$.

Useful work $= mAV^2.(v - V)$.

∴ Lost work $= Rv - RV$.

    $= R(v - V)$.

    $= mAV(v - V)^2$.

Loss in race $= \frac{1}{2}mAV(v - V)^2$ since $(v - V)$ is the absolute velocity of the water in the race.

∴ Loss due to shock of floats and water

    $=$ Total work lost $-$ loss in race

    $= \frac{1}{2}mAV(v - V)^2$.

In the jet propeller the work lost is only $\frac{1}{2}mAV(v - V)^2 = \frac{1}{2}$ of the above if v is the same. It is to be observed that A is assumed to be the sectional area of a continuous stream in steady flow, but in actual paddles the stream is a series of blocks of water in more or less vortex-like motion, to which the floats have given motion, principally astern, but also in some other directions.

$(v - V)$ the velocity of slip will bear a proportion to the linear velocity of the paddle v.

$$v = \pi D n \qquad D = \text{diameter of wheel.}$$

$$n = \text{number of revolutions.}$$

$$\therefore \ v - V = k\pi D n \qquad k \text{ is a constant. In this case it is}$$

called the "Apparent Slip."

$$\therefore \qquad V = Dn(1 - k)\pi.$$

$$\text{But} \qquad R = mAV(v - V)$$

$$= mA\pi^2 D^2 n^2 k(1 - k).$$

$$\therefore \qquad A = \frac{R}{m(\pi Dn)^2 k(1 - k)}.$$

If A' is the area of the floats,

$$A'v = AV.$$

$$\therefore \qquad A' = \frac{AV}{v}$$

$$= \frac{R}{m(\pi Dn)^2 k},$$

which will determine the size of float if a value for k is selected and R is known. Usually, however, the diameter of the wheel remains to be determined from the intended speed of ship, slip, and the number of revolutions. At first sight it appears that the way to increase paddle efficiency is to make $(v - V)$ small, or v and V nearly equal. To do this, however, it would be necessary to make A very large, but there is a practical limit to A, so that the limit of efficiency is soon reached. The losses peculiar to a paddle are due (1) to the vertical motion of the floats through the water, and (2) loss due to the shock of the floats when entering the water. Feathering paddle-wheels are designed to obviate the latter source of loss. A sketch of the feathering arrangement is given in fig. 191. The floats are geared by connecting-rods to an eccentric so that the plane of any float when entering the water lies in the line of the resultant of the forward velocity of ship and the tangential velocity of float.

Let O in fig. 189 be the paddle centre at any instant and C the relative position of the centre of a float A B entering the water, C being on the surface. Join O C. Draw C D perpendicular to O C, and make $CD = \pi Dn$, i.e. velocity of float about the centre O. Draw D E horizontal and equal to V. Then C E is the resultant in magnitude and direction of the velocities of the float and ship.

If A B lies in C E the float will then be entering without shock. This only determines the inclination of float for one point, C. If we consider any other point in A B, say B, the direction of B E' the resultant of the velocity of B will be different from C E. Therefore the float should be such that the direction of the resolved velocity of each point should be a tangent to the curve of the float at that point : C E is tangential to the float at the surface. The section A B of the float must be a curve which can be roughly approximated to by making it a circular arc of radius equal to O C. It is evident that a float fixed in relation to the periphery of the wheel at an angle to be effective when entering the water would be very ineffective when leaving. It therefore becomes necessary to change this angle during the motion of the paddle-wheel. This is done by mechanism known as the feathering gear. Each paddle float is hinged on an axis a little above its centre. To the float is attached a lever connected by a rod to an eccentric which has a centre a little forward and slightly above the paddle centre. This arrangement causes the paddle floats to revolve round the axis on which they are hinged. See fig. 191.

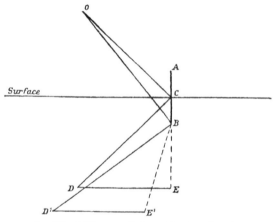

FIG. 189.—B D' is perpendicular to O B and equal to C D.
D' E' is equal and parallel to D E.

Various methods are used for the determination of the eccentricity which produces the desired motion of float. In some paddles the float is designed so that its plane when it strikes the water always passes through the highest point of the circle concentric with the paddle centre. The centre of the eccentric circle is called the "Jenny Nettle Centre." It can be found by drawing the planes of the floats in two or three desirable positions after the length of the smaller lever is fixed.

In the construction for a wheel so as to give the floats the required motion the designed speed must be fixed. The following is a method of fixing the position of the Jenny Nettle centre. But the more frequent practice is to fix it by relation to previous successful practice.

A circle A B C is drawn through the lower edge of entering float.

B D represents the tangential velocity of float edge, D K represents the velocity of the vessel. Produce D K to E making D E = B D. K E will

represent the velocity of slip.   Draw L B, where L is the middle point of
K E.   Draw the curve of float radius = radius of float centres.   L B is a
tangent to the float at B.   At C draw the tangent C G = D B and G H
parallel to B C and = D E.   Join C H.   Draw the curve of float so that C H
is a tangent to it at C.   Let the chord to the lowest position Q of the float
be vertical.   Make the length of the float levers three-fifths of the depth of
the float and find the centre M of the circle through the extremities of the
levers.   This gives the eccentric circle.

The revolutions of a paddle vary from about 40 to 60 per minute in this
country.   In America a paddle-wheel is frequently driven by a very long

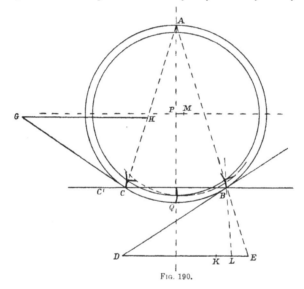

Fɪɢ. 190.

stroke engine attached to a beam and connecting-rod which rotates a radial
or non-feathering wheel at about one-half the number of revolutions usual
in this country.

The slip we have seen to be $(v - V)$.

$$\text{Slip ratio} = \frac{v - V}{v}.$$

∴   Slip per cent. is $\frac{v - V}{v} 100.$

If the slip per cent. is 20, this is good efficiency for a paddle.   Some paddles
work with as low as 16 per cent.

$$\text{Assume}\qquad \frac{v-V}{v}100 = 20,$$

$$\text{then}\qquad v - V = \frac{v}{5},$$

$$v = \frac{5}{4}V.$$

$$\therefore\quad \text{Loss in race} = \tfrac{1}{2}mAV(v - V)^2$$

$$= \tfrac{1}{2}mAV\frac{v^2}{25}$$

$$= \frac{mAV^3}{32}.$$

$$\text{Effective horse-power (E.H.P.)} = RV = mAV(v - V)V$$

$$= \frac{mAV^3}{4}.$$

$$\therefore\quad \text{Loss in the race} = \frac{1}{8}\text{E.H.P.}$$

Here, again, it must be observed that A is the sectional area of an ideal stream of continuous motion astern.

$$R = \frac{mAV(v - V)}{g}\text{ in lbs.}$$

$$m = 64 : g = 32.$$

$$\therefore\quad R = 2AV(v - V) = 2A'v(v - V).$$

$$\therefore\quad A' = \frac{R}{2v(v - V)}\text{ where } A' = \text{area of two floats in sq. ft.}$$

$$\text{Now } (v - V) = \frac{v}{5}, \text{ and } \therefore\ v = \frac{5}{4}V.$$

$$\therefore\quad A' = \frac{8R}{5V^2}\text{ for a slip of 20 per cent.}$$

Analysis of the I.H.P. of Paddle Engines.—The actual values of the ratios can only be determined by experiment or by comparison of successful vessels. An estimate has been made, and the following are supposed to be fairly accurate percentages for a good working set of paddle engines.

Horse-power required to overcome resistance of ship $= 1 \times$ E.H.P. . . (1)

,,   lost due to race . . . . $= \cdot125$,, . . (2)

,,   ,,   shocks, etc. . . . $= \cdot125$,, . . (3)

,,   ,,   vertical motion of floats . $= \cdot1$,, . (4)

$\therefore$ Total loss which is proportional to E.H.P. $= \cdot35$ E.H.P.

No. 2 is only $\frac{1}{2}$ of total loss due to race.

No. 4 is a variable quantity, and depends on form of floats, etc.

Initial friction of engine = ·11 I.H.P.   .   .   . (1)

Live load friction   = ·15 „   .   .   .   . (2)

Losses due to pumps   = ·04 „   .   .   .   . (3)

Total loss proportional to I.H.P. = ·3 I.H.P.

No. 2 includes frictional loss in parts of paddle that cannot be lubricated as in a screw engine. They run in water.

$$\text{E.H.P.} + \text{sum-total loss} = \text{I.H.P.}$$

$i.e.$ 1·35 E.H.P. + ·3 I.H.P. = I.H.P.

1·35 E.H.P. = ·7 I.H.P.

∴ $\dfrac{\text{E.H.P.}}{\text{I.H.P.}} = ·52$, which is a very good result for a paddle engine.

Examination of Efficiency—according to the Blade Theory.—

The method just considered depends upon the dynamical changes that take place in a quantity of water which can be acted upon by the propeller. Rankine considered the question of propeller efficiency in this way, and to his theory as applied to screw propellers the name "disc theory" was given. It was assumed that the volume of water that caused the change of momentum was measured by the area of the disc of the tips of the propeller and the slip.

However, when it is necessary to examine what effect the variation in shape or design of the propeller having a giving disc area and slip has upon the efficiency, this method offers no assistance. Experience has shown that considerable differences exist in such cases, and therefore an examination of the relations between all the forces acting on the propeller is necessary before the effect on efficiency of variations in the design can be stated. The general conclusions based on the disc theory are that large disc area and small slip are necessary for high efficiency. Experience has not borne this out, and it becomes necessary to investigate the subject of screw propellers in full detail. This can be done by considering first the simple case of a small element of the surface of the propeller. The theory of the propulsive efficiency of the element of a propeller blade was enunciated by the late Mr W. Froude. To this theory the name of "blade theory" has been given.

The simplest kind of propeller that one can imagine is a plane which is constrained to move in a definite straight line by some power within the ship.

Examination of the Efficiency of a Small Plane Propeller.—Let

C C,' fig. 192, be the small plane fixed in direction placed so that its normal is at an angle θ with the line of motion A B of the ship. A force T acting along C A causes the ship to move in direction A B with velocity u, and in direction C A with velocity v. A C is at an angle a to A B.

Let the reaction of the plane C C' be R along a line C R inclined at β to A B. This reaction propels the ship in the direction A B. We can resolve this reaction into components.

R cos $(\beta - \theta) = P$, say, perpendicular to C C', and R sin $(\beta - \theta) = Q$, say, parallel to C C'. P represents the normal reaction of the plane. Q represents

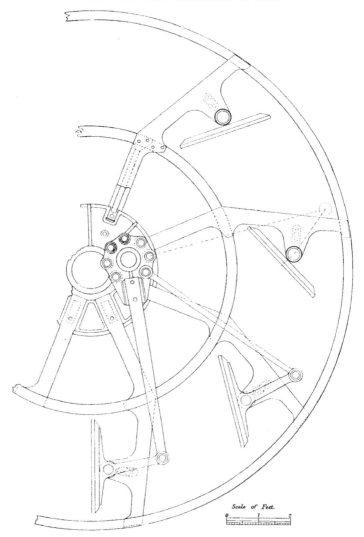

Scale of Feet.

FIG. 191.—Feathering arrangements of paddle-wheel.

the friction of the plane.   Then the total available thrust for overcoming the resistance to the motion of the ship along A B

$$= R \cos \beta$$
$$= P \cos \theta - Q \sin \theta.$$

For uniform motion along A B this must equal the resolved part of the thrust T along $A B = T \cos \alpha$.

Also the component of R along A C must be equal and opposite to the thrust T,

i.e. $T = P \cos (\alpha - \theta) + Q \sin (\alpha - \theta)$.

Therefore the *useful work*, which equals work done against resistance by

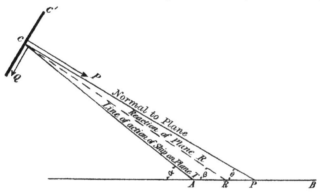

FIG. 192.

thrust $T \cos \alpha$ at speed u is equal to $Tu \cos \alpha = (P \cos \theta - Q \sin \theta)u$.   The *total work* is the work done in moving the propeller plane against resistance $= Tv$

$$= \{ P \cos (\alpha - \theta) + Q \sin (\alpha - \theta) \} v.$$

The efficiency $= \dfrac{\text{Useful work}}{\text{Total work}} = \dfrac{(P \cos \theta - Q \sin \theta) u}{\{ P \cos (\alpha - \theta) + Q \sin (\alpha - \theta) \} v}$

In the case of a perfectly smooth plane $Q = 0$.

So that $\epsilon = \dfrac{P \cos \theta}{P \cos (\alpha - \theta)} \dfrac{u}{v} = \dfrac{u}{v} \dfrac{\cos \theta}{\cos (\alpha - \theta)}$.

If the plane is moved in the direction of its normal then $(\alpha - \theta) = 0$.

So that $\epsilon = \dfrac{u}{v} \cos \theta$

and $T = R$.

Again, if the plane is moved in the direction of its normal, and also if the plane is perpendicular to line of motion of ship, then $\theta = 0$,

$$\text{and therefore} \quad \epsilon = \frac{u}{v},$$

$$\text{and} \quad T = R.$$

In the general case the expression for the efficiency of a smooth plane propeller is

$$\epsilon = \frac{u \cos \theta}{v \cos (\alpha - \theta)}.$$

If we suppose that the water is solid, yet penetrable by the plane edgewise without effort, the condition will be the same as if the plane were pushed along a smooth unyielding surface parallel to itself. In such a case, there being no loss of work, the work done in pushing the plane would equal the total work done.

$$\text{Hence} \quad \epsilon = 1.$$

$$\therefore \quad \frac{u \cos \theta}{v \cos (\alpha - \theta)} = 1.$$

$$\therefore \, u, \text{ the velocity of the ship, } = \frac{v \cos (\alpha - \theta)}{\cos \theta}.$$

This is the theoretical maximum velocity.

In the actual case of the plane working in water, u is always less than $\frac{v \cos (\alpha - \theta)}{\cos \theta}$.

The difference of these two velocities, $\frac{v \cos (\alpha - \theta)}{\cos \theta} - u$, is called the velocity of slip.

In the case considered above, where the plane is perpendicular to the line of motion of ship, the velocity of slip $= v - u$.

" Slip ratio " is defined to be

$$\frac{\dfrac{v \cos (\alpha - \theta)}{\cos \theta} - u}{\dfrac{v \cos (\alpha - \theta)}{\cos \theta}} = S.$$

$$\therefore \quad S = 1 - \frac{u \cos \theta}{v \cos (\alpha - \theta)} = 1 - \epsilon.$$

We may now apply the above general proposition to particular cases.

Paddle.—Consider one immersed float, as in fig. 193, of a radial paddle-wheel.

Let $W\,W_1$ be the water surface. O is the paddle centre. A B the float. O A B a radial arm.

The resistance of the water can be represented by a force R acting at the centre of pressure of the float.

Let P and Q be the components of this resistance perpendicular and parallel to the plane of the float respectively.

Let the inclination of A B to the vertical be θ. Then the angle of inclination of P to the horizontal is θ.

The angle between P and the direction of motion is therefore θ.

Applying the formula as in the case of the plane propeller,

$$T = P \cos \theta - Q \sin \theta,$$

where T represents the useful thrust, *i.e.* the thrust to overcome R, the resistance of ship.

Let v = tangential velocity of the float at the instant under consideration.

Let u = resulting velocity of ship.

Useful work done $= Tu$
$= (P \cos \theta - Q \sin \theta)u.$

Now the component of the resistance R, to the motion of the plane along the line of motion of float, $= P$.

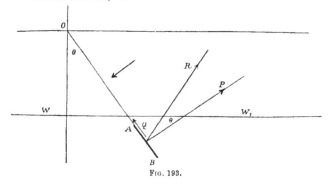

Fig. 193.

∴   Total work done $= Pv$

∴ $\epsilon = \dfrac{(P \cos \theta - Q \sin \theta)u}{Pv}.$

For a perfectly smooth float $Q = 0,$

and $\epsilon = \dfrac{u \cos \theta}{v}.$

When the float is vertical $\theta = 0,$

and $\epsilon = \dfrac{u}{v}.$

Feathering Floats.—Consider a point in the float at a distance r from the paddle centre. The principle of a feathering float has already been dealt with, but it may be interesting to examine the question from another point of view.

If the tangential velocity v of the point equals the velocity of forward motion u of the paddle centre or ship, the point will describe a cycloid. A cycloid is the path of a point on the circumference of a circle which rolls on its circumference without slipping.

If by some mechanism we could feather the float so that its plane would be

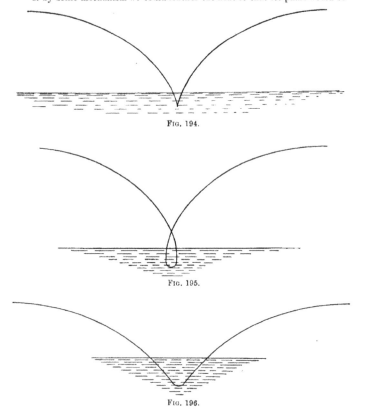

FIG. 194.

FIG. 195.

FIG. 196.

always tangential to the cycloid in fig. 194, then there would be a minimum of shock.

In the actual case of a paddle driving a ship a certain amount of slip necessarily takes place, thus making u less than v, and the path traced out by a point whose radius is r would be a curtate trochoid (fig. 195). A curtate trochoid is traced out by a point on the circumference if the circle slipped with a uniform velocity. This is equivalent to the point being on the circumference of a circle whose radius is greater than the radius of the rolling circle.

Again, if the floats be feathered so that the plane of one float follows a curtate trochoid as in fig. 195, the resulting path of a point in the float when driving the ship would be a trochoid more curtate than the one in the figure.

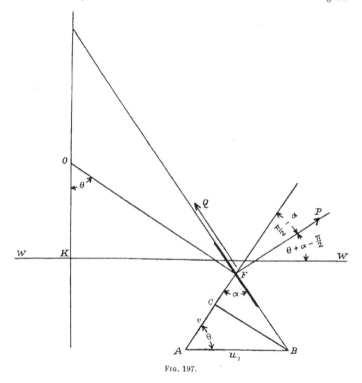

Fig. 197.

Thus we see that in order to have the forward motion equal to a certain amount u, when the tangential velocity of the paddle floats is v we should feather the floats to a curtate trochoid formed by the velocities v and u_1, where u_1 is greater than u by an amount depending upon the velocity of slip. In practice this method for finding the amount of feather is not adopted, a practical method being to feather the float so that its plane passes through the highest point of the paddle circle.

It is also interesting to see what feather should be given to the floats when u is greater than v. A velocity u_1 greater than u is chosen, and the resultant curve of u_1 and v then found.

The form is as in fig. 196 and is a trochoid.

For any desired values of v and u we can construct floats to the required feather if we know what the velocity of slip is likely to be.

Efficiency of a Feathering Float.—

Let the forward motion of ship $= u$.

Let the tangential velocity of float $= v$.

Consider the float at any instant, when centre is at F, say (fig. 197).

Choose velocity u_1 greater than u by an amount depending upon the slip.

In some paddles $u_1 = v$, that is, when the float is designed to pass through the top part of the circle.

This makes $\alpha = \dfrac{\pi}{2} - \dfrac{\theta}{2}$.

The velocity of slip is $(v - u)$, an assumption that was made in the treatment of paddle efficiency by the other method.

We also have $\qquad \tan \alpha = \dfrac{BC}{CF} = \dfrac{u_1 \sin \theta}{v - u_1 \cos \theta} = \dfrac{\sin \alpha}{\cos \alpha}$.

Set off triangle of velocities F B A, B A $= u_1$ and F A $= v$ as shown, and is perpendicular to O F. Then F B is the plane of float.

Let O be the paddle centre, and the angle F O K $= \theta$. O K is the vertical.

Let P and Q be the components of the resistance of the water to the motion of the float.

Let $\angle$ AFB $= a$.

Then the angle between P and A F produced is $\left(\dfrac{\pi}{2} - a\right)$ and the angle between P and W W produced is $\left(\theta + a - \dfrac{\pi}{2}\right)$ where W W is the water surface, and is therefore the direction of ship's motion.

Let T $=$ component of resistances in direction of motion.

Then T$u = $ useful work done.

$$\therefore \quad \text{Useful work} = \left\{ P \cos\left(\theta + a - \frac{\pi}{2}\right) - Q \sin\left(\theta + a - \frac{\pi}{2}\right) \right\} u.$$

Total work done $=$ work done against resistances to tangential motion

$$= \left\{ P \cos\left(\frac{\pi}{2} - a\right) + Q \sin\left(\frac{\pi}{2} - a\right) \right\} v.$$

$$\therefore \quad \text{Efficiency} = \frac{\left\{ P \cos\left(\theta + a - \frac{\pi}{2}\right) - Q \sin\left(\theta + a - \frac{\pi}{2}\right) \right\} u}{\left\{ P \cos\left(\frac{\pi}{2} - a\right) + Q \sin\left(\frac{\pi}{2} - a\right) \right\} v},$$

in the general case.

$$i.e. \quad \epsilon = \frac{\{P \sin (\theta + a) + Q \cos (\theta + a)\} u}{\{P \sin a + Q \cos a\} v}$$

$$= \frac{\{P \sin \theta \cos a + P \cos \theta \sin a + Q \cos \theta \cos a - Q \sin \theta \sin a\} u}{\{P \sin a + Q \cos a\} v} .$$

Substituting the value given above for $\dfrac{\sin a}{\cos a}$,

$$\epsilon = \frac{\{P \sin \theta(v - u_1 \cos \theta) + P \cos \theta u_1 \sin \theta + Q \cos \theta(v - u_1 \cos \theta) - Q \sin \theta u_1 \sin \theta\} u}{\{Pu_1 \sin \theta + Q(v - u_1 \cos \theta)\} v}$$

$$= \frac{\{vP \sin \theta + vQ \cos \theta - Qu_1\} u}{\{u_1 P \sin \theta - u_1 Q \cos \theta + Qv\} v}.$$

If $u_1 = v$, then $a = \dfrac{\pi}{2} - \dfrac{\theta}{2}$

$$\text{and } \epsilon = \frac{\left\{ P \cos \dfrac{\theta}{2} - Q \sin \dfrac{\theta}{2} \right\} u}{\left\{ P \cos \dfrac{\theta}{2} + Q \sin \dfrac{\theta}{2} \right\} v}.$$

These cases just considered

Radial float $\epsilon = \dfrac{(P \cos \theta - Q \sin \theta)u}{Pv} = \dfrac{u \cos \theta}{v}$, when $Q = 0$ . . . (1)

First feathering float $\epsilon = \dfrac{\left\{ P \cos \dfrac{\theta}{2} - Q \sin \dfrac{\theta}{2} \right\} u}{\left\{ P \cos \dfrac{\theta}{2} + Q \sin \dfrac{\theta}{2} \right\} v} = \dfrac{u}{v}$, when $Q = 0$. (2)

General case $\epsilon = \dfrac{\left\{ P \sin \theta + Q \cos \theta - Q\dfrac{u_1}{v} \right\} uv}{\left\{ P \sin \theta - Q \cos \theta + Q\dfrac{v}{u_1} \right\} u_1 v} = \dfrac{u}{u_1}$, when $Q = 0$. (3)

The velocity of slip in $(1) = v - u \cos \theta$

$(2) = v - u.$

$(3) = u_1 - u.$

Screw Propellers.

—A screw propeller is an apparatus which by its rotation about a straight line produces motion in the direction of that line. The surface of an ordinary screw propeller blade is a helical surface. Its action in producing thrust can be seen by considering a small element of the surface, which we may consider as a small plane. Let this element be supposed rigidly fixed to a rod perpendicular to the axis of rotation. Suppose that the rod in turning creates no resistance. The small plane will be oblique to this radius rod, and its effect when rotated round the axis of the shaft will be to tend to move the radius rod forward or backward (according to the direction of turning) along the shaft axis.

Let us first examine the nature of a helical surface. Consider an axis with a radius bar so attached to it that it can be moved along the axis while rotating. If we impart to the radius a uniform angular and at the same time a uniform forward motion it will trace out a helical surface.

Pitch of a Helical Surface.

—Let A B, fig. 198, be the axis, and b the radius. Let C C′ be position of the radius at one instant, and C_1 C′$_1$ its position after a complete revolution. Then the pitch of the surface is the distance C C_1. Pitch, properly speaking, only refers to a unit area of surface.

Thus we speak of the pitch at any point of the surface, meaning the pitch of the element of area at the point.

If either the angular or forward motions of the radius were independently accelerated, the pitch would vary from point to point of the surface. The pitch at any point of a helical surface is therefore defined to be the length that the radius of the point would travel along the axis during one revolution if its forward velocity and angular velocity remained constant through that revolution.

Consideration of Leading Features of a Screw Propeller.—An ordinary screw propeller is usually made up of 2, 3, or 4 blades, identically alike, and more or less conforming to a helical surface. They are united by means of bolts, or are cast into what is called the boss, which can be keyed on to the driving shaft. There are various shapes of blades, but the modifications in shape do not affect the question of efficiency very much.

Figures 199, 200, 201 show—

(1) An ordinary four-bladed propeller, slow merchant ship.
(2) Admiralty bronze propeller, cruiser or battleship.
(3) Small propeller, high speed, on turbine-driven shaft.

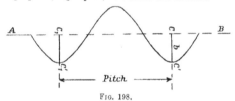

FIG. 198.

A propeller is right-handed if, when viewed from aft, it turns in the direction of the hands of a watch and drives the vessel ahead.

The "driving face" is the after side, and it is this surface which is designed to produce the required speed.

The "back" of a blade is the other or forward side, and its surface depends on the thickness of material necessary to give the blade sufficient strength.

The "leading edge of the blade" is the edge that cuts the water first when the screw is turning ahead.

The "following edge" is the other edge of the blade.

The "disc circle" is the circle swept out by the tips or outermost parts of the blades.

The "disc area" is the area of the disc circle.

The "diameter" of the propeller is the diameter of the disc circle.

The "pitch" of the propeller as a whole is the linear distance that the propeller would travel per revolution if its driving face worked in a solid fixed nut of the same form of surface.

If the "pitch" of a propeller is not uniform, an average has to be taken. The pitch at a point we have already seen.

The pitch, if not uniform, can vary in two ways — radially and axially.

We can find the variation in radial pitch by considering the variation of pitch at different points of a radius. We can find the variation in axial pitch by considering the variation of pitch on a circumference of a circle drawn on the blade with the axis as centre. The intersection of a cylinder with the blade will give a line, the pitch of which from point to point may be measured.

The "area" of a blade refers to the developed area of the driving face of one blade, and is the "helicoidal" area.

The "area or surface of a propeller" is the area of all the blades of it.

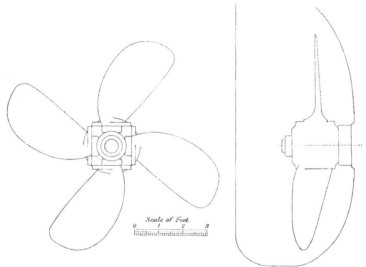

Fig. 199.—Four-bladed Propeller for a Slow Merchant Ship.

The "projected" area is the projection of the helicoidal area on a plane perpendicular to the axis.

$$\text{The "pitch ratio"} = \frac{\text{Pitch}}{\text{Diameter}} = \frac{p}{d}.$$

$$\text{The "diameter ratio"} = \frac{\text{Diameter}}{\text{Pitch}} = \frac{d}{p}.$$

We have seen in the case of a plane propeller that a certain slip necessarily takes place in order to obtain the thrust. In the same way, considering the propeller and its forward motion as a whole, its actual speed when driving a ship or when developing a thrust will be less than its speed if working in a solid fixed nut at the same rate of revolutions.

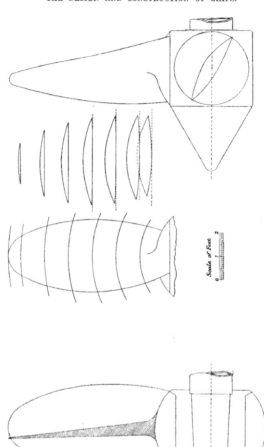

Scale of Feet

Fig. 200.—Bronze Propeller, Admiralty pattern.

Let n = revolutions per second.

p = pitch of propeller in feet.

V = speed of ship in ft. secs. = actual speed of propeller relatively to still water.

Speed of propeller worked in a solid fixed nut = pn.

$$\text{Slip} = pn - V.$$

$$\text{Slip ratio} = \frac{pn - V}{pn}.$$

$$\therefore \quad pn\,(1 - \text{slip ratio}) = V.$$

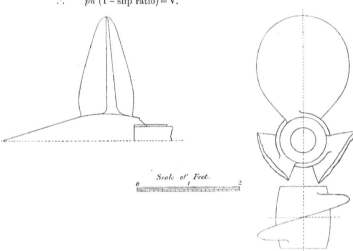

Scale of Feet.

FIG. 201.—Small High-speed Propeller for Turbine Steamer.

Efficiency of a Small Element of a Screw Propeller.—Let the element be a small plane fixed to a radius which offers no resistance to turning. Let the angle of inclination of the plane to the perpendicular transverse plane be ϕ. Fig. 202 gives a view of the plane element, the radius being perpendicular to the plane of the paper. This angle ϕ is called the pitch angle. Let the plane be moving at the instant with velocity v, and let the resulting motion of the ship be u.

Adopting the nomenclature of the case of the plane propeller in the preceding chapter,

$$\epsilon = \left\{ \frac{P\cos\phi - Q\sin\phi}{P\sin\phi + Q\cos\phi} \right\} \frac{u}{v},$$

since the direction of u is perpendicular to direction of v. We are here still considering the water round the plane element as being at rest.

Suppose we represent the velocity v by a line A B (fig. 203). Then the velocity u of ship is perpendicular to A B.

Let B C be drawn $= u$. Then A C represents the distance the elemental plane has actually travelled in a unit of time. The plane is, however, inclined to the transverse plane at an angle ϕ, the pitch angle.

Draw A D meeting B C produced in D such that angle D A B $= \phi$.

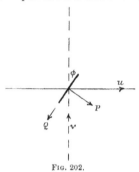

Fig. 202.

If now we suppose the propeller to be working in a solid fixed nut it will follow the line represented by A D, but being in water, where a certain amount of slip takes place, it will follow the line A C.

C D therefore represents the velocity of slip that takes place.

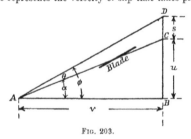

Fig. 203.

The angle D A C is called the slip angle, and the angle C A B is called the virtual pitch angle.

Call D A C, θ; and call C A B, a.

Then $\qquad (a + \theta) = \phi$

and $\qquad \tan \phi = \dfrac{u + s}{v}$

$$\tan a = \frac{u}{v} \cdot$$

The element of the blade is moving in the direction A C inclined to A D at the angle θ.

$\therefore$ Expression for efficiency becomes, when in the above expression we write $\phi = (a + \theta)$ and $\dfrac{u}{v} = \tan a$,

$$\epsilon = \frac{\{P \cos (a + \theta) - Q \sin (a + \theta)\} \tan a}{P \sin (a + \theta) + Q \cos (a + \theta)}.$$

Theoretically, it appears from this equation that to increase ϵ, all that is necessary is to decrease θ or the slip angle; but in doing so it will be necessary to run the propeller plane at a very much higher number of revolutions in order to get the forward speed u.

The value of Q in relation to P is dependent on the velocity, as we shall see, and therefore a contrary element may come in, tending to reduce the efficiency as we decrease the slip.

It becomes, therefore, a question of giving certain values to P and Q in terms of the velocity V, and finding what relation of pitch and slip gives maximum efficiency. The force Q is called the edgewise friction. This was the method adopted by the late Dr Froude in determining the best pitch angle and slip angle for maximum efficiency, and the values he took for P and Q were based on the following.

If we have a small plane of area A moved obliquely through water at a speed V, at an angle of λ to its line of motion, the normal pressure $P = p A V^2 \sin \lambda$, and the edgewise or surface friction $Q = f A V^2$, where p and f are coefficients representing the pressure and friction per unit area of surface at unit velocity respectively. Mr Froude gave for A in square feet, V in feet per second, P and Q in lbs.,

$$p = 1\cdot7 \text{ and } f = \cdot008.$$

The resultant speed of plane in this case through the water is represented by the line A C (fig. 203), which is v sec a and $\lambda = \theta$.

$$\therefore \quad P = p A v^2 \sec^2 a \sin \theta,$$
$$Q = f A v^2 \sec^2 a.$$

$$\therefore \quad \frac{Q}{P} = \frac{f}{p} \cdot \frac{1}{\sin \theta} = \frac{k}{\sin \theta} \quad \text{where} \quad k = \frac{f}{p}.$$

Making these substitutions in the equation above for efficiency we have

$$\epsilon = \tan a \; \frac{\sin \theta \cos (a + \theta) - k \sin (a + \theta)}{\sin \theta \sin (a + \theta) + k \cos (a + \theta)}.$$

Since θ the slip angle is seldom greater than $10°$, we may take $\sin \theta = \theta$ and $\cos \theta = 1$.

$$\therefore \quad \epsilon = \tan a \frac{\theta \cos a - \theta^2 \sin a - k \sin a - k\theta \cos a}{\theta \sin a + \theta^2 \cos a + k \cos a - k\theta \sin a}$$

$$= \frac{\theta(1 - k) - (\theta^2 + k) \tan a}{\theta(1 - k) + (\theta^2 + k) \cot a}.$$

In this equation k is constant and the angles θ and a are variables. It is necessary, therefore, to find what values of a and θ will give maximum efficiency. To do this, if we find first what value of a gives maximum ϵ when θ is constant, and second what value of θ gives maximum ϵ when a is constant, we can then find $(a + \theta)$.

Suppose θ is the only variable, a is constant.

$$\frac{d\epsilon}{d\theta} = 0 \text{ for maximum efficiency.}$$

From this we get $\theta = \sqrt{k}$.

When a is the only variable,

$$\text{from } \quad \frac{d\epsilon}{da} = 0 \text{ we get } \tan 2a = \frac{\theta}{\theta^2 + k}.$$

So that $\quad \tan a = \sqrt{1 + \left(\frac{\theta^2 + k}{\theta}\right)^2} - \left(\frac{\theta^2 + k}{\theta}\right).$

But $\quad \tan (a + \theta) = \dfrac{\tan a + \tan \theta}{1 - \tan a \tan \theta}$

$$= \frac{\sqrt{\theta^2 + (\theta^2 + k)^2} - (\theta^2 + k) + \theta \tan \theta}{\theta - \tan \theta \{ \sqrt{\theta^2 + (\theta^2 + k)^2} - (\theta^2 + k)\}}.$$

Putting $\theta = \sqrt{k}$,

$$\tan (a + \theta) = \frac{\sqrt{1 + 4\theta^2} - 2\theta + \tan \theta}{(1 - \tan \theta \sqrt{1 + 4\theta^2} + 2\theta \tan \theta)}.$$

Again making an approximation, since θ is a small angle, putting $\tan \theta = \theta$.

$$\therefore \quad \tan (a + \theta) \doteqdot \frac{1 - \theta + 2\theta^2}{1 - \theta + 2\theta^2 - 2\theta^3} \text{ since } \sqrt{1 + 4\theta^2} \doteqdot 1 + 2\theta^2 \text{ very nearly,}$$

$$= 1 \text{ very nearly.}$$

$$\therefore \quad a + \theta = 45°.$$

This is therefore the pitch angle that gives maximum efficiency. It will be noted that $(a + \theta)$ is independent of the value of k.

The slip angle corresponding to angle 45° maximum efficiency is in this case dependent upon k and equals $\sqrt{k}$.

From the above we can therefore say that if the slip angle is increased or decreased by a certain small amount, the pitch angle has approximately to receive the same amount of increment or decrement to obtain maximum efficiency.

To prove this. Suppose now we are given a certain slip angle θ_1 other than $\theta = \sqrt{k}$ which gives maximum efficiency and we want to find a_1 so that the pitch angle $a_1 + \theta_1$ may give a maximum efficiency in the new condition, i.e. suppose we want to find what change to make in a. When θ is constant the value of a which gives maximum efficiency is given by

$$\tan a = \sqrt{1 + \left(\theta + \frac{k}{\theta}\right)^2} - \left(\theta + \frac{k}{\theta}\right) \quad . \quad . \quad . \quad (1)$$

Since $\quad \theta = \sqrt{k}$

$$\tan a = \sqrt{1 + 4k} - 2\sqrt{k} \quad . \quad . \quad . \quad . \quad (2)$$

Let $\theta_1 = c \sqrt{k}$ where c is a constant $= \dfrac{\theta_1}{\theta}$.

$\therefore$ from (1) $\tan a_1 = \sqrt{1 + k\left(c + \dfrac{1}{c}\right)^2} - \sqrt{k}\left(c + \dfrac{1}{c}\right)$.   .   (3)

This equation (3) gives us the new value for a_1 which must be associated with the given value θ_1 to give maximum efficiency.

If no great departure from $\sqrt{k}$ is made in the given slip, c will be only a little greater or less than unity, and therefore $\left(c + \dfrac{1}{c}\right)$ may be regarded as equal to 2. Looking at equations (3) and (2), this means that practically $\tan a$ and $\therefore a$ remain unaltered.

Let slip angle for maximum $\epsilon = \theta_1$ when pitch angle $= 45°$, $i.e.$ $\theta_1 = \sqrt{k}$.
Let new slip angle be θ.
Let $a = 45° - y$.

$\therefore$ $\tan a = \dfrac{1 - \tan y}{1 + \tan y}.$ y is a small angle,

$\therefore$ $\tan a = \dfrac{1 - y}{1 + y} = 1 - 2y + 2y^2.$

But it has already been proved that

$$\tan a = \sqrt{1 + \left(\theta + \dfrac{k}{\theta}\right)^2} - \left(\theta + \dfrac{k}{\theta}\right).$$

$\therefore$ $1 - 2y + 2y^2 = 1 + \dfrac{\left(\theta + \dfrac{k}{\theta}\right)^2}{2} - \left(\theta + \dfrac{k}{\theta}\right)$ nearly.

$$y^2 - y = - \dfrac{\left(\theta + \dfrac{k}{\theta}\right)}{2} + \left\{\dfrac{\theta + \dfrac{k}{\theta}}{2}\right\}^2$$

$$= - \dfrac{\theta + \left(\dfrac{\theta_1^2}{\theta}\right)}{2} + \left(\dfrac{\theta + \dfrac{\theta_1^2}{\theta}}{2}\right)^2$$

$$y = \tfrac{1}{2} - \sqrt{\tfrac{1}{4}\left\{1 - 4\left(\dfrac{\theta + \dfrac{\theta_1^2}{\theta}}{2} - \left[\dfrac{\theta + \dfrac{\theta_1^2}{\theta}}{2}\right]\right)^2\right\}}$$

Call this first function of θ, X.

So that $y = \tfrac{1}{2} - \tfrac{1}{2}\sqrt{1 - 4X}$
$i.e.$ $y = \tfrac{1}{2} - \tfrac{1}{2}(1 - 4X)^{\frac{1}{2}}.$
Expanding the binomial $y = \tfrac{1}{2} - \tfrac{1}{2}(1 - 2X - 2X^2 - 2X^3, \text{ etc.})$
$= X + X^2 + X^3 + \text{etc.}$

Substituting orig. values $y = \left\{\dfrac{\theta + \dfrac{\theta_1^2}{\theta}}{2} - \left(\dfrac{\theta + \dfrac{\theta_1^2}{\theta}}{2}\right)^2\right\} + \text{higher powers.}$

$\therefore$ neglecting powers of θ above 2

we get $\quad y = \frac{1}{2}\left(\theta + \frac{\theta_1^{\,2}}{\theta}\right).$

Let $\qquad \theta = \theta_1(1 + h).$

Then $\qquad y = \theta_1\left(1 + \frac{h^2}{2} - \frac{h^3}{2} + \frac{h^4}{2} + \text{etc.}\right),$ substituting $\theta_1(1 + h)$ for θ.

But $\qquad a + \theta = 45° - y + \theta$

$\therefore \qquad a + \theta = 45° + \theta_1\left(h - \frac{h^2}{2} \ \text{etc.}\right)$

$\therefore$ if the slip angle θ is increased by a small amount $= \theta_1 h$, then for maximum efficiency the pitch angle $(a + \theta)$ has to be increased by approximately the same amount, which proves the proposition.

We have seen $\qquad \tan a = \sqrt{1 + 4k} - 2\sqrt{k}$

$\therefore \qquad \cot a = \dfrac{1}{\sqrt{1 + 4k} - 2\sqrt{k}}$

$\qquad\qquad\qquad = \sqrt{1 + 4k} + 2\sqrt{k} \ \text{nearly.}$

also $\qquad \theta = \sqrt{k}.$

Substituting these values for θ, $\tan a$, and $\cot a$, in the general expression for efficiency, viz.

$$\epsilon = \tan a \ \frac{\theta - \tan a \ (\theta^2 + k)}{\theta \tan a + (\theta^2 + k)}, \ \text{Froude's formula (see below)},$$

we get $\qquad \epsilon = \dfrac{\sqrt{k} - 2k \tan a}{\sqrt{k} + 2k \cot a} = \dfrac{1 - 2\sqrt{k} \tan a}{1 + 2\sqrt{k} \cot a}.$

$\therefore \qquad \epsilon = \dfrac{1 - 2\sqrt{k} \ \sqrt{1 + 4k} + 4k}{1 + 2\sqrt{k} \ \sqrt{1 + 4k} + 4k}$

$\qquad\qquad = \dfrac{\sqrt{1 + 4k} - 2\sqrt{k}}{\sqrt{1 + 4k} + 2\sqrt{k}} = \tan^2 a.$

$\therefore \qquad \epsilon = 1 + 8k - 4\sqrt{k}(1 + 2k).$

Putting a value for k, Mr Froude calculates $\cdot0047$ as a common value.

$\therefore \quad \sqrt{k} = \cdot07.$

$\therefore \qquad \epsilon = 1\cdot0376 - \cdot28 \times 1\cdot0094 = \cdot75 \ \text{nearly.}$

$\therefore \qquad \epsilon = \cdot75 \ \text{nearly.}$

$\text{Tan } a = \sqrt{\epsilon} = \cdot86 \ \text{nearly.}$

The greatest efficiency that can be obtained with the above value for k is about 76 per cent.

Froude's equation to the efficiency is based on the assumption that the frictional force Q acts along the resultant of the plane's motion A C, and hence is inclined a instead of $(a + \theta)$ to transverse.

Taking Q as acting along the plane, we get

$$\epsilon = \frac{1 - k - 2 \sqrt{k} \tan a}{1 - k + 2 \sqrt{k} \cot a},$$

substituting $\quad = \dfrac{1 + 3k - 2 \sqrt{k} \sqrt{1 + 4k}}{1 + 3k + 2 \sqrt{k} \sqrt{1 + 4k}}.$

All the investigations we have hitherto considered in the question of the efficiency of a small plane propeller involved the assumption that the particles of water in the vicinity of the plane were at rest relatively to one another, so that we could thereby give a definite value to the velocity of the water as it met the plane, or, as it is called, the velocity of feed. From what we have seen regarding the efficiency of a small helical surface element, we can hardly make direct deductions for an actual propeller, or even for one blade, because the pitch might vary from point to point; and even if this were not the case, we could not say with certainty what the action at any small element of the blade area would be, on account of the fact of its only being a part of the whole blade, and not isolated, as was the case previously under consideration.

The Standard of Efficiency of the Screw Propeller.—Professor J. B. Henderson of the R.N. College, Greenwich, has recently proposed a theory respecting the action of the screw propeller from the following considerations :—

The propulsive effect on a body moving through a medium is due to the projection of a stream of the medium in a sternward direction. In a perfect fluid this would set up a stream-line motion which would form a closed kinematic chain, and, providing there were no discontinuities in the stream lines, the nett thrust on the body would be nil. To produce a thrust we must have a discontinuity in the stream-line motion. Thus a jet propeller in a perfect fluid, with submerged inlet and outlet, would have no losses, and therefore its efficiency would be unity ; but no thrust would be developed. Thus, in order to get thrust we must necessarily have a certain waste of energy, since a discontinuity of motion will cause the formation of eddies, which is a source of loss. Hence our efficiency must be less than unity. As a standard of efficiency we can consider the jet propeller, working in a perfect fluid, to have the greatest efficiency possible, and therefore this will be our standard of efficiency. In order to obtain thrust, energy must be imparted to the jet ; a portion of this must be lost. As we can have no eddy motion in a perfect fluid, we must cause a discontinuity in the stream-line system by discharging the jet above the surface of the fluid. This will then represent our ideal propeller, which will develop thrust with a minimum waste of energy. Its efficiency may be regarded as a standard, above which it is impossible to go in a propeller working under the conditions of ordinary practice in a viscous fluid, and the expression for this efficiency may be obtained as follows :—

Let V = speed of advance of propeller.

v_o = speed of jet at outlet, relative to the propeller.

v_i = speed of fluid at inlet, relative to the propeller,

F = the mass flux through the propeller.

Then   thrust $= F(v_0 - v_i)$

useful power $= F(v_0 - v_i)V$.

Total power = flux of kinetic energy into the jet = $\frac{1}{2}F(v_0^2 - v_i^2)$. Hence the efficiency is given by

$$\epsilon = \frac{(v_0 - v_i)V}{\frac{1}{2}(v_0^2 - v_i^2)} = \frac{2V}{v_0 + v_i}.$$

Now $(v_0 - V)$ is the *nominal slip* of the propeller ; it would be the actual slip if the fluid ahead of the propeller race were not accelerated so as to flow to meet the propeller. And $(v_0 - v_i)$ is the *actual slip*. If we call S_n and S_a the nominal and actual slip ratios respectively we have

$$S_n = \frac{v_0 - V}{v_0} \quad \therefore \quad V = v_0(1 - S_n),$$

$$S_a = \frac{v_0 - v_i}{v_0} \quad \therefore \quad v_i = v_0(1 - S_a).$$

And $\quad \therefore \quad \epsilon = \frac{2V}{v_0 + v_i} = \frac{2v_0(1 - S_n)}{v_0(2 - S_a)} = \frac{1 - S_n}{1 - \frac{S_a}{2}}.$

This is therefore our ideal efficiency which cannot be exceeded. To apply this conception to the case of the screw propeller we imagine the tube of a submerged jet propeller to become quite short. The stream-line system will then become what is known as a free vortex. The generation of a free vortex would not, however, cause a thrust, which must therefore be due to the discontinuity caused in the wake.

Thus the water ahead of the screw flows towards it in stream lines, but in passing through the screw it becomes accelerated and discontinuous with the surrounding fluid, and is projected sternwards as a jet. The main conclusions of this method of analysis of the phenomena of propulsion are :—

(1) A propeller forms the centre of a system of stream tubes, the configuration of which moves forward with the propeller. In a perfect fluid the system consumes no energy, but in a viscous fluid the energy required for its maintenance is supplied by the propeller.

(2) In a perfect fluid—and also in a viscous fluid, apart from the small thrust required to maintain the stream-line system—thrust would be impossible of attainment without a discontinuity in the stream-tube system. In a jet propeller this discontinuity occurs at the outlet, and in a screw propeller most probably in the wake beginning at the screw disc.

(3) The acceleration of the fluid ahead of the propeller does not contribute to the thrust, but is brought about by a circulation of energy from the wake, as in a moving source and sink combination ; hence all the energy in the wake as it leaves the propeller is not lost. The thrust produced by a screw propeller is due to an acceleration of the whole or part of the fluid as it passes through the screw disc, the accelerated portion being discontinuous with the surrounding fluid, thus forming a jet.

(4) In the case of a screw propeller there must be a flux of rotational momentum into the surrounding fluid equal to the torque. This rotational momentum is most probably confined to the immediate wake behind the screw, and the screw is continuously imparting rotational velocity to new fluid, this rotational energy constituting one of the losses in the propeller. Since this rotational system, unlike the stream-tube system in the fore and aft direction, cannot move forward with the screw unchanged, the rotational motion is not cumulative.

CHAPTER XVIII.

PROPELLERS AND PROPELLER EFFICIENCY.

In coming to the question of the efficiency of a screw propeller driving a ship, let us first of all examine what effect the ship has on the water immediately behind it, as that is the place where it is found most convenient to have the propeller. The efficiency of the combination of ship and propeller is determined, not by the screw working alone in still water against a resistance equal to that of the ship for a certain speed, but by the efficiency of the screw in conjunction with the hull, or working in the wake of the hull. Let us first examine the conditions that thus influence the efficiency.

Conditions of Wake.—When the hull is passing through the water the motion of the stream lines aft depend to a great extent on the form of the after-body. The particles of the water in the vicinity of the wake have an inward velocity perpendicular to the line of motion of the ship. The propeller has a forward velocity equal to that of ship. The result is, therefore, that the particles of water meet the propeller in an oblique direction, or, which is the same effect, as if the propeller were working in still water, but placed obliquely to its line of motion. The loss due to this cause is not very considerable, but it becomes important in the question of "vibration due to propellers."

In a very bluff ship, bluff at the stern, a certain amount of eddying takes place, the water at the stern being in a state of disturbance or eddy, but the particles possessing a certain forward velocity.

If the propeller were placed in the eddy, and if we neglected any loss that might occur due to the turbulence of the water, the effect would be that the propeller would develop a greater thrust for the same speed of ship. That is, the propeller would be placed in a stream of water having a forward velocity relatively to still water, and thus would work with greater efficiency relatively to the still water. The propeller thus gains a little of the lost energy which must have been spent in creating the eddying wake. In fine forms there is practically no eddying wake of this description at all.

Frictional Wake.—There is another kind of wake caused by skin friction, which is more evidenced in the finer forms. The effect of the skin friction in imparting a certain forward velocity to particles in the vicinity of the skin produces the resultant effect of a certain amount of frictional wake at the stern, the particles having more or less a definite forward velocity relatively to still water. Those particles near the middle line will have the greatest velocity, and for this reason the wake will have more effect on a single screw than on a twin screw. This wake is also dependent to a great extent on the amount of skin friction, or on the character of the skin surface.

These disturbances already noted are caused by the ship moving through the water, and effect a change in the efficiency of the propeller because of its position in the region of these disturbances. They can be briefly noted as the influence of the hull on the propeller, or change in efficiency due to wake. Further on, while considering this change in its relation to the nett efficiency of the hull and propeller, it will be referred to as the " wake factor."

Action of Propeller on Ship.—To understand clearly the action that a propeller if placed in the vicinity of the stern has upon the resistance of the ship, it will be better first to examine the action of the propeller on the surrounding water. Suppose we have a propeller fixed on a horizontal shaft in water, this shaft being controlled so that it can be turned at any desired number of revolutions. Also suppose that we can cause the whole body of water to flow past the propeller at any desired speed. Let the propeller be loose on the shaft ; then no matter what may be the speed of the water, the screw will turn without slip.

If we run the water at speed v, and the pitch of propeller be p,

$$\text{then the revs. for no slip} = n = \frac{v}{p}.$$

Suppose now the propeller to be fixed to the shaft. The condition of no slip will be $pn = v$. Now increase the number of revolutions to n_1, still keeping the speed v. There will now be a certain amount of slip, viz. $pn_1 - v$, and the propeller will develop a forward thrust.

It therefore requires this relation pn_1 greater than v before a forward thrust can be developed. The development of this thrust can be seen better by supposing v to be zero. In this case the propeller does not move relatively to the water, and the slip is $pn - 0 = pn$.

As the propeller is turning round, the driving face of each blade exerts a pressure on the water behind it and the back face exerts a suction. The sum of the components of these resultant forces will equal the thrust of the blade. The resultant effect of the blade is to displace the water behind it in a direction normal to the surface, and immediately before the blade to draw the water after it. The excess of pressure on the driving face and the defect of pressure on the back will depend on the inertia of the water and the pressure due to the head. What we have, then, as the propeller turns, is that the water in the vicinity of the propeller must have a rotary motion, and at the same time a sternward motion. There must therefore be a steady flow of water from the region in front of the propeller to that behind it. It is to be supposed that it will flow in from a large area, and be gradually accelerated both in a rotary and sternward direction. Consider the water to have a certain speed v_1 less than pn there will be less slip, but there will still be the same characteristics as above described in the motion of the water to the propeller, though to a less degree.

Suppose this propeller working when the speed of water $= V$, the speed of ship (known), and at such a rate of revolutions N, which give a thrust ρ equal to the resistance of ship. Consider the propeller situated at the stern of the ship. If driven at revolutions N, one might think that the resultant speed of ship should be V, since the propeller is developing a thrust ρ, the resistance of ship at that speed, wake not being considered ; but in this condition we have to examine the tendency of the propeller to draw water away from the hull ; this will therefore cause a defect of pressure on the hull, and hence an addition will be made to the resistance of the ship, so that the propeller in order to drive the ship at the intended speed V will have to develop a proportionately greater thrust.

The effect of the change on the resistance of the ship due to the propeller is called the "Augment of Resistance." This term is most commonly used when we refer to its effect on the resistance of the ship.

Experimental data furnish proof that this change, which we can see will depend to a great extent on the pitch of the propeller, varies as the revolutions, and therefore as the thrust. It is therefore found more convenient, when we are relating it to the thrust of the propeller required to drive the ship at speed V, to call it a "thrust deduction." This was the term that was introduced by Mr Froude in his work on the experimental methods of arriving at the best size of propeller to use for maximum efficiency.

We have now examined two factors that will affect the efficiency of a propeller working behind the hull, viz. "wake factor" and "thrust deduction." The first named increases the apparent efficiency of the screw. Also due to this factor there is sometimes noted in actual cases a negative slip, which is only apparent however.

Let V = speed of ship,

v = forward speed of wake,

p = pitch of propeller,

n = rate of revolutions.

The apparent slip is $pn - V$, and in some cases of full ships, with propellers of small slip, V is observed to be greater than pn. This may be the case. The speed of the propeller relatively to the water in wake is $V - v$, i.e. speed relatively to the water in which it works.

The true slip is therefore $= pn - (V - v)$.

Froude's Experiments on Screw Propellers. — The limit of application of the mathematical deductions as to the efficiency of a small element of a blade has been seen to be reached when we begin to sum up the thrusts and turning moments of separate elements of the blade, because we cannot say what effect is produced on the factor p in the equation $P = pAv^2 \sin \lambda$ when several blade elements are contiguous to each other. To find the effect of this change of condition, Mr W. Froude carried out a series of experiments in the Experimental Tank at Torquay, and subsequently Mr R. E. Froude carried out for the Admiralty in the Haslar Tank another series of experiments, with a view to obtaining a method of finding the efficiencies of screw propellers by means of model screws in conjunction with models of ships. The latter investigation was divided into two principal sections—(1) the efficiency of screws working by themselves in undisturbed water; and (2) the change in efficiency due to bringing the screw into conjunction with the hull. These two divisions are termed "screw efficiency proper" and "hull efficiency" respectively. Previously, at Torquay and Haslar, a fairly complete and accurate determination (in model screws) of the characteristics of performance which are common to all screws of ordinary pattern had been made, and some ideas were obtained of the variations of efficiencies due to alterations of design. The method of experimenting was as follows :—The model screws on which the experiments were made were each mounted on the forward end of a shaft, the bearings of which were bracketed down from a frame above the water-level. The shaft was driven by a geared vertical spindle, the top bearing of which was in the above water-frame. This frame was mounted on a delicate parallel motion free only to move fore and aft wise. This motion, which consists of the forward thrust of the screw minus the resistance of the mechanism in the water, was measured automatically by recording the extension of a spiral spring. The whole apparatus was mounted on a truck running on a straight and level railway which extended throughout the length of the experimental tank. Any speed could be assigned to the screw or truck. When twin screws were used, each screw had a separate frame mounted in its position on the same parallel motion. The resistances of the mechanism in itself and through the water were eliminated as far as possible from the recorded results. A somewhat similar truck running on the same railway was used for experimenting on the resistance of models, the model being for this purpose attached underneath it. By joining the two trucks the model may either be attached in its place or omitted, and the screw experiments made either behind the model or in undisturbed water. The model can also be run with or without the screw behind it. Fig. 130 shows the screw truck.

The screw truck records for each screw the thrust, speed, turning moment, and revolutions per minute, and, when the experiments are made without the ship model in front, the screw efficiency is determinable. When the model is run alone, the amount of energy necessary to overcome the resistance of the model at a certain speed is determinable. If the joint trucks be run with the screw in combination with the hull, the modifications in (1) resistance of the model caused by the presence of the screw, and (2) in efficiency of screw caused by the presence of the model, are determinable. The first of these two has been called the "augmentation" of resistance, and is of necessity a loss of efficiency. The second is due to the fact that the screw is working in water which has been disturbed by the passage of the model through it, so that generally a less amount of driving power is required to maintain a given thrust at a given speed behind the model than in undisturbed water. "The cause of this reduction of power is the forward motion of the wake water in which the screw is working, and the nett efficiency of the screw in this disturbed water is practically identical with that *which would be produced by a mere uniform forward current*, the forward speed of which, and the saving in driving power due to which, may be measured."

Efficiency of Screw in Undisturbed Water.—To determine the screw efficiency in undisturbed water, a series of experiments upon any given screw is made, without the model in front, at a constant speed of advance, but at a varying number of revolutions per minute, ranging from that which gives almost no thrust to about double that number. These correspond to from no slip to 50 per cent. slip. The records of turning moment and thrust for one speed of advance can be shown as in fig. 204.

$$\text{Efficiency} = \frac{\text{Thrust} \times \text{travel per rev.}}{\text{Turning moment} \times 2\pi} = \frac{\text{Thrust}}{\text{T.M.} \times \dfrac{2\pi}{\text{travel per rev.}}}$$

If we multiply all turning-moment ordinates by $\dfrac{2\pi}{\text{travel per rev.}}$ we get a curve which may be called "turning force" measured at radius =

$\dfrac{\text{travel per rev.}}{2\pi}$ because the ratio of thrust to this force gives the efficiency ordinate. The thrust and turning-force curves are slightly concave upwards, but do not become even approximately tangential to the base line. The ordinates of the efficiency curve must be zero where the thrust is zero, and, like the thrust curve, the efficiency curve intersects the base at an angle. It rises steeply and uniformly as the rotary speed increases, somewhat suddenly reaching a maximum, from which it slowly falls off. It will be seen that the point of actual maximum efficiency is rather vague, and it follows that a given screw, advancing through the water at a given speed, is almost equally efficient within a somewhat large range of thrust values.

Other diagrams can be obtained for any other speed of advance required, but this is not necessary, as there is a theoretical law of comparison for screws similar to that for models which expresses the relation between such curves for different speeds of advance, which is tolerably correct for the largest differences of speed, and is practically accurate for small differences.

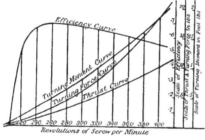

FIG. 204.

On a diagram for a given speed of advance V take one value of R (= revs. per minute) giving a thrust T and a turning force F. Suppose the speed of advance be changed to V_1. If the revolutions R be altered in the same proportion as the speed has been and become $R_1 = R\dfrac{V_1}{V}$, then the travel per revolution remains the same, so does the slip ratio, and so do the angles at which the different parts of the blade cut the water. The speeds in the different parts of the stream-line system will all be changed in the same ratio as the linear speed of advance, and the directions of all the forces acting on all parts of the blades, whether due to friction or to pressure, will be unaltered, and *their magnitude will be directly proportional to the square of the linear speed of advance.*

In changing V into V_1 the original thrust and turning force are each multiplied by $\left(\dfrac{V_1}{V}\right)^2$, so that the efficiency, which is thrust divided by turning force, remains unaltered at *corresponding revolutions*, which are in the ratio $\dfrac{V_1}{V}$. The travel per revolution and slip ratio are unaltered.

Fig. 205 illustrates the relations between the diagrams severally expressing the performances of a given screw at different speeds.

$A_1 E_1$ is the thrust curve, $a_1 e_1$ the turning-force curve, and $b\, b_1\, d\, d_1$ the efficiency curve for a speed of advance of V_1. To obtain the respective curves for a speed of advance V_2 we must alter the abscissæ scales of revolution directly as the speeds of advance, the ordinate scales of thrust and turning force directly as the square of the speed, while the ordinates of the efficiency curves will remain unaltered.

Take any points B_1, C_1, D_1 on the thrust curve $A_1 E_1$ for a speed of advance of V_1, and corresponding points b_1, c_1, d_1 on the corresponding turning-force curve at certain rotary speeds. Take points at the "corresponding revolutions" to these in the thrust and turning-force curves of the other speed of advance V_2, that is, at revolutions $R_1 \dfrac{V_2}{V_1}$, as shown at B_2, C_2, D_2 and b_2, c_2, d_2. Pass through the points B_1, B_2, etc., also b_1, b_2, etc., parabolas, with their origin at the zero of revolutions, their ordinates varying as $\left(\dfrac{V_2}{V_1}\right)^2$, V_2 having different successive values.

We can see from this construction that any number of additional thrust curves can be drawn for a series of values of the speed of advance. Any number of parabolas can be drawn similar to B_1, B_2, B_3, etc., and the successive intersections of any one of these parabolas with the individual thrust curves will be points of corresponding revolutions per minute, and will have the same travel per revolution, the same slip ratio, and the same efficiency. Each parabola will have assigned to it its appropriate efficiency value, so that *a single efficiency curve in addition to the thrust curves and parabolas* is sufficient without any turning-force curves to enable us to show, for any given screw within the limits of pitch ratio 1·2 to 2·2, its complete performances at any speed whatever. What has been shown and proved above refers to one particular screw. We can establish another law which enables us to express the relations between the *performances of similar screws of different absolute dimensions.* This law is that "at the corresponding revolutions the efficiency is constant, the thrusts and turning forces being for a given linear speed proportional to the square of the dimensions." Hence, from one thrust and one efficiency curve for a given screw we can find the turning force, thrust, and efficiency of any similar screw of modified dimensions for all speeds of advance and revolution.

Efficiency of Screw behind Ship Model.—We shall now show that there is a gain in the efficiency of the screw when working behind a model in a wake which is travelling at a speed relatively to the surrounding water of v feet per minute. The speed of the model through the water is V. Suppose that its speed through the wake water in which the screw acts to be V_1, so that the forward speed of the wake water relatively to the model is $V - V_1 = v$, it follows that the screw will be working under the same conditions as when working in undisturbed water at speed V_1. As the revolutions remain unchanged the thrust will be the same as in undisturbed water at V_1, and so will the turning moment. The advance per revolution will be greater in the case of the screw working behind the model in the ratio of V to V_1, and the turning force as a measure of efficiency will necessarily be less in the same ratio, and the efficiency of the screw working behind the model which is $\dfrac{\text{thrust}}{\text{turning force}}$ will also be greater than when working in undisturbed water in the ratio V to V_1, that is, $E \times \dfrac{V}{V_1}$.

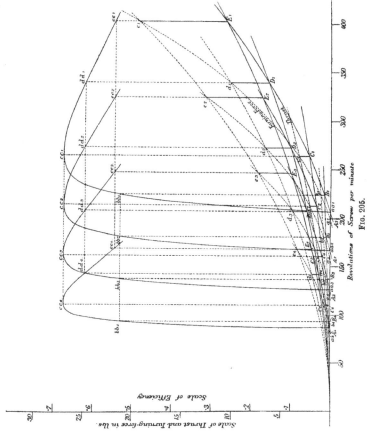

Fig. 205.

Hence, if we find that with a model at speed V we get a certain thrust for certain revolutions with the screw working behind, and that we get the same thrust for the same revolutions in still water at speed V_1, we know that the speed of the wake must be $V - V_1$, and that the efficiency of the screw when working behind the model must be its efficiency in still water multiplied by $\dfrac{V}{V_1}$; so that to find the speed of the wake we have to get a comparison between the thrust curves given in still water and those taken behind the model.

Character of Wake.—So far, in our consideration of the wake, we have taken it as being a uniform homogeneous forward moving current, and, in its resultant action, we may take this as being correct, and infer from this that the turning moment behind the model will be the same as in still water, and that the turning force will therefore be less in the ratio that V_1 is to V. Now, from the comparison of records of turning moment made in conjunction with the hull and the records of the same in still water, it has been found that there is very little difference between them, and that, in fact, the turbulence of the wake tends to increase rather than diminish the efficiency of the screw, so that we are justified in our assumption regarding the wake. Hence, what we have to do now in order to find the hull efficiency is to get (1) the resistances of the model with and without the screw, which gives us the loss by "augmentation" of resistance ; and (2) thrusts of the screw with and without model, which give us the gain in efficiency due to wake. These two results give us the value of the elements "augmentation" and "wake," which together form hull efficiency ; any other information required for the total propulsive efficiency can be got from experiments with the screws alone.

Fig. 206 given below is typical of all other such ; it shows the results for a complete set of experiments for ascertaining the augmentation and wake values for a single model with its screw at a constant speed V. The figure embodies the three essential experiments—(1) model without screw, (2) model and screw together, (3) screw alone.

As the experiment has been tried in order to find the augmentation and wake for a particular speed of model, it is imperative that the experiments involving the model should be made at that speed, but with the screw it is different, as it is not necessary that it should be run at any exact speed, but it is desirable that the speed of the screw should be sufficiently nearly equal to V_1 to enable the thrust curve for speed V_1 to be inferred by the law giving the relations between the thrust curves of the same screw at different speeds.

Results of Ship Model and Screw in Combination.—Let us look at a few of the features of the curves as shown in fig. 206. Take first the results of the model and screw in combination. Here we have a curve of thrust of screw, and a curve of resistance of model corresponding. It will be seen that as the thrust increases so also does the augmented resistance, showing that the augmentation is not due to the position of the screw, but to the amount of thrust produced, the suction exerted in front of the blades having as its reaction the sternward ejectment of water which produces the thrust. As the augmentation is distinctly a loss of thrust from the total thrust generated, it is better, instead of using "augmentation of resistance," to use "thrust deduction," as this term much more correctly expresses the state of affairs.

The amount of thrust deduction is not exactly proportional to the thrust, but may be supposed to consist of two terms, one proportional to the thrust and the other a constant, this constant being the value for the thrust deduction when the thrust is zero, and is accounted for by the non-uniformity of the speed over any cross section of the water operated on by the screw.

Consider now the thrust curves of the screw with and without model. These curves will coincide more or less closely according as the speed of the experiments without the model (U) approximates to V_1, *i.e.* the speed of the

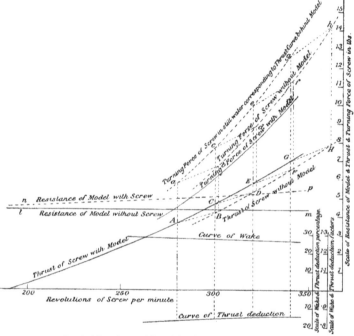

Speed of Experiment with Model and Screw = 297 ft. per min.
  ,,   ,,   Screw without Model = 250 ft. ,,   ,,

Fig. 206.

model minus the speed of the wake. When the curves coincide, it follows that $U = V_1$ and the wake factor of efficiency becomes $\dfrac{V}{U}$. If the curves do not coincide, we must then determine the value of V_1 by calculation from the known U. This is done as follows :—

In the thrust curve behind the model take a point A (fig. 206) corresponding to revolutions R per minute ; through this point describe a parabola with its origin at the zero of revolutions, and continued so as to cut the curve of thrust without model at the point B which corresponds to, say, R_1 revolutions per minute.   Then $V_1 = U\dfrac{R}{R_1}$ and the wake factor is $\dfrac{VR_1}{UR}$.   We want the thrust at V_1 and the R without model.   We can only get the thrust at corresponding revolutions, so the thrust at V_1 without model and thrust at V with model at the same revolutions are required.   Hence the corresponding velocity to V at R_1 is V_1 at R, and the wake factor is $\dfrac{V}{V_1}$.   Since the wake is caused by the passage of the model, there does not seem to be any reason why the wake should not be the same for all revolutions of the screw, or why the thrust curves with and without the model should not either coincide exactly, or if not at all, that the revolutions at any point D should have the same proportion to the revolutions at the corresponding point C as the revolutions at B have to the revolutions at A.   This is, however, not the case, and the cause seems to be the non-uniform velocity of the water across any cross section of wake. The values thus obtained for "wake" and "thrust deduction" may now be plotted at the correct positions relatively to the revolutions, and curves drawn.

On fig. 206 are also shown curves of "turning force" of screw with and without model.   These are put on not because they are of any actual use in the determination of the efficiency (as shown before), but because they act as a check on our assumption that we may take the wake to be of uniform velocity throughout.   For a method of obtaining the turning force, suppose V is not equal to U, then the first thing to be done is to infer from the thrust and turning-force curves without model at speed U the turning forces corresponding in still water at a speed V_1 to the thrust recorded behind the model. We proceed thus:—At the revolutions for the point A in the thrust curve behind model we know the still-water efficiency for a speed V to be equal to the efficiency at the point B in the thrust curve without the model at speed U.   Hence the still-water turning forces will individually bear the same ratios to the thrusts A, C, E, etc., as the ordinates b, d, f, etc., of the turning force without the model do to the thrusts B, D, F, etc.   In this way we obtain the ordinates a, c, e, etc., forming a new curve ace of still-water turning force, which corresponds to the thrust behind the model, and the ratio of the ordinates of this curve to the ordinates of the actual curve of turning force behind the model should be equal to the value of the wake factor as deduced from the curves of thrust.   This does not always come exact, by an amount varying from 0 to 2 per cent., due, most likely, to the cause before stated.   For further information on the subject of the interaction between the ship and screw, the reader is referred to the paper by W. J. Luke in the *Trans. I.N.A.*, 1910.

CHAPTER XIX.

PRACTICAL APPLICATION OF EXPERIMENTAL MODEL RESULTS.

WE may now consider what, if any, of the foregoing we can make use of in practical work. In considering the experiments in connection with models, we are concerned only with the "hull efficiency," or, as has been shown, with "wake" and "thrust deduction" factors of efficiency, and we have seen that these latter differ somewhat at different parts of the curve, as shown in fig. 206. The diagram at the point where the thrust curve with model intersects the curve of augmented resistance shows what the conditions would be if the model were self-propelled. At the higher values the conditions are examples of what would be the case in a self-propelled model against a head wind, or, say, towing another model. Now look more closely into the conditions of affairs on the ship under the first circumstances. We must remember that before applying the law of comparison of resistances of ships and models we must take into account a skin correction which is due to the lessened friction on the wetted surface of the ship as compared with the friction of the surface of the model. Hence this condition of thrust equal to augmented resistance in the model corresponds to the condition of the ship with a very foul skin. For comparison with a ship in her condition of a clean shell we must use the thrust equal to the resistance as corrected for skin friction, but even this is not all, as the wake depends on the friction of the model in its passage through the water, and this friction is very much more excessive in the case of models than with the actual ships, and it is only possible by another series of experiments to determine the laws of the effect of this variation in friction upon the amount of wake, and also to what extent such variation affects the "thrust deduction." Again, we have to take into account a similar correction to "skin correction" in models in the case of model screws. But assume that we are able to supply all or nearly all these corrections, then the problem most commonly put before us is such a one as this: A design of a vessel is required to fulfil certain conditions. Experiments are thereupon made with models to determine the form that is best suited to the particular requirements. These results only give us the resistance of the model. But we can proceed to find the effect of any particular screw on the model, *i.e.* we wish to try to find as nearly as possible its propulsive efficiency. However, the value of this factor will greatly depend on the design of the screw, which is not always known definitely when the models are being tried. So it happens that the experiments should determine the propulsive efficiencies of the designs with whatever screw may turn out to be the most suitable for each. They should also determine the design of the most suitable screw.

Now it is possible by means of the treatment of the proposition, as indicated in these pages, and with the aid of a few general preliminary experiments, to obtain the desired information sufficiently closely for all practical purposes from a single set of experiments in connection with each model screw at one speed, and to tabulate the results as shown in fig. 206. When it is said that one single set of experiments will give us all the data required, it is taken for granted that we are able by means of calculation alone to determine the efficiency of a screw of any given design, proportions, and dimensions, etc., when maintaining a given thrust at a given linear speed of advance through the water. The ratio of pitch to diameter, the number and width of blades are the main features of a propeller on which the screw efficiency depends ; and when we take into consideration that in practical work we do not have to deal with screws of more than four blades, or less than two, and that the variation in range of pitch ratio and proportionate width of blades is not large, we see that it will not require a great number of experiments on screws to get sufficient knowledge for practical use. We ought also to have some idea of how the hull efficiency is affected by (1) variations in speed ; (2) the design and the position, relatively to the hull, of the screws, before we can make use of our data with confidence. The general conclusions of the investigations on hull efficiency are as follows :—

"(1) The variation of the elements of hull efficiency with variation in speed is generally slight, and so far regular in its character that in most cases experiments on a model at about the speed corresponding to the intended working speed of the ship will be sufficient for practical purposes.

"(2) Variation of number of blades or pitch ratio of screw does not practically affect the values of hull efficiency elements.

"(3) On the other hand, variation of diameter of screw, or of its position in reference to the hull, does affect these values, and in a manner which we have not thus far been able satisfactorily to reduce to rule."

Propulsive Efficiency.—The manner of setting about the determination of the probable propulsive efficiency for any intended design of hull is as follows.

Suppose the diameter and position of screw to be fixed by circumstances connected with the design of the ship. One set of experiments must be made upon the model with any screw of the correct diameter and in the correct position. We shall thus be able to determine the wake and thrust deduction factors which jointly form the hull efficiency. By the aid of data on screw efficiency, the design of screw is selected which will give with a maximum efficiency the required thrust at a linear speed of advance equal to the intended speed of ship *minus* speed of wake. This will be the most suitable design of screw, and the product of its still-water efficiency under these conditions into the wake and thrust deduction factors will give the total efficiency.

To investigate the other factor which, with hull efficiency, forms the total factor of propulsive efficiency, namely, screw efficiency ; first let us make a sort of resumé of our method of experiment and any assumptions we have made. Consider the case of a ship being propelled by a screw at a speed V, the ship's nett resistance at this speed is, say, P. Let the screw be working with revolutions R per minute and delivering a thrust T ; this value of T is greater than P by the value of the thrust deduction. The power delivered to the screw which enables it to produce the thrust T is less than the I.H.P. of the engines as recorded by the cards, by an amount which is absorbed in overcoming the friction in the cylinders, bearings, and shafts. This amount of loss may, at full speed, be taken as a constant of percentage of the total I.H.P. As we are not to treat so much with the actual efficiency as with the differences in efficiency caused by the variations of propellers and propelling conditions we may, to simplify matters, reckon that the power delivered to the screw is the I.H.P. as generated at the cylinders. The nett total efficiency is expressed as the product of the nett resistance P into the speed V, i.e. PV, or E.H.P. divided by the total power consumed, i.e. I.H.P. Hence the propulsive coefficient $= \dfrac{\text{E.H.P.}}{\text{I.H.P.}}$. Consider now that the ship in front of the propeller has as an agent for producing wake ceased to exist, or, in other words, suppose we have a phantom ship. This phantom ship is to be capable of resisting the thrust as supplied by the screw, but, on the other hand, it passes through the water without causing any disturbance. The speed V and revolutions R of the screw are supposed to remain unaltered. Now, as we have seen earlier in this chapter, the thrust exerted by the screw in the phantom ship will be less than T, supposing, of course, it to be working at revolutions R. We could by increasing the revolutions raise the thrust until it was of the same magnitude as in the real ship, but we could not then consider that the conditions were the same as exerted in propelling the actual ship. We have, however, another method of increasing the value of the thrust and at the same time keeping the revolutions per minute unaltered, namely, by decreasing the speed of the advance to some speed V_1 at which the screw exerts a thrust T at R revolutions. Thus we have the screw propelling the phantom ship and working in undisturbed water at the speed V_1, corresponding in its conditions of working to the same screw propelling the real ship at a speed V and exerting the same thrust at the same number of revolutions. If the wake operated on by the screw were of uniform forward speed throughout its section we should have no reason to doubt that the I.H.P. driving the screw and maintaining the thrust T in undisturbed water at a speed V_1 would not be the same as that driving the screw and maintaining a thrust T behind the actual ship at a speed V. From experiments it has been found that these thrusts do differ, but so little that we may treat the I.H.P. of the screw propelling the phantom ship and exerting a thrust T at R revolutions per minute at a speed V_1 as being identical with the I.H.P. exerted by the same screw on the actual ship working at the same number of revolutions, but at a speed V. The efficiency of the screw driving our phantom ship may be deduced as follows : The speed is V_1 and the resistance is equal to the thrust T, therefore the E.H.P. of the phantom ship is TV_1, which we will call T.H.P. ; so that the efficiency of the screw working under conditions corresponding to those of the same screw propelling the actual ship is $\dfrac{\text{T.H.P.}}{\text{I.H.P.}}$.

The efficiency of this screw in propelling the real ship is $\dfrac{\text{E.H.P.}}{\text{I.H.P.}}$, therefore the coefficient of "hull efficiency" is $\dfrac{\text{E.H.P.}}{\text{I.H.P.}} \div \dfrac{\text{T.H.P.}}{\text{I.H.P.}} = \dfrac{\text{E.H.P.}}{\text{T.H.P.}}$. Again

E.H.P. = PV, and T.H.P. = TV_1, so hull efficiency = $\dfrac{PV}{TV_1}$, which may be written

as $\dfrac{P}{T} \times \dfrac{V}{V_1}$. This gives us the hull efficiency divided up into two factors, the

first of which $\dfrac{P}{T}$ represents the thrust deduction factor, and the other $\dfrac{V}{V_1}$ the

wake factor.

Laws of Comparison between Different Size Screws.

—To deal more in detail with the effect of change of dimensions and of proportions in screws on the factor of screw efficiency. A long series of experiments

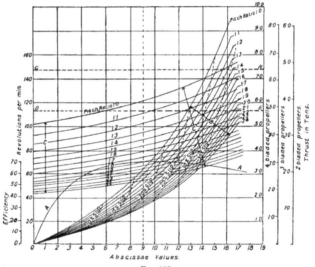

Fig. 207.

on model screws of different pitch ratios has been conducted, and the results are shown diagrammatically on fig. 207. This diagram, as will be seen later, can be put into what is perhaps a form more suitable for practical use. An explanation of fig. 207 requires some preliminary statements, which can be put most conveniently in the form of propositions.

" (i) The performance of any given screw advancing at any given speed through the water and turning at various numbers of revolutions per minute (*i.e.* working at various slip ratios) may be represented by a diagram such as fig. 208, where the abscissæ values are those of slip ratio, the ordinates of curve B B the corresponding thrust, and those of A A the corresponding efficiencies.

" (ii) With given slip ratio, the thrust of a given screw varies as the square of the speed of advance through the water.

" (iii) With given slip ratio and given speed of advance, with given design of screw and varying size, the thrust varies as the square of the dimension of the screw.

" (iv) With given slip ratio and given design of screw, the efficiency is unaffected by variations of speed or of size of screw.

" (v) Consequently a single diagram, such as that in fig. 208, will represent the performance of any number of screws of a given design, but of differing sizes, advancing at any different variety of speeds through the water, if the ordinates of the thrust curve are taken to represent, not thrust simply, but values of the expression $\dfrac{T}{D^2 V_1{}^2}$, where T = thrust, D = diameter of screw, and V_1 = speed of advance through the water."

Thus we see that a single diagram such as fig. 208 represents for any variety of conditions the performances of any number of screws of any size, but of uniform design. The only differences of design with which we shall at first deal are two in number, namely, (1) differences in number of blades, and (2) differences in pitch ratio within the limits of 1·2 to 2·2.

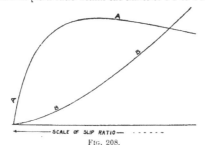

FIG. 208.

Effect of Number of Blades and Pitch Ratio on Efficiency.—

With reference to the differences in number of blades, it has been found from a series of experiments on model screws that the respective thrusts of screws of four, three, and two blades, of the same diameter, of the same pitch ratio, with the same design of blade, and working at the same slip ratio, are proportional to one another as the values 1, ·865, ·65. From these figures it will be noticed that with constant slip ratio the thrust per blade decreases somewhat with increase of number of blades : in the meantime we shall treat the efficiency as independent of the number of blades. Again, consider the effect of differences in pitch ratio. We have found from the experiments carried out on screws of various pitch ratios that if all the results are brought together on a common base of slip ratio we should get a combined diagram such as fig. 209. B_1, B_2, and B_3 are the thrust curves of a series of screws with successively increasing pitch ratios ; A_1, A_2, and A_3 the corresponding efficiency curves. The relations between the several curves on such a diagram may be perhaps best explained by saying that the individual thrust and the individual efficiency curves are (approximately) replicas of each other on different abscissæ scales, the differences in the abscissa scale of the thrust curves being greater than those for the efficiency curves. It should be particularly noticed that this statement implies that there is practically no difference in maximum efficiency between screws of different pitch ratios; and one proof of this is that over so large a range of pitch ratios with which these experiments were conducted, viz. from 1·2 to 2·2, there is so little, if indeed any, difference in maximum efficiency. We can therefore consider that, for practical purposes, the maximum efficiency is unaffected by pitch ratio varying, at any rate, from 1·2 to 2·2. We have just seen that, so far as efficiency is concerned, no particular pitch ratio (within this range) is much to be preferred before another, and we know that in practice each different class of ships requires a different pitch ratio in order to suit the revolutions per minute to the I.H.P. of engines. Besides this, since in any given ship or class of ships the revolutions per minute may be regarded as fixed, any variation in diameter necessitates an accompanying change in pitch ratio. So, in calculating the dimensions of screws, we have to remember that the pitch and the diameter of the screw are so interdependent that it is impossible to determine the one without the other. As a first stage in the

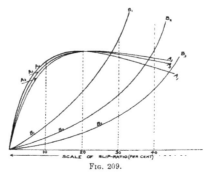

Fig. 209.

determination of the most suitable dimensions for a screw, let us suppose all screws to have one and the same pitch ratio, and that for such an invariable pitch ratio we have a diagram, fig. 208, carefully prepared. The efficiency is then designated directly by the slip ratio, and each degree of slip ratio corresponds to a certain value of $\dfrac{T}{D^2 V_1^2}$, as indicated by the thrust curve; then, to determine the diameter of screw to suit any given values of T and V_1, all we have to do is to find the value for D which gives $\dfrac{T}{D^2 V_1^2}$, the value which corresponds to the slip ratio for maximum efficiency. Should this diameter not suit, on account of its impracticable or inconvenient size, we are able to judge from our curve of efficiency by how much we are warranted in decreasing D, and so increasing $\dfrac{T}{D^2 V_1^2}$ and slip ratio, without making an un-justifiable sacrifice of efficiency. Now, if it were not that such a compromise were often needed, or if it were that the curve of efficiency were more marked at the point of maximum efficiency, and thereby more strictly limited the range within which there is nearly equal efficiency, it would be sufficient if we

specified once and for all the slip ratio and the value of $\dfrac{T}{D^2 V^2}$ which corresponds to maximum efficiency. But what we have to do is really just to keep
in mind the form of the efficiency curve, and to have means of finding the
position on its abscissæ scale which is appropriate to any proposed dimensions
of screw and values of thrust and speed. This position in the abscissæ scale
of the efficiency curve is really a mark of the standing of the screw with
reference to efficiency ; and in our hypothetical case of invariable pitch ratio
the criterion of this abscissæ position is given by the value of the slip ratio, or
by the value of $\dfrac{T}{D^2 V_1^2}$. It is obvious from a consideration of fig. 209 that
neither of these characteristics will be of use as a common criterion of
abscissæ value position in reference to the efficiency curve for screws of
different pitch ratios, nor have we any other *natural* characteristic which
would serve this purpose. In consequence, then, of this state of affairs, we
can do nothing but introduce an *artificial* one, and this has been done by

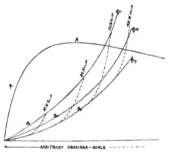

Fig. 210.

empirically modifying the several abscissæ scales of the diagram for the
successive pitch ratios of screw, as in fig. 209, so as to bring these several
efficiency curves into coincidence, as shown in fig. 210.

Method of Plotting Model Screw Results.—The reading on the
arbitrary abscissæ scale to which the curves are plotted, which shows for
screws of different pitch ratios the position relatively to the abscissæ scale
of the efficiency curve, is called the *abscissæ value*. The dotted lines
indicate degrees of slip ratio. The function of these curves is to specify the
slip ratio proper to the points at which they intersect the thrust curves
for the several pitch ratio values, and they thus enable the revolutions per
minute proper to these points of intersection to be determined for any given
diameter and speed of advance of screw. Now suppose we have a diagram
such as fig. 210, that this diagram has been obtained with sufficient care and
accuracy, and that it includes curves of sufficiently close gradations in pitch
ratio, then we see that from this diagram we can obtain all the information
necessary to determine for any given diameter, pitch ratio (inside the experimental limitations) and values of T and V_1, the abscissa value, and also the
number of revolutions at which the screw would work. We should thus be

able to select the dimensions of screw for maximum efficiency for any given values of V_1 and T, and also revolutions per minute, and at the same time we should be enabled to form an opinion as to what extent these dimensions might be altered with impunity to suit the peculiar needs of the case. Such a diagram is shown in fig. 207. We shall now go more into detail regarding the manner in which the experimental results have been put into the form of fig. 207, and also to what extent this diagram requires to be corrected for application to full-sized screws for propelling actual ships. The model screws on which the experiments were carried out were all of uniform diameter, viz. 0·68 feet, and of four different pitch ratios, namely, 1·225, 1·4, 1·8, and 2·2. In order to satisfactorily interpolate results for closer gradations of pitch ratio than those obtained from the given screws, and to ensure that in the diagrams the results should be given with sufficient accuracy and also to show the nature of the differences caused by the variation of pitch ratio, the minor inaccuracies and irregularities due to experimental error had to be faired in. This was done during the reduction of the data into the diagram fig. 207 as follows: "An analysis of the results showed (a) that the relations between the thrust curves of the several screws could be expressed empirically, within the limits of error of the results, by the propositions that with given slip ratio the thrust $\left(\text{or value of } \dfrac{T}{D^2 V_1{}^2}\right)$ varies as the reciprocal of the pitch ratio *minus* a constant, the value of this constant being 0·17. (This, although it held good empirically throughout the range of variation of pitch ratio (1·225 to 2·2), could not, obviously, hold good for unlimited range.) It also showed (b) that the thrust $\left(\text{or value of } \dfrac{T}{D^2 V_1{}^2}\right)$ for constant efficiency might be taken to vary inversely as the power 0·8 of the pitch ratio." So, putting (a) and (b) in the form of equations, we have for constant slip ratio

$$(a) \qquad \frac{T}{D^2 V_1{}^2} \propto \frac{\text{Diameter}}{\text{Pitch}} - ·17 \, ;$$

$$(b) \text{ for constant efficiency} \quad \frac{T}{D^2 V_1{}^2} \propto \left(\frac{\text{Diameter}}{\text{Pitch}}\right)^{·8}.$$

"Thrust curves for the several screws were then drawn so as to most nearly agree with the actual results of experiment consistent with proposition (a), and, by means of the same proposition, thrust curves were deduced from these for intermediate gradations of pitch ratio, as well as for other gradations extending somewhat beyond the limits of 1·225 and 2·2 covered by experiment." The abscissa scales were then so modified that the ordinates of the several thrust curves at any common abscissa value should be proportioned as by proposition (b). In doing this the abscissa scale of one of the curves, viz. that for 2·2 pitch ratio, remained unchanged; hence for this pitch ratio abscissa value is exactly proportional to slip ratio. The thrust curves were then plotted with such an ordinate scale as to show, not actual thrust for the experimental diameter and speed, but values of $\dfrac{T}{D_2 V_1{}^2}$, where T = thrust in tons, D = diameter in units of 10 feet, and V_1 = speed in units of 10 knots; hence the curve may be considered as showing absolute thrust for a screw of unit diameter of 10 feet at a unit speed of 10 knots. The screws were four-bladed, but the data can be corrected to two- or three-bladed screws by the propositions before mentioned.

The revolutions per minute corresponding to each of the curves were calculated for a unit diameter of 10 feet and a unit speed of 10 knots, and were plotted as ordinates at the abscissa values of the respective intersections. Hence curves were obtained showing for varying pitch ratio, revolutions per minute for varying abscissa values. But as with constant pitch ratio and constant slip ratio revolutions vary directly as speed, and inversely as the diameter, the ordinates obtained as above can be considered as showing values of $\frac{RD}{V_1}$, where R = revolutions per minute, D = diameter in tens of feet, and V_1 = speed in tens of knots.

Relation between Model Results and Full-Sized Screws.— We must next consider the manner (if any) in which the results will be affected by a change from model to full-sized screws. Although the diagrams are stated in such a way as to make them applicable to screws of any size and travelling at any speed, yet these curves were obtained from the results of experiments on screws of ·68 feet diameter, travelling at 206 feet per minute ; but by virtue of the five propositions before enunciated, these results are applicable to screws of any size, travelling at any speed. These propositions are based on the assumption that the skin-friction resistance of the screw blades varies directly as the area of the surface and as the square of the speed. In view of the probable inaccuracy of this, it is obvious that these diagrams need a correction for full-sized screws which is analogous to the skin correction, and which is introduced into the comparison of the resistances of a ship and her model. Regarding the accurate determination of the amount of this correction, we have so far no satisfactory method. Now supposing this diagram to be correct for full-sized screws, it seems to determine the best diameter of screw for given values of T and of V_1, but in the actual case we generally have to determine the most suitable dimensions, having given, not T or V_1, but the resistance (or E.H.P.) and speed V. Now, from experiments on "hull efficiency," we know the value of the "thrust deduction" and "wake" factors for many forms of hull, and we can fairly correctly infer from a model of similar form to the one presented to us the correct values of these factors for this particular case. Hence we can generally convert the values of resistance and of speed V for any given ship into values of T and V_1 if we assume that the "thrust deduction" and "wake" factors are identical in ship and model. There is some foundation for the belief that both these factors will be somewhat less in the actual ship than in the model, by reason of the relatively lessened surface friction of the former. This, it will be seen, brings in an element of uncertainty.

We are here called on to consider two principal sources of inaccuracy, namely, (1) the inaccuracy of the diagram itself as applied to full-sized screws ; (2) the error in the estimate of the values of T and V_1 for a full-sized ship, by which the diagram has to be applied to each individual case. Now if we follow the reasoning of the late Mr W. Froude's paper of 1878 " On the Elementary Relation between Pitch, Slip, and Propulsive Efficiency," W. Froude, *Trans. I.N.A.*, 1878, given in Chapter XVII., we see that we have here two contending factors (since the diagram is based on model experiments), the one tending to overestimate the abscissa value, the other tending to underestimate it. So, in the use of this diagram for the purpose of determining how a ship's screw stands in regard to efficiency as shown by the position in the abscissæ scale, these two factors tend to counteract each other. In a very similar way we have the factors tending to neutralise each other if we use the diagram for finding the correct rotary speed of screw. Thus we see that we have to deal with conflicting errors, either of which, if taken separately, would be important, but if taken together the difference caused in the result may be almost, if not quite, neglected, and it is thus possible to use the diagram for full-sized ships. As a test of the correctness of this statement, a comparison has been made between the revolutions per minute recorded in the steam trials of various ships of which models had been made and the revolutions per minute assigned to these ships by the diagram at the recorded speeds, with the recorded dimensions of screw, and it has been found that the revolutions as obtained from the diagram exceeded the revolutions (trial trip) of twin screws, and underestimated the revolutions of single screws (trial trip) by about 2 or 3 per cent.

In a similar manner, tests have been made on the theoretical efficiency as compared with efficiency shown from trial data. These show the character of the curve to be correct, but there seems to be some factor governing the efficiency which has not been taken into account.

Thus, to summarise, we can rely on (1) the model screw efficiency curve, as sufficiently correct in character; (2) the abscissa values calculated for screws of full-sized ships from fig. 207 in the manner shown, as sufficiently correct relatively to one another, but (3) perhaps erroneous by some uncertain amount relatively to the true efficiency curve.

Relation between Dimensions and Efficiency.—We have then to find the information needed to answer—(1) what size of screw may be chosen if efficiency is the only consideration; and (2) how much may the size so chosen be altered if required by circumstances. Now, when we look at the character of the efficiency curve and the comparatively large range of abscissa value within which the maximum efficiency is practically constant, and although it is not possible to fix the point of maximum efficiency absolutely, we see that we get an answer to our first question pretty simply. All that we really require is to fix on an abscissa value which will give us a performance not sensibly less than the maximum possible, and this we can quite readily do. Probably any value between 8·0 and 11·0 would suit, but, for convenience in manipulating the data, we should adopt one particular standard value, and the value which has been chosen as being the most suitable is 9·0. With regard to the amount of liberty we can take in altering the diameter of the screw which is proper to an abscissa value of 9·0, we would require to know when to stop reducing the diameter, as there is a certain point beyond which we cannot go without a great sacrifice in efficiency. Unfortunately we cannot say with anything approaching confidence where this point is. Now, with reference to the form in which the information in fig. 207 has been reduced so as to be more convenient for handling, the data will be used for the purpose of enabling us to choose the dimensions of propellers most suitable for any given design of ship. We must know, before we can do anything, the speed at which the vessel is to be run, and the I.H.P. necessary to be produced. In order to develop this I.H.P. with most advantage, the different types of engines require to run at certain numbers of revolutions per minute; hence we can suppose that the revolutions per minute are also fixed. We may therefore consider that the speed I.H.P. and revolutions per minute form the basis upon which we work. Then we first of all find the size of screw which, for these values of speed, etc., will give an abscissa value of 9·0, and then, should such dimensions not conform to practical use, we have to determine what change of abscissa value would accompany a change of diameter, and what corresponding change we would require to make in the pitch ratio in order to retain the revolutions per minute unaltered.   For this purpose we do not require a diagram such as

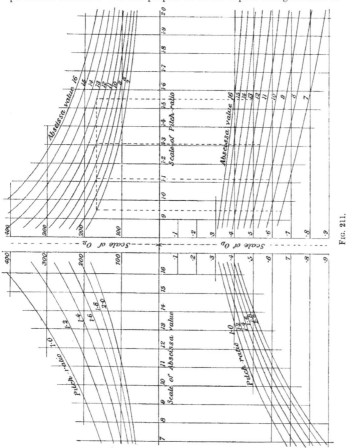

Fig. 211.

fig. 207, but one which will show (1) dimensions of screw for an abscissa value of 9·0, and (2) the alterations of diameter and pitch ratio which are entailed by a change of abscissa value from 9·0 to any other.   Such a diagram is shown in fig. 211.

In determining the dimensions of screw for an abscissa value of $9\cdot0$ (*i.e.* constant abscissa value), let us first suppose we are dealing with constant pitch ratio also, whence we have constant slip ratio.

$$\therefore \quad \mathrm{T} \propto \mathrm{D}^2\mathrm{V}_1{}^2$$

$$\text{and} \quad \mathrm{TV}_1(\text{or T.H.P.}) \propto \mathrm{D}^2\mathrm{V}_1{}^3.$$

We may take the hull efficiency as a constant of value equal to unity (since the product of the "wake" and "thrust deduction" factors varies little from unity).

$$\text{So} \quad \text{E.H.P.} = \text{T.H.P.}$$

$$\text{Let} \quad \frac{\text{E.H.P.}}{\text{I.H.P.}} = \text{P},$$

$$\text{then} \quad \text{P} \times \text{I.H.P.} \propto \mathrm{D}^2\mathrm{V}_1{}^3.$$

Now, since pitch ratio and slip ratio are supposed constant,

$$\text{revs. per min.} \quad \propto \frac{\mathrm{V}_1}{\mathrm{D}}.$$

Again, assume revolutions per minute as constant,

$$\text{then} \quad \mathrm{V}_1 \propto \mathrm{D}.$$

$$\therefore \quad \text{P} \times \text{I.H.P.} \propto \mathrm{D}^5 \propto \mathrm{V}_1{}^5.$$

$$\text{Now let} \quad \frac{\mathrm{V}}{\mathrm{V}_1} = 1 + \omega(\omega = \text{increase of V over } \mathrm{V}_1),$$

$$\text{then} \quad \mathrm{V}_1{}^5 = \left(\frac{\mathrm{V}}{1+\omega}\right)^5,$$

and so, if we assume certain constant values for P (the propulsive coefficient) and $1 + \omega$ (the wake factor),

$$\text{the values} \quad \frac{\text{IHP}^{\frac{1}{5}}}{\mathrm{V}} \quad \text{and} \quad \frac{\mathrm{D}}{\text{IHP}^{\frac{1}{5}}} \quad \text{are constant.}$$

The ordinates of the curves in fig. 211 show the value of two constants O_R and O_D, which are such that

$$\mathrm{O}_\mathrm{R} = \mathrm{R}\mathrm{I}^{\frac{1}{5}} \times \left(\frac{\mathrm{W}}{\mathrm{V}}\right)^{2\cdot5}$$

$$\text{and} \quad \mathrm{O}_\mathrm{D} = \frac{\mathrm{D}}{\mathrm{I}^{\frac{1}{5}}} \times \left(\frac{\mathrm{V}}{\mathrm{W}}\right)^{1\cdot5},$$

where $\mathrm{R} = $ tens of revolutions per minute,

$\mathrm{I} = $ I.H.P. (for each set in twin screws),

$\mathrm{D} = $ diameter of screw in feet,

$\mathrm{V} = $ speed of ship in tens of knots,

$\mathrm{W} = $ multiplier for wake correction.

Now, as regards values of W, the value of $1 + \omega$ (the wake factor) depends mainly upon the form of hull and the position of the screws in reference to the hull. Curves in fig. 211 are plotted for assumed standard values of

$p = 0{\cdot}5$ and $(1 + \omega) = \dfrac{1}{0{\cdot}9}.$ So that $\dfrac{V}{V_1} = \dfrac{10}{9},$ where V = speed of ship and V_1 = speed of advance of screw through wake, hence O_R and O_D are expressed in terms of $\dfrac{V}{W}$ where $\dfrac{V}{W} \times \dfrac{1}{V_1} = \dfrac{10}{9}$ or $W = \dfrac{9}{10} \cdot \dfrac{V}{V_1}.$

Now let "b" and "c" represent the ordinates of curves of thrust and revolutions per minute in fig. 207, and put "t," "v," "r," and "d" to represent thrust, speed, revolutions per minute, and diameter *in the units of fig. 207* : since we have assumed a propulsive coefficient of $\cdot5$ we have

$$I = 2 \times E.H.P.$$
$$= 2 \times 68{\cdot}78t.v.$$

and $\dfrac{V}{W} = \dfrac{10}{9} v$; also $R = \dfrac{r}{10}$ and $D = 10d.$

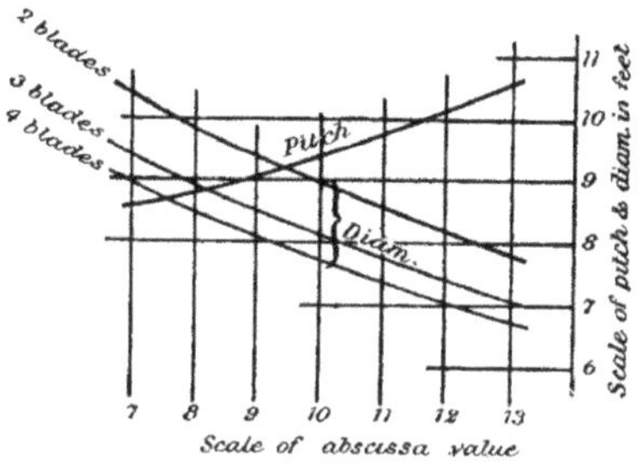

Scale of abscissa value

FIG. 212.

Hence $O_R = \dfrac{r \times (137{\cdot}56tv)^{\frac{1}{4}}}{10 \times \left(\dfrac{10}{9}v\right)^{2\cdot5}}$

$= {\cdot}901 \dfrac{rd}{v} \times \dfrac{t^{\frac{1}{4}}}{dv}$

$= {\cdot}901c \sqrt{b}.$

and $O_D = \dfrac{10d \times \left(\dfrac{10}{9}v\right)^{1\cdot5}}{(137{\cdot}56tv)^{\frac{1}{4}}}$

$= {\cdot}999 \times \dfrac{dv}{t^{\frac{1}{4}}} = \dfrac{{\cdot}999}{\sqrt{b}},$

which shows how fig. 211 is deduced from fig. 207.

Now from fig. 211 we wish to determine the most suitable diameter and pitch for a given I.H.P., revolutions per minute and speed of ship.   First of all obtain the value for O_R given by the specified conditions, then by means of the construction shown by dotted lines in fig. 211 a series of corresponding value of O_D are got for a series of abscissa values within a convenient range.

These values of O_p, taken in conjunction with the pitch ratio values of the vertical dotted lines, give a series of values of diameter and pitch which are then plotted to a base of abscissa values as shown in fig. 212. By using this diagram, sizes can be easily selected with due regard to limitations imposed by space, and of abscissa and pitch ratio values as affecting efficiency.

Effect of Number of Blades on Dimensions.—The diagram, fig. 211, is for four-bladed screws, but it can be used for two- or three-bladed propellers by first dividing the. given I.H.P. by 0·65 or 0·865 respectively, but it is more simple and almost as accurate to first work out fig. 212 for four-bladed propellers, and thence obtain similar curves for two- or three-bladed screws by multiplying all the diameter ordinates by 1·16 or 1·05 and the pitch ordinates by ·985 or ·995. The left-hand part of fig. 211 shows exactly the same data as the right-hand side, but are only plotted differently. This second form is sometimes more handy to use when the problem is given differently from that supposed.

CHAPTER XX.

THE RELATION BETWEEN TYPE, AREA, DIMENSIONS, AND EFFICIENCY OF SCREW PROPELLERS.

Mr R. E. Froude gave to the Institution of Naval Architects in 1908 the results of further experiments on screws enabling the effects of variation in form and pitch ratio to be determined. It has been already shown that results for propellers of the same design as that experimented upon can be obtained from one standardised diagram. This comparatively simple form of recording results was based on the observed result that the efficiency curve was the same for variation of pitch ratio of 1·2 to 2·2. The development of engine design involved increase of revolution to such an extent that much smaller propellers had to be used. To ensure sufficient thrust, these propellers had to be made of small pitch ratios and large relative surface. This necessitated designs very different from those upon which model experiments had been made, and involved pitch ratios much below the ratio 1·2.

Scope of Experiments.—To find the effect of variation in design and to test the truth of the assumption of a practically common efficiency curve for these lower pitch ratios, propeller models of three and four blades of elliptical shape and varying blade area were tried. Others of three blades, but of shapes having wide tips, were also experimented with ; the developed outlines of the propellers are shown in fig. 213. These results covered the range of ratio of developed to disc area from ·30 to ·80 and of pitch ratio from ·8 to 1·5. The model propellers tried were all ·8 foot in diameter, and the immersion to the centre of the shaft was uniformly ·8 of the diameter, i.e. ·64 of a foot : the speed of advance at which the model propellers were tried was 300 feet per minute, and they were run " in the open," with no ship model preceding them ; consequently the slip is "real," and not " apparent."

Method of Recording Results.—The introduction of the variants of blade shape and area and pitch ratio necessarily added to the complexity of the basis of recording the results. To obviate this as much as possible, Mr Froude invented a method of simplifying the results by the introduction of a formula giving the relation of revolutions per minute for a screw of any diameter and pitch. This formula is one for horse-power in terms of diameter of propeller and other particulars, based on the simple formula $T = aR^2 - bR$, where T is the thrust, R is the number of revolutions per minute, a is a coefficient depending on the dimensions, etc., of the screw, and b is a coefficient depending on the speed and pitch. By taking R_0 for zero thrust, b can be eliminated, being equal to aR_0, there being no slip. P, the pitch, will equal $\dfrac{V}{R_0}$, where V is the speed of advance corresponding to zero thrust : the general equation then becomes

$$T = aR^2 - aR_0R = aR^2\left(1 - \frac{R_0}{R}\right) = aR^2S \quad \text{where} \quad S = \text{slip ratio.}$$

Assuming the coefficient a to have been correctly obtained for a screw of specific design and unit diameter, and remembering that the thrust per unit

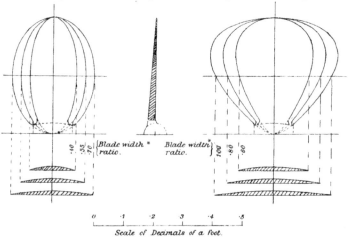

Blade width * ratio.   Blade width * ratio.

Scale of Decimals of a foot.

FIG. 213.

area varies as the square of the diameter, as does also the area, the equation for all diameters of propellers becomes

$$T = aD^4R^2S.$$

This can be written in an altered form independent of R by substituting for R^2 its value $\dfrac{V^2}{p^2D^2(1 - S)^2}$ derived from $(1 - S) = \dfrac{V}{RP}$ and $p = \dfrac{P}{D}$ (P being the actual pitch and p the pitch ratio) when the equation becomes

$$T = \frac{a}{p^2}D^2V^2\,\frac{S}{(1 - S)^2}.$$

The two principal elements governing the value of a for any difference in propeller design are (1) pitch ratio, and (2) type and blade-width proportions. It was found that these two were independent of one another, and that as regards (1) a is proportionate to $p(p + 21)$. From this it follows $\dfrac{a}{p(p + 21)}$

---

* Blade-width ratio is the ratio of the width of the expanded blade at half the radius of the tips to the radius of tips.

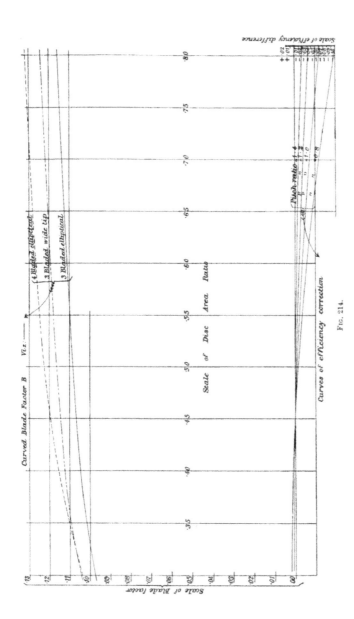

Fig. 214.

is constant for varying pitch ratios.   This expression was called blade factor B, whence $a = pB(p + 21)$.

Values of B, as obtained from experiments and dependent on these variants, are given here in fig. 214.

The thrust values obtained from all available experiments were compared with the results given by the formula, and it was found that the formula required correction by multiplying the right-hand side by $1\cdot02(1 - \cdot08\ S.)$

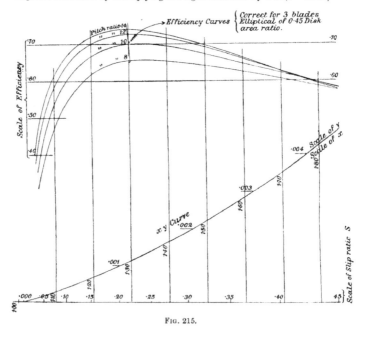

FIG. 215.

Making this correction, and substituting for a its value $Bp(p + 21)$, the final thrust formula becomes

$$T = D^2V^2 \times B\left(\frac{p + 21}{p}\right) \times \frac{1\cdot02S(1 - \cdot08S)}{(1 - S)^2}.$$

This may be written

$$\frac{TV}{D^2V^3} = B\left(\frac{p + 21}{p}\right) \times \frac{1\cdot02S(1 - \cdot08S)}{(1 - S)^2}.$$

Converting this to units of thrust horse-power (H) and speed in knots, from thrust in lbs. and speed in hundreds of feet per minute, the expression becomes

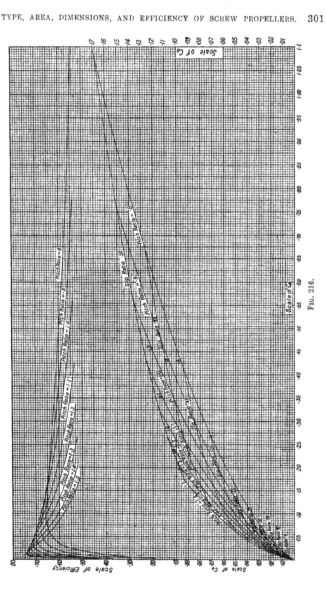

Fig. 216.

$$\frac{H}{D^2V^3} \frac{p}{B(p+21)} = \cdot 0032162 \frac{S(1 - \cdot 08S)}{(1 - S)^2}.$$

To facilitate the use of this expression, curves of

$$y = \frac{H}{D^2V^3} \frac{p}{B(p+21)} = \cdot 0032162 \frac{S(1 - \cdot 08S)}{(1 - S)^2}$$

were constructed and are here reproduced in terms of $x = \dfrac{RpD}{V} = \dfrac{1\cdot 0133}{(1 - S)}$

(fig. 215). An alternative to the use of the foregoing formula is the series

of curves of C_0 in terms of C_A where $C_A = \dfrac{R^2H}{BV^5} = \dfrac{p+21}{p^3} x^2 y$

and $C_0 = \dfrac{H}{D^2V^3B} = \dfrac{p+21}{p} y$ (fig. 216).

In these latter the C_A value can be calculated for any conditions of V, R, B, and H, and the value of C_0 read from the curves, whence D can be determined : the efficiencies belonging to each curve are set off on the same diagram and can be read off.

These efficiency curves are correct for the 3-bladed elliptical type of propeller having a disc area ratio of ·45. It should be noted that this disc area ratio includes the ellipse to the centre of the shaft in these model propellers : when reducing to actual ship figures a reduction of 20 per cent. should be made. To correct the efficiency curves for the other propellers a uniform efficiency deduction of ·02 must be made in the case of the 3-bladed wide-tip ones, and a similar reduction of ·0125 for the 4-bladed elliptical ones : also a deduction as indicated by the curves in fig. 214 dependent on the disc area ratio and pitch ratio.

The pitch P has throughout been taken as equal to the travel per revolution for zero thrust, and p and S corresponding. Comparison of trial results have led to the conclusion that the pitch or pitch ratio figures used in or obtained from these calculations should be taken as $1\cdot 02$ times the driving-face pitch for ship.

For a complete understanding of the reasons which have led to the adoption of this method, the reader is referred to Mr Froude's paper, "Results of further Screw Propeller Experiments," but for the practical application of the results the study of a few examples will suffice. These have been worked out in a later chapter. See Chapter XXIV.

CHAPTER XXI.

TAYLOR'S EXPERIMENTS ON THE DETERMINATION OF DIMENSIONS FOR SCREW PROPELLERS.

Taylor's 1904 Paper.—Other results of a recent investigation of the powers and efficiencies of propellers are those given to the American Inst. of N.A. 1904 by Constructor Taylor. In these experiments there has been a variation both in blade area and in pitch, while, as we have seen in the foregoing pages, Froude had practically only one variable, namely, the pitch. The chief object of these experiments was the determination of the power and efficiency of model screws of the common three-bladed type throughout the range of pitch ratio and blade area likely to occur in practice, but, in view of the increased rotary speed of propellers on turbine-driven vessels, the pitch ratio variation has been extended to the unusually low value of 0·4. The series of experiments comprised thirty propellers. They were all 16″ in diameter, three-bladed, of uniform pitch, diameter of boss $3\frac{1}{8}$″, with a thickness of blade at the centre of $\frac{9}{32}$″ at root and $\frac{3}{32}$″ at tip. There were six pitch ratios used, namely, ·4, ·6, ·8, 1·0, 1·2, and 1·5, and for each pitch five widths of blade were used : the mean width ratios, total blade area, and blade area as a fraction of the disc area are shown in the table below. The blades were approximately elliptical in shape (see fig. 217). The driving faces of the screws were trued up in a special machine, the backs of the blades were finished by hand, and both back and driving faces were, before experiment, carefully smoothed with emery cloth. The apparatus used was very similar in principle to that used by Froude, only that Taylor could call to his aid many scientific devices which were not in existence about twenty years ago. The method of getting the recorded data reduced to diagrams will be treated below. The results were faired by cross curves, and if not satisfactory the par-

PROPELLER VARIABLES.

	Pitch ratio.						Mean width ratio.	Total developed area, sq. in.	Developed area ÷ disc area.
	·4	·6	·8	1·0	1·2	1·5			
No. of screw.	1	6	11	16	21	26	·075	24·28	·1207
	2	7	12	17	22	27	·125	40·46	·2012
	3	8	13	18	23	28	·200	64·74	·3220
	4	9	14	19	24	29	·275	89·02	·4427
	5	10	15	20	25	30	·350	113·30	·5635

ticular screw was re-tested.   As to the method of conducting the experiments, the general rule was, after calibrating the apparatus, to put the propeller in place and make a run at a speed of advance of 4 knots.   The necessary number of revolutions of screw to give a negative slip of about 5 per cent. was known from previously prepared diagrams, and so the carriage was put in motion at the desired speed and the requisite number of revolutions per minute obtained by adjusting the rheostats.   The pens and revolution counters were then thrown into gear and the run commenced.   On the completion of the run it was quite easy to see from the number of revolutions from point to point if the desired slip had been obtained.   If so, then the next run was started at the same speed of advance, but with the propeller revolving at a number of revolutions corresponding to a positive slip of, say, 2 per cent. or 3 per cent.   The runs were continued until a slip of about 40 per cent. was obtained.   The zeros were then checked, and the resistance of the shaft itself to moving forward through the water at a speed of 4 knots and 5 knots was determined.   The propeller was then replaced and a similar series of runs at 5 knots was commenced.   Similar experiments were carried out at speeds of advance of 6 and 7 knots.

Method of Recording Results.—In reducing the records obtained from the experimental apparatus to diagrams the procedure followed is shortly outlined below.

From the records the number of revolutions over the last 64 feet of run is obtained.   Call this number ρ.   The time occupied by the truck in passing over this 64 feet is also given on the records.   Let it be i seconds.   Then from the average value of i the speed of advance is given by $V = \dfrac{37 \cdot 895}{i}$.

The values of torque proper are now obtained from the deflections of the torque pen, and these values of T (say) are entered opposite to the values of i and ρ according to the number of the run.   The value of the final thrust (P) is now obtained from the value of the thrust given on the record plus the head end pressure on the propeller shaft, which is overcome by the propeller before any thrust can be recorded.   Curves of T and P at different speeds are then plotted to a base of ρ.   For the same value of pitch each value of ρ corresponds to a certain slip.   P and T are taken off on even values of slip at intervals, say, of 5 p.c. on the range covered.   These results of T and P in lbs. are plotted on two separate sheets to abscissæ at the constant speeds of the experiments.   These faired values of P and T at 5 knots speed were, for the above slips, tabulated for the calculation of efficiency and the value of a coefficient S which Taylor has introduced, and which he calls the power coefficient, and it is such that if G denote the horse-power absorbed by the propeller, D denote the diameter of the propeller in feet, n the number of blades, and V denote the speed of advance of the propeller in knots, then

$$G = \cdot 00312\, n S D^2 V^3.$$

This is obtained from the following considerations :—

At a constant speed of advance, say five knots, if U = the useful work and G the power absorbed by propeller,

$$\frac{U}{G} = E, \text{ the efficiency.}$$

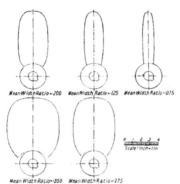

Fig. 217.—Model Propeller Experiments. Shape of Taylor's Blades.

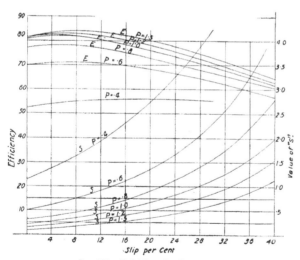

Fig. 218.—Model Propeller Experiments.

2 Blades. ·2 Width ratio.
" E," Efficiency curves for constant pitch ratio.
" S," Power coefficient curves for constant pitch ratio.

Then at a pitch p in feet and R revolutions per minute a slip s can be determined, and

$$E = \frac{U}{G} = \frac{PpR(1 - s)}{TR \times 2\pi} = \frac{Pp(1 - s)}{2\pi T} \qquad . \qquad . \qquad . \qquad (1)$$

where T and P are the effective torque at 1 foot radius and the push or thrust of the propeller respectively.

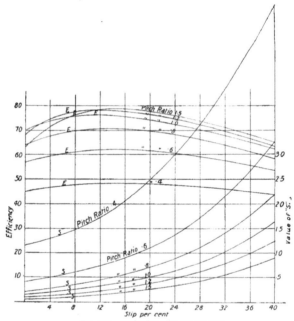

Fig. 219.—Model Propeller Experiments.

3 Blades.   ·200 Width ratio.
" E," Curves of efficiency for constant pitch ratio.
" S," Power coefficient curves for constant pitch ratio.

From the investigations upon the thrust, torque, and efficiency of an elementary oblique plane rotating about an axis, it may be shown that the total horse-power absorbed in turning an aggregation of these elements in the form of a screw propeller may be expressed by a formula

$$G = 3n\left(\frac{pR}{1000}\right)^3 D^2(asX + fZ)$$

where a is a reaction or push and f a friction or rubbing constant; X and Z are characteristics of the blade depending on the diameter ratio, the proportions and the shape of the blade, and n is the number of blades.

Now
$$p\mathrm{R} = \frac{101 \cdot 3\mathrm{V}}{(1 - s)}, \ \mathrm{V} \ \text{being in knots} ;$$

so that if we put
$$\mathrm{S} = \frac{a s \mathrm{X} + f \mathrm{Z}}{(1 - s)^3}$$

we have by substitution
$$\mathrm{G} = \cdot 00312 . n . \mathrm{SD}^2 \mathrm{V}^3 . \qquad . \qquad . \qquad . \qquad . \qquad (2)$$
and
$$\mathrm{U} = \mathrm{EG} = \cdot 00312 . \mathrm{E} . n . \mathrm{SD}^2 \mathrm{V}^3 \qquad . \qquad . \qquad . \qquad . \qquad (3)$$

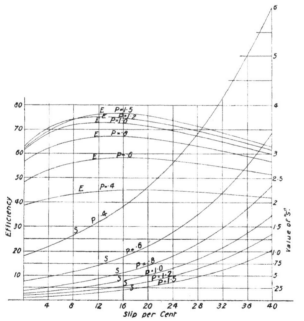

Fig. 220.—Model Propeller Experiments.

3 Blades.   ·275 Width ratio.
" E," Curves of efficiency for constant pitch ratio.
" S," Power coefficient curves for constant pitch ratio.

S for a given propeller depends only upon the slip, so that a curve of G's of a given propeller plotted to a base of slip will give us a curve of S's.

But
$$G = \frac{2\pi R}{33,000} \cdot U = \frac{2\pi T}{33,000} \cdot \frac{101 \cdot 33 V}{p(1-s)} \; ;$$

$$\therefore \quad \frac{2\pi T}{33,000} \cdot \frac{101 \cdot 3V}{p(1-s)} = \cdot 00312 . n . SD^2 V^3 \; ;$$

$$\therefore \quad S = \frac{6 \cdot 18 T}{pn(1-s)} D^2 V^2.$$

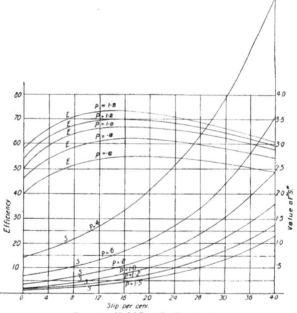

Fig. 221.—Model Propeller Experiments.

3 Blades.   ·35 Width ratio.
" E," Efficiency curves for constant pitch ratio.
" S," Power coefficient curves for constant pitch ratio.

In the experimental propellers

$$V = 5, \; D = 1\tfrac{3}{4} \text{ feet} \; ;$$

$$\therefore \quad S = \frac{\cdot 139 T}{np(1-s)} \qquad . \qquad . \qquad . \qquad . \qquad (4)$$

Also from equation (1) $$S = \frac{\cdot 022 P}{En} \qquad . \qquad . \qquad . \qquad . \qquad (5)$$

Hence for a given propeller we can plot values of S when either P or T and E are known. If therefore S and E are known and plotted for a given propeller, we have its characteristics complete, and can apply the formula (2) to find the power expended in a larger propeller at other speeds and revolutions by the methods formerly explained.   The efficiency of the model propeller at the corresponding revolutions or at the same slip per cent. will enable us to determine the power utilised.

Similar experiments were subsequently carried out on four-bladed,

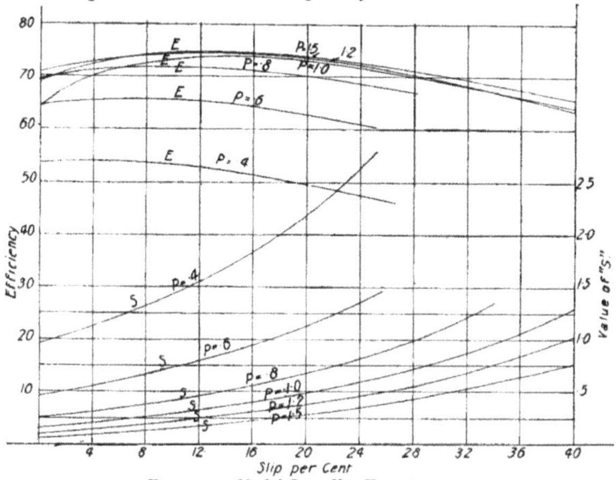

Fig. 222.—Model Propeller Experiments.

4 Blades.   ·125 Width ratio.
" E," Efficiency curves for constant pitch ratio.
" S," Power coefficient curves for constant pitch ratio.

six-bladed, and two-bladed propellers. The experiments on the six-bladed and two-bladed propellers were not so extensive as those on the three-

Figure number.	Number Blades.	Mean width ratio of Blade.	Corresponding ratio. Total developed area / Disc area .
218	2	·200	·214
219	3	·200	·322
220	3	·275	·442
221	3	·350	·563
222	4	·125	·268
223	4	·200	·429
224	4	·275	·590

bladed and four-bladed. The shapes of blades that were tried are shown in fig. 217.

Results obtained.—The curves in figs. 218 to 224 have been selected from the results of the above experiments on two-, three-, and four-bladed propellers. They have been grouped together as follows :—

In each of the above figures which fix number and shape of blades, according to the preceding table, we have the S and the E curves for six different pitch ratios plotted on a base of slip per cent.

The pitch ratios chosen in each case were ·4, ·6, ·8, 1·0, 1 2, 1·5 respectively.

It will be seen that the field of exploration is fairly complete. Numbers,

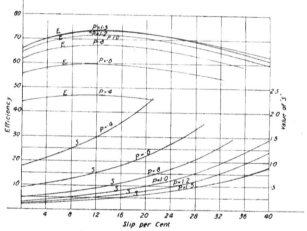

FIG. 223.—Model Propeller Experiments.

4 Blades. ·2 Width ratio.
" E," Efficiency curves for constant pitch ratio.
" S," Power coefficient curves for constant pitch ratio.

areas, shapes, and pitch ratios have been varied over an extent sufficient for all practical purposes. The wide range of the experiments enabled the investigators to conclude "that within working limits the propeller forces vary as the square of the speed of advance," that is, what we have called *speed of ship*. It was only necessary, therefore, to give results at one speed of advance, viz. five knots. The power absorbed in turning a propeller having n blades of any diameter D at a speed of advance V can be got from the formula (2),

$$G = ·00312n.SD^2V^3,$$

S being obtained from the curve for the particular type of propeller whose area ratio, pitch ratio, and revolutions or slip ratio are known. The corresponding value of E, the efficiency, can be read off from the curves, and the value of the useful power U developed by the thrust of the propeller can be found. It may be noticed that for the constant speed of five knots at which all these results are set off, the variables are number of blades, pitch ratio, slip ratio, and area ratio, and the results we obtain by experiment are power absorption and efficiency. We can show a series of any two of these variables on one set of curves by assuming the other two to be constant throughout the series. If we select number of blades and area ratio as constant, we can set off a series of S values for varying pitch and slip ratios, and we can set off a series of E values for the same pitch and slip ratios. We cannot treat the number of blades as a continuous variable, so that for one set of curves it must always be constant, and we must always have a different set of

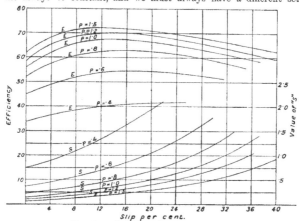

FIG. 224.—Model Propeller Experiments.

4 Blades.   ·275 Width ratio.
" E," Curves of efficiency for constant pitch ratio.
" S," Power coefficient curves for constant pitch ratio.

curves for each number of blades. But with the pitch, slip, and area ratios we may make one constant and plot values of S and E for varying values of the other two. In figs. 218 to 224 each figure shows the values of S and E for a constant pitch ratio, each curve of the series being for a specified width ratio, the base being slip ratio. We are then able to see how S and E each vary according as pitch or area ratios are altered.

By inspection it may be seen that—

(1) For propellers of the same number and area ratio of blades S increases rapidly with decrease of pitch ratio.

(2) For propellers of the same number of blades *for small pitch ratios* the narrow blades absorb a little more power at low slips than the wide blades up to a certain point, after which, as the slip increases, the wide blades gradually absorb greater power than the narrow ones. *For large pitch ratios* the wide blades absorb slightly more power at all slips.

(3) Maximum efficiency occurs at lower slips as the pitch and area ratios decrease.

(4) The value of the maximum efficiency increases as pitch ratio increases for the smaller area ratios up to 1·2, but slightly decreases afterwards, but in the larger area ratio it continuously increases with increase of pitch ratio.

(5) The value of maximum efficiency increases between area ratios ·075 and ·125, but decreases with further increase.

In order to make use of the curves given in figs. 218 to 224, figs. 225 to 234 have been made.

Consider the formula $G = ·00312 n SD^2 V^3$. If we are given G and V, we

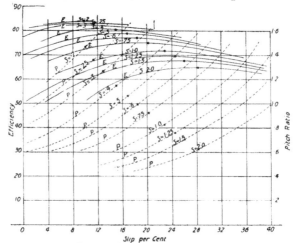

Fig. 225.—Model Propeller Experiments.

2 Blades.   ·2 Width ratio.
" E," Curves of efficiency for constant value of " S."
" P " Curves of pitch ratio for constant value of " S."

can select n and D, and hence get a value of S. If then we can draw a horizontal line in any of the figs. 218 to 224 at this value of S and set up ordinates at the intersections of this line with the S curves, we get the corresponding efficiencies at the points where these ordinates cut the efficiency curves. Hence an efficiency curve corresponding to the given value of S may be drawn to the same abscissæ, slip per cent. We also know the corresponding pitch ratio at each of these ordinates, and hence a curve of pitch ratios can be set up for the given value of S and in terms of slip per cent.

This has been done in order to get curves as in the figs. 225 to 231. Fig. 225 is derived from 218, fig. 226 is derived from 219, etc.

The efficiency curves are lettered E, and the pitch ratio curves are lettered P.

The value of S to which each curve corresponds is also noted, and the

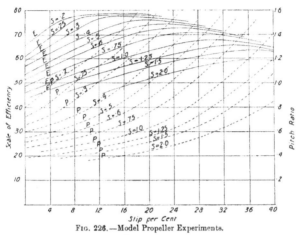

Fig. 226.—Model Propeller Experiments.

3 Blades. ·200 Width ratio.
" E," Curves of efficiency for constant value of " S."
" P," Curves of pitch ratio for constant value of " S."

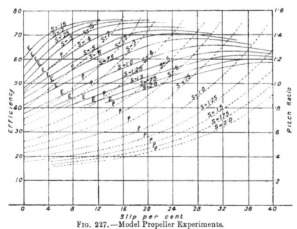

Fig. 227.—Model Propeller Experiments.

3 Blades. ·275 Width ratio.
" E," Curves of efficiency for constant value of " S."
" P," Curves of pitch ratio for constant value of " S."

range of values that has been chosen depends upon the range of S in the original S and E curves.

From inspection of the E and P curves in the figs. 225 to 231, it will be seen that for any of the chosen values of S we are able to fix the maximum efficiency point.

Drawing the ordinate at this maximum efficiency point, we can get the corresponding pitch ratio, and the abscissa gives the slip ratio. For example, in fig. 225, which gives the E and P curves for two-bladed propellers of ·2 width ratio, the S values chosen range from ·2 to 2·0.

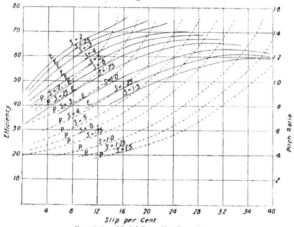

Fig. 228.—Model Propeller Experiments.

3 Blades.   ·35 Width ratio.
" E," Curves of efficiency for constant value of " S."
" P," Curves of pitch ratio for constant value of " S."

The following table gives the maximum efficiencies and the corresponding pitch ratios and slip ratios for each selected value of S :—

Value of S.	Maximum Efficiency.	Pitch Ratio.	Slip per cent.
2·0	65	·625	28·2
1·5	67·7	·705	26·0
1·25	69·5	·76	24·5
1·0	71·6	·825	22·9
·75	74·9	·92	20·3
·6	77·0	·99	18·5
·5	78·8	1·06	16·8
·4	80·6	1·14	15·0
·3	82·2	1·25	13·0
·25	83·2	1·35	11·3
·2	84·0	1·465	10·0

The figures in the above table have been plotted on a base of S *value*. The curves are shown in diagram 232. For each of the figs. 225 to 231 a similar table was made, and the results plotted. Fig. 233 gives the results for all the three-bladed propellers, and fig. 234 shows the curves for all the four-bladed propellers.

These figures, 232, 233, and 234, are final diagrams, and can be made use of directly to determine the maximum efficiency, the pitch ratio, and the slip ratio corresponding to maximum efficiency for any given value of S.

Suppose that for any given value of S we have determined E, P, and *s*

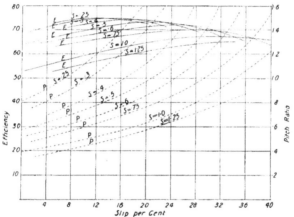

FIG. 229.—Model Propeller Experiments.

4 Blades.   ·125 Width ratio.
" E," Curves of efficiency for constant value of " S."
" P," Curves of pitch ratio for constant value of " S."

(slip ratio) from the final diagram. Let the diameter which has been selected to give S be D.

Then the pitch $p = P \times D$
and $p R(1 - s) = V(101 \cdot 33)$;
$\therefore R = \dfrac{V(101 \cdot 33)}{p(1 - s)}$.

We can thus obtain the revolution corresponding to maximum efficiency for any given value of S.

It will be seen from the figures that the very best three-bladed propeller may have an efficiency as high as about 80 per cent., while the very best four-bladed only reaches about 75 per cent. The pitch and area ratios of this three-bladed propeller are about 1·6 and ·28 (of disc area), while in the four-bladed these values are 1·1 and ·24 respectively.

Relation between Efficiency, Pitch Ratio, and Slip Ratio.—It

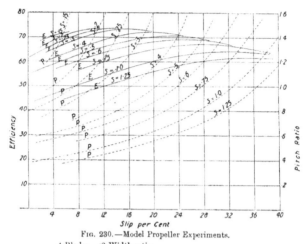

Fig. 230.—Model Propeller Experiments.
4 Blades.   ·2 Width ratio.
" E," Curves of efficiency for constant value of " S."
" P," Curves of pitch ratio for constant value of " S."

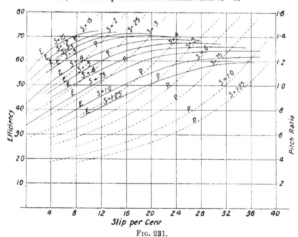

Fig. 231.
4 Blades.   ·275 Width ratio.
" E," Curves of efficiency for constant value of " S,"
" P," Curves of pitch ratio for constant value of " S."

will also be seen that in both the three- and four-bladed propellers maximum efficiency is consistent with a very large range of pitch ratio, and corresponds in the three-bladed to about 12 per cent. slip ratio, and in the four-bladed to 13 per cent. slip ratio.   Of course the value of the maximum efficiency will vary very much with pitch ratio, but the position of it in relation to slip will not alter.   It may be interesting to notice that as between the three- and four-bladed propellers, while maximum efficiency occurs at about the same slip ratio, *i.e.* at about the same revolutions in the same diameter propellers, that the corresponding area ratios are ·27 and ·36, the excess of the latter over the former being simply that due to the extra blade, viz. about

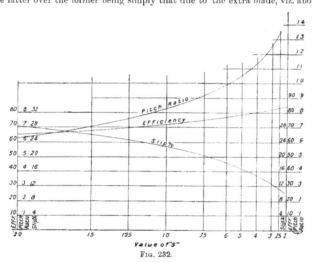

Fig. 232.

Curves of { Maximum efficiency } for two-bladed
{ Pitch ratio } propellers.
{ Slip ratio } ·200 Width ratio.
" S " obtained from formula $G = ·00312nSD^2V^3$.

one-third.   The effect of this extra blade only seems to be to detract from efficiency, as it lowers the maximum possible from 80 per cent. in the three-bladed to 75 per cent. in the four-bladed.

It has been shown that the values of S increase with decrease in pitch ratio, *i.e.* increase of diameter ratio, ranging in four-bladed propellers having narrow blades (of, say, area ratio ·17) from ·1 at pitch ratio of 1·6 to 1·0 at pitch ratio of ·4, and in broad blades (say, of area ratio of ·65) from ·1 to 2·0. These are very significant figures, and show the wide range of power absorption of different propellers.   The value of S, except for small areas, increases with increase of area ratio for the same pitch ratio, the rate of increase being much greater for small pitch ratios than for large.   Taking these two statements together, it is seen that to get a large value of S small pitch ratios and large area ratios are necessary.

Elements affecting Powers and Efficiencies of Propellers.— There are *four* principal elements which affect the powers and efficiencies of propellers : these are (1) the diameter ; (2) the pitch ; (3) the blade area ; and (4) the shape of the blade section. The first three we are accustomed to taking into account, but the last has not been looked upon as an element which required any special attention, but which, judging from Taylor's results, is a factor which will require to be reckoned with as much as any of the other three. With reference to this factor of efficiency,

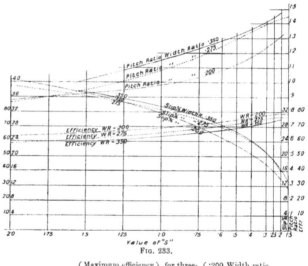

Fig. 233.

Curves of { Maximum efficiency Pitch ratio Slip ratio } for three-bladed propellers { ·200 Width ratio. ·275   ,,   ,, ·350   ,,   ,, }
" S " obtained from formula $G = ·00312nSD^2V^3$.

we understand, when talking about pitch, that we are referring to the pitch, uniform or otherwise, of the face of the propeller, but we must remember that the back of the propeller has also a pitch, and that this pitch varies from point to point. As the thickness of the blade is very often fixed in a most arbitrary manner, generally only taking into account the diameter of the propeller, and not the width of blade, it follows that we shall have a very great difference of pitch over the back of the propeller, especially in long narrow blades, with heavy metal at the centre line of blade, and a fine pitch. Now as the water is supposed to remain in contact with the back of the blade at all times when driving ahead, it is obvious that the pitch of the back of the blade must be a controlling factor in the final efficiency.

We have been accustomed to reckon the highest efficiency attainable as about 70 per cent., but we have from these experiments a maximum efficiency of 78·8 per cent. for propeller No. 28. In calculating this efficiency the action of the propeller boss has not been taken into account, and so the efficiency will be slightly greater than would have been obtained if this action had been taken into consideration. Taylor is, however, confident that this extreme efficiency has been obtained. He cites as factors confirming his results the extreme accuracy with which the propellers were finished, the comparative thinness of the blades, and the steady falling off in efficiency as the

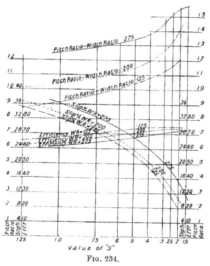

FIG. 234.

Curves of ⎰ Maximum efficiency ⎱ for four- ⎰ ·200 Width ratio.
         ⎰ Pitch ratio   ⎱ bladed ⎰ ·275   ,,   ,,
         ⎰ Slip ratio   ⎱ propellers ⎰ ·350   ,,   ,,
"S" obtained from formula G = ·00312nSD²V³.

pitch ratio was decreased, a result one would have expected from theoretical considerations.

Influence of Blade Width and Area.—Another result of these experiments is the fact that it has been shown that as the pitch ratio is decreased the influence of the blade width and area upon the final results becomes gradually less, until for propellers of very fine pitch ratio the narrow blades actually absorb the greater power. For the propellers of ·6 pitch ratio the experiments show, at a slip of 26 per cent., that it makes practically no difference what the width of blade is, for the same power is absorbed by the propeller, although the narrow blades show somewhat greater efficiency. Below 26 per cent. slip the narrow blades absorb greater power, while above this percentage the wider blades take the greater power, until at the highest pitch ratios experimented with the greater width of blade absorbs most power at all slips.

One other feature of the results is the fact that, as the pitch ratio is decreased, the power absorbed and the efficiency at low slips are both very great, e.g. taking propellers 6 to 10 for the narrowest blade, the efficiency at zero slip is 66·8 per cent., while the maximum efficiency of this propeller is 67·4 per cent., but as the width of blade is increased this effect is diminished.

Cavitation.—It is generally admitted that experiments on model propellers are of very little use as regards the phenomenon of cavitation,[1] owing to the fact that the model propellers working under the combined pressure of air and water have a virtual immersion much greater than the full-sized ones.

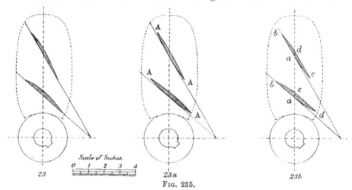

Fig. 235.

Diameter 16″.
Pitch 19·2″.
Total Blade area 64·7 sq. inches.
Mean Width ratio ·200.

For many of the propellers tested there seemed to be a tendency towards a reduction in thrust and torque when travelling at the 7-knot speed, but there was no pronounced cavitation, except in the case of propeller No. 1, at 7 knots. This propeller had its results carefully noted, and they showed that at 5 knots the curves were normal, at 6 knots it showed signs of cavitation at about 0 per cent. slip and 115 lbs. thrust, and at 7 knots strong signs of cavitation at about – 15 per cent. slip and 80 lbs. thrust. It should be noted that the cavitation occurred at a very low thrust per square inch of projected surface, and it is here that Taylor makes a remark, which ought to be paid particular attention to, in reference to the cavitation which exists in the models and is said to exist in the actual screws when running at a high speed of revolution such as turbine-driven destroyers, viz.: "It seems reasonable to suppose that all cavitation is largely of the same nature, and a function not only of the thrust, but also of the speed of revolution

[1] See also Chapter XXIII., p. 339.

and shape of blade section, and that it could probably be mitigated in many cases or deferred by modifying suitably the blade section."

Effect of Blade Section.—With reference to his contention as to the effect of blade section on efficiency, etc., Taylor shows the two diagrams, figs. 235 and 236.

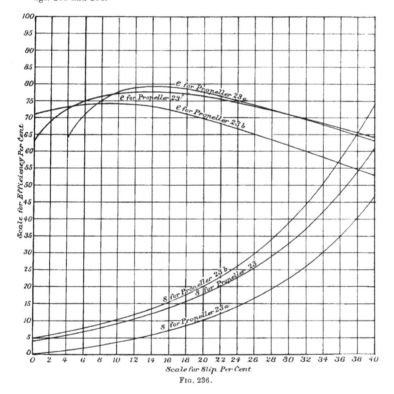

Fig. 236.

Fig. 235 shows shapes of blade section for the propellers whose results are given as curves in fig. 236. Propeller 23 was one of the regular series, 16 inches diameter, 19·2 inches pitch, 64·7 square inches blade, and ·200 mean width ratio and ·322 ratio of surface to disc area. Nos. 23a and 23b had the same diameter and blade area as No. 23, but had blade sections as shown in fig. 235. The pitch of the line A A was in 23a, 19·2 inches, i.e. the face and back were similarly convex. For 23b the pitch of the portion a b of the face and portion cd of the back was the same as before, viz. 19·2 inches. Fig. 236 shows the curves of efficiency and S for these three propellers. This diagram emphasises the statement made by Taylor with reference to the blade section. It may be here noted that the value of S should be kept as high as possible, as this enables the propeller to be made smaller, and it is necessary when the pitch is small, as it must be with quick-running engines, to keep the diameter down as small as possible, and it is probable that with warships there may be something gained with quick-running propellers by making them four-bladed instead of three-bladed.

Importance of these Results.—The introduction of the Parsons and other steam turbines as propelling engines has led to great increases in revolutions of propellers. This necessitated reduction of pitch ratios and diameters. The earlier experiments of the Froudes did not cover pitch ratios of much less than 1·2. Taylor's experiments carry these results to ratios as low as ·4, and in the regions between 1·2 and ·4 lead to conclusions somewhat different to those above 1·2. The method of Froude which is given in fig. 207 is found to be not applicable to the lower pitch ratios. The efficiency curve given in that figure, which is assumed to be applicable to all the pitch ratios covered by the diagram, is not applicable in the much lower ratios.

CHAPTER XXII.

EFFECT OF THICKNESS, RAKE, AND SHAPE OF BLADE UPON PROPELLER EFFICIENCY.

FOLLOWING up the experiments which we have just considered, there was made a series of experiments undertaken by the Model Basin authorities at Washington in order to ascertain the effect of "rake" on propeller blades, the influence of thickness and section of blade, and also the result on the efficiency of the propeller due to alteration of shape of blade. Investigations were carried out in two other directions, viz. with reference to the suction forward of the propeller, and, as the truth of the law of comparison as applied to propellers had been often questioned, to obtain proof or otherwise of this law by means of experiments on propellers. These latter experiments were not carried out to such a degree of completion as those which have gone before, but they supply us with very useful data, and will, as Mr Taylor says, "furnish a basis for more complete investigation of other explorers in this wide field." It is well known that in order to give more clearance to the propeller in the aperture, or for other purposes, the blades are often raked back, very rarely forward, and it has been a much discussed question as to the effect of this on the efficiency of the propeller. Experiments were made on propellers of two different pitch ratios, viz. ·6 and 1·2 ; in all, six propellers were tried, one of each pitch ratio with the blades set at right angles to the shaft, one at a rake of 10° forward, and one at a rake of 10° aft : the area ratio was in all cases ·313 and the blade thickness fraction ·0425. This last particular is a new one, and is the ratio between the maximum thickness of the blade at the axis and the diameter, a section being taken in a radial direction, the lines of the front and back supposed extended to the centre of the shaft. From the results of these experiments it is shown that for the pitch ratios in ordinary use the efficiency is practically unaltered by the blades being raked within the limits of the experiments, either in a fore. or aft direction. With the finer pitch ratios there seems to be a tendency for the forward-raked blade to decrease in efficiency, so that, other things being favourable, there is no reason why we should depart from the perpendicular blade so far as the propeller itself is concerned. The details of the propellers are given below in the following table and fig. 237.

Thickness of Blade.—The thickness of propeller blades has up to the present been a very arbitrarily chosen quantity, each designer generally having his own ideas on the subject, and taking very little thought as to the effect on the efficiency of his increasing the thickness of the blade. In 1904 Taylor called attention to this point, and stated that the thickness of the blades seemed to

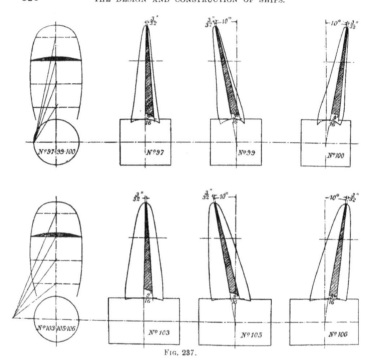

FIG. 237.

TABLE.

No.	Diameter.	Pitch.	M. W. R.	Rake of Directrix.	No. of Blades.	Total developed area.	Root thickness.	Blade thickness fraction.
97	16″	9′6″	·200	0°	3	62·9	9⁄16″	·0425
99	16	9·6	·200	10 aft	3	62·9	9⁄16	·0425
100	16	9·6	·200	10 for'd	3	62·9	9⁄16	·0425
103	16	19·2	·200	0	3	62·9	9⁄16	·0425
105	16	19·2	·200	10 aft	3	62·9	9⁄16	·0425
106	16	19·2	·200	10 for'd	3	62·9	9⁄16	·0425

have an important bearing on the final results obtained, and that he hoped to be able to show this. We are now in possession of the results of experiments made by him in this direction, and they amply bear out the prophecy made. Twelve propellers were tried, the blade outlines of which were such as shown in fig. 238. The sections were in all cases the ordinary type, with pitch

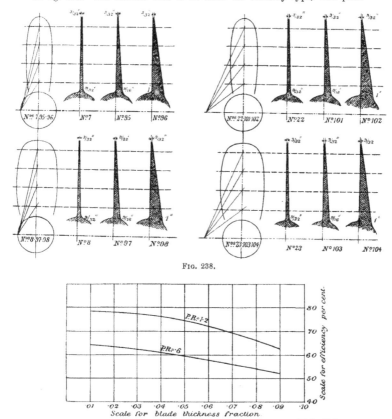

Fig. 238.

Fig. 239.—Average Maximum Efficiencies. Results of Experiments on Blade thickness.

ratios of ·6 for the half, and 1·2 for the remaining six. Two different widths of blade were chosen, viz. ·125 and ·200, with three values of thickness fraction, ·0205, ·0425, and ·0768. The results obtained show clearly that there is a falling off in efficiency with an increase of blade thickness, and that such increase causes a marked increment in the power absorbed and thrust

delivered. It seems to be a fair conclusion that, if the type of blade section
remains constant, any increase of blade thickness will cause a loss of efficiency,

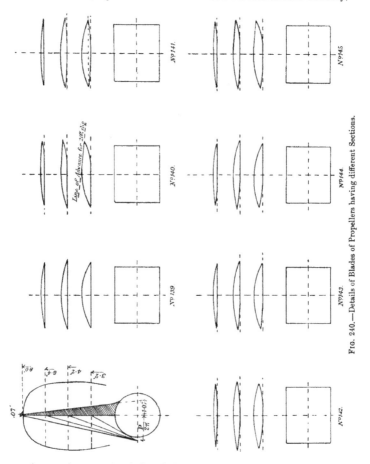

FIG. 240.—Details of Blades of Propellers having different Sections.

an increase in power absorbed, and also an increased thrust from the propeller,
but not in proportion to the extra power absorbed. Fig. 239 shows the value
of the efficiency obtained by various thickness fractions for the two pitch
ratios treated, the propellers being supposed to be of ordinary proportions

and the common ogival section. What we require now is a set of experiments combining those just described with those detailed below, so that we would have complete information as to the variation on efficiency produced by alteration in thickness of blade, in conjunction with variation in type of section, pitch, and area ratios : this would give us all the particulars (some

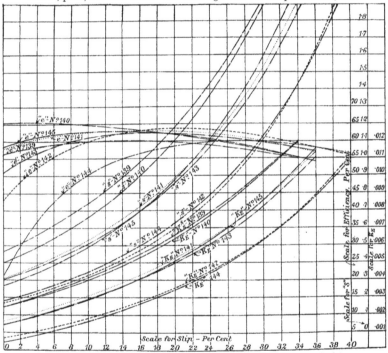

Fig. 241.—Curves of efficiency and coefficients for various Blade Sections. Derived from experiments with Model Propellers, Nos. 139-145 inclusive.

of which have been previously obtained) required to give the most efficient propeller to fulfil a given set of conditions.

Blade Section.—To the question of thickness of blade there is closely allied the question of the form of blade section, and in connection with the latter a few experiments were made with propellers all as nearly as may be with the same developed blade outline and the same thickness of blade in the centre, but of various sections. The forms of sections used were those shown in fig. 240. They are all of a fine pitch ratio ·7875. For the purposes of comparison the nominal pitch was taken as the same, although the variation in form of section would, of course, influence the virtual pitch. The nominal pitch lines, or at any rate the portions of the blade which are assumed to have nominal pitch, are shown in fig. 240. Model (139) is the ordinary ogival section; model (140) is of the same type with regard to the larger portion, but the leading edge is set forward. Model (141) has a rounded driving face, the leading and following edges being both set forward two-tenths of the maximum blade thickness. Model (142) is of a similar type, but the leading and following edges are set forward a distance equal to four-tenths of the maximum thickness. Model (143) combines the forward half of (139) with the rear portion of (141), and model (144) combines with the forward half of (139) the rear half of 142. Model (145) combines with the forward portion of (140) the rear of (141). Fig. 241 shows in the usual way the results of these experiments, and exhibits in a very telling manner the large influence which the shape of the blade section has on the efficiency of the propeller. The coefficient K_E here used is a coefficient similar to S, expressing the useful work done; the formula for the value of this coefficient being

$$K_E = \frac{\cdot0030707 VT}{d^2 V^3} = \frac{EP}{d^2 V^3} = \cdot00312 n ES,$$

the letters having the same significance as in the preceding chapter. Looking now at the results as depicted by the curves, we notice that the following edge seems to influence the power and thrust to a greater extent than the leading edge, a result which certainly was not anticipated, and which comes rather as a surprise. Comparing Nos. 139 and 140, Nos. 141-3-5 and Nos. 142 and 144, we see the truth of this, the forms having similar tails falling closely together as regards power and thrust. With reference to efficiency, it will be seen that the commonly used ogival section with the rounded back is not the most efficient; the leading edge can be improved with regard to the efficiency, especially at the lower slips. None of the propellers shown has very high efficiency, but this is easily accounted for by the broad, thick blades and fine pitch.

Shape of Blade.—On the subject of shape of blade much has been said

No.	Diameter.	Pitch.	Diameter of Boss.	No. of Blades.	M. W. R.	Value of "n."	Total developed area.	Blade thickness fraction.
167	16″	12″·8	3·125	3	·178	1·5	56·0	·0575
168	16	12·8	3·125	3	·185	2·0	58·1	·0575
169	16	12·8	3·125	3	·194	2·5	60·7	·0575
170	16	12·8	3·125	3	·200	3·0	62·9	·0575
171	16	12·8	3·125	3	·203	3·5	63·8	·0575
172	16	16	3·125	3	·178	1·5	56·0	·0575
173	16	16	3·125	3	·185	2·0	58·1	·0575
174	16	16	3·125	3	·194	2·5	60·7	·0575
175	16	16	3·125	3	·200	3·0	62·9	·0575
176	16	16	3·125	3	·203	3·5	63·8	·0575
177	16	19·2	3·125	3	·178	1·5	56·0	·0575
178	16	19·2	3·125	3	·185	2·0	58·1	·0575
179	16	19·2	3·125	3	·194	2·5	60·7	·0575
180	16	19·2	3·125	3	·200	3·0	62·9	·0575
181	16	19·2	3·125	3	·203	3·5	63·8	·0575

and written, much virtue and no faults being claimed by many inventors for their peculiar form of blade. The short series of experiments which was undertaken to find, if possible, some guide as to the influence of the developed

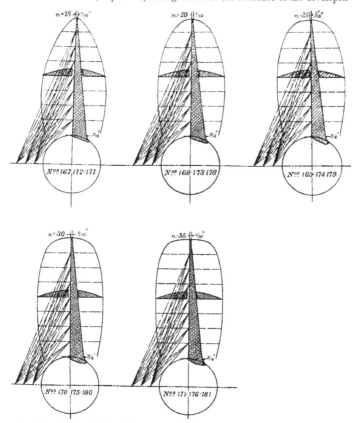

FIG. 242.—Details of Blades of Propellers used in experiments on effect of Shape of Blades.

shape upon the efficiency, dealt with five shapes of blade, each shape being used for three propellers of different pitches. The table given above gives the data for these propellers, and fig. 242 gives shapes and sections.

In each case the portion of the blade inside of the mid-radius was the same, being an ellipse which, if it had been continued, would have touched the centre line of the shaft. The outer portion of the area was bounded by a mathematical curve of the general equation

$$\left(\frac{x}{r/2}\right)^n + \left(\frac{y}{b}\right)^n = 1,$$

where "r" is the radius of the blade, "x" represents the distance out from

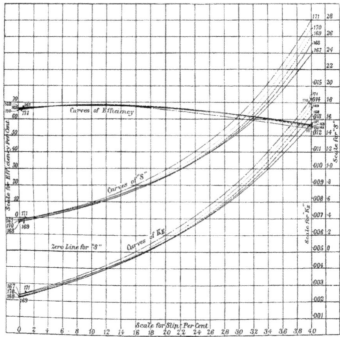

FIG. 243.—Curves of efficiency and coefficients for various Blade Contours. Derived from experiments with Model Propellers Nos. 167-171 inclusive. Pitch ratio ·8.

the mid-radius, and "y" is the breadth of the blade, "b" being the breadth at mid-radius. The five outlines used were those determined by giving to "n" the values 1·5, 2, 2·5, 3, and 3·5 : when $n = 2$ the outer portion of the area forms a complete ellipse with the inner portion. When $n = 3$ the derived shape is one of which Taylor advocates the use. The thickness of the blade was kept the same in all cases, regardless of width. Each blade outline was used with the three pitch ratios, ·8, 1·0, and 1·2. The results obtained were as shown in figs. 243, 244, 245. The information to be gathered from these curves is of much value as corroborating previous results. As one would have expected, the broad-tipped blades absorb more power and deliver more thrust, with the exception that at a pitch ratio of ·8 and small slips the narrow-tipped

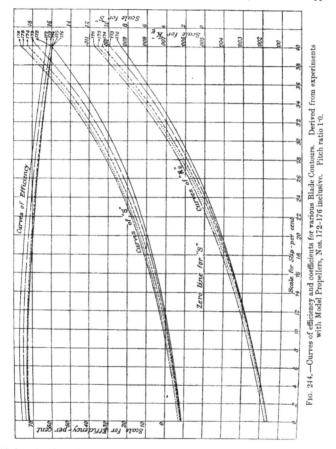

Fig. 244.—Curves of efficiency and coefficients for various Blade Contours. Derived from experiments with Model Propellers, Nos. 172-176 inclusive. Pitch ratio 1·0.

blades absorb at least as much power and deliver as much thrust as the widest blades. The reason of this is not far to seek : the virtual pitch of the outer portion of the narrow blades is a good deal in excess of that in the broad-tipped ones : at large slips this difference of virtual pitch has little effect, but when it comes to small slips, this difference has a considerable influence, and so we find an increase of both power absorbed and thrust delivered in the case of the narrow-tipped blades.

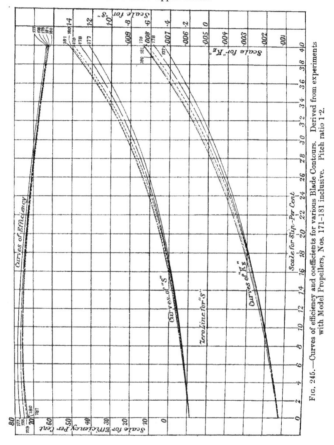

Fig. 246.—Curves of efficiency and coefficients for various Blade Contours. Derived from experiments with Model Propellers, Nos. 171–181 inclusive. Pitch ratio 1·2.

Influence of Blade Shape on Efficiency.—In the matter of efficiency the very narrow tips certainly show the best results unless at fine pitches, and the elliptical blades seem to be more efficient than the broad-tipped blades. The difference is nowhere great, and it is to be noted that the differences between the power curves at higher slips are greater than are warranted by the addition of the extra area, but it must be remembered that this additional area is put on the place where it will tell most, and is not, as would commonly be done, distributed round the whole circumference of the blade.   In conclusion, it would seem that these experiments, as far as they go, show that as the narrow-tipped blades are more liable to cavitation, especially at fine pitches, than the broad ones, it would be preferable to use the elliptical blade for coarse pitches not liable to cavitation, and broader-tipped blades for fine pitches, and especially where cavitation is feared.

CHAPTER XXIII.

PRESSURES NEAR PROPELLER. TEST OF LAWS OF COMPARISON AND CAVITATION.

Mr Taylor has produced some useful data with reference to the pressure in the water proximate to a revolving propeller which is delivering thrust, and the experiments here briefly summarised give the first experimental information on this subject. The apparatus used was as follows :—A vertical plane surface was fitted parallel to the centre line of shaft with a number of tubes in the rear, each tube was connected to a particular measuring spot on the plane designated, as shown in fig. 246, *e.g.* A₂, B₅,

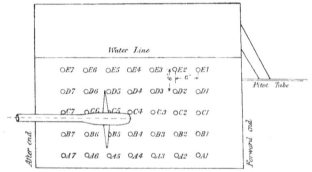

FIG. 246.

etc. At each of these measuring spots there was a thin cap flush with the face of the plane, and having a large number of very small holes forced through it with the object of allowing the pressure in the moving water to be communicated to the water in the tubes. Each tube was connected at the top of the plane to a glass tube, and these tubes were in turn connected by a common pipe to a receiver from which the air could be partially exhausted this arrangement being simply to raise the water in the tubes to a convenient height for measuring. In addition to these tubes, a pitot tube was fitted forward of the plane for measuring the undisturbed pressure of the water. Each tube below the glass part was supplied with a shut-off cock, and all the cocks could be closed simultaneously. The method of experiment was very simple : first runs were made without the propeller at the speed at which it was proposed to run the carriage when the propeller was in place, and so calibrate the tubes, etc., as the plane, not being an ideal one, raised a quite perceptible wave, and consequently there was a definite change of pressure at each measuring point when travelling from the still-water condition. Knowing this, if we put the propeller in place and run the

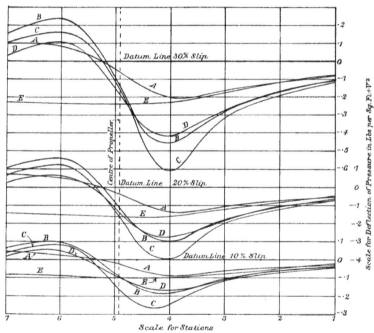

Fig. 247.—Curves of Pressure for Propeller. Holes of Row C 1¼″ above centre line of shaft. Rows and Stations each 6″ apart.

carriage at the aforesaid speed, and the propeller at a number of revolutions to give the chosen slip, we can get from the tubes the excess or diminution of pressure over the plane caused by the rotation of the propeller. Of course we get the power absorbed, thrust delivered, and efficiency at the same time. The vertical plane was tested for three positions parallel to the shaft with four different propellers ranging in pitch from 12·8 inches in the finest to 24 inches in the coarsest 16-inch propeller. The mean width ratio was ·2 in all cases, and the plane was ⅜ inches, 5⅞ inches, and 11⅞ inches from the propeller tips in the three occasions. A horizontal plane 7 inches above the tips was also tried several times in conjunction with the vertical one. With the vertical plane only in place, the results of torque, thrust, and efficiency do not differ appreciably from the results obtained for the propeller in the open. With the horizontal plane also in place there is a slightly increased thrust and torque, but practically no difference in the efficiency. Fig. 247 shows a specimen of the results for one propeller when the vertical plane was ⅜ inch from the tips of the blades. Three groups of curves corresponding to nominal slips of 10, 20, and 30 per cent. are shown with a line in each group indicating the excess or defect of pressure along a horizontal row of measuring points. It will be seen that the point of greatest suction is 6 inches forward of the centre of the propeller, and on a line with the centre of the shaft. It is worthy of note that there is a diminution of pressure for an appreciable distance abaft the screw. The results for the other propellers are fairly represented by the above figure, and the general characteristics seem to be pretty constant, no matter whether the pitch is coarse or fine. When the vertical plane is only 11⅞ inches away from the tips of the propeller the diminution of pressure extends over practically the whole plane, behind as well as in front of the screw. When the horizontal plane is also in position there is an excess of pressure close behind the screw, even to the line marked E in fig. 246. The differences of pressures are plotted in lbs. per square foot divided by V^2. Fig. 248 gives the results in another manner, showing for certain selected measurement spots on the plane the ratio between the reduction of pressure per square inch and the mean thrust per square inch over the disc area. These results corroborate the practice of Froude in taking the thrust deduction as a constant fraction of the thrust.

Comparison between Model and Full-sized Screws.—It has been found on several occasions that the results of full-sized propellers did not agree with the results which had been expected from information derived from experiments with models of these, and the law of comparison began to be looked upon with something like suspicion. There were two chief reasons for this, viz. either the law of comparison did not hold, or the model did not accurately represent the full-sized propeller. To anyone who knows about the manufacture of propellers it is not at all difficult to imagine that the large propeller *did* differ from its model, and to a much greater extent that it would be believed possible. We have already seen that a comparatively slight difference in blade section, etc., leads to a considerable difference in the final result. A set of experiments was undertaken in order to prove the law of comparison for propellers, or to show that it did not hold. There were fifteen propellers in all used in the experiments, viz. five of the different diameters 8-inch, 12-inch, 16-inch, 20-inch, and 24-inch, and each diameter with pitch ratios ·6, 1·0, and 1·5. The mean width ratio was kept constant at ·2 and the blade thickness fraction also constant at ·0425. The area ratio in all was ·3151. These propellers were exceedingly carefully made, the greatest care being taken that they were exactly alike to scale : they were similar to each other to a degree not to be obtained between a tank-made model and an ordinary foundry casting. It was an unfortunate circumstance that necessitated the use of very fine springs for the 8-inch propellers and very heavy ones for the 24-inch ones : if it had been possible to use the same springs right through for torsion and for thrust, the result would have been more satisfactory. Figs. 249, 250, 251 show the results of the tests : if the law of comparison applied exactly and if the experiments were accurate, then there ought to have been only one curve of S and K_E for the five different sizes of propeller. As it is, there are five curves ; and the question

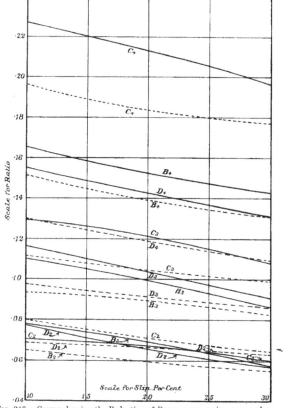

Fig. 248.—Curves showing the Reduction of Pressure per sq. in. expressed as a fraction of the mean thrust per sq. in. of disc area, taken at particular points.

Full lines correspond to case in which the vertical plane is only in place, and is ⅜″ from propeller tips.

Dotted lines are for case in which vertical plane is in same position, but horizontal plane also in place. C_1 D_1 etc. correspond to the points on fig. 246.

comes to be, is it possible to explain away this difference, and show that the law holds almost exactly ? We say "almost," as we know that the law of comparison is based upon the assumption of exactly similar motions in the case of a model and full-sized propeller, and this entails in fluids the perfect continuity of motion. In the actual case there is discontinuity of motion and the resultant eddy motion. So that it seems as if the law might hold to a

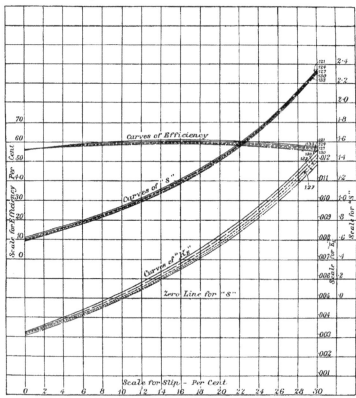

FIG. 249.—Curves of efficiency and coefficients for various diameters. Pitch ratio ·8.

very great degree of approximation, but never could hold exactly. One source of error in the experiments was the disturbance caused by the 20-inch and 24-inch screws; with the smaller propellers this disturbance could be neglected, but with the larger ones the disturbance was great, and pressure of time did not allow a proportionate time interval to be admitted between the runs of the larger propellers. It is not thought, however, that this error will

have any appreciable effect on the results. A much more serious source of
error, and one whose effect is rather difficult to gauge without experiment, is
that the centres of all the propellers were the same distance below the waterline, viz. 16 inches. This, of course, gives a depth of water equal to one and
a half times the diameter for the 8-inch screw, but only equal to one-sixth
diameter in the case of the 24-inch propellers. A few preliminary experiments were made with 16-inch propellers, and these seemed to show that there
was a slight falling off in thrust and torque as the depth of water over the
tips was decreased, until, of course, when air began to be sucked, there was a
sudden fall. This error, combined with the previous one, makes the curves of

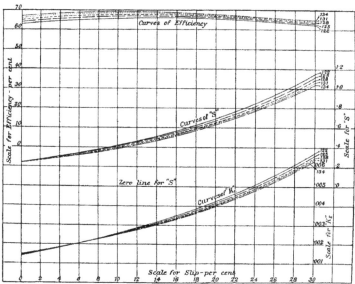

FIG. 250.—Curves of efficiency and coefficients for various diameters. Pitch ratio 1·0.

figs. 249, 250, 251 exaggerate the effect of increase of diameter. Even not
allowing for this error, it is seen that the difference in actual slip of the
24-inch propeller and the slip calculated by the law of comparison from the
8-inch propeller is only about 2 per cent., so that if all error were eliminated
the difference would be practically negligible. It appears reasonable to
conclude that, in the absence of more complete information, which can only
be obtained by elaborate experiments with full-sized propellers, we can rely
with a good deal of confidence upon model propeller results extended by the
law of comparison to full-sized propellers.

Cavitation.—In a propeller the propulsive effect is obtained by imparting to a body of water an absolute sternward velocity. Thus the propeller is

continually acting on new water, the continuity of the supply being, as was pointed out in 1873 by Professor Osborne Reynolds, regulated by the power the water has to follow the propeller.

Consider a simple case of a flat vertical board moving horizontally through the water in the direction of its normal, and having part of the board above the surface. Consider a small area on the back of the plane "h" feet below the surface. However fast the plate may move, the pressure on this part of the surface can never be less than atmospheric pressure, because, if the pressure is reduced below atmospheric pressure, air will flow in at the

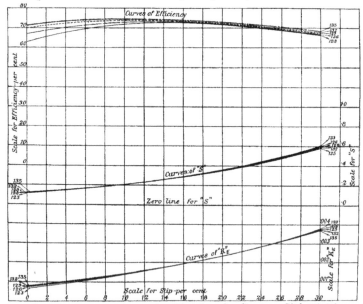

FIG. 251.—Curves of efficiency and coefficients for various diameters.   Pitch ratio 1·5.

back of the plate if the water does not, and so keep the pressure up to that of the atmosphere. The limiting velocity in this case at which air instead of water flows in will be given by $v^2 = 2gh$, where v is in ft. sec. units, because the maximum velocity at which the water can flow is that of a particle from the surface falling to the depth h feet. If, however, the plate is wholly beneath the surface, and we consider a small area h feet below the surface, the limiting velocity will be such that the total energy in the water is converted into energy of motion, i.e. the velocity is given by

$$v^2 = 2g(h + 34),$$

where 34 feet is the head of water due to atmospheric pressure. If the velocity of the plate exceeds this, the water is not capable of attaining a greater velocity than that due to its head, and thus will be incapable of maintaining a continuous flow.   Cavities will consequently be formed in the water at the back of the plate.   This phenomenon has been called Cavitation.*

To extend this to the case of the screw propeller, it is necessary to note that the propeller acts partly by pressure upon the face and partly by suction at the back.   In addition, we have a rotary motion of the water about the axis of the shaft, and hence a centrifugal action.   Thus the effect in this case will be more marked than in the simple case of the vertical plate.   It may be seen, therefore, there is a limit to the rotary speed of a propeller, depending upon the immersion, especially if it is not entirely submerged.

Messrs Thornycroft & Barnaby's Experiments.—Cavitation was first noticed in 1894 during the trials of the T.B.D. "Daring," which was designed to have a speed of not less than 27 knots.   This vessel was of 7 feet draught, and the stern was shaped so that the screws had little

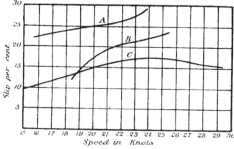

Speed in Knots
FIG. 252.

immersion.   This immersion was less at full speed than when at rest, owing to the wave formation.   The vessel was fitted with narrow-bladed screws of elliptical form, the minor axis being 4/10ths of the major axis.   The pitch was an increasing one from the leading to the following edge.

Curve A, fig. 252, shows the performance of these screws.   The slip was too great at all speeds, and the curve A shows a large increase from 22 to 24 knots.   The pitch of the screws was slightly reduced, and then gave a performance shown by curve B.   There was an appreciable reduction of slip at moderate speeds, but it increased more rapidly than was anticipated at the higher speeds.   This led to the conclusion that too high a thrust per unit of area of blade was demanded of these blades, and new propellers were made having blades of increased area, the pitch being the same as in the original screws.   The performance of these new screws is shown by curve C.   It is seen that the slip is the same as for B at about 19 knots, but at higher speeds it is less, and rises to a maximum at about 24 knots.

With the narrow blades, excessive vibration was experienced at the stern. With the blades removed and with the engines running at the same speed

* See remarks on p. 320.

there was no vibration, thus indicating that some vibratory action was taking place at the propellers.

Comparing the new screws with the original ones, from which they only differ in area of blade, at 24 knots the slip is reduced from 30 per cent. to 17¾ per cent., and the I.H.P. from 3700 to 3050. The number of revolutions required to give 24 knots with original screws gave 28·4 with the new ones. The excessive vibration at the stern disappeared.

In screws of elliptical form, cavitation appears to be produced when the mean negative pressure exceeds 6¾ lbs. per square inch of projected area, or the whole thrust exceeds 11¼ lbs. per square inch, and probably varies for differently shaped blades.

Results precisely similar to the above were obtained, at the same time, on the trials of some torpedo-boats.

The Hon. Chas. Parsons's Experiments.—These were undertaken in connection with the "Turbinia," which was the first turbine-driven vessel. The engines were designed previously to the experiments on the "Daring," referred to above; and as a turbine is more efficient at high than at low revolutions, the engines were designed to run at 2500 revolutions per minute and to develop 1500 H.P., and the vessel was originally designed for a single screw. On the trials, cavitation was experienced in a very aggravated form, although several screws of various patterns were used. In order to thoroughly investigate the phenomenon, a series of experiments were made upon model screws in a tank of water heated nearly to boiling-point. This was done to make the head of water above the propellers as near as possible to the same scale as that to which the model screw represented the actual ones in the "Turbinia." The revolutions were arranged to give the same slip ratio as that at which the actual screws were working. By using heated water the phenomenon of cavitation took place at a smaller rate of revolutions than it would have. By means of suitable apparatus the formation and growth of the cavities were traced. A cavity first formed near the tip of the blade, just behind the leading edge, and increased as the revolutions increased. At a speed corresponding to the "Turbinia's" propeller it covered a sector of the screw disc of 90°. At higher revolutions the screw revolved in a cylindrical cavity, scraping off layers from the forward end and delivering them to the after end.

These experiments led to the replacing of the single screw by three screws, when no further trouble was experienced.

Thus there appears to be a limit to the amount of thrust per projected area of screws that can be developed. This limit will probably depend to some extent upon the immersion. The solution of the problem is obtained by dividing the work between a large number of screws and adopting a larger blade area. The experiments of Dr Wm. Froude had led to the adoption of screws having a ratio for maximum efficiency of developed blade area to disc area of ·25 to ·3. The experience of engineers in many cases led them to adopt for special purposes a larger ratio. Dr R. E. Froude, in his later experiments, found that a ratio as high as ·5 in some cases gave high efficiency. Mr Parsons and other engineers have used a ratio as high as ·6 with advantage.

The reasons that have led to this increased area are that it has been found that for average seagoing work the thrust which the propellers may have to meet may be increased 20 per cent. to 30 per cent. on account of the head seas and winds, and in such circumstances it is probable that cavitation may occur in propellers which show little or no sign of it in smooth-water conditions. The extra blade area is a margin available for such contingencies. The fear that such great areas would be associated with inefficient results on account of increased frictional resistance has not been borne out either by experiments on models or experience in ships. The results of Taylor's experiments on screws with small pitch ratios show that in this case great blade area is more efficient than small.

CHAPTER XXIV.

APPLICATION OF MODEL EXPERIMENTAL RESULTS TO THE DESIGN OF PROPELLERS AND THE DETERMINATION OF EFFICIENCY IN FULL-SIZED SHIPS.

HAVING described these experiments, we may now, by concrete examples, see their application to the design of screw propellers. Let us apply Taylor's results to the case of a vessel developing 9000 I.H.P., having three screws driven by three turbines or other motors, each capable of giving off 3000 H.P. to each screw shaft, and collectively driving the vessel at 23 knots. From the formula

$$G = \cdot 00312n SD^2 V^3 \quad \text{we get} \quad 3000 = \cdot 00312 \times 3 \times S \times D^2 \times 23^3 \,;$$
$$\therefore \quad SD^2 = 26 \cdot 3.$$

From this value, if we choose D, we can find a value for S. It is better to select different values for D and to draw curves of efficiency, pitch, slip, and revolution in terms of D. The most favourable propeller to the given set of conditions can thereby be obtained. Selecting values of D from 4 to 10 feet we obtain values of S at which we can set up ordinates in the final curves. The following table shows the results obtained :—

$$SD^2 = 26 \cdot 3.$$

D.	S.	E.	Slip.	P.	Pitch p.	$p(1-s)$.	$R = \dfrac{V \times 101 \cdot 33}{p(1-s)}$.
4	1·65	60·5	37·2	·92	3·68	2·32	1008
5	1·05	65·0	33·0	1·06	5·30	3·55	655
6	·73	69·0	29·6	1·185	7·11	5·00	466
7	·536	71·4	26·7	1·275	8·92	6·55	356
8	·411	73·5	24·2	1·340	10·72	8·10	288
9	·325	75·0	21·8	1·380	12·42	9·72	240
10	·263	76·0	19·5	1·410	14·10	11·38	205

The first column gives the diameters that have been selected. The corresponding values of S are put in the next column. We are now left to choose width ratio. In this case the width ratio ·275 has been chosen. We therefore get our results from fig. 233, and the series of ·275 curves. Setting up

344

ordinates at the values of S given in the second column, we can read off the results for E the maximum efficiency, s the slip, and P the pitch ratio.   These results have been tabulated in the next three columns.

Multiplying P by D, we get the pitch p in feet.   The sixth column gives the values of the pitch.

In the seventh column the values of $p(1 - s)$ have been put, and the last column is the revolutions which are calculated from the formula $R = \dfrac{101\cdot33 \times V}{p(1 - s)}$.   These results have been plotted in curves in terms of D, and are shown in fig. 253.

Other examples are given.

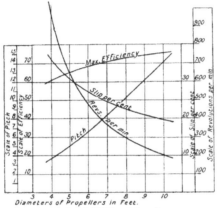

Vessel of 9000 I.H.P. and three Screws.

FIG. 253.—3000 I.H.P. to one Propeller having three Blades.

Selected width ratio = ·275.
Selected area ratio = ·4427.
Speed = 23 knots.

Fig. 254 shows the curves for the propellers of the same vessel, only in this case there are two screws ; the I.H.P. per screw is therefore 4500.   The speed being the same, we get in this case an SD^2 value of 39·6.

Fig. 255 shows the curves for the case of a vessel of 24,000 I.H.P.   There are three propellers, each three-bladed.

Fig. 256 shows the curves for two different cases of large vessels, each with four screws.

Fig. 257 shows the curves for the propellers of the same vessel as in fig. 255, only in this case there are two screws ; I.H.P. per screw therefore is 12,000.   The speed is the same as before.

Application of Froude's 1908 Paper.—In giving an example of the method of applying Froude's 1908 paper it will be of interest to assume the same I.H.P. and speed as in a case for which Taylor's results have been applied.

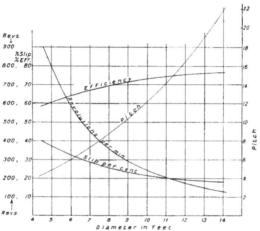

Vessel of 9000 I.H.P. and two Screws.

FIG. 254.—4500 I.H.P. in each Propeller having three Blades.

Selected width ratio = ·275.
Selected area ratio = ·4427.
Speed = 23 knots.

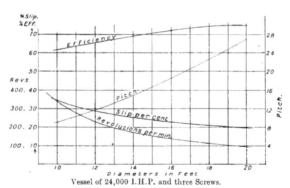

Vessel of 24,000 I.H.P. and three Screws.

*FIG. 255.—8000 I.H.P. in each Propeller having three Blades.

Selected width ratio = ·275.
Selected area ratio = ·4427.
Speed = 19 knots.

Take the case of a vessel having three screws, driven by separate engines, each capable of developing 3000 I.H.P. and driving the vessel at 23 knots. Revolutions 500 per minute. Propellers to be three-bladed elliptical.

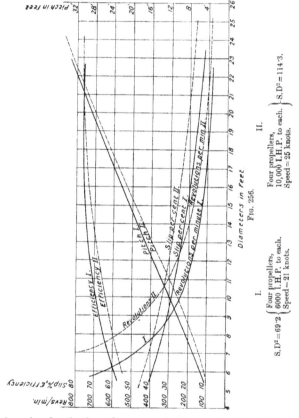

Fig. 256.

Assuming that the thrust horse-power is 45 per cent. of the I.H.P., thrust horse-power per propeller

$$= H = 3000 \times 0.45 = 1350.$$

Let the selected disc area ratio* be ·4427 as chosen in one of the cases already dealt with.

* Disc area ratio is the ratio of area of propeller blades to area of disc circle.

This problem is similar to that on p. 344, except that, for Froude's results, we must fix on a definite number of revolutions. The results, according to Taylor, are given in fig. 253.

Application.—For purposes of design, the C_A and C_0 curves are to be used and the method of procedure is as follows :—Select two or more pitch ratios, for which curves on fig. 216 are drawn, *e.g.* 1·0, 1·2, and 1·4, and from fig. 214 select two values of the disc area ratio, between which the selected value—·4427—lies. Take values of ·4 and ·45. We must determine the diameter and efficiency for each of the above values of pitch ratio, for each of the two values of the selected disc area ratios. That is, we must obtain in all six values of diameter and the corresponding six values of efficiency.

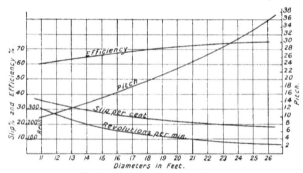

Vessel of 24,000 I.H.P. and two Screws.

FIG. 257.—12,000 I.H.P. to each Propeller having three Blades.

Selected width ratio = ·275.
Selected area ratio = ·4427.
Speed = 19 knots.

In order to do this we must first find values of C_A. For values of C_A we have—

(*a*) ·4 disc area ratio.
From fig. 214 we see that B = ·105

$$C_A = \frac{R^2 H}{BV^5} = \frac{5^2 \times 1350}{·105 \times (23)^5} = ·0500.$$

R is in hundreds of revolutions per minute,
H is in horse-power,
V is in knots.

(*b*) ·45 disc area ratio.

B = ·107.

$$\therefore \quad C_A = \frac{5^2 \times 1350}{·107 \times (23)^5} = ·0490.$$

If we now read off from fig. 216 the values of C_0, corresponding to the above values of C_A, for the pitch ratios we have chosen we get the following values for C_0 :—

Pitch ratio.	Value of C_0 corresponding to	
	$C_A = \cdot 0500.$	$C_A = \cdot 0490.$
1·0	·0285	·028
1·2	·03475	·03425
1·4	·04075	·04025

$$\text{Now} \quad C_0 = \frac{H}{BD^2V^3}$$

$$\text{and} \quad C_A = \frac{R^2H}{BV^5}.$$

$$\therefore \quad \frac{C_0}{C_A} = \frac{V^2}{D^2R^2}$$

$$\text{and} \therefore \quad D^2 = \frac{V^2C_A}{C_0R^2}.$$

Hence, from the values of C_0 and C_A already obtained, we can find the values of D, as V and R are known quantities.

The values of D so found are

Pitch ratio.	Values of D.	
	$C_A = \cdot 0500.$	$C_A = \cdot 0490.$
1·0	6·09 feet.	6·08 feet.
1·2	5·52 ,,	5·50 ,,
1·4	5·10 ,,	5·08 ,,

Efficiency.—From fig. 216 we find that, for a three-bladed elliptical propeller of disc area ratio 0·45, the values $C_A = \cdot 0500$ and $\cdot 0490$ give the values of ϵ for the different pitch ratios, as in the following table :—

Pitch ratio.	Value of ϵ corresponding to $C_A =$	
	·0500.	·0490.
1·0	·7	·7
1·2	·705	·7075
1·4	·68	·6825

These results of diameters and efficiencies have to be plotted to a base of total blade areas.

In calculating the total area a discount of 20 per cent. is allowed for the bossing.

Hence, total blade area $= \dfrac{8}{10} \dfrac{\pi D^2}{4} \times$ disc area ratio.

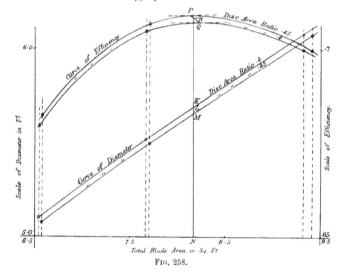

FIG. 258.

The values in these cases are

Pitch ratio.	Total blade area for disc area ratios of	
	·4	·45
1·0	9·32 sq. ft.	9·41 sq. ft.
1·2	7·66 ,,	7·70 ,,
1·4	6·54 ,,	6·57 ,,

Having plotted the values of ϵ and D for the two disc area ratios under consideration, we can find the points P and Q, fig. 258, which are the points of maximum ϵ for these two conditions. By interpolation we can find R the point of maximum, ϵ for disc area ratio ·4427 from the relation

$$\frac{RQ}{QP} = \frac{·4427 - ·4}{·45 - ·4} = \frac{427}{500}.$$

If we draw an ordinate R N through R this will cut the curves of D at the points K and M. If we then find L such that

$$\frac{LK}{MK} = \frac{427}{500}$$

we get the value of $D = N L$ corresponding to the maximum $\epsilon = R N$ and the disc area ratio ·4427.

A correction for disc area ratio from ·45 to ·4427 should be applied to

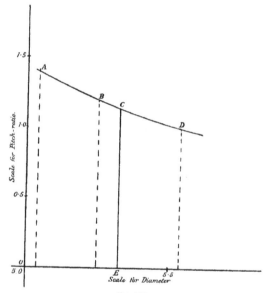

FIG. 259.

the value of ϵ so found, and is obtained from fig. 214. In this case it is negligible.

Thus maximum $\epsilon = 70·85$ per cent.
and $D = 5·67$ feet.

For Pitch Ratio.—If we consider the propeller of disc area ratio ·45, and plot the values of D for this propeller as abscissæ, and the corresponding values of the pitch ratio as ordinates, we get a curve A B C D above, fig. 259.

If we set off O E = diameter indicated by point M in fig. 258, then the ordinate C E in fig. 259 will show the pitch ratio of required propeller. This is found to be 1·13. The same value is found for the pitch ratio of the point K. If these were different we should need to interpolate between K and M, and so find the value of p corresponding to L. Hence the pitch $= pD = 1\cdot13 \times 5\cdot67 = 6\cdot41$ feet.

According to Froude, the "Analysis" pitch is $1\cdot02$ times the driving face pitch. Hence these values have to be divided by $1\cdot02$. Thus $p = 1\cdot11$ and $P = 6\cdot28$.

From fig. 253 at 500 revolutions Taylor gives pitch $= 6\cdot3$ feet,
and efficiency $= 68$ per cent.
Diameter $= 5\cdot8$ feet.

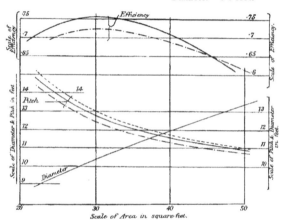

FIG. 260.—Dimensions and Efficiencies of Screws.

Developing 4800 thrust horse-power at 25 knots at 275 revolutions per minute.
— · — · — Froude Elliptical ⎱ segmental section.
——————— Taylor ⎰
– – – – – – Taylor, equal double convex section.
Screws three-bladed disc area ratio ·357.

Hence a final comparison of the results obtained by the Froude and Taylor methods can be obtained. It is shown in the following table :—

	Efficiency.	Diameter.	Pitch.	Pitch ratio.
Froude	70·85 per cent.	5·67 feet	6·28 feet	1·11
Taylor	68 ,,	5·8 ,,	6·3 ,,	1·09

—which shows a very close agreement between their experimental results. It should be, however, noted that the forms of Froude's blades differ from Taylor's.

This question of the comparison of the experimental results of Froude and Taylor has been investigated by Mr T. B. Abell, R.C.N.C., and the results published in the *Transactions of the Institution of Naval Architects* for 1910. In making such a comparison, consideration must be given to the different systems employed of fairing the experimental results, the difference in the notation in which the results are expressed, and the difference in the forms of the blades. The chief differences in type of blade are the proportions of boss diameter and of root thickness to screw diameter. Taylor's experimental screws are much larger than Froude's, their diameters being respectively 16 and 9·6 inches. As Taylor only experimented with three-bladed screws, the comparison is only made for this type.

The conclusion of the analysis is that the two sets of results are very fairly consistent, due allowance being made for the differences noted above. The greatest inconsistency is in the variation of efficiency with disc area ratio. Froude states that the decrease of efficiency due to alteration in the area of a propeller by widening the blades is constant for all slips, while Taylor states that the advantage of narrow blades is greater at large than at small values of slip.

Fig. 260 shows the results of a case worked out on the two bases. It will be noticed that the pitch of Taylor's blades are slightly greater than Froude's, as is also the efficiency until we reach large diameters. This shows a fairly close agreement with the case we have already dealt with, the results of which are given on p. 352.

Determination of Efficiency of Propellers in a Ship from Results of Steam Trials.

From steam trials giving the relation between I.H.P. or S.H.P. revolutions and speed it is possible for a given design of propeller, upon which model experiments have been made, to determine the efficiency of the propellers in the ship. Taking the case of a turbine-driven vessel we have

S.H.P. = 18000   Revs. = 500.   Speed = 25 knots.
D. = 75″   Blade area   2871 sq. ins.
P. = 79″   Projected area 2649 ,,
4 shafts   Disc area   4418 ,,

By means of Froude's curves we can find the propulsive coefficient $\left(\dfrac{\text{T.H.P.}}{\text{S.H.P.}}\right)$ of the vessel, and the efficiency of the screw.

Analysis.—"*Analysis*" *Disc area ratio.*—The blade area given above is the total area of the outline of the blade to the root of the blade. In computing the total blade area for the ship propeller from the diameter and disc area ratio, a discount of 20 per cent. is allowed for the bossing. Hence to obtain the disc area ratio for analysis a correction of 20 per cent. has to be applied.

$$\text{Hence disc area ratio} = \frac{100}{80} \times \frac{2871}{4418}$$

$$= 0.8125.$$

The Analysis pitch is 2 per cent. greater than the pitch of the driving face of the screw = 1·02 × 79″ = 80″·58,

and $\therefore$ " Analysis " pitch ratio $= \dfrac{80.58}{75} = 1.074.$

Speed of propeller = Revolutions per minute × " Analysis pitch "

$$= 500 \times 80\cdot58 \text{ inches per minute}$$

$$= \frac{500 \times 80\cdot58 \times 60}{12 \times 6080} \text{ knots}$$

$$= 33\cdot13 \text{ knots}$$

and $\therefore$ slip ratio $= \dfrac{\text{Speed of propeller} - \text{speed of ship}}{\text{Speed of propeller}}$

$$= \frac{33\cdot13 - 25}{33\cdot13} = \frac{8\cdot13}{33\cdot13}$$

$$\therefore \quad S = \cdot245.$$

For purposes of analysis of steam trials Froude recommends the x, y curve, fig. 215. From the above value for S we have

$$x = \frac{1\cdot0133}{1 - S} = \frac{1\cdot0133}{\cdot755} = 1\cdot342.$$

and from the curve fig. 215 $y = \cdot00133$.

Now
$$y = \frac{p}{B(p + 21)} \times \frac{H}{D^2 V^3}.$$

We know y and have now to find B. The propellers are three-bladed wide tip. From fig. 214 we get for disc area ratio $\cdot8125$ a value of $B = \cdot127$, and from this the Thrust Horse-Power,

$$H = \frac{\cdot00133 \times \cdot127 \times 22\cdot074 \times (75)^2 \times (25)^3}{(12)^2 \times 1\cdot074}$$

$$= 2118.$$

If we assume hull efficiency as unity, and therefore T.H.P. = E.H.P., and write I.H.P. for S.H.P., we cannot be very far wrong.

Then propulsive coefficient $= \dfrac{\text{E.H.P.}}{\text{I.H.P.}} = \dfrac{2118}{4500}$

$$= 47\cdot1 \text{ per cent.}$$

Efficiency of Propeller.—From fig. 215. For $x = 1\cdot342$ and pitch ratio $1\cdot074$

$$\epsilon = \cdot709.$$

This is for a three-bladed elliptical propeller of 0·45 disc area ratio.

The propeller is a three-bladed wide tip of 0·8125 disc area ratio and 1·074 " analysis " pitch ratio.

We must therefore apply the following *corrections* :—

    Correction for three-blade wide tip = ·020 deduction.

    Correction due to disc area ratio $\left.\right\}$ = ·052 deduction
       and pitch ratio from fig. 214

    Hence total deduction = ·072

    and $\therefore$ correct efficiency = ·709 − ·072 = ·637

$$= 63\cdot7 \text{ per cent.}$$

This assumes that the actual blade is of the same form as Froude's " wide tip " blade.

We have thus determined the propulsive coefficient of the ship and the efficiency of the propeller.

CHAPTER XXV.

RELATION BETWEEN INDICATED AND SHAFT HORSE-POWER. PROGRESSIVE SPEED TRIALS.

In reciprocating engines the power developed is measured by means of indicators, which give a graphical representation of the pressures in the cylinder during the whole stroke of the piston. Knowing the length of stroke, area of piston, and number of revolutions per minute, the horse-power developed in the cylinder can be calculated. The power thus obtained is called the indicated horse-power, or I.H.P.

With turbines we are necessarily forced to adopt some other method of measuring the power developed. This is effected by the use of torsion meters (sometimes called torsiometers), which register the amount of twist in a given length of shafting. From the modulus of rigidity of the shaft, its dimensions and revolutions per minute, the amount of horse-power actually passed through the shaft can be measured. This is known as shaft horse-power, or S.H.P.

For comparison between reciprocating and turbine installations it is necessary to know the relation between the I.H.P. as developed in the cylinder and the S.H.P. actually transmitted to the shaft. In reciprocating engines the I.H.P. developed is spent partly in friction of pistons, glands, bearings, and thrust block; also in the auxiliary machinery which is worked off main shaft (air pumps, etc.); and the rest is transmitted to the screw through the shaft. Experiments have been made to determine these losses, but these could not be made on a very large scale owing to the difficulty of constructing a dynamometer capable of consuming sufficient power. From the experiments it was found that 12½ to 15 per cent. of the I.H.P. is used before reaching the screw. In the case of modern vessels the loss may be as low as 7 per cent., but usually is from 10 to 12 per cent.

Hence a vessel with reciprocating engines, the measure of whose power is 10,000 I.H.P., can only deliver 9000 S.H.P. to the propellers. The efficiency of turbine machinery is, however, greater than reciprocating, so that generally for the same boilers a greater S.H.P. is delivered to the propellers. It is usually considered that the turbine is 15 per cent. more efficient in the use of the steam, while the friction losses are about 2 per cent.

Thus, for a given boiler installation, we have the following comparison between reciprocating and turbine machinery.

For every 115 H.P. developed in the turbine we have 100 H.P. in the reciprocating engine. Friction losses are 2 per cent. in the former and 10 per cent. in the latter. Thus in actual S.H.P. we have

$$\left(115 - \frac{2 \times 115}{100}\right) \text{ in the turbine against}$$

$$(100 - 10) \qquad \text{in the reciprocating engine,}$$

$$\textit{i.e.} \quad (115 - 2\cdot3) : 90$$
$$112\cdot7 \qquad : 90$$
$$1\cdot25 \qquad : 1.$$

Thus, in any system of boilers, if we add 25 per cent. to the S.H.P. that would be developed by reciprocating engines, we get the S.H.P. developed by the same boilers in a turbine. In other words, the turbine is 25 per cent. more efficient. Some of this gain is lost in the propeller (see Chap. XXIV.).

Progressive Speed Trials.—When a ship is ready to be tried under steam a series of trials is made, as far as possible under the conditions of service for which she is intended, with a view to determine the relation of speed and power, and to test the working of the machinery. For this purpose the vessel is run at successive speeds over an approved course, and records are taken of—

(a) Revolutions of engines.
(b) Power developed.
(c) Speed of ship.

(a) *Revolutions of Engines.*—These are measured by means of mechanical counters in the engine-room, and sometimes by graphic records on time cylinders.

(b) *Power developed.*—In the case of reciprocating engines this is measured by engine indicators, and by torsiometers in the case of turbines.

(c) *Speed of Ship.*—This is taken over a measured distance, usually a nautical mile of 6080 feet. Four poles P (fig. 261) are placed on the seashore such that the lines P P joining them as shown are a mile apart.

The course taken is perpendicular to these lines, and is shaped by compass. In some cases buoys B give the best channel and approximate path. The ship must be run on the straight before reaching the mile, so that when she enters the measured mile the speed is uniform and up to the desired amount. After finishing the mile she is kept on the same course for nearly another mile, so that after turning she will have sufficient distance to run to get to a uniform speed again when running through the measured mile in the opposite direction.

Conduct of Trial.—Shortly before entering the measured mile the telegraph bell is rung from the bridge to the engine-room as a warning. As soon as the course is entered a stop-watch is started and the telegraph bell is again rung to the engine-room, so that the counters may be read and diagrams or torsiometer readings taken. When the mile is completed the watch is stopped and the telegraph bell rung to engine-room. Thus a complete account of the revolutions and horse-power while running through the mile is obtained, together with the time taken.

Sources of Error.—The course may be too oblique or is not straight. This will cause an error in the speed measurement. If too short a turn be taken, the ship may not be at uniform speed on the return journey. Some of the thrust will then be used in acceleration. The rudder may be worked too much, causing an erratic course and also a drag. The other factors affecting the results are the tide and wind effects. These are generally present.

Effects of Tide and Wind.—The effect of the wind may not be the same positively and negatively in the two directions on the mile, and may not cancel out on both. Helm may have to be carried each way. The effects are augmented if the wind is variable. The lofty erections of modern passenger steamers add appreciably to resistance, so that estimates based on old steamers or model experiments alone must be modified to allow for the character of the deck erections.

The effects of a varying tide during the trial are eliminated by taking the *Admiralty mean*, or *mean of means*. Usually where tides are about two miles per hour, for a large ship four runs at each speed is sufficient. For

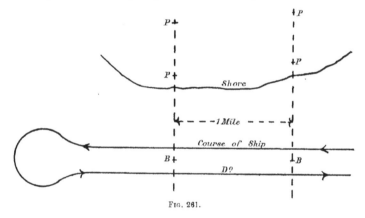

FIG. 261.

special accuracy six are made. This is done in the case of small vessels, such as torpedo-boats or destroyers. With a tide speed not exceeding one mile per hour little inaccuracy is likely to result from taking only two runs. The greater the maximum tidal speed the greater must be the variation in speed if the time over which the variation takes place is constant. The rule for the mean of means in the case of four runs is

$$v = \tfrac{1}{8}(v_1 + 3v_2 + 3v_3 + v_4),$$

where v_1, v_2, v_3, and v_4 are the individual speeds registered. In the case of six runs the rule becomes

$$v = \tfrac{1}{32}(v_1 + 5v_2 + 10v_3 + 10v_4 + 5v_5 + v_6).$$

It is essential that the runs should be taken at equal intervals of time.

Another method of eliminating the error due to change of tide, and, incidentally, to obtain from the records the speed of tide at any time during trial, is as follows :—

Let v_1, v_2, etc., be the actual speeds relatively to the water during the

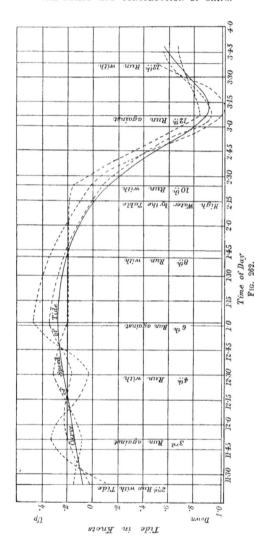

Fig. 262.

successive runs, and V_1, V_2, etc. the recorded speeds.   Then, supposing the first run is against the tide, we have

tide during run $1 = t_1 = kv_1 - V_1$
,,   ,, $2 = t_2 = V_2 - kv_2$
,,   ,, $3 = t_3 = kv_3 - V_3$

and so on, where k is practically constant, and will be very nearly unity. The values of v_1, v_2, etc. can be obtained by observing a floating object

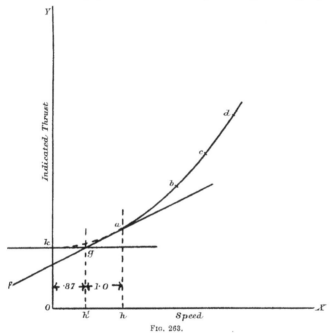

FIG. 263.

which is far enough away from the vessel so as not to have its position influenced by the wave motion due to the ship's progress.

If we assume values of k and plot t in terms of the time of day at which the successive experiments were made, we shall get a curve of tide in terms of time of day.   This curve should be a fair one.   The curves deduced for different values of k are zigzag in form, but by trying several values of k a fair curve can be found.

This has been done in a special case, and the curves so obtained are shown in fig. 262.

Analysis of Speed Trials.—For the purpose of analysis of speed trials W. Froude introduced the term "indicated thrust," which is

$$\frac{33000 \times \text{I.H.P.}}{\text{pitch of propeller} \times \text{revolutions}}.$$

This is the thrust which the propeller would be exerting if the force of the steam were employed in creating thrust only. It may be divided into the following parts :—

(1) The useful thrust, or ship's true resistance.

(2) The augment of resistance, or thrust deduction.

(3) The frictional resistance of propeller.

(4) The initial or dead-load friction of the engine, due to the weight of the moving parts causing friction on the bearings, the friction due to piston and glands packings.

(5) Friction of working load which is due to pressure on the bearings due to steam.

(6) Power absorbed in air, feed, and bilge pumps worked off main engines.

Dead-load Friction of Engines.—The use to which the results of the speed trials are put is in the determination of (4), the dead-load friction. This is done as follows :—

Let a, b, c, d, fig. 263, represent the several values of the indicated thrusts as obtained from the trials at different speeds.

A fair curve is drawn through these spots. We require the shape of the curve below the lowest speed, so as to get the ordinate at zero speed.

To do this, assume that the resistance of a ship at low speeds varies as $V^{1.87}$, and draw a parabola of this order so as to form a continuous curve with that already obtained.

Through a, the lowest point of the curve obtained, a tangent af is drawn to the curve and a line ah is drawn parallel to OY.

Divide Oh at h' so that $\dfrac{Oh'}{hh'} = 0.87$, and draw a line through h' parallel to OY to cut af at g.

Then if gk be drawn parallel to OX, Oh gives the ordinate at zero speed which is the indicated thrust required to overcome the dead-load friction. gk is a tangent to the curve at k.

This construction was made for several cases and gave results which coincided so well at the point a and for some distance above it that the assumption seems to be justified.

PART VII.

OSCILLATIONS OF SHIPS.

CHAPTER XXVI.

GENERAL CONSIDERATIONS OF THE MOTION OF A SHIP WHEN AT SEA.

WHEN a ship is in motion at sea it is usually acted upon by many forces. The wind, the sea, the thrust of the propeller, the action of gravity, all produce forces varying in amount and direction. To consider the effect of all these forces upon the vessel, it is necessary for some purposes to consider them in detail. For instance, for purposes of determination of strength locally, it is necessary to consider local forces. For purposes of general determination of strength, the forces must be considered in combination. For the motion of a ship as a whole, under the action of many forces, we may consider these forces in detail, to determine the motions of parts of the structure in relation to each other. But these motions in all cases produce forces or resistances to relative motion which balance the forces producing the motion. The bending of a beam produces resistance to bending, in the form of tension on one side of the beam and compression on the other, to an extent that just balances the forces applied. But these resistance forces can only be developed if the end of the beam, or some part of it, is connected or supported to some other part of the structure. The reaction of this support will similarly develop resistances in the other part of the structure, and in turn will demand support from another part, until every part has been acted upon and has reacted, and has in each case developed resistance forces and has called for support from adjacent parts. Thus the whole structure has transmitted through it the effect of each single force, until finally there is nothing left to give support and the body has to move. It is evident that as each resistance force is developed only by, and exactly to the amount of, each applied or reactive force, that these resistance forces must all balance the internally applied reactions, and leave finally the external system of forces which tends to move the body. While these forces balance each other internally, they cannot be neglected, as we have already seen in the part dealing with Strength. They are of the utmost importance in determining the character of the structure and its scantlings. But, except to the extent which change of form affects the external forces, they do not affect the actual motion of the body as a whole, though they determine the change of form which takes place in the body. Thus, as this change of form is generally very small, in studying the motion of the structure as a whole, the forces acting from the outside may be considered as if they were acting on a body that is absolutely rigid, and contained no material which could change its form, and thereby develop resistance forces.

We will consider the effect of the forces upon the motion of the body.

Take the usual principal planes in a ship as planes of references, with G as origin (fig. 264).

Instead of studying the complex motion of the ship as a whole, we can divide the motion into a motion of translation of the C.G. and a motion of rotation about it. The rotational motion with which we are now principally concerned is that about the axis G X, and is spoken of as a *"rolling" motion.* If we asume the ship to rotate about this axis, the wedges of submersion and

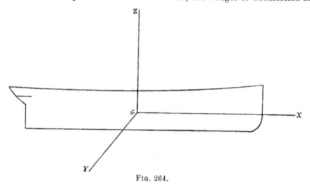

Fig. 264.

emersion tend to equalise, but are not equal, and hence their vertical resultant causes a motion of translation of G along G Z (fig. 264). This is called a *dipping motion,* and will be dealt with later. We have also a motion of rotation about G Y, which is known as *"pitching,"* and will also be referred to later.

A Consideration of the Forces acting upon a Ship when inclined in Still Water.—The forces acting on a ship when heeled over and in equilibrium will keep her there. These forces (see fig. 265) must form a couple, applied in such a manner as to balance the righting couple W.GZ. If some of the forces, such as wind pressure, were suddenly removed, we should have an unbalanced couple = W.GZ – whatever is left of the external couple.

This unbalanced couple will be effective in setting the ship in motion; and if there were no resistance offered, would cause the vessel to be in a continual state of motion. Under these conditions, since the only forces acting on the ship are the balanced vertical forces of weight and buoyancy, G cannot move horizontally. Also, as the displacement is constant, F the centre of flotation (fig. 265) cannot have a vertical motion. Hence if we drew a vertical line F C and a horizontal one G C, an axis through the point

C will be the "instantaneous axis of rotation" of the ship.* This is known as "Moseley's Construction" for the instantaneous axis. Mons. Bertin made

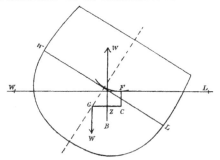

FIG. 265.

a series of experiments on an actual vessel to determine the exact position of this axis, and found it to be very near the C.G. of the ship.

Consider the general case of the motion of a body about a fixed axis. By

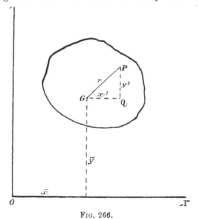

FIG. 266.

the principle enunciated by D'Alembert, the internal forces balance, and the external forces with the forces of inertia reversed form another balanced system.

Let the fixed axis be perpendicular to the paper through O (fig. 266). Let G be the C.G. of body and its coordinates be $(\bar{x}, \bar{y})$ referred to the fixed axes O X, O Y.

Let P be any particle of mass m and (x, y) its coordinates. Then, if X

* See also p. 424.

and Y are the external forces acting on the body in the directions parallel to the axes O X, O Y respectively,

$$X = \Sigma m \frac{d^2 x}{dt^2}$$

$$Y = \Sigma m \frac{d^2 y}{dt^2}.$$

Shift the origin to G, and let (x', y') be the coordinates of P relative to the new axes.

Then $\quad x = \bar{x} + x'$
$$y = \bar{y} + y'$$

also $\quad \left.\begin{matrix} \Sigma m x = M \bar{x} \\ \Sigma m y = M \bar{y} \end{matrix}\right\}$ where M is whole mass of body

and $\quad \left.\begin{matrix} \Sigma m x' = 0 \\ \Sigma m y' = 0 \end{matrix}\right\}$ since G is the C.G. of body.

and $\therefore \quad \Sigma m \dfrac{d^2 x}{dt^2} = M \dfrac{d^2 \bar{x}}{dt^2}$

$$\Sigma m \frac{d^2 y}{dt^2} = M \frac{d^2 \bar{y}}{dt^2}$$

$$\Sigma m \frac{d^2 x'}{dt^2} = 0$$

$$\Sigma m \frac{d^2 y'}{dt^2} = 0.$$

Hence if we substitute in the values of X and Y the values above of x and y we obtain

$$X = \Sigma m \left(\frac{d^2 \bar{x}}{dt^2} + \frac{d^2 x'}{dt^2} \right) = M \frac{d^2 \bar{x}}{dt^2}$$

$$Y = \Sigma m \left(\frac{d^2 \bar{y}}{dt^2} + \frac{d^2 y'}{dt^2} \right) = M \frac{d^2 \bar{y}}{dt^2}.$$

Hence for the motion of translation of body we can suppose the whole of the mass to be concentrated at the C.G.

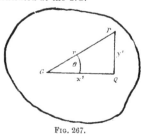

FIG. 267.

For rotation about G. In fig. 267
Let PG $= r$
and angle PGQ $= \theta$.

Then the acceleration of P at any time t perpendicular to G P is $= r\dfrac{d^2\theta}{dt^2}$.

Hence force of inertia perpendicular to G P of particle at $P = mr\dfrac{d^2\theta}{dt^2}$.

And $\therefore$ total moment of forces of inertia about G

$$= \Sigma mr^2\frac{d^2\theta}{dt^2}$$

$$= I\frac{d^2\theta}{dt^2}$$

where I is the moment of inertia of body about an axis through G perpendicular to the paper. Hence the moment of the external couple is equal to $I\dfrac{d^2\theta}{d^2t}$. It is this equation that is the basis of the mathematical treatment of rolling of ships. We will now go on to consider the case of—

The Simple Pendulum.—This is the simplest case of an oscillating body; and as the equations of motion are of exactly the same nature as those we have in the case of the rolling of a ship, it is instructive to study the motion.

Let l be the length of pendulum, m the mass of the bob (fig. 268), θ the inclination to the vertical at any instant, and T the tension of the string.

As the motion of the bob is always perpendicular to the string, since the string is assumed to be inelastic, the tension T will not affect the motion.

At any time t the acceleration of the bob in the direction of θ increasing is

$$l\frac{d^2\theta}{dt^2}.$$

The resolved force in this direction is

$$- mg \sin \theta,$$

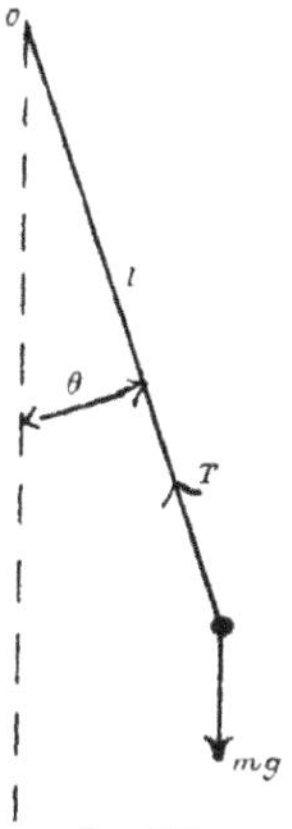

and therefore the equation of motion is

$$ml\frac{d^2\theta}{dt^2} = - mg \sin \theta.$$

$$\therefore \quad \frac{d^2\theta}{dt^2} + \frac{g}{l}\sin \theta = 0 \quad . \qquad . \quad . \quad (1)$$

FIG. 268.

Small oscillations.—If θ is small, then for $\sin \theta$ we can write θ. Equation (1) then becomes

$$\frac{d^2\theta}{dt^2} + \frac{g}{l}\theta = 0 \quad . \qquad . \qquad . \quad . \quad (2)$$

The solution of this equation is of the form

$$\theta = A \sin pt + B \cos pt,$$

where A and B are arbitrary constants, their particular values in any one case depending upon the circumstances of that particular case.

From this value of θ we have

$$\frac{d^2\theta}{dt^2} = -Ap^2 \sin pt - Bp^2 \cos pt.$$

Substituting these values in equation (2) we get

$$-Ap^2 \sin pt - Bp^2 \cos pt + \frac{g}{l}(A \sin pt + B \cos pt) \equiv 0.$$

Since the left-hand side of the equation is identically equal to zero for all values of t, we must have the coefficients of $\sin pt$ and $\cos pt$ each separately zero.

$$\therefore \quad Ap^2 = \frac{g}{l}A$$

$$\text{or} \quad p = \sqrt{\frac{g}{l}}.$$

Hence the solution of equation (2) is

$$\theta = A \sin t\sqrt{\frac{g}{l}} + B \cos t\sqrt{\frac{g}{l}} \quad . \quad . \quad . \quad . \quad (3)$$

Inspecting this equation, we see that if

$$t\sqrt{\frac{g}{l}} = a \text{ or } (2\pi + a) \text{ we get the same value for } \theta.$$

Hence between the times given by

$$t = a\sqrt{\frac{l}{g}} = t_1$$

$$\text{and} \quad t = (2\pi + a)\sqrt{\frac{l}{g}} = t_2$$

the motion has gone through a complete cycle, and is in precisely the same state as before. The time elapsed between t_1 and t_2 is obviously the time taken to go through this cycle. This time is called the *mathematical period* of the motion. If we denote this by T we have

$$T = (t_2 - t_1) = 2\pi\sqrt{\frac{l}{g}},$$

which is the usual formula for the period of a simple pendulum when making small oscillations.

When the motion is not small,

we have the equation $\qquad \dfrac{d^2\theta}{dt^2} + \dfrac{g}{l}\sin\theta = 0 \quad . \quad . \quad . \quad . \quad (1)$

This equation cannot be solved exactly, and methods of approximation have to be applied. The usual method is to solve for $\dfrac{d\theta}{dt}$.

If we multiply equation (1) all through by $2\dfrac{d\theta}{dt}$ we get

$$2\frac{d^2\theta}{dt^2}\frac{d\theta}{dt} + 2\frac{g}{l}\sin\theta\frac{d\theta}{dt} = 0.$$

$\therefore \left(\dfrac{d\theta}{dt}\right)^2 = A + \dfrac{2g}{l} \cos\theta$, where A is a constant whose value is determined as follows.

Let α be the maximum angle of swing from the upright. Then when

$$\theta = \alpha$$

$$\dfrac{d\theta}{dt} = 0 \quad \text{since the pendulum is then at rest.}$$

And $\therefore$ $\qquad 0 = A + \dfrac{2g}{l} \cos\alpha.$

$\therefore$ $\qquad A = -\dfrac{2g}{l} \cos\alpha$

and $\qquad \left(\dfrac{d\theta}{dt}\right)^2 = \dfrac{2g}{l}(\cos\theta - \cos\alpha).$

$\therefore$ $\qquad \dfrac{d\theta}{dt} = \dfrac{2\pi}{T}\sqrt{2(\cos\theta - \cos\alpha)}$ since $T = 2\pi\sqrt{\dfrac{l}{g}}$.

$\therefore$ $\qquad dt = \dfrac{T}{2\pi} \dfrac{d\theta}{\sqrt{2(\cos\theta - \cos\alpha)}}$

where T is the time of a small oscillation,

or $\qquad T_\alpha = \dfrac{T}{2\pi}\int_{-\alpha}^{\alpha} \dfrac{d\theta}{\sqrt{2(\cos\theta - \cos\alpha)}}$

where T_α is the time of a complete oscillation for an angle α to the upright. The above integration has to be performed approximately, and the results are as follows:—

Values of α.	Small.	30°.	60°.	90°.	120°.	150°.	180°.
Values of T_α	T	1·017T	1·073T	1·183T	1·373T	1·762T	∞

where $\qquad T = 2\pi\sqrt{\dfrac{l}{g}}.$

From this it will be seen that for angles of oscillation up to 30° from the upright the period is less than 2 per cent. above that for a small oscillation.

CHAPTER XXVII.

UNRESISTED ROLLING IN STILL WATER.

Definitions.—The *Arc* of *Oscillation* is the angle from extreme roll to Port to extreme roll to Starboard, or *vice versa*. This is generally spoken of as from "out to out." The *Period* is the time taken by the vessel to roll through the arc of oscillation. This is half the "mathematical period."

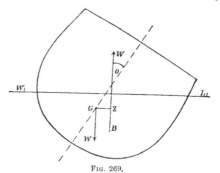

FIG. 269.

Period of Oscillation of a Ship in Still Water.—Consider the ship to be heeled over to an angle θ, fig. 269. Let I be the mass moment of inertia of ship about the axis of rotation, which is assumed to pass through G.

Then $I\dfrac{d^2\theta}{dt^2}$ = external couple, and is reckoned positive in the direction of θ increasing.

Hence

$$I\frac{d^2\theta}{dt^2} = -\,\mathrm{W.GZ, \ fig.\ 269,}$$

or

$$I\frac{d^2\theta}{dt^2} + \mathrm{W.GZ} = 0.$$

To integrate this equation we must express G Z as some simple function of θ. If θ is small we can write $GZ = m\theta$, where $m = GM$ the metacentric height.

368

With this assumption the equation becomes

$$I\frac{d^2\theta}{dt^2} + Wm\theta = 0.$$

$$\therefore \quad \frac{W}{g}K^2\frac{d^2\theta}{dt^2} + Wm\theta = 0$$

where K is the radius of gyration of the ship about the longitudinal axis through its C.G.,

$$\text{or} \quad \frac{d^2\theta}{dt^2} + \frac{gm}{K^2}\theta = 0 \quad . \quad . \quad . \quad (1)$$

Comparing this with the case of the pendulum, we see that the mathematical period of motion is

$$2\pi\sqrt{\frac{K^2}{gm}},$$

or the period of roll, as defined, is given by

$$T = \pi\sqrt{\frac{K^2}{gm}}.$$

T is called the "Natural Period" of the ship. We see that it is independent of θ up to the angle at which the G Z curve coincides with its tangent, and that the rolling is "Isochronous" within these limits.

If the "Metacentric Evolute" is the involute of a circle of radius G M and centre G, we have (fig. 270),

GZ = PQ, where Q is a point on the "Metacentric Evolute"
= arc PM
= $m\theta$.

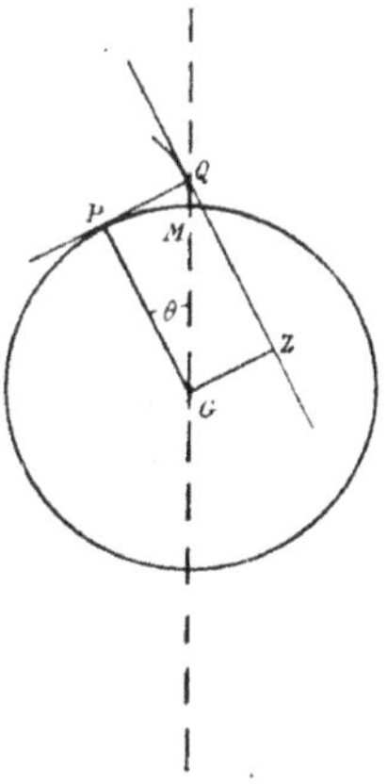

FIG. 270.

Near the value $\theta = 0$ the M curve is approximately of this nature, and we get isochronous rolling for a fairly good range of θ.

The General Solution of the above equation, comparing it with the pendulum case, is seen to be

$$\theta = A\sin t\sqrt{\frac{gm}{K^2}} + B\cos t\sqrt{\frac{gm}{K^2}},$$

which may be written

$$\theta = A\sin\frac{\pi t}{T} + B\cos\frac{\pi t}{T}, \text{ since } T = \pi\sqrt{\frac{K^2}{gm}}.$$

The values of A and B are determined from the particular circumstances of the motion. Thus, suppose the ship starts initially at an angle α to the vertical, with angular velocity U.

Then when $t = 0$, $\theta = \alpha$.

$\therefore \quad \alpha = B$.

Also when $t = 0$, $\frac{d\theta}{dt} = U$.

Now $\dfrac{d\theta}{dt} = \dfrac{\pi}{T}A \cos \dfrac{\pi t}{T} - \dfrac{\pi}{T}B \sin \dfrac{\pi t}{T}.$

∴ $U = \dfrac{\pi}{T}A,$ or $A = \dfrac{TU}{\pi}.$

And ∴ for this particular case the solution becomes

$$\theta = \dfrac{TU}{\pi} \sin \dfrac{\pi t}{T} + a \cos \dfrac{\pi t}{T}.$$

Similarly, the values of A and B for any other set of conditions may be found, the general solution being the same for all cases.

We have seen that $T = \pi \sqrt{\dfrac{K^2}{gm}}.$

It is essential, especially in the case of warships, that T should be as large as possible. The value of K cannot be altered much, so that m should be kept as small as possible.

The following are the values of T for a few cases. Knowing T and m, K can be calculated. The ratios of K to B the beam are also given.

Vessel.	G.M.	T.	Values of K.	B.	$\dfrac{K}{B}.$
	feet	secs.	feet	feet	
" Resolution "	3·5	7·5	25·4	75	·34
Paris and New York . .	1·0	10·0	18·1	63	·29
Large Atlantic Liners . .	1·5–2·5	5–8·7	18·8–20	50	·38–·4
(400 feet and over)					
Gunboats and Destroyers .	2·0–2·5	5–2	5·7–12·8	24	·24–·53

In small boats K is small, and so T cannot be very great.

Cargo-carrying vessels, when light, fill up their ballast tanks. This may cause a great G M, and hence a very quick rolling ship. To get over this difficulty various methods of fitting these tanks have been suggested. Two of the best known are shown in fig. 271.

If the GZ Curve is a Sine Curve.—This is the case of a submarine or circular vessel. It is sometimes true for an ordinary vessel up to a fairly large angle of heel. In this case (see fig. 272) M is at the centre of the circle and

$$GZ = GM \sin \theta$$
$$= m \sin \theta.$$

Thus the equation of roll becomes

$$\dfrac{d^2\theta}{dt^2} + \dfrac{\pi^2}{T^2} \sin \theta = 0.$$

This is precisely the same case as for large oscillations of a pendulum, and has already been dealt with. See p. 366.

In the report on the loss of H.M.S. "Captain," Professor Rankine proposed a solution for a low freeboard ship. He considered the curve

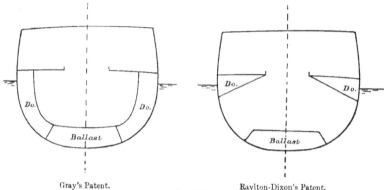

Gray's Patent.   Raylton-Dixon's Patent.

FIG. 271.

to be a curve of sines. Suppose such a vessel to have a range of R° and to be oscillating to an angle a. Then, if we find ϕ such that $\dfrac{\phi}{180} = \dfrac{a}{R}$, we should expect that the period at angle a would exceed the period for a small roll in the same ratio that the period of a pendulum at ϕ degrees exceeds the period for a small oscillation of the pendulum; *e.g.* — Let R = 60° and a = 30°.

Then $\dfrac{\phi}{180} = \dfrac{30}{60}$ or $\phi = 90°$,

and from the table given on page 367 the ratio is 1·183. Thus the period of ship rolling through 30° should be 1·183 times the period when rolling through a small angle.

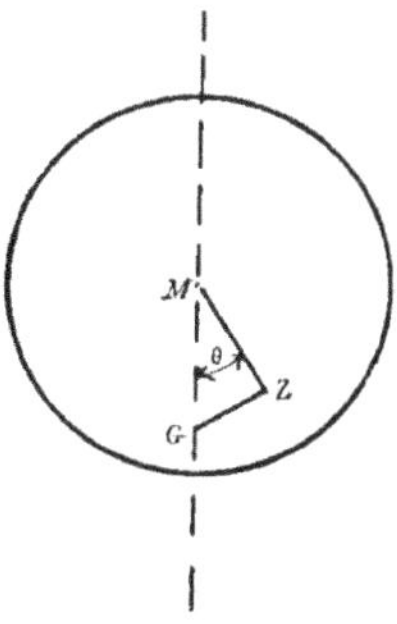

Unresisted Still - Water Rolling in the Case of Vessels of Small Metacentric Height. — It was pointed out by Professor Scribanti in 1904 that in the case of a vessel with small metacentric height the approximation for GZ = $m\theta$ will lead to erroneous results. We have seen that the equation of unresisted rolling is

FIG. 272.

$$\frac{d^2\theta}{dt^2} + \frac{g}{K^2}GZ = 0.$$

Scribanti assumes that, in the region of the waterline, the ship has vertical sides. Hence the "wall-sided" formula for the value of G Z in the case of a rectangular box will apply.　This formula is

$$GZ = \sin \theta (GM + \tfrac{1}{2} BM \tan^2 \theta).*$$

If θ is small we can write

$$\theta = \sin \theta = \tan \theta.$$

Hence the equation of roll becomes

$$\frac{d^2\theta}{dt^2} + \frac{gm}{K^2}\theta + \frac{g\rho}{2K^2}\theta^3 = 0.$$

Where $BM = \rho$.

This differs from equation (1), p. 369, in the last term.　It should be noted

---

* **Wall-sided Formula.**—If a wall-sided ship be inclined, then within the region of wall-sidedness the inclined waterline $W_1 L_1$ passes through C the centre of W L (fig. 273). Let $B_0 B_1$ be the C.B. in upright and when inclined through angle θ respectively.　Let x, y

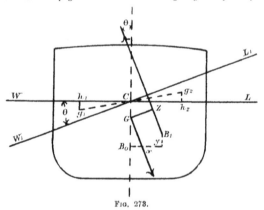

FIG. 273.

be the shift of C.B. parallel to and perpendicular to W L respectively.　An elemental length dl of submerged and emerged wedges forms triangular prisms.

Let b be the half-breadth of ship at this elemental wedge, $g_1 g_2$ are the centres of gravity of wedges, and $g_1 h_1$, $g_2 h_2$ are perpendicular to W L.　Then $h_1 h_2 = \tfrac{4}{3} b$ and $g_1 h_1 + g_2 h_2 = \tfrac{2}{3} b \tan \theta$. Volume of elemental wedge $v = \tfrac{1}{2} b^2 \tan \theta dl$.　Let V be volume of displacement of ship.

Then　　$Vx = \Sigma v.h_1 h_2 = \Sigma \tfrac{1}{2} b^2 \tan \theta dl \tfrac{4}{3} b$

　　　　　　$= \tan \theta \tfrac{2}{3} \Sigma b^3 dl = I \tan \theta$

where I is the moment of inertia of the waterplane W L about its centre line.

Similarly,　　$Vy = \Sigma v(g_1 h_1 + g_2 h_2)$

　　　　　　　$= \Sigma \tfrac{1}{2} b^2 \tan \theta dl \tfrac{2}{3} b \tan \theta$

　　　　　　　$= \tfrac{1}{3} \tan^2 \theta \Sigma \tfrac{2}{3} b^3 dl$

　　　　　　　$= \tfrac{1}{2} I \tan^2 \theta.$

∴　　$x = \dfrac{I}{V} \tan \theta = B_0 M \tan \theta$, and $y = \dfrac{I}{V} \tfrac{1}{2} \tan^2 \theta = \tfrac{1}{2} B_0 M \tan^2 \theta.$

Now　　$GZ = x \cos \theta + y \sin \theta - B_0 G \sin \theta$

　　　　　$= \sin \theta (B_0 M + \tfrac{1}{2} B_0 M \tan^2 \theta - B_0 G)$

　　　　　$= \sin \theta (GM + \tfrac{1}{2} B_0 M \tan^2 \theta).$

that the smaller m is, the smaller is the second term, and the motion depends more upon the value of ρ than m. The solution of the above equation is of a very complex nature, and leads to the following results.

If T_m is the period calculated from the equation and T the period calculated from the formula $T = \pi \sqrt{\dfrac{K^2}{gm}}$,

(*a*) For a battleship of G M 3 feet . . . . . . $\dfrac{T_m}{T} = 1\cdot04$.

(*b*) For a large Atlantic liner of weak initial stability, G M 4 inches . . . . $\dfrac{T_m}{T} = 1\cdot31$.

(*c*) As an extreme case of very weak initial stability, G M = $\tfrac{3}{8}$ inch . . . . $\dfrac{T_m}{T} = 2\cdot98$.

Scribanti also studied the case in which $m = 0$. Then equation becomes

$$\frac{d^2\theta}{dt^2} + \frac{g\rho}{2K^2}\theta^3 = 0.$$

The rolling is not now isochronous. The solution of this equation is

$$T = \frac{5\cdot25}{a}\sqrt{\frac{K^2}{g\rho}},$$

where a is the maximum angle from the upright. Thus the greater the angle rolled through the smaller is the period. Scribanti verified the results by making experiments upon a model.

Stresses set up in a Body due to Harmonic Oscillations.—Take the case of a rigid body suspended by an axis through 0, fig. 274. Let G be its centre of gravity, distant h from 0.

Let θ be the inclination of O G to the vertical. M the mass of the pendulum. Then the equation of motion of the body is

$$MK^2\frac{d^2\theta}{dt^2} + Mgh \sin \theta = 0$$

where K is the radius of gyration of body about O.

$$\therefore \quad \frac{d^2\theta}{dt^2} + \frac{gh}{K^2}\sin \theta = 0.$$

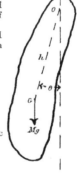

FIG. 274.

If θ is small we get the usual equation for harmonic oscillations, viz.

$$\frac{d^2\theta}{dt^2} + \frac{gh}{K^2}\theta = 0.$$

Now consider a mass m distant l from 0. Let a be the maximum angle reached. Then, neglecting sign, the maximum value of $\dfrac{d^2\theta}{dt^2}$ is $\dfrac{gh}{K^2}a$.

Hence the maximum linear acceleration of the small mass will be

$$l\frac{gh}{K^2}a.$$

That is, a force $ml\dfrac{gh}{K^2}a$ is acting on this small mass. Similar forces are acting on all other parts of the body, and these will induce stresses. The stresses induced in this manner due to Heaving and Pitching have been dealt with in Vol. I. If we now consider the case of Rolling, our equation is

$$\frac{d^2\theta}{dt^2} + \frac{\pi^2}{T^2}\theta = 0.$$

Hence, for maximum roll a, the force acting on a mass m distant l from the axis of oscillation is

$$ml\frac{\pi^2}{T^2}a.$$

If **T** is small and a is large, which is often the case, we then get large transverse forces on bodies that are distant from the axis of oscillation, such as bodies at the top of a mast. This problem was investigated in the case of the loss of H.M.S. "Atalanta." She was a vessel of 1075 tons, G M 6 feet and T $4\frac{3}{4}$ seconds for a roll from 40° to leeward to 25° to windward. Assuming harmonic roll through the mean angle $32\frac{1}{2}$° we get

$$\frac{d^2\theta}{dt^2} = \frac{\pi^2}{(4\cdot75)^2} \times \frac{32\frac{1}{2}}{180}\pi$$
$$= \cdot248.$$

Thus, at a point 100 feet above axis of oscillation, linear acceleration $= 24\cdot8 \dfrac{\text{ft.}}{\text{sec.}^2}$, and therefore at this point a body would receive a transverse force of magnitude $\dfrac{24\cdot8}{32\cdot2}$ times its weight, *i.e.* more than $\frac{3}{4}$ the weight of the body.

In the case of a mast, each part will have a transverse force acting upon it, the magnitude of which will depend upon its weight and distance from the axis of oscillation. Thus the problem is similar to a beam loaded in a definite manner, fixed at one end—viz. the deck—and having intermediate supports such as shrouds.

CHAPTER XXVIII.

RESISTED ROLLING IN STILL WATER
(EXPERIMENTAL INVESTIGATIONS).

It is evident that if there were no resistances to the rolling of a ship, once a motion was started it would never cease.
The main natural causes of resistance to rolling are—
I. Skin frictional resistance.
II. Keel resistances, *i.e.* the action of bilge keels, rudders, and any other projection on the outside of the ship.
III. Stream-line action at the bilge keels.
IV. The formation of surface waves due to the motion of the ship.
The precise nature of the resistances caused by these and their effect upon extinction of rolling will be dealt with later. The method of investigation employed is to treat the subject—
(1) Experimentally.
(2) The experimental results are analysed and extended mathematically.
Experimental Investigations. — These have been made by Dr Froude, Sir Philip Watts, several French investigators, and various others, from time to time, and the laws governing the resistances thoroughly analysed.
To carry out an experiment on a large ship, she is caused to roll by men running across the deck, and so timing their motion that they are always running up hill. Thus, in the "Sultan," a vessel of 9000 tons, 600 men produced a roll of 15° to each side. As soon as a good roll is started, the men are massed as nearly as possible on the middle line, and at each successive roll the extreme angle reached is recorded, and thus a complete history of the damping of the oscillations is obtained. The methods used for measuring the angles of roll should be accurate. The chief methods are—
(1) Pendulums.
(2) Gyrostatic apparatus.
(3) Batten or horizon apparatus.
(4) Mallock's rolling indicator.
(5) Froude's automatic recording apparatus.
We will consider each of these in detail.
(1) **Pendulums.**—The value of the pendulum as an apparatus for recording the angle of roll depends upon its vertical position in the ship. Suppose we have a pendulum suspended from a point P, fig. 275, at height h above the axis of oscillation O. If θ is the inclination to the upright at any time t, the angular velocity of ship is $\dfrac{d\theta}{dt}$ and angular accleration $\dfrac{d^2\theta}{dt^2}$.

∴ P has a transverse linear acceleration $h\dfrac{d^2\theta}{dt^2}$. Also, as P is moving in the arc of a circle of radius h, it will have a linear acceleration of $h\left(\dfrac{d\theta}{dt}\right)^2$ towards 0. Hence if m is the mass of the bob of the pendulum, the forces acting upon it are

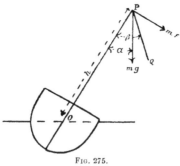

(1) mg vertically,

(2) $mh\dfrac{d^2\theta}{dt^2}$ transversely,

(3) $mh\left(\dfrac{d\theta}{dt}\right)^2$ along PO,

and the pendulum will set itself along the line of action of the resultant of these forces. (2) is zero at the upright and a maximum at the maximum angle of swing. (3) is a maximum at the upright and zero at the maximum angle of swing. Hence if a is the maximum angle of swing, and we assume

FIG. 275.

isochronous rolling, so that the equation of motion is

$$\frac{d^2\theta}{dt^2} + \frac{\pi^2}{T^2}\theta = 0,$$

the maximum value of $\dfrac{d^2\theta}{dt^2}$ is $\dfrac{\pi^2}{T^2}a$, and the maximum linear acceleration of P is $f = h\dfrac{\pi^2}{T^2}a$.

Hence the forces acting on pendulum are as shown in fig. 275, and consist of a vertical force mg, and a force $mf = mh\dfrac{\pi^2}{T^2}a$ perpendicular to P O.

Thus the pendulum will set itself along the line P Q, making an angle β with the upright. Resolving the forces in the direction perpendicular to P Q, we have

$$mg \sin(\beta - a) = mh\frac{\pi^2}{T^2}a \cos \beta.$$

If the angles are not very large, we can write

$$\sin(\beta - a) = \beta - a,$$

and $$\cos \beta = 1.$$

Then $$mg(\beta - a) = mha\frac{\pi^2}{T^2},$$

and ∴ $$\beta = \left(1 + \frac{h}{g}\frac{\pi^2}{T^2}\right)a.$$

Hence $\dfrac{h}{g}\dfrac{\pi^2}{T^2}a$ represents the error of the pendulum, and this increases as the height of suspension above the axis of oscillation increases, and also is greater for a vessel of small period. Also, as long as the pendulum is above the axis of oscillation, the recorded angle β is greater than the real angle a. If the pendulum is below the axis, β will be less than a. The best position is obviously at the axis of oscillation, but as this varies for different degrees of lading, there will generally be a slight error.

By using two pendulums, however, we can get the correct value of a and also the position of the axis of oscillation.

Let h_1, h_2 be the heights of pendulums above the axis of oscillation, β_1 and β_2 the angles recorded when the ship swings through an angle a.

Then
$$\frac{\beta_1}{a} = 1 + \frac{h_1}{g}\frac{\pi^2}{\mathrm{T}^2},$$

$$\frac{\beta_2}{a} = 1 + \frac{h_2}{g}\frac{\pi^2}{\mathrm{T}^2}.$$

Hence
$$\frac{\beta_1 - \beta_2}{a} = \frac{\pi^2}{g\mathrm{T}^2}(h_1 - h_2).$$

Now β_1, β_2, $(h_1 - h_2)$ are known, and T can be found by actually rolling the ship, hence a can be determined.

Then from the formula
$$\beta_1 = \left(1 + \frac{h_1}{g}\frac{\pi^2}{\mathrm{T}^2}\right)a$$

we can find h_1, and hence the position of the axis of rotation. This method has been put into practice and the centre of oscillation has been shown to be quite close to the C.G. of ship.

In the above mathematical investigation the pendulum has been assumed to be a very short one and of short period. If this were not so the pendulum would attain a considerable momentum, and hence the error would be enlarged.

(2) **Gyrostatic Apparatus for Recording Rolling.**—This consists of a heavy fly-wheel spinning around a vertical axis which is supported by two gimbal rings. The first ring has its plane vertical and in a longitudinal direction. The second ring carries the first and has its plane horizontal, and is carried on horizontal pivots whose axis is transverse. The principle of the apparatus is, that if the wheel be set spinning at a high angular velocity its axis will be maintained in direction. In this case the motion of the first ring will measure the roll of the ship, and of the second ring will measure the pitch. If the frame of the machine is turned on its side it will measure the yawing.

This apparatus has the advantage of accuracy for still-water rolling. At sea there is the disadvantage of not knowing the true vertical, and thus only the complete arc of oscillation is registered.

(3) **Batten or Horizon Apparatus.**—These are more generally used than the foregoing, and have the advantage of simplicity. One form, fig. 276, consists of a vertical semicircle, A B C, graduated in degrees. At P a bar is pivoted with sights at each end. An observer keeps this bar so that the line of sights points to the horizon, while another records the angle. This instrument will give the correct roll as long as the horizon is visible. Another form, fig. 277, consists of vertical battens, and is more accurate than the pivoted bar instrument just described. It consists of observation brackets $b\,b$, each having a slit S. These brackets are fitted on the bridge so that

the slits are on about a level with a man's eye. Vertical battens B B are painted white and graduated in a scale of tangents, so that upon looking through S at the horizon the tangent of the inclination of the ship to the

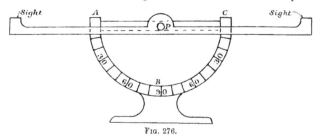

FIG. 276.

vertical can be at once read. These instruments can also be used at night by taking observations from a star of known altitude.

(4) **Mallock's Rolling Indicator** (fig. 278).—This consists essentially of a short cylindrical metal vessel with a glass front, filled with some non-freezing liquid, and carrying at the centre a light cylindrical box with projecting

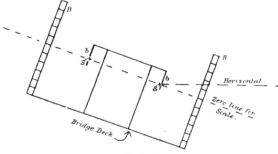

FIG. 277.

vanes, the extremities of which do not approach within 1 inch of casing. The front pivot is carried by three threads thus ⅄ and the top one serves as an index. A light circular metal strip is fastened to the moving part and graduated in degrees. Weights w can be shifted, and so give the wheel a definite zero position, and also cause it to form a pendulum of very long period. Generally, in air the period is 4 seconds, and in the liquid it is 40 seconds. The weight of the wheel and vanes and size of central barrel are so adjusted that there is no weight on the pivots. This is a very reliable instrument, and, together with the vertical battens, form the apparatus usually fitted to war vessels.

(5) **Froude's Apparatus.**—This was designed by W. Froude in order to determine accurately the effect of the resistances to roll experienced by a vessel, both in still water and amongst waves. A diagrammatic view of the

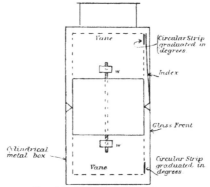

FIG. 278.—Mallock's Rolling Indicator.

apparatus is shown in fig. 279. It consists of two pendulums, one of very long period and the other of very short period. Only the long-period pendulum is required for still-water rolling.

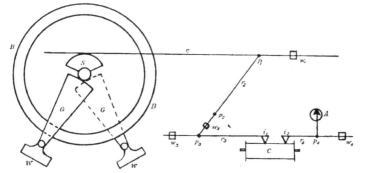

FIG. 279.—Froude's Automatic Rolling Indicator.

B is the long-period pendulum, and consists of a large metal wheel 3 feet in diameter, and weighs 200 lbs. It is carried on a 1-inch steel axle, which is fixed in a longitudinal direction, and is itself carried on steel sectors G G. The sectors are mounted on spindles, and are themselves counterbalanced about these spindles by weights W W. There are two of these sectors at each end of the wheel axle. The wheel is weighted so that its C.G. is ·006 inches below the centre of suspension, and its period is from 34–35 seconds, and it remains practically upright as the ship rolls. Sector S is carried by B and has a rod r_1 geared to it. The weight of r_1 is balanced about p_1 by means of weight w_1. Rod r_2 carries the pivot p_1 and oscillates about p_2, which is part of the framework of the machine. r_2 is balanced about p_2 by weight w_2. At the lower end of r_2 there is a third rod r_3, pivoting about p_3, and carrying a stylo i_1 and a balance-weight w_3.

A is the short-period pendulum, which consists of a brass tube $2\frac{1}{2}$ inches diameter, 20 inches long, and is filled with lead, and carried on knife-edges at the upper part of the circumference of the tube. Its period is 0·2 seconds. It is connected to a rod r_4, which is pivoted about p_4, carries the stylo i_2, and is balanced by w_4.

The stylos i_1 and i_2 record upon a cylinder C, which is rotated by clockwork, and there is a third pen, not shown, that indicates the time. When rolling in a seaway the force is in the direction of the normal to the effective wave-slope, and the short-period pendulum A then records the effective wave-slope acting upon the ship.

CHAPTER XXIX.

RESISTED ROLLING IN STILL WATER (*continued*).

Mathematical Analysis of Experimental Results of Rolling.—
Having described the various types of apparatus used to determine the
rolling of a ship, we will now proceed to analyse the records so obtained,
in order to ascertain the laws of extinction. The chief work that has been done

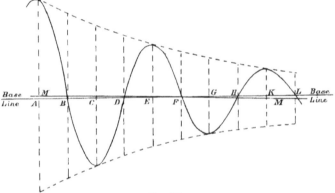

Fig. 280.

on this subject in this country is that of W. Froude, who made a long series
of experiments upon actual ships, using the apparatus described above, and
subjecting the records to a searching analysis.

**Analysis of the Records of Froude's Apparatus for Still-Water
Resisted Rolling.**—In this case we need only to use the long-period
pendulum B, fig. 279.

The apparatus then gives us the wavy curve as shown in fig. 280. By
drawing vertical lines as shown through the points of maximum and minimum
ordinates we find that A B, B C, etc., are all equal, so that the period of
rolling is practically constant.

We can put the dotted curves shown through the points of maxima and
minima. If we then square across from A, B, C, etc., to the dotted curves,
the base line should bisect these lines. If the wheel has any motion of its

381

own, the base line will not bisect them.   In this case we bisect the ordinates
and put a curve M through these points as shown.   The period of this curve
is the same as that of the wheel, *i.e.* 34–35 seconds.   The true rolling of the
ship should be measured from this curve.   If we do this for the dotted curve
above and set off the ordinates to a base of number of rolls, we get a curve

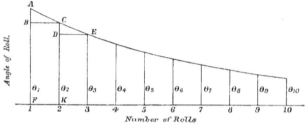

FIG. 281.—Curve of Declining Angles.

like fig. 281, which is called the "Curve of Declining Angles." (*Note.*—If
A F represents the angle rolled to port, C K represents the succeeding roll to
starboard, and so on.)

Draw C B and E D parallel to the base line.   We can consider A B as the
decrement of roll in the first complete swing, *i.e.* from θ_1 to θ_2; C D the
decrement from θ_2 to θ_3, and so on.   Thus we can express the decrement of

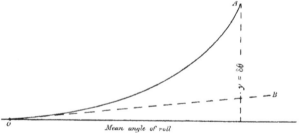

FIG. 282.—Curve of Extinction.

roll in terms of the mean angle for the two sides; *i.e.*, if $AB = \delta\theta_1$, express
$\delta\theta_1$ in terms of $\dfrac{\theta_1 + \theta_2}{2}$.

We can thus draw the curve in fig. 282, in which the abscissæ
show the mean angles of roll, and the ordinates show the corresponding decrements.   This curve is called the "Curve of Extinction,"
and may be considered as consisting partly of a straight line O B and partly
of a parabola O A.   Its equation is

$$y = \delta\theta = a\theta + b\theta^2.$$

French experimenters also carried out a series of experiments on rolling. These were analysed by M. Bertin. He states that the $a\theta$ part was not very distinguishable, and that the results were given quite well by

$$\delta\theta = N\theta^2.$$

Attempts were made by Froude to account for the a and b coefficients in the above formula from the nature of the various resistances acting upon the ship. Mathematical considerations led to the following results.

The a coefficient is produced by the formation of surface waves due to the motion of the ship.

The b coefficient is due to the resistance caused by skin friction, keel resistances, and stream-line action.

The following are values of a and b for the vessels named, and were obtained either from experiments made upon the vessels themselves or upon models.

Name of Ship.		Period T Seconds.	a.	b.
" Sultan "	. . .	8·87	·0267	·0016
" Devastation "	. . .	6·75	·072	·015
" Inconstant"	. . .	8·0	·035	·0051
" Inflexible"	. . .	5·35	·040	·008
"Revenge " { with Bilge Keels		7·75	·065	·017
without ,, ,,		7·60	·0123	·0025

A Consideration of the Nature of the Resistances that give rise to the a and b Constants in Froude's Formula for the "Curve of Extinction."

—The following mathematical considerations were suggested by W. Froude, who, after ascertaining the laws of resisted rolling by experiment, subjected the results to a very searching analysis in order to account for the nature of the resistances experienced.

I. Consider a vessel acted upon by a resistance to rolling which varies as $\dfrac{d\theta}{dt}$.

Let $K_1\dfrac{d\theta}{dt}$ be the moment of resistance.

Suppose the ship starts swinging from an angle a to the upright, and swings to an angle β to the upright on the other side. Then the total work done against resistance is

$$\int_a^0 K_1\frac{d\theta}{dt}d\theta + \int_0^\beta K_1\frac{d\theta}{dt}d\theta.$$

We assume, for the purposes of analysis, that the ship rolls harmonically, and that each half-swing from a to 0 and 0 to β takes place in the time $\dfrac{T}{2}$, the half-period of the unresisted oscillation.

With these assumptions, consider the roll from $\theta = a$ to $\theta = 0$. The resistance experienced is the same as for a harmonic roll from 0 to a.

We have, as our equation of motion,

$$\theta = a \sin \frac{\pi t}{T}.$$

$$\therefore \quad \frac{d\theta}{dt} = \frac{\pi a}{T} \cos \frac{\pi t}{T}.$$

$\therefore$ energy expended against resistance from $\theta = 0$ to $\theta = a$ is

$$\int_0^a K_1 \frac{\pi a}{T} \cos \frac{\pi t}{T} d\theta.$$

$$\text{But} \qquad d\theta = \frac{\pi a}{T} \cos \frac{\pi t}{T} dt.$$

Also, when $\theta = a$, $t = \frac{T}{2}$, and when $\theta = 0$, $t = 0$,

and $\therefore$ energy expended

$$= \int_0^{\frac{T}{2}} K_1 \frac{\pi^2 a^2}{T^2} \cos^2 \frac{\pi t}{T} dt$$

$$= \frac{1}{2} K_1 \frac{\pi^2 a^2}{T^2} \int_0^{\frac{T}{2}} \left(1 + \cos \frac{2\pi t}{T}\right) dt$$

$$= K_1 \frac{\pi^2 a^2}{2T^2} \frac{T}{2}$$

$$= \frac{K_1 \pi^2 a^2}{4T}.$$

Similarly, for the other part of the swing from $\theta = 0$ to $\theta = \beta$ the energy expended is $\dfrac{K_1 \pi^2 \beta^2}{4T}$.

Hence total loss of energy is

$$\frac{K_1 \pi^2}{4T} (a^2 + \beta^2)$$

$$= \frac{K_1 \pi^2}{4T} 2\theta_m{}^2 \text{ approximately,}$$

where θ_m is the mean of a and β.

This loss of energy must be equal to the loss in dynamical stability between a and β.

Now dynamical stability at a

$$= \int_0^a W . GZ d\theta.$$

In this investigation we are assuming harmonic rolling, and therefore small angles of roll in which $GZ = m\theta$, where m is the metacentric height. And therefore dynamical stability at $a = \int_0^a W . m . \theta d\theta = \frac{1}{2} W m a^2$.

Similarly, the dynamical stability at $\beta = \frac{1}{2} W m \beta^2$.

Hence total loss of dynamical stability from a to β

$$= \tfrac{1}{2} W m (a^2 - \beta^2)$$

$$= W m \frac{a + \beta}{2} (a - \beta)$$

$$= W m \theta_m \delta\theta,$$

where $\delta\theta = (a - \beta)$ is the decrement or extinction of roll between successive swings.

Hence $\quad \dfrac{K_1 \pi^2}{4T} 2\theta_m{}^2 = W m \theta_m \delta\theta$, or $\delta\theta = \dfrac{K_1 \pi^2}{2 W m T} \theta_m$,

and therefore $\delta\theta$ is proportional to the mean angle of swing, or the existence of a resistance varying as the first power of the angular velocity gives rise to the extinction represented by O B, fig. 282, and therefore to the a coefficient in the formula

$$\delta\theta = a\theta + b\theta^2.$$

II. Consider the case in which the moment of resistance varies as $\left(\dfrac{d\theta}{dt}\right)^2$.

Let $K_2 \left(\dfrac{d\theta}{dt}\right)^2$ be the moment of resistance.

We deal with this case in precisely the same manner as the preceding case. The total work done against the resistance from a to β is

$$\int_a^0 K_2 \left(\frac{d\theta}{dt}\right)^2 d\theta + \int_0^\beta K_2 \left(\frac{d\theta}{dt}\right)^2 d\theta.$$

Considering the first part of the above expression, we have

$$\theta = a \sin \frac{\pi t}{T}.$$

$$\therefore \quad \frac{d\theta}{dt} = \frac{\pi a}{T} \cos \frac{\pi t}{T}$$

and $\quad \left(\dfrac{d\theta}{dt}\right)^2 d\theta = \dfrac{\pi^3 a^3}{T^3} \cos^3 \dfrac{\pi t}{T} dt.$

As before, our limits are now 0 and $\dfrac{T}{2}$.

Hence energy expended from $\theta = a$ to $\theta = 0$ is

$$\int_0^{\frac{T}{2}} K_2 \frac{\pi^3 a^3}{T^3} \cos^3 \frac{\pi t}{T} dt$$

$$= K_2 \frac{\pi^3 a^3}{T^3} \int_0^{\frac{T}{2}} \cos \frac{\pi t}{T} \left(1 - \sin^2 \frac{\pi t}{T}\right) dt$$

$$= K_2 \frac{\pi^3 a^3}{T^3} \frac{2T}{3\pi} = K_2 \frac{2\pi^2 a^3}{3T^2}.$$

Similarly, from $\theta = 0$ to $\theta = \beta$, energy expended $= K_2 \dfrac{2\pi^2 \beta^3}{3T^2}$.

Hence total loss of energy

$$= K_2 \frac{2\pi^2}{3T^2}(\alpha^3 + \beta^3)$$

$$= K_2 \frac{2\pi^2}{3T^2} 2\theta_m{}^3 \text{ approximately,}$$

where $\theta_m = \frac{\alpha + \beta}{2}$.

Equating this, as in the previous case, to the loss of dynamical stability we have

$$W m \theta_m \delta\theta = K_2 \frac{4\pi^2}{3T^2} \theta_m{}^3,$$

and $\therefore$ $\delta\theta = \frac{4}{3} \frac{K_2 \pi^2}{W m T^2} \theta_m{}^2,$

and therefore a resistance that varies as $\left(\dfrac{d\theta}{dt}\right)^2$ will give rise to the extinction represented by O A, fig. 282, and therefore to the b coefficient in the formula

$$\delta\theta = a\theta + b\theta^2.$$

Hence in this formula we have the coefficients a and b, which are respectively due to a resistance varying as $\dfrac{d\theta}{dt}$ and $\left(\dfrac{d\theta}{dt}\right)^2$.

Thus the general equation of resisted rolling of a ship is

$$I\frac{d^2\theta}{dt^2} + K_1\frac{d\theta}{dt} + K_2\left(\frac{d\theta}{dt}\right)^2 + W.GZ = 0,$$

and the decrement of θ corresponding to these resistances is given by

$$\delta\theta = \frac{K_1 \pi^2 \theta_m}{2 W m T} + \frac{4}{3} \frac{K_2 \pi^2 \theta_m{}^2}{W m T^2},$$

where θ_m is the mean angle of roll from out to out.

Analysis of the Extinctive Effect produced by the Formation of Surface Waves due to the Rolling Motion of a Ship in Still Water.—As we have already pointed out on p. 375, one of the causes of resistance to rolling of a ship in still water is the formation of waves due to the oscillatory motion of the ship. This is due to the amount of difference between the shipshape and a circular form in the region of the waterplane. To obtain an insight into the precise nature of the resistance offered in this manner, Dr W. Froude proposed the following mathematical analysis. He assumed—

I. The breadth of the wave varies as the length of the ship.

II. The length of the wave from crest to crest is such that its period is the same as that of the ship. Now the period of a wave of length l is $T = \sqrt{2\pi\dfrac{l}{g}}$ (see p. 127), and therefore T varies as the square root of l. The period of rolling of a ship is $T = \pi\sqrt{\dfrac{K^2}{gm}}$, and therefore, for similar ships, as both K and m are linear dimensions, T will vary as the square root of the linear dimensions. Hence for the period of wave to equal that of the ship, the length of the wave must vary as the linear dimensions of the ship.

III. The height of wave varies as the beam of the ship multiplied by the angle of roll.

It is found that, when conducting rolling experiments upon dynamical models of ships, the curves of extinction are precisely the same for the models as for the actual ships. Thus the decrement of roll must be independent of linear dimensions of the ship.

Now we have seen (p. 133) that the energy of a wave varies as lbh^2, where l is its length, b its breadth, and h its height. In this case, if L stands for the linear dimensions of the ship and θ is the angle of roll, then—

$$l \text{ varies as } L$$
$$b \quad ,, \quad ,, \quad L$$
$$h \quad ,, \quad ,, \quad L\theta$$
$$\text{and} \quad lbh^2 \quad ,, \quad ,, \quad L^4\theta^2$$

The ship has therefore, in each roll, to impart to the surrounding water an amount of energy that varies as $L^4\theta^2$. We have seen (p. 385) that if the ship rolls through an angle θ, and $\delta\theta$ is the decrement, the loss of dynamical stability is $Wm\theta\delta\theta$, which varies as $L^4\theta\delta\theta$. If this decrement is caused by the formation of the wave, the loss of dynamical stability must be equal to the energy of the wave.

$$\therefore \quad L^4\theta\delta\theta \text{ varies as } L^4\theta^2$$
$$\text{or} \quad \delta\theta \quad ,, \quad ,, \quad \theta$$

and is independent of the size of the ship. Hence such a wave will account for the " a " coefficient in the formula $\delta\theta = a\theta + b\theta^2$. Also, the rolling of the ship and the model will be identical, since the decrement is independent of linear dimensions.

Dr W. Froude gave, as an example of this, a case in which the calculated resistance to rolling of a ship 150 feet long and period 4 seconds was 4700 ft.-lbs. The estimated amount of resistance due to surface friction and keel effect was 820 ft.-lbs., which left 3880 ft.-lbs. unaccounted for. Assuming that all this was due to the formation of a wave, the dimensions of the wave are, length 320 ft. from crest to crest and height from hollow to crest $1\frac{1}{4}$ ins. Thus the wave would be imperceptible under ordinary circumstances.

CHAPTER XXX.

ROLLING AMONGST WAVES.

In dealing with this we have to consider the forces acting on the ship due merely to the wave structure, as well as the usual forces of stability. At any point upon the upper surface of a wave, the resultant force will be normal to the surface at this point; hence in the case of a small floating body its

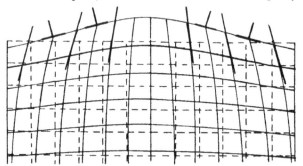

Fig. 283.—Diagram of Wave Structure.

instantaneous position of equilibrium will be in the direction normal to the surface. In the case of a ship which penetrates to some extent into the water, the portions below the surface are influenced by the subsurface wave-slopes, which are less steep than at the surface. Hence the "*Effective Wave-Slope*" acting on the whole body is not as steep as the surface slope; so that, in treating this subject, if we deal with the surface conditions only, we are making an error on the safe side.

If we consider the wave structure we notice that columns of water that were originally vertical are now inclined towards the crest, as shown in fig. 283. Hence a deep narrow vessel would always tend to incline towards the crest of the wave. On the other hand, a raft will always have its mast inclined away from the crest. A ship is an intermediate stage between these two conditions. Hence, due to mere wave structure alone, the tendency to roll is negligible; and in dealing with the subject we may confine our attention merely to the effect of stability on rolling, the equilibrium position being assumed normal to the wave surface.

388

Froude's General Solution for Rolling amongst Waves. — A

mathematical solution was proposed by the late Dr W. Froude. In order to
deal with the subject mathematically he makes the following assumptions :—
  (1) The waves form a regular parallel series.
  (2) The ship is supposed to be broadside on to the waves and rolling
passively.
  (3) The waves are very long compared to the beam of the ship.
  (4) The rolling is isochronous, or approximately so ; *i.e.* we may write
stability = $Wm\theta$ within these limits.
  (5) Variations in virtual weight, due to the wave structure, are neglected.

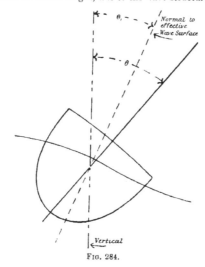

FIG. 284.

  (6) The length of the wave is so long compared to the height, that its
form may be assumed to be a sine curve.
  The justification for these assumptions is that the conditions are the
worst possible.
  Let θ_1 be the inclination of the wave normal to the upright (fig. 284).
  Let θ be the inclination of the ship to the upright.
  Then the moment of stability

$$= Wm(\theta - \theta_1).$$

Hence the equation of motion is

$$1\frac{d^2\theta}{dt^2} + Wm(\theta - \theta_1) = 0.$$

$$\therefore \quad \frac{d^2\theta}{dt^2} + \frac{gm}{K^2}(\theta - \theta_1) = 0.$$

Now $\qquad T = \pi \sqrt{\dfrac{K^2}{gm}}$,

and $\therefore \qquad \dfrac{d^2\theta}{dt^2} + \dfrac{\pi^2}{T^2}(\theta - \theta_1) = 0.$

This differs from the equation for still-water roll by the term in θ_1. Now θ_1 is a function of the time, as it obviously changes continuously. To find the relation between θ_1 and t we assume a sinusoidal wave. Let H be its

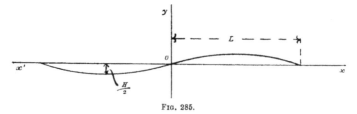

FIG. 285.

height, 2L its length, and T_1 the half period of wave. Then, with axes as shown (fig. 285), the equation to the wave is

$$y = \frac{H}{2} \sin \frac{\pi x}{L},$$

and $\therefore \qquad \dfrac{dy}{dx} = \dfrac{\pi H}{2L} \cos \dfrac{\pi x}{L} = \theta_1$, for a small angle,

so that the maximum wave-slope is $\dfrac{\pi H}{2L}$.

Having now found θ_1 in terms of x, we must find the connection between x and t, and hence find θ_1 in terms of t.

If we measure time from the instant the wave is as shown in the above fig. 285, we get

$$\frac{x}{L} = \frac{t}{T_1},$$

and $\therefore \qquad \theta_1 = \dfrac{\pi H}{2L} \cos \dfrac{\pi t}{T_1}.$

This value of θ_1 is the wave-slope at O, t secs. after the passage of the mid height of the wave. Or, measuring our time from the passage of the trough of the wave, which is more convenient, we get

$$\theta_1 = \frac{\pi H}{2L} \sin \frac{\pi t}{T_1}.$$

Hence $\qquad \dfrac{d^2\theta}{dt^2} + \dfrac{\pi^2}{T^2}\left(\theta - \dfrac{\pi H}{2L} \sin \dfrac{\pi t}{T_1}\right) = 0$ is our equation of motion

The solution of this equation consists of a particular and a general solution, and is effected by the general methods of solving differential equations. The solution is

$$\theta = \frac{\pi H}{2L} \left(\frac{1}{1 - \frac{T^2}{T_1^2}} \right) \sin \frac{\pi t}{T_1} + A \sin \frac{\pi t}{T} + B \cos \frac{\pi t}{T},$$

in which we have the two constants A and B which depend upon the initial conditions. If we assume that in the trough the inclination is a and angular velocity U, then when $t = 0$, $\theta = a$ and $\frac{d\theta}{dt} = U$. From these we get

$$\theta = \frac{\frac{\pi H}{2L}}{1 - \frac{T^2}{T_1^2}} \sin \frac{\pi t}{T_1} + \sin \frac{\pi t}{T} \left(\frac{UT}{\pi} - \frac{T}{T_1} \frac{\frac{\pi H}{2L}}{1 - \frac{T^2}{T_1^2}} \right) + a \cos \frac{\pi t}{T},$$

which is Froude's general equation for rolling amongst waves.

If we take this solution and separate out the parts that are influenced by the wave, we get

$$\theta = \frac{\frac{\pi H}{2L}}{1 - \frac{T^2}{T_1^2}} \left(\sin \frac{\pi t}{T_1} - \frac{T}{T_1} \sin \frac{\pi t}{T} \right)$$

$$+ \frac{UT}{\pi} \sin \frac{\pi t}{T} + a \cos \frac{\pi t}{T}.$$

The last two terms are identical with the general solution for unresisted rolling in still water. We thus see that the still-water rolling takes place just as if the waves had no existence, and the effect of the waves is to superpose upon the still-water rolling the motion represented by the first part of the above equation. This motion consists of two simple harmonic motions, one being in the ship's natural period T, and the other in the wave period T_1. The amplitude of these imposed motions depends directly upon the maximum wave-slope $\frac{\pi H}{2L}$ and also upon the ratio of $\frac{T}{T_1}$. We will now consider in detail the motions corresponding to the three values of this ratio : (I.) when $\frac{T}{T_1} = 1$, (II.) when $\frac{T}{T_1}$ is very small, and (III.) when $\frac{T}{T_1}$ is large.

I. **Synchronism.**—This is the case in which the period of wave is equal to the period of the ship, $i.e.$ $T = T_1$. We can simplify Froude's general equation if we consider the ship to be initially upright and at rest in the trough.

Then $a = U = 0$, and the equation becomes—

$$\theta = \frac{\frac{\pi H}{2L}}{1 - \frac{T^2}{T_1^2}} \left(\sin \frac{\pi t}{T_1} - \frac{T}{T_1} \sin \frac{\pi t}{T} \right) = \frac{\beta \left(\sin \frac{\pi t}{T_1} - \frac{T}{T_1} \sin \frac{\pi t}{T} \right)}{1 - \frac{T^2}{T_1^2}}$$

where $\beta = \frac{\pi H}{2L}$ = maximum wave-slope.

For synchronism $T = T_1$, and this value for θ becomes $\dfrac{0}{0}$ which is indeterminate.

If we differentiate the numerator and denominator with respect to T_1, we get—

$$\theta = \text{Limit of } \dfrac{\beta\left(-\dfrac{\pi t}{T_1{}^2}\cos\dfrac{\pi t}{T_1} + \dfrac{T}{T_1{}^2}\sin\dfrac{\pi t}{T}\right)}{\dfrac{2T^2}{T_1{}^3}} \text{ when } T = T_1$$

$$= \dfrac{\beta}{2}\left(\sin\dfrac{\pi t}{T} - \dfrac{\pi t}{T}\cos\dfrac{\pi t}{T}\right).$$

If we now consider the ship at successive points of the maximum wave-slope, we have—

when $\qquad t = \dfrac{T}{2}, \dfrac{3T}{2}, \dfrac{5T}{2}$, etc.

then $\qquad \theta = \dfrac{\beta}{2}, \dfrac{-\beta}{2}, \dfrac{\beta}{2}$, etc.,

which means that when the maximum wave-slope passes under the ship the masts are always inclined at $\dfrac{\beta}{2}$ to the vertical.

Also, if we consider the passage of each half wave-length from the trough, we have—

when $\qquad t = 0,\ T,\ 2T,\ 3T$, etc.

then $\qquad \theta = 0,\ \dfrac{\pi\beta}{2},\ -\pi\beta,\ \dfrac{3\pi\beta}{2}$, etc.,

and therefore the passage of each half wave-length adds $\dfrac{\pi\beta}{2}$ to the actual inclination from the vertical, the masts being inclined in one direction in the troughs, and in the opposite direction at the crests, the passage of each complete wave adding π times the maximum wave-slope to the inclination of the ship. Hence, in the absence of resistances to rolling, the vessel would soon capsize. The result can be represented graphically as follows (see fig. 286). In this case the vessel is supposed to be upright and at rest in the trough, as shown by position 1. A series of regular waves is then supposed to pass in the direction indicated by the arrow, and the ship takes up successive inclinations as shown, the dotted lines being vertical.

Thus synchronous rolling must be avoided, and this is done by altering the course of the ship. Also, even if synchronism exists at small angles as the angle of roll increases, the period of the ship does not remain constant, and so synchronism breaks down.

II.—*When* $\dfrac{T}{T_1}$ *is Small.*

This is the case in which T, the period of the ship, is very short, *e.g.* the case of a raft. We have seen that $T = \pi\sqrt{\dfrac{K^2}{gm}}$, so that a small value of T corresponds to a large value of m, the metacentric height.

With the same simplification of the general equation as is adopted in the case of synchronism, we have—

$$\theta = \frac{\beta}{1 - \frac{T^2}{T_1^2}}\left(\sin\frac{\pi t}{T_1} - \frac{T}{T_1}\sin\frac{\pi t}{T}\right),$$

which, when $\frac{T}{T_1}$ is small, reduces to

$$\theta = \beta \sin\frac{\pi t}{T_1}.$$

This is also the equation of the wave-slope. In other words, the inclination of the masts to the upright is equal to the inclination to the horizontal of the tangent to the wave; that is, the masts are in the direction of the normal to the wave-surface.

III.— *When $\frac{T}{T_1}$ is Large.*

This case corresponds to a vessel of relatively small metacentric height. With the same assumptions as before, our equation is

$$\theta = \frac{\beta}{1 - \frac{T^2}{T_1^2}}\left(\sin\frac{\pi t}{T_1} - \frac{T}{T_1}\sin\frac{\pi t}{T}\right).$$

In order to simplify this expression we multiply the terms inside the bracket by $\frac{T_1^2}{T^2}$ and the term outside by $\frac{T^2}{T_1^2}$.

Then

$$\theta = \frac{\beta\frac{T^2}{T_1^2}}{1 - \frac{T^2}{T_1^2}}\left(\frac{T_1^2}{T^2}\sin\frac{\pi t}{T_1} - \frac{T_1}{T}\sin\frac{\pi t}{T}\right)$$

$$= \frac{\beta}{\frac{T_1^2}{T^2} - 1}\left(\frac{T_1^2}{T^2}\sin\frac{\pi t}{T_1} - \frac{T_1}{T}\sin\frac{\pi t}{T}\right)$$

$$= \frac{\beta}{\frac{T_1^2}{T^2} - 1}\frac{T_1}{T}\left(\frac{T_1}{T}\sin\frac{\pi t}{T_1} - \sin\frac{\pi t}{T}\right).$$

Then when $\frac{T}{T_1}$ is large, or $\frac{T_1}{T}$ is small, this reduces to

$$\theta = \frac{T_1}{T}\beta\sin\frac{\pi t}{T},$$

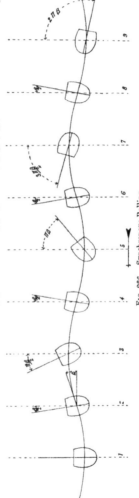

Fig. 286.—Synchronous Rolling.

and therefore the motion of the ship is independent of the wave motion, excepting that it influences her maximum amplitude of roll, which is $\frac{T_1}{T}\beta$.

But $\frac{T_1}{T}$ is small, and therefore the ship oscillates through a small angle in her own natural period.

This is the condition aimed at in designing a steady ship. Hence small metacentric heights are conducive to steadiness in a seaway.

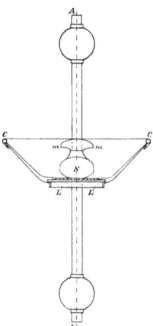

Fig. 287.

Mechanical Illustrations of Rolling amongst Waves.—In the case of still-water rolling, experiments can easily be made on models in a tank and the phenomena carefully studied. In rolling amongst waves model experiments are impracticable owing to the difficulty of producing in the tank a regular series of waves of convenient size and period. We have therefore, in order to make a complete study of the rolling motion of a ship amongst waves, to either resort to graphic integration, which is a slow process, or else adopt some mechanical representation of the phenomenon.

Captain Russo's Navipendulum.—This is an apparatus invented by Captain Russo of the Royal Italian Navy, and may be utilised to study both the resisted and unresisted rolling of a ship in still water or amongst waves. In this the ship is represented by a pendulum-shaped body which he calls a navipendulum, and the motion of the water is represented by a specially constructed apparatus which produces precisely the same effect upon the motion of the pendulum as the wave motion does upon the motion of the ship.

The principle of the navipendulum is that for the purposes of studying the transverse rolling of a ship she may be represented by a cylinder whose C.G. coincides with the C.G. of the ship, and the shape of the section of which is an involute of the metacentric evolute, since the righting couple acting upon the cylinder in any inclined position will be proportional to the couple acting upon the ship when similarly inclined. Thus, if the cylinder be made dynamically similar to the ship, its motion will be precisely similar to that of the ship. The pendulum is shaped as shown in A A, fig. 287, being supported on a platform L by means of steel sectors S, which are shaped to an involute of the metacentric evolute. In order to obtain a resistance corresponding to that experienced by the ship, a sector m is attached, the upper part of which is in contact with an elastic band C C, and its shape is obtained experimentally from a knowledge of the resistance to rolling in still water experienced by the ship or its model.

The principle of the wave-motion apparatus is as follows :—If we consider a small line of particles $a\,b$, fig. 288, lying on the surface of a wave of length L, height H, and period T, this line will assume during the passage of the wave

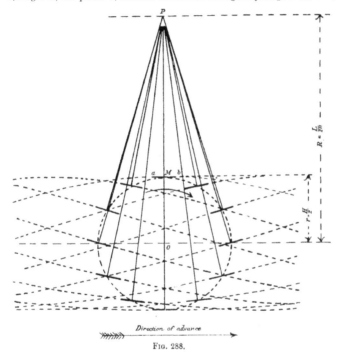

FIG. 288.

all the positions indicated, the normal always passing through the point P which is vertically above O, a height $PO = \dfrac{L}{2\pi}$. In rolling amongst waves it is the inclination to the normal to the effective wave-slope that determines the motion. Thus if we can make the base plate L of the navipendulum, fig. 287, assume all the inclinations of $a\,b$ in their regular order, the motion of the pendulum will correspond to that of the ship in a regular series of waves. This is effected by the mechanical device shown in fig. 289, in which the rods r and r_1 are caused to turn at the same angular velocity, and thus to always remain parallel to each other. In this way the line $M\,M_1$ always passes through a fixed point on the line $O O_1$ produced. By suitably proportioning r and r_1 the motion of $a\,b$, fig. 289, can be made precisely that of $a\,b$ in fig. 288, and hence $M\,M_1$ is always in the direction of the normal to the effective wave-slope. The lever $M\,M_1$ passes through a slot in the base plate L of the navi-pendulum so that L is always perpendicular to $M\,M_1$. Thus there is imposed upon L a motion precisely similar to the motion of the normal to the effective wave-slope, and hence the motion of the pendulum is precisely that of the ship.

To test the apparatus a pendulum was constructed to represent the case

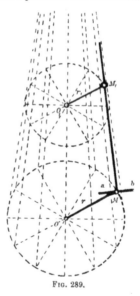

FIG. 289.

of an actual ship, and the results of experiments actually carried out on the ship were compared with those given by the pendulum, and they were found to agree very closely with one another.

For purposes of lecture-room demonstration to students of the effect of imposing a wave motion upon the ordinary unresisted and resisted rolling motion of a vessel, the author has since 1891 often made use of the following simple apparatus, see fig. 290.

A represents a vessel, and is mounted on curved rockers R which represent the curve of buoyancy. Trestles B carry a horizontal plate C upon which the rockers R rest. Attached to A are wings W, which can support weights, and hence the moment of inertia of A can be altered, and thus its period of oscillation. An index arm I is attached to A, and records on a scale S the angle of heel. In order to obtain resistance to rolling, water chambers or similar apparatus may be placed inside A. The apparatus will thus illustrate the unresisted and resisted rolling in still water. For the purposes of illustrating the rolling amongst waves the whole thing is slung up by means of ropes attached to

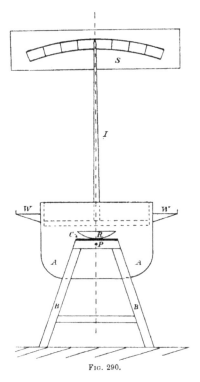

FIG. 290.

points P and hung from a beam overhead. The whole apparatus then swings bodily with a long-period motion, the period of which can be adjusted by suitably raising or lowering the apparatus. We thus get a combination of the two motions, and by suitable arrangements the effects of synchronism and similar phenomena may be practically demonstrated.

CHAPTER XXXI.

THE GRAPHIC PROCESS OF INTEGRATING THE EQUATION OF ROLLING FOR A SHIP.

Still-Water Unresisted Rolling.—We have seen that the equation of motion in still-water unresisted rolling is

$$\frac{d^2\theta}{dt^2} + \frac{g}{K^2}GZ = 0. \quad \text{See fig. 291.}$$

If we assume $GZ = m\theta$, we can obtain an exact mathematical solution of this. If we assume $GZ = m\sin\theta$ we can integrate once, but not a second time. In general GZ cannot be expressed as a simple function of θ, and we cannot mathematically integrate the expression at all. We have thus to fall back upon a graphical process which can be used whatever be the nature of the GZ curve, and is a strictly correct solution, no assumptions or approximations having to be made.

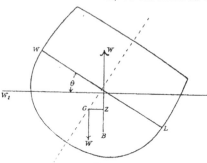

Fig. 291.

When θ is small, $T = \pi\sqrt{\dfrac{K^2}{gm}}$, and therefore the above equation may be written—

$$\frac{d^2\theta}{dt^2} + \frac{\pi^2}{T^2}\frac{GZ}{m} = 0,$$

or $\quad \dfrac{d}{dt}\left(\dfrac{d\theta}{dt}\right)$ numerically equals $\dfrac{\pi^2}{T^2}\dfrac{GZ}{m}$

or $\quad d\left(\dfrac{d\theta}{dt}\right) \qquad ,, \qquad ,, \qquad \dfrac{\pi^2}{T^2}\dfrac{GZ}{m}dt,$

or, for finite increments,

$$\delta\left(\frac{d\theta}{dt}\right) = \frac{\pi^2}{T^2}\frac{GZ}{m}\delta t.$$

398

If we know G Z, T, and m, we can calculate the right-hand side of the equation for a small finite increment δt, and so get the corresponding increment of angular velocity in time δt, supposing δt to be small. For our purpose the most convenient value for δt is $\dfrac{T}{10}$.

Then $\delta\left(\dfrac{d\theta}{dt}\right)$ is numerically equal to $\dfrac{GZ}{m}\dfrac{\pi^2}{T^2}\dfrac{T}{10}$

$$=\dfrac{GZ}{m}\dfrac{1}{1\cdot013T}$$

where θ is in circular measure. It is more convenient to work in degrees. If we express θ in degrees we get in $\dfrac{T}{10}$ secs. the increment $\delta\left(\dfrac{d\theta}{dt}\right)$ is numerically equal to $\dfrac{GZ}{m}\dfrac{180}{\pi}\dfrac{1}{1\cdot013T}$.

If now we lay out a base line A C representing a time $1\cdot013T$, fig. 292,

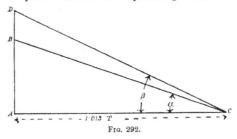

FIG. 292.

and draw A D perpendicular to A C, and C B making an angle α with A C so that the value of tan α is equal to the angular velocity of the ship at the beginning of an interval of time $\dfrac{T}{10}$, and then set up from B a length

$BD = \dfrac{180}{\pi}\dfrac{GZ}{m}$ and join DC,

$$\tan\beta = \dfrac{BA + DB}{AC}$$

$$= \dfrac{BA}{AC} + \dfrac{DB}{AC}$$

$$= \tan\alpha + \dfrac{180}{\pi}\dfrac{GZ}{m}\dfrac{1}{1\cdot013T}$$

$$= \dfrac{d\theta}{dt} + \delta\left(\dfrac{d\theta}{dt}\right),$$

where $\dfrac{d\theta}{dt}$ is the angular velocity at the beginning of the interval and $\delta\left(\dfrac{d\theta}{dt}\right)$ is the increment of angular velocity during the interval. In other words, $\tan \beta$ is the angular velocity at the end of the interval. Then from A D, by a similar process, we can get the angular velocity at the end of the next interval, and so on.

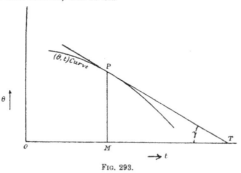

Fɪɢ. 293.

Suppose a curve, fig. 293, is drawn such that the abscissæ represent values of time, and the ordinates the corresponding values of θ, the inclination of the

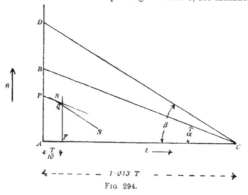

Fɪɢ. 294.

ship. For convenience this may be called the (θ, t) curve. Then the slope of the tangent to this curve at any point represents the angular velocity $\dfrac{d\theta}{dt}$ of the ship at that instant. Thus $\tan \gamma$ is numerically equal to the angular velocity of the ship at the time represented by O M and the inclination P M. Then, knowing the value of G Z corresponding to the inclination P M, we can carry out the graphic process described above in fig. 292, and so get the slope of the tangent to the (θ, t) curve at a time $\dfrac{T}{10}$ secs. later. Now it is the

(θ, t) curve that we are trying to get, as this represents the complete history of the rolling motion. We have therefore to work backwards, and, finding the slopes of the tangents to the (θ, t) curve for intervals of $\dfrac{T}{10}$ secs. by the method described, use this to enable us to set out our (θ, t) curve.

Thus, suppose the ship to be held over initially to an angle A P, fig. 294, and given an initial angular velocity U, set out $AC = 1 \cdot 013 T$ and A B perpendicular to A C, so that $\tan a = U$. Then if we draw P R parallel to B C, P R will be the tangent to the (θ, t) curve at P. If we then go through the construction given in fig. 292 and find the line C D, this line will be parallel to the tangent to the (θ, t) curve at an interval $\dfrac{T}{10}$ secs. later. Set out $AF = \dfrac{T}{10}$. Then if Q is the point on the (θ, t) curve, Q S parallel to D C will be the tangent to the (θ, t) curve at this point. This is not sufficient information to enable us to draw the line Q S as we do not know Q, and we require some more knowledge respecting its exact position. This is obtained from the following considerations. The first differential of the (θ, t) curve is a curve of angular velocities. The second differential will be a curve of angular accelerations, and therefore a curve of force expressed in a different scale, or a (force, t) curve which is the second differential of the (θ, t) curve. There is thus this relation between the curves, that if they be both drawn on the same base of t, the tangents to the (θ, t) curve at any two points will intersect above the C.G. of the corresponding portion of the (force, t) curve.*

---

* Let $y = f(x)$ be the equation of the (force, t) curve.

Then $y_1 = \displaystyle\int f(x)dx = f_1(x)$ is the equation of the $\left(\dfrac{d\theta}{dt}, t\right)$ curve

and $y_2 = \displaystyle\int f_1(x)dx = f_2(x)$ is the equation of the (θ, t) curve.

From these expressions we have the following relations :—

$$\frac{dy_2}{dx} = f_1(x) = y_1$$

$$\frac{dy_1}{dx} = f(x) = y.$$

Let these curves be as shown in fig. 295. Take any two ordinates whose abscissæ are x and x^1. Let y, y_1, and y_2 be the ordinates of the three curves at abscissa x, and y^1, y_1^1, and y_2^1 the ordinates at x^1. Then if $\bar{x}$ is the abscissa of the C.G. of part A B C D of (force, t) curve,

$$\bar{x} = \frac{\displaystyle\int_x^{x^1} x f(x)dx}{\displaystyle\int_x^{x^1} f(x)dx} = \frac{\displaystyle\int_x^{x^1} x \left(\dfrac{dy_1}{dx}\right)dx}{\left[y_1\right]_x^{x^1}}$$

$$= \frac{\left[xy_1\right]_x^{x^1} - \displaystyle\int_x^{x^1} y_1 dx}{y_1^1 - y_1} = \frac{x^1 y_1^1 - xy_1 - \left[y_2\right]_x^{x^1}}{y_1^1 - y_1}$$

$$= \frac{x^1 y_1^1 - xy_1 - y_2^1 + y_2}{y_1^1 - y_1}.$$

If now we consider the abscissa of the point of contact of the tangents to the (θ, t) curve at the points whose abscissæ are x and x^1. The equation of the curve is

$$y_2 = f_2(x).$$

From fig. 295 we have

$$\tan a = \frac{dy_2}{dx} = y_1 \text{ from the preceding formula}$$

$$\tan \beta = \frac{dy_2^1}{dx} = y_1^1 \qquad ,, \qquad ,, \qquad ,,$$

Let X be the abscissa of P, the point of contact of the tangents.

Then $KL = KQ + QL = (x^1 - X)\tan \beta + (X - x)\tan \alpha$

$= (x^1 - X)y_1^1 + (X - x)y_1.$

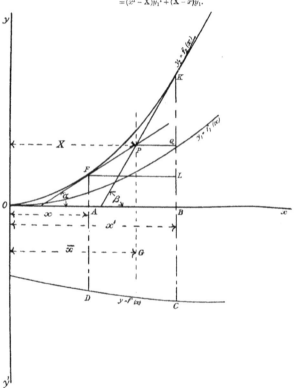

FIG. 295.

Also $KL = KB - AF = y_2^1 - y_2.$

And $\therefore$ $y_2^1 - y_2 = (x^1 - X)y_1^1 + (X - x)y_1.$

$\therefore$ $X(y_1^1 - y_1) = x^1 y_1^1 - x y_1 + y_2 - y_2^1,$

or $X = \dfrac{x^1 y_1^1 - x y_1 + y_2 - y_2^1}{y_1^1 - y_1}.$

$\therefore$ $X = \bar{x},$

i.e. the tangents at any two points in the (θ, t) curve meet over the C.G. of the corresponding portion of the (force, t) curve.

To apply this to our case, the force curve is our G Z curve. We have seen that the numerical value of $\delta\left(\dfrac{d\theta}{dt}\right)$ in time $\dfrac{T}{10}$ is

$$\frac{180}{\pi}\frac{GZ}{m}\frac{1}{1\cdot013T};$$

thus it is more convenient for us to work with values of $\dfrac{180}{\pi}\dfrac{GZ}{m}$ than with

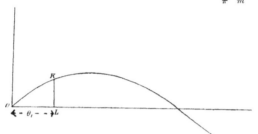

FIG. 296. — "*Modified Force Curve.*"

G Z. Our first step is therefore to construct a "*modified force curve*" from our G Z curve by multiplying all the ordinates by $\dfrac{180}{\pi m}$. This is shown in

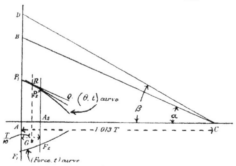

FIG. 297.

fig. 296. A convenient scale is $\frac{1}{8}'' = 1°$ and $\frac{1}{8}'' = 1$ unit of force. With these scales the curve will always start off from the origin making an angle of 45° with the base.

Now, as before, set out $AC = 1\cdot013T$ (fig. 297). Set up $AP_1 = \theta_1$ the initial angle of heel. Let U be the initial angular velocity. Draw through P_1 the line $P_1 Q$ at a slope corresponding to U, that is $P_1 Q$ is parallel to B C where $\tan a = U$.

Set down A F₁ equal to K L in fig. 296, the value of the modified force at θ_1. Now guess in the first portion of the (force, t) curve $F_1 F_2$. Guess in also the corresponding portion of the (θ, t) curve $P_1 P_2$. Scale the mean ordinate of the (force, t) curve between F_1 and F_2 and set it up at B D. Join D C, then the tangent to the (θ, t) curve at P_2 is parallel to D C, and also the tangents at P_1 and P_2 intersect at a point R vertically over G, the C.G. of the (force, t) curve A F₁ F₂ A₂.

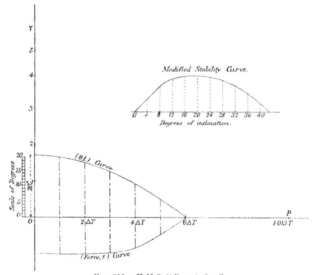

FIG. 298.—H.M.S. "Devastation."
Graphical Integration of Unresisted Rolling in Still Water.

$$T = 6\cdot75 \text{ secs.} \quad \Delta T = \frac{T}{10}.$$

Thus the tangent to the (θ, t) curve at P_2 is obtained. Then by exactly the same process the tangent at the next increment $\dfrac{T}{10}$ is found, and so a series of spots $P_1 P_2$, etc., on the curve, and the directions of the tangents at these points is found, and the curve can be sketched in. Each step carries us forward through an interval $\dfrac{T}{10}$ and is self-checking, since the ordinate $A_2 F_2$ must equal the ordinate of modified force curve corresponding to the angle $A_2 P_2$.

The above process is one of trial and error, and at first sight appears to be rather tedious of application, but when actually solving a problem in this manner it is found that after a very short time the eye is able to foretell almost exactly the directions of the curves, and generally the first attempt proves successful, and the second always is.

An example worked out by this method is shown in fig. 298. This has been done for the "Devastation." She is assumed to be heeled over to an angle of 20 degrees and then allowed to roll freely. The points marked 1, 2, 3, etc., on O Y are such that when joined to P they give the inclination of the tangents to the (θ, t) curve at the abscissae ΔT, $2\Delta T$, $3\Delta T$, etc., where $\Delta T = \dfrac{T}{10}$. We see in this case that the ship becomes upright in time $6\Delta T$, or her period of roll is $2 \times \dfrac{6}{10} T = 1\cdot2T$ when started of at 20 degrees inclination. As the motion is unresisted, the ship will roll over on the other side of the vertical to 20 degrees, and the motion will continue indefinitely.

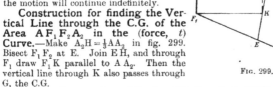

Construction for finding the Vertical Line through the C.G. of the Area $A F_1 F_2 A_2$ in the (force, t) Curve.—Make $A_2 H = \frac{1}{3} A A_2$ in fig. 299. Bisect $F_1 F_2$ at E. Join E H, and through F_1 draw $F_1 K$ parallel to $A A_2$. Then the vertical line through K also passes through G, the C.G.

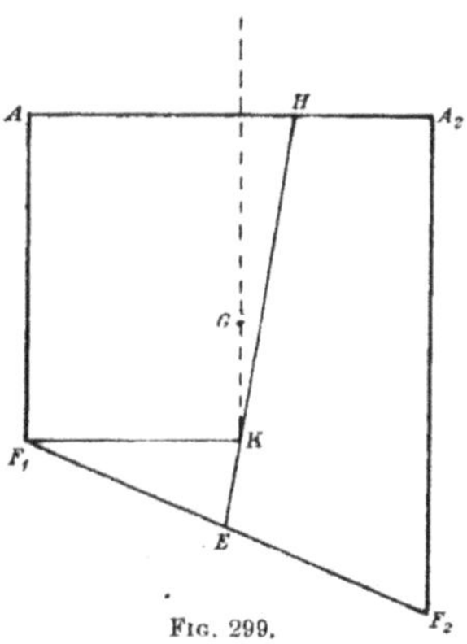

Fig. 299.

Graphic Integration of Resisted Rolling in Still Water.—This is an extension of the above. The mathematical equation for resisted rolling is

$$1\frac{d^2\theta}{dt^2} + K_1\frac{d\theta}{dt} + K_2\Big(\frac{d\theta}{dt}\Big)^2 + W.GZ. = 0 \; ;$$

and it has been shown mathematically (see p. 386) that with this equation the decrement of θ is given by

$$\delta\theta = \frac{K_1\pi^2\theta_m}{2WmT} + \frac{4}{3}\frac{K_2\pi^2\theta_m^2}{WmT^2},$$

where θ_m is the mean angle of roll from port to starboard. The above equation is in circular measure. If we turn it into degrees we get

$$\frac{\pi}{180}\,\delta\theta = \frac{K_1\pi^2\theta_m}{2WmT}\frac{\pi}{180} + \frac{4}{3}\frac{K_2\pi^2\theta_m^2}{WmT^2}\Big(\frac{\pi}{180}\Big)^2.$$

$$\therefore \quad \delta\theta = \frac{K_1\pi^2\theta_m}{2WmT} + \frac{4}{3}\frac{K_2\pi^2\theta_m^2}{WmT^2}\frac{\pi}{180}.$$

Comparing this with Froude's equation for the decrement of θ, viz.—

$$\delta\theta = a\theta_m + b\theta_m^2 \quad \text{where} \quad \theta_m$$

is in degrees, we see that

$$a = \frac{K_1\pi^2}{2WmT} \quad \text{or} \quad K_1 = \frac{2WmT}{\pi^2}a$$

$$b = \frac{4}{3}\frac{K_2\pi^2}{WmT^2}\frac{\pi}{180} \quad \text{or} \quad K_2 = \frac{3}{4}\frac{WmT^2}{\pi^3}\,180b.$$

And therefore the expression for the resistance moment becomes

$$\frac{2WmT}{\pi^2} a \frac{d\theta}{dt} + \frac{3}{4} \frac{WmT^2}{\pi^3} 180b\left(\frac{d\theta}{dt}\right)^2.$$

When finding the value of K_1 and K_2 in terms of Froude's a and b

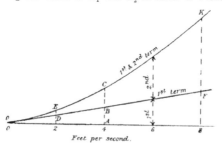

FIG. 300.—Resistance Indicator.

constants we had to convert the expressions for $\delta\theta$ into degrees. In the same manner, the above expression for the resistance moment is in circular measure, and for our purpose is required in degrees. Expressing θ in degrees, the resistance moment becomes

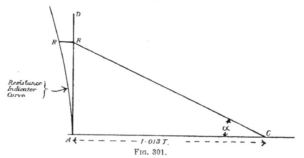

FIG. 301.

$$\frac{2WmT}{\pi^2} a \frac{\pi}{180} \frac{d\theta}{dt} + \frac{3}{4} \frac{WmT^2}{\pi^3} 180b\left(\frac{\pi}{180}\right)^2\left(\frac{d\theta}{dt}\right)^2$$

$$= W\left[\frac{\pi m}{180}\left\{\frac{2Ta}{\pi^2} \frac{d\theta}{dt} + \frac{3T^2b}{4\pi^2}\left(\frac{d\theta}{dt}\right)^2\right\}\right].$$

The resistance moment being necessarily of the dimensions of a weight multiplied by a length, the quantity multiplied by W in the foregoing equation is the arm of a resistance couple corresponding to G Z of the stability couple. In the graphic integration we make use, not of G Z simply, but of a modified G Z which is $\dfrac{180}{\pi}\dfrac{GZ}{m}$. Dealing with the arm of the resistance couple in the same way, we get a modified resistance lever which has to be added to or subtracted from the modified G Z in order to take account

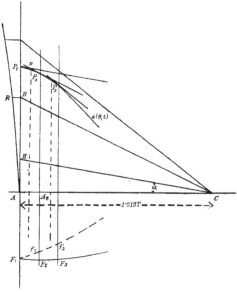

FIG. 302.

of the resistance. Multiplying the arm of resistance couple by $\dfrac{180}{\pi m}$ we get, as the modified lever,

$$\frac{2\mathrm{T}a}{\pi^2}\frac{d\theta}{dt}+\frac{3}{4}\frac{\mathrm{T}^2 b}{4\pi^2}\left(\frac{d\theta}{dt}\right)^2.$$

This was named by W. Froude the "*Resistance Indicator*," and has to be added to or subtracted from the modified force according as the ship is swinging away from the upright or towards it.

To calculate the "Resistance Indicator."—Take any value of $\dfrac{d\theta}{dt}$, say 4° per second, and from the known values of T, a, and b calculate the two terms of the expression separately. Let A B, fig. 300, represent the first term and B C the second. The first term varies as $\dfrac{d\theta}{dt}$, and ∴ if we draw the straight line O B this will represent the first term for all values of $\dfrac{d\theta}{dt}$.

The second term varies as $\left(\dfrac{d\theta}{dt}\right)^2$, hence at 2 feet per second make DE = $\frac{1}{4}$BC

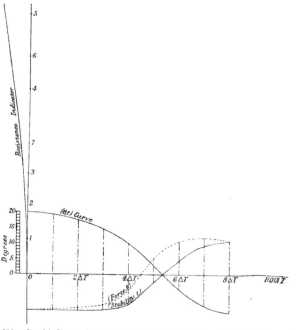

Fig. 303.—Graphic Integration of Still-Water Resisted Rolling of H.M.S. "Devastation."

$$a = \cdot072.$$
$$b = \cdot015.$$
$$T = 6\cdot75 \text{ secs.}$$
$$\Delta T = \frac{T}{10}.$$

and at 8 feet per second make FK = 4BC. Then a curve through O E C K will give us the arm of the "Resistance Indicator" for all values of $\dfrac{d\theta}{dt}$.

Application of the "Resistance Indicator" to Graphic Integration.—As before, make AC = 1·1013T, fig. 301. The most convenient scale is T = 10 inches, then AC = 10″·3. Draw A B D perpendicular to A C. We make A D the base line of the resistance indicator, so that B R is the value of the indicator corresponding to the angular velocity tan α. The vertical scale of the indicator curve has to be arranged to suit this, and it is done in the following manner :—

Suppose tan α represents 4 degrees per second,

$$AC = 1\cdot013T \text{ seconds, and } \therefore AB = AC \tan \alpha$$
$$= 4 \times 1\cdot013T \text{ degrees.}$$

The scale for degrees, measured along A D, is $\frac{1}{8}$ inch = 1 degree. Hence the distance along A D corresponding to 4 degrees per second is

$$AB = \frac{4 \times 1\cdot013T}{8} \text{ inches.}$$

Similarly for any other angular velocity. Thus the indicator curve can

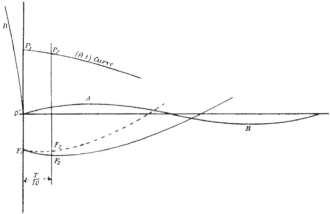

FIG. 304.

be set up with A D as base, such that any ordinate B R represents the "Resistance Indicator" for the angular velocity tan α.

Having set up the curve in this manner, we proceed in the same way as for unresisted motion.

Suppose the vessel to be heeled over to an angle $\theta_1 = AP_1$, fig. 302, and given an angular velocity = tan α. Draw $P_1 p$ parallel to C H. Set down A F_1 = ordinate of modified force curve at angle θ_1. Sketch in the first portion of the force curve $F_1 F_2$ for *unresisted motion*, and guess in the curve $F_1 f_2$ for *resisted motion*. Find, as before, the C.G. of the effective force curve A $F_1 f_2 A_2$, then the tangents to the (θ, t) curve at P_1 and P_2 must intersect above this. Set up H B = mean ordinate of A $F_1 f_2 A_2$. Then the tangent at P_2 to the (θ, t) curve is parallel to B C. We have the additional check that $F_2 f_2$ = B.R., and $A_2 F_2$ must equal the ordinate of modified force curve at the angle $A_2 P_2$. We go on for increments of $\frac{T}{10}$. The curves of (θ, t) and $F_1 F_2 F_3$, etc., cross on the base line. The dotted curve $F_1 f_2 f_3$, etc., meets the

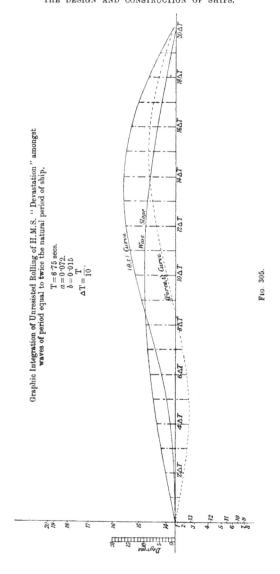

Graphic Integration of Unresisted Rolling of H.M.S. "Devastation" amongst waves of period equal to twice the natural period of ship.

$T = 6.75$ secs.
$a = 0.072$.
$b = 0.015$
$\Delta T = \dfrac{T}{10}$.

Fig. 305.

curve $F_1 F_2 F_3$, etc., at the extreme angle of roll.   An example of this method, for the same ship as fig. 298 is drawn, is shown in fig. 303.   The values of a and b, the constants in the formula of extinction, were obtained from experiments.   As in fig. 298, the ship is supposed to be heeled over to $20°$ from the upright, in still water, and allowed to roll freely.   She becomes upright again in time $5\cdot36\Delta T = 0\cdot536T$, and reaches the extreme angle on the other side of the upright in time $8\Delta T = 0\cdot8T$, the angle reached being $11°$.

Rolling amongst Waves — Resisted and Unresisted.— The graphical method of dealing with this differs from that for still water in the fact that the stability is now that given by the inclination to the wave normal instead of to the vertical, otherwise the process is exactly the same as for still water.

We start by drawing O A B, the curve of the wave-slope, to a base of time (see fig. 304).   This is generally assumed to be a sine curve.   As before, set up our "Resistance Indicator" O R.   There is no indicator in the case of unresisted rolling.   The (θ, t) curve starts according to the initial conditions of heel and angular velocity in precisely the same manner as before.   Guess in the first part of the (θ, t) curve $P_1 P_2$.   The difference between the ordinate of this curve and that of the curve of wave-slope gives the inclination for the stability, and the ordinate of the modified G Z curve at this inclination gives us the force for unresisted rolling.   We can thus get in our curve $F_1 F_2$, then by the process already given we can get our curve $F_1 f_2$ of effective force. The process in this case is rather tedious, but each step is self-checking, and the correct solution can be obtained.   An example of the application of this method to the case of unresisted rolling amongst waves is shown in fig. 305, which has been worked out for the same ship as figs. 298 and 303 have been drawn.   The ship is supposed to be initially at rest in the trough of a wave of maximum slope $10°$ and of period twice the natural period of ship.   She reaches a maximum inclination of $16\cdot6°$ at $1\cdot35T$, and then comes back to an inclination of $0\cdot8°$ in time $2T$ from the start.

CHAPTER XXXII.

METHOD OF REDUCING ROLLING BY
BILGE KEELS.

MECHANICAL methods have been adopted to reduce the rolling of ships. External keels increase the resistance. When such a projection is fitted other than at the middle line of the ship it is called a bilge keel. The action of bilge keels is different from the other methods that have been adopted to restrict rolling in that they are fitted on the outside of the ship with the intention of developing a greater resistance to motion in the surrounding water, whereas the other methods depend upon the motion of some loose weight or weights which operate against the motion of the ship and are fitted internally.

Mr W. Froude's Experiments.—In 1871 Mr W. Froude conducted a series of experiments on a model of H.M.S. "Devastation" in order to test the relative efficiency of various depths of bilge keels. The model was made to a scale of $\frac{1}{36}$th full size, and was so weighted that its C.G. was in the correct position, it floated at the proper waterline, and the period of roll was proportional to that of the ship. The model was tried under the following conditions :—

(1) Without bilge pieces.

(2) With one keel on each side, representing a 21-inch bilge keel in the actual ship.

(3) With one keel on each side, representing a 36-inch bilge keel in the actual ship.

(4) With two keels on each side of same size as in (3).

(5) With a single keel on each side equivalent to 6 feet in the actual ship.

The model was tried in still water, being heeled over to an angle of $8\frac{1}{2}°$, when the middle part of the upper deck edge was just immersed. It was then set free and allowed to oscillate until coming to rest. The following are the recorded results :—

Condition.	Number of Double Rolls before coming to rest.	Period of Double Roll. Seconds.
(1) No bilge keels	$31\frac{1}{2}$	1·77
(2) Single 21″ keels on both sides	$12\frac{1}{2}$	1·9
(3) ,, 36″ ,, ,,	8	1·9
(4) Double 36″ ,, ,,	$5\frac{3}{4}$	1·92
(5) Single 72″ ,, ,,	4	1·99

Thus, fitting bilge keels has a small effect upon the period of the vessel's roll. A single bilge keel is more effective than two of half the size.

A series of experiments were carried out with the same model to determine the steadying effect of bilge keels when rolling amongst waves of approximately the same period as the ship. It should be noted that these waves are relatively steeper in the case of the model than they would be for the ship, so that the results should not be taken as an indication of what would be likely to happen to the ship. The results were—

	Maximum angle reached.
With a 6-feet keel on each side . . .	5 degrees.
„ 3 „ . „ . . .	13½ „
„ none.	model upset.

This again shows the relative advantage of employing deep keels.

Mr W. Froude also made a series of experiments on full-sized ships. The "Greyhound" was fitted with bilge keels 100 feet long and 3 feet 6 inches deep. Another ship, the "Perseus," had no bilge keels, but was trimmed until she rolled in still water at the same natural period as the "Greyhound." These vessels were taken out to sea and allowed to roll. It was found that, upon all occasions, the "Perseus" rolled just twice as much as the "Greyhound." The largest rolls recorded were 23° for the "Perseus" and 11½° for the "Greyhound." On one occasion the "Greyhound" was observed to be behaving rather worse than usual, and it was found that one of her bilge keels had been torn off, it having been fixed on temporarily with bolts.

Experiments on the "Repulse" and "Revenge."—These are the only experiments carried out in large-sized vessels, and the results obtained are of great importance. From experiments and observations it had been decided that, in ships of large dimensions and inertia, practicable sized bilge keels would have very little steadying effect (see page 416). It was therefore decided not to fit them to ships of the "Royal Sovereign" class, but, for purposes of experiment, the "Repulse," a ship of that class, was fitted with bilge keels 200 feet long and 3 feet deep, and tried in company with other vessels of her class that had no bilge keels. One of these vessels, the "Resolution," had been purposely kept in the same condition of stability as the "Repulse." It was found, when at sea, that the maximum angle reached by the "Resolution" was 23°, whereas that for the "Repulse" was 11°. As a result of the experience gained from these trials, it was decided to fit all the ships of that class with bilge keels.

In order to throw more light upon the subject, with the view of obtaining information for guidance in future designs, it was arranged that still-water rolling experiments should be carried out on the "Revenge," a sister ship to the "Resolution." These experiments were conducted by Dr R. E. Froude and consist of two series. The first series was made before the bilge keels were fitted, and the second after they had been fitted. In each series trials were made by rolling the ship in her condition of maximum G.M. and also in the condition of the minimum G.M. likely to be reached on service. Trials were also made, when bilge keels had been fitted, with the ship under way as well as with no headway. The particulars of the ship during the trials are—

	Without Bilge Keels.		With Bilge Keels.	
	1st Trial.	2nd Trial.	1st Trial.	2nd Trial.
Mean draught	27' 6"	26' 0½"	26' 0¼"	27' 11¼"
Displacement, tons . . .	14,300	13,370	13,370	14,620
Metacentric height, feet . .	3·78	3·25	3·29	3·86
Period of single swing, seconds .	7·6	8·0	8·4	7·75

The bilge keels were 200 feet long and 3 feet deep. The results of all the experiments are given in fig. 306, which are "Curves of Declining Angles." The abscissæ values correspond to successive swings from port to starboard, or *vice versa*, and the ordinates are the extreme inclinations to the vertical for each swing. It will be seen that, starting from an inclination of 6° to the vertical, after 18 swings the angle reached is 3¾° without bilge keels and 1° with them. Also without bilge keels it takes from 45 to 50 swings to reduce the angle from 6° to 2°, and with bilge keels it only takes 8 swings. Another striking effect noticed is that the fitting of the keels destroyed the isochronism of the roll at large angles, the period being greater at the greater angles.

The effect of headway on rolling is that the rate of extinction is increased (see fig. 306). This is apparent from the following table, which shows the angle of inclination reached by the ship when started initially at 5° from the upright.

	Speed of Ship.		
	Nil.	10 knots.	12 knots.
	Degrees.	Degrees.	Degrees.
After 4 swings	2·95	2·35	2·2
,, 8 ,,	1·95	1·12	1·05
,, 12 ,,	1·45	·55	·45
,, 16 ,,	1·15	·20	·25

The reason for this increased rate of extinction is, when the ship has no headway, the rolling motion sets up a corresponding motion in the water, and once its inertia has been overcome it offers less resistance to the motion of the ship. When under way, however, the ship is constantly meeting water at rest, and has to be continuously overcoming the inertia of the water at rest as she has at the beginning of each roll in still water. This involves a greater expenditure of energy for a given roll than when in still water, and so causes a greater extinctive effect.

This experience is familiar to those who have noticed that a ship that has been going ahead in a rolling sea will roll more when the headway is taken off the ship by stopping the engines.

Mathematical Analysis of Effect of Bilge Keels.—Consider a small elemental area dA, fig. 307, of keel, distant r from the axis of oscillation.   The law of resistance of a plane moving normally through a fluid is

$$R = CAV^2,$$

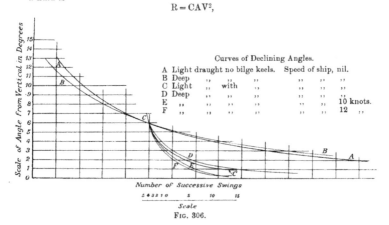

Curves of Declining Angles.

A Light draught no bilge keels.   Speed of ship, nil.
B Deep   ,,   ,,   ,,   ,,   ,,   ,,
C Light   ,,   with   ,,   ,,   ,,   ,,
D Deep   ,,   ,,   ,,   ,,   ,,   ,,
E   ,,   ,,   ,,   ,,   ,,   ,,   10 knots.
F   ,,   ,,   ,,   ,,   ,,   ,,   12   ,,

Scale of Angle from Vertical in Degrees

Number of Successive Swings

Scale

Fig. 306.

where R is the resistance, C a constant, A the area of the plane, and V its velocity.

If $\dfrac{d\theta}{dt}$ is the angular velocity of the ship, this law applied to the element dA of bilge keel will give us

$$R = CdA\left(r\frac{d\theta}{dt}\right)^2,$$

and ∴ the moment of resistance will be

$$\int CdAr^3\left(\frac{d\theta}{dt}\right)^2 = CAl^3\left(\frac{d\theta}{dt}\right)^2,$$

where $Al^3 = \int r^3 dA$, or l is the cube root of the mean cube of r.

Comparing this with the formula on p. 385 where the moment of resistance is $K_2\left(\dfrac{d\theta}{dt}\right)^2,$

Fig. 307.

we see that $K_2 = CAl^3$.

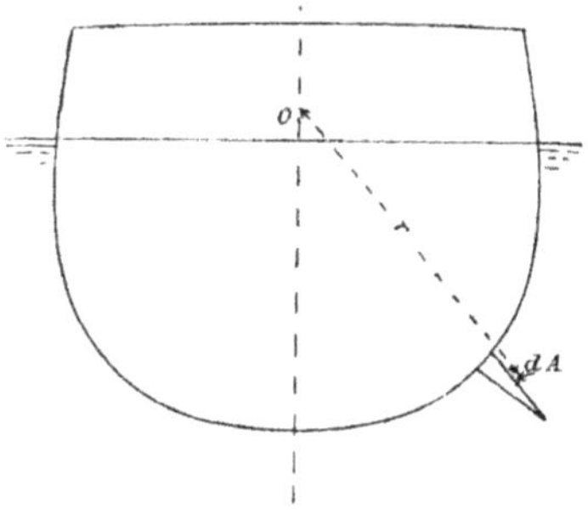

We have seen, p. 386, that with such a resistance the decrement of roll is given by

$$\delta\theta = \frac{4}{3}K_2\frac{\pi^2}{WmT^2}\theta_m^2,$$

where θ_m is the mean angle of roll from out to out.

Hence $\quad \delta\theta = \dfrac{4CAl^3\pi^2}{3WmT^2}\theta_m{}^2.$

Now $\quad T = \pi\sqrt{\dfrac{\overline{K}^2}{gm}}.$

And $\therefore \quad \delta\theta = \dfrac{4CAl^3\pi^2 gm}{3Wm\pi^2K^2}\theta_m{}^2$

$\qquad\qquad = \dfrac{4CAl^3 g}{3WK^2}\theta_m{}^2$

$\qquad\qquad = \dfrac{4}{3}\dfrac{CAl^3}{I}\theta_m{}^2$

where $I = \dfrac{W}{g}K^2 =$ moment of inertia of ship about a longitudinal axis through its C.G.

In similar ships l^3 varies as the displacement, and therefore a given area of bilge keel will produce a decrement of roll proportional to the displacement of the ship, and inversely proportional to the moment of inertia about the axis of oscillation. Thus a given area of keel is more effective in a small ship than in a large one. Also, with the same form and displacement, and same area of bilge keel, the decrement is inversely proportional to the mass moment of inertia. This led to the omission of the keels in the vessels of the "Royal Sovereign" class, see p. 413.

The reason for the difference between the above theoretical result and the experiments is, that we have assumed the whole of the extinctive effect of the keel to be due to head resistances, whereas a considerable amount is due to the stream-line action at the keels when the vessel is rolling.

CHAPTER XXXIII.

MEANS OF RESTRICTING ROLLING BY MOVING WEIGHTS.

In addition to bilge keels already considered, various methods have been devised by which rolling can be restricted. These have mostly taken the form of a loose weight or weights which are set in motion by the ship rolling, and are such that their centre of gravity moves so that a righting couple is created.

Water Chambers.—In 1884 Sir Philip Watts made a series of experiments on the effect of water chambers on H.M.S. "Inflexible." These were fitted athwartships, and the width across the deck could be made either 67 feet, 51 feet, or 43 feet. Several depths of water were tried, and the effect upon the extinction of rolling observed. The main conclusions were—

(1) Best extinctive effect was obtained with a certain depth of water, this being such that a wave of translation moved across from side to side in the same period as the ship's roll.

(2) With this critical depth of water, the resistance begins at a very small angle and increases rapidly up to a certain point, and then remains practically constant.

(3) With other depths the resistance did not begin until at larger angles, and the greater the departure from the critical depth the greater the roll had to be before any resistance was observed.

(4) At large angles the disadvantage of departure from the critical depth was not marked. The water rushed across the deck in the form of a breaking wave or bore.

A comparison was also made between the effect of increasing the depth of the bilge keels by 2 feet and taking the full breadth of water chamber with the water at its critical depth. The results were that the addition to the bilge keels added about $\frac{2}{3}$ extra resistance to the ship at ordinary angles, whereas the water at 5° added three times the original extinctive effect, at 12° once, and at 18° one-half. So that below 15° the water chamber has an enormous extinctive effect, and is the most effective means of damping and preventing oscillations.

Sir J. I. Thornycroft's Apparatus.—In 1892 Sir J. Thornycroft gave to the Institution of Naval Architects the results of a series of experiments he had made upon a mechanical device to prevent rolling. The apparatus is shown in fig. 308, and consists of a ballast tank, shaped as shown, mounted upon a shaft, and free to turn completely around it, the shaft being inclined aft so that the weight tended naturally to take up a position of equilibrium along the centre of the vessel.

The motion of the ballast was controlled by a water cylinder containing a piston, and having loaded valves which limited the resistance to motion offered by the water on the piston. The piston was connected to a crank on the shaft. This cylinder was also available for giving motion to the ballast, which was effected by an electrical device actuated by a short pendulum which was fixed at the C.G. of the ship. This pendulum always tends to set itself normal to the effective wave-slope, the consequence being that the vessel is always kept normal to this wave-slope, and thus does not experience a large roll, as the greatest slope of the wave is about 9°. The weight itself, when moved out at the greatest distance from the centre line, inclined the vessel about 2°. On one occasion the apparatus was effective in reducing the roll at once from 18° to 9°.

Herr Schlick's Gyrostatic Apparatus.—This was introduced by Dr Schlick at the 1904 meetings of the Institution of Naval Architects. It consists essentially of a heavy fly-wheel fixed to a vertical axis that is mounted in a case, the case itself being mounted on an athwartships shaft, and free to oscillate about it. The wheel is caused to rotate very rapidly; then, as the vessel rolls, the axis of the wheel tends to move in a vertical fore-and-aft plane, and thus to become inclined to the vertical. Its oscillations are damped by means of a brake attached to the outside of the casing, so that

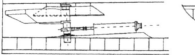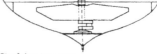

FIG. 308.—Thornycroft's Steadying Apparatus.

the wheel is caused to pitch in the vertical plane with an angular velocity proportional to, and in phase with, the rolling couple causing it. The gyroscopic action of the wheel has then its maximum effect in preventing roll.

The two primary effects of the apparatus are that, due to the gyroscopic action, a couple is induced acting in the direction opposite to that of the external rolling couple, and also the period of oscillation of the vessel is increased. Hence, due to these causes, the rolling motion is very greatly damped.

This apparatus was fixed to a torpedo-boat, and a series of experiments was carried out both in still water and at sea. The particulars of the gyroscope are:—

Outside diameter of fly-wheel . . . 1 metre.
Weight of wheel (without spindle) . . 1106 lbs.
Peripheral velocity . . . . 274·8 feet-seconds.
Revolutions per minute . . . . 1600.

The particulars of the vessel are—

Length at the waterline . . . . 116 feet.
Extreme breadth . . . . : . 11·7 ,,
Mean draught . . . . . . 3·4 ,,
Displacement . . . . . . 56·2 tons.
Metacentric height . . . . . 1·64 feet.
Period of oscillation with gyroscope at rest   2·068 seconds.

In still water, with the gyroscope free to move, the period increased to 3 seconds. The vessel was heeled over to different angles, and the number of rolls taken to reduce the inclination to half a degree was noted with and without the gyroscope. The results were—

Angle of Heel.	No. of Rolls to reduce inclination to $\frac{1}{2}°$.	
	With Gyroscope.	Without Gyroscope.
10°	2	20
13° 40′	3	25

With the apparatus in use at sea the following results were noted :—

ARC OF OSCILLATION.

Gyroscope fixed.	Gyroscope free.
30°	1°
23°	1°
30°	1° to 1½°

so that the total arc, from extreme port to starboard, never exceeded 1½° with the apparatus working freely.

M. Crémieu's Apparatus.—In 1907 the author made a series of model experiments upon a roll-destroying apparatus invented by M. Crémieu of Paris. The apparatus consists essentially of a chamber shaped to the arc of a circle, as shown in fig. 309. This chamber is fixed with the plane of the

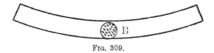

FIG. 309.

circle in the vertical transverse plane, and is filled with water or some more viscous liquid. A heavy ball B is placed in the chamber, and can move in the athwartships plane only, its motion being damped by the liquid. The apparatus is so arranged that there is a phase difference of 180° between the motion of the ship and the ball, and then the righting couple has its maximum effect.

The model upon which the experiments were made was 1/49th the size of an actual ship, and was accurately weighted and adjusted so that its C.G. was in the correct position and the model dynamically represented the ship. Since $T = \pi \sqrt{\dfrac{K^2}{gm}}$, and both K and m are to scale, the period of the model was 1/7th that of the ship.

For purposes of experiment the apparatus was tested against water chambers having the same weight.   Two forms of water chambers were used. One was the ordinary rectangular box form, and the other had a restriction in the middle and was of the form indicated in plan in fig. 310.   The results of the experiments are given in fig. 311 and table.

It will be noticed that curves C and D, given by placing plain rectangular water chambers with 1 inch depth of water in the model, show an increase in the rolling compared to A, the normal condition, and also lengthen the period of roll.   This latter effect probably results from a decrease in the metacentric height, due to the presence of free water in the ship.

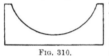

FIG. 310.

A comparison of curves b and c with B and C shows that a decided gain has been effected by using only half the same depth of water in the chamber, with the same amount of free surface.

This is because the lesser depth is more nearly equal to the depth of water in which a wave of translation will move across the chamber during a single roll.

By using an obstruction for the passage of water at the middle of the chamber a still further gain in roll extinction, due to damping, is effected with the same weight of water used.   Compare K B, K C, and K D with B, C, and D.

Curves K, d, and b indicate the best results, as with least weight of apparatus the longest period and quickest extinction is observed.

The Crémieu apparatus placed in the model has the advantage of occupying less space than the water chambers, and, owing to the absence of any free liquid surface, there is no change in the metacentric height, as is evidenced by there being no change in the period.

This apparatus was also tested in a model of a shipshaped section that was caused to oscillate by being mounted on curved rockers R, fig. 312, which were shaped to the curve of buoyancy and rested on a horizontal plane. It was found that, with the Crémieu apparatus

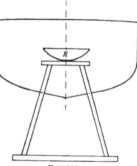

FIG. 312.

in position, the model when inclined at 60° comes to rest in 21 seconds after six double rolls.   With no roll-destroying apparatus, and body quite free to oscilliate, it comes to rest in 20 minutes after 240 double rolls.   This shows the great effect produced by the apparatus.

Comparing the effects of the Crémieu apparatus and the water chambers upon the apparatus sketched in fig. 312, it is found that the water chambers are roughly twice as effective as the Crémieu apparatus.   The noise of the water chamber is much greater than the Crémieu apparatus.   These chambers have been fitted in some warships and a passenger ship, but their use was soon discontinued.   In the case of the passenger ship the rolling was reduced by the use of the chamber by as much as 60 per cent. of the amount of roll which the ship had when the water chamber was empty.   Herr Flamm has recently invented a modified form of water chamber which is said to give satisfactory results.

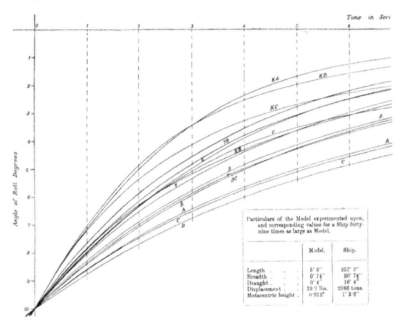

Time in Seconds

Angle of Roll Degrees

Particulars of the Model experimented upon, and corresponding values for a Ship forty-nine times as large as Model.

	Model.	Ship.
Length . .	5' 3"	257' 3"
Breadth . .	0' 7½"	30' 7½"
Draught . .	0' 4"	16' 4"
Displacement . .	39·7 lbs.	2080 tons.
Metacentric height .	0·312"	1' 3·3"

Fig. 311.—Curves of De

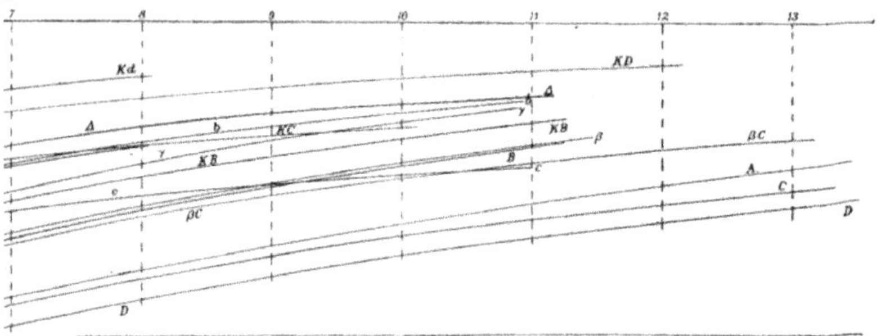

[Plate IV.

ls

ing Angles.

Letter of Curve.	Description of kind of Roll-destroying Apparatus placed on board.	Number of Pieces.	Weight of Apparatus expressed as per cent. Total Displacement.	Period of one complete Oscillation.	Remarks.
A	None. All fixed weights	...	...	2·2 seconds,	
β	Crémieu Tube. Solid weight in mixture of water and glycerine	1	0·82	2·25 ,,	
γ	,, ,, ,, ,,	2	1·64	2·2 ,,	
Δ	,, ,, ,, ,,	3	2·4	2·17 ,,	
B	Water Chamber, plain rectangular box, about half full of water	1	0·82	2·4 ,,	
C	,, ,, ,, ,,	2	1·64	2·9 ,,	Worse than original condition.
D	,, ,, ,, ,,	3	2·4	3·25 ,,	,, ,, ,,
b	Water Chamber, plain rectangular box, about one-quarter full of water	1	0·41	2·5 ,,	
c	,, ,, ,, ,,	2	0·82	3·0 ,,	
KB	Water Chamber, with constricted passage at middle, about half full of water	1	0·82	2·4 ,,	
KC	,, ,, ,, ,,	2	1·64	2·8 ,,	
KD	,, ,, ,, ,,	3	2·4	3·0 ,,	Very good.
Kd	Water Chamber, with constricted passage at middle, about one-quarter full of water .	3	1·23	3·0 ,,	,,
βB	{ Crémieu Tube (as at β) . . . . . . Water Chamber (as at B) .	1 / 1	} 1·64	2·4 ,,	Identical with curve γ.
γB	{ Crémieu Tube (as at γ) . Water Chamber (as at B)	2 / 1	} 2·4	2·36 ,,	
βC	{ Crémieu Tube (as at β) . Water Chamber (as at C) .	1 / 2	} 2·4	2·8 ,,	

CHAPTER XXXIV.

PITCHING AND DIPPING OSCILLATIONS.

Pitching.—This has already been considered in Vol. I., Chapter XXV., where an attempt has been made to determine the stresses produced in the structure of a ship due to pitching amongst a regular series of waves. Here

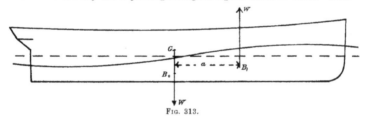

Fig. 313.

we are concerned with the motion of the ship as a whole. The disturbing force in this case is the change of distribution of buoyancy due to the ship passing through waves obliquely or at right angles to her length.

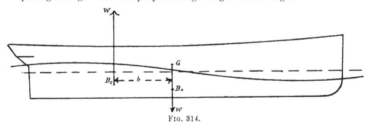

Fig. 314.

Thus, the effect of a wave as it passes along the ship's length is, in fig. 313, to shift the C.B. forward from B_0 to B_1, and hence cause a disturbing couple Wa. Then, when the crest passes aft, the C.B. moves to B_2 (fig. 314), and causes a couple Wb in the opposite direction to the former couple. The motion is approximately harmonic, and its magnitude is not as great as in the case of rolling, while the fluid resistances are much greater. Thus we do not get as large angles of pitching as of roll. The period of pitching is about half that for roll. A vessel pitches heavily when steaming fast against a head sea because the pitching couple changes sign much more rapidly than when the vessel is at rest or running away from the sea.

Combination of Rolling and Pitching.—In 1898 Captain Kriloff of the Russian Imperial Navy gave to the Institution of Naval Architects the results of a series of calculations made upon a vessel to determine the combined effects of rolling, pitching, and yawing when steaming obliquely to a regular series of waves. The particulars of the ship and waves are—

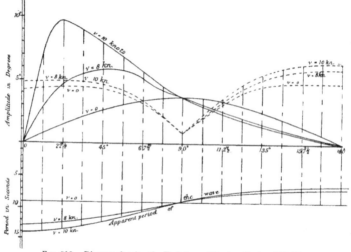

Fig. 315.—Diagram showing the Variations of the Amplitudes of Pitching and Rolling with the course, head and speed of the ship.
——————— Amplitude of Rolling.
.... ,,   Pitching.

Length of ship	350 ft.
Beam .	48' 6".
Draught	19'.
Displacement	5000 tons.
Length of waves	420 ft.
Height .	16' 6".
Period .	9 seconds.

Fig. 315 shows the amplitudes of rolling and pitching for the vessel at rest, and also moving at 8 knots and 10 knots. The abscissæ are the angles which the line of motion of ship make with the line of motion of the wave. From 0° to 90° she is steaming away from the waves, and from 90° to 180° she is steaming towards them. It is instructive to note that, with motion ahead, the amplitude of rolling is greatest when steaming away from the waves, and the greater the speed of the ship the smaller the angle between the line of advance of the ship and the wave at which this maximum occurs. On the contrary, the amplitude of pitching is greater when steaming towards the waves ; but whether steaming away from or towards the waves, the pitching amplitude is in each case greater than when the ship is stationary.

In the same manner as synchronism in rolling is conducive to violent motion, so it is with pitching. The author remembers a case when, just off the coast of Newfoundland, the vessel met a smooth, glassy sea with just a slight, almost imperceptible swell, and the vessel pitched so heavily as to cause the water to break completely over her bows. Generally, however, the period of the ship for pitching is greater than the period of the wave, and we get the effect as in the corresponding case for rolling, which has been dealt with on p. 393. See also p. 154, Vol. II.

Heaving Oscillations.—These have already been dealt with in Vol. I., Chapter XXV., for the case of a ship steaming head to sea and not rolling.

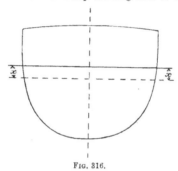

Fɪɢ. 316.

It was shown there that the passage of the wave relatively to the ship caused an inequality in the forces of weight and buoyancy, which produces a vertical oscillation of the C.G. of the ship. When a ship rolls about a longitudinal axis, the amount of displaced volume depends partly on the form of the ship and partly upon the vertical position of that axis. If at any instant the forces of weight and buoyancy are not equal there will be a tendency to produce vertical oscillations similar to those due to the passage of the waves when moving against a head sea. The oscillations caused in this way have been called " Dipping Oscillations."

Dipping Oscillations.—A ship's complete motion in rolling has been considered as (1) a motion of rotation about an axis through the C.G., and (2) the motion of the C.G. itself. The former has been already treated, and we will now consider the motion of the C.G., which must necessarily be in a closed path. This may be divided into a vertical and a horizontal oscillation. The former is the more important, and we will confine our attention to that only.

When a ship rolls through a fairly large angle, the inclined waterplane may or may not cut off the same volume of displacement. If it does not, the unbalanced force will cause a vertical or " *dipping* " oscillation.

The same effect is produced if we suddenly add or subtract a weight from the ship. Suppose this is done and the vessel suddenly rises or sinks a distance x, fig. 316. Let A be the area of the waterplane. Then the force acting $= Axw$ where w is the weight of a unit volume of water, and if W is the weight of the ship in the new condition, its equation of motion will be

$$\frac{W}{g}\frac{d^2x}{dt^2} + Axw = 0.$$

$$\therefore \quad \frac{d^2x}{dt^2} + \frac{Awg}{W}x = 0,$$

and $\therefore$ the ship oscillates harmonically with a mathematical period

$$T = 2\pi\sqrt{\frac{W}{Awg}} = 2\pi\sqrt{\frac{W}{12tg}},$$

where t is the tons per inch immersion of the ship. It is found that this period is about half the period of roll.

Complete Motion of Axis of Rotation of Ship during a Roll in Still Water.—In the *Transactions* of the Institution of Naval Architects for 1909, Mr A. W. Johns has endeavoured to build up the complete motion of the axis of rotation for the case in which the wedges of submersion and emersion are equal. He considers a ship in a perfect fluid, and shows that the path is a symmetrical curve of four loops, the loops intersecting at the C.G. Thus the axis passes through the C.G. when the ship is upright, and also when she is at her extreme angle of roll on either side. If we pass from this to the case of an imperfect fluid, the lower loops are increased and the upper ones diminished. If the ship has bilge keels their effect is to further increase the lower loops, and also to pull the intersection of the curves below the C.G. The axis of oscillation will be generally below the waterplane, and thus the tendency will be to form surface waves, *i.e.* the a coefficient in the formula

$$\delta\theta = a\theta + b\theta^2$$

will be increased.

INDEX.

Lightning Source UK Ltd.
Milton Keynes UK
UKHW010033070223
416578UK00002B/333

9 783368 498573